"King's lyrical style shines in a tender tale of how love and forgiveness heal broken hearts and restore a family and a community. With its Missouri setting, King offers us a knowing look into a different Amish settlement. Readers will look forward to more Cedar Creek stories."

—Marta Perry, author of the Pleasant Valley series

"*Abby Finds Her Calling* is a heartwarming story, beautifully told, of forgiveness, redemption, and the healing power of love in its many forms: love between individuals, family love, love within a community, and God's love. This story touched my heart."

—JoAnn Grote, author of "Image of Love" from *A Prairie Christmas Collection*

"Naomi King writes with a heartwarming honesty that will stay with the reader long after the last page."

—Emma Miller, author of the Amish Matchmaker series

"What distinguishes this from many other Amish romances is how it shows that forbearance and forgiveness take a good deal of work, and the Amish, like everybody else, gossip, bicker, and sometimes have less-than-ideal family lives. . . . King has created enough open-ended characters to entice the reader back to Cedar Creek for more."

—*Publishers Weekly*

"A new contemporary series, Home at Cedar Creek, from a talented author who writes from her heart. The story line's been around for decades, but King freshens it up and brings new life to it."

—RT Book Reviews

Emma Blooms at Last

HOME AT CEDAR CREEK

Naomi King

JOVE
New York

A JOVE BOOK
Published by Berkley
An imprint of Penguin Random House LLC
penguinrandomhouse.com

Copyright © 2014 by Charlotte Hubbard
Penguin Random House supports copyright. Copyright fuels creativity, encourages
diverse voices, promotes free speech, and creates a vibrant culture. Thank you for buying
an authorized edition of this book and for complying with copyright laws by not
reproducing, scanning, or distributing any part of it in any form without permission.
You are supporting writers and allowing Penguin Random House to continue to
publish books for every reader.

A JOVE BOOK, BERKLEY, and the BERKLEY & B colophon are registered
trademarks of Penguin Random House LLC.

ISBN: 9780593198391

New American Library trade paperback edition / November 2014
Jove mass-market edition / December 2020

Printed in the United States of America
1   3   5   7   9   10   8   6   4   2

Cover design by Judith Lagerman
Cover image of woman by Claudio Marinesco and Tom Hallman;
image of Amish buggy by Dennis MacDonald/AgeFotostock/MediaBakery

*For Johnny Lynn, my lifelong friend,
who—like Emma—had to wait awhile for the right man
to come along and bless her life!*

Fear thou not; for I am with thee: be not dismayed; for I am thy God: I will strengthen thee; yea, I will help thee; yea, I will uphold thee with the right hand of my righteousness. —ISAIAH 41:10

Chapter 1

This is what a Monday morning should look like, Amanda mused. Her kitchen was thrumming with activity as her family finished breakfast—and everyone appeared happily intent on getting where they needed to go next. In the six weeks since she'd married Wyman Brubaker, they'd known some rough moments, yet it seemed their eight kids and the four adults had finally figured out a morning routine that worked. Today they'd all been dressed and ready to eat on time, without any squabbling or drama. It was a minor miracle.

"What a wonderful-gut meal," Wyman said as he rose from his place at the head of the table. "The haystack casserole had all my favorite things in it. Lots of sausage and onions and green peppers."

"And cheese!" five-year-old Simon piped up. "So much cheese. The hash browns were really gooey and really, really gut."

"What are you three fellows doing this morning?"

Wyman asked. He tousled Simon's dark hair, looking from Eddie to Jerome. "Did I hear you say we might have baby mules by the end of the day?"

"That's my best guess," Jerome replied as he, too, stood up. "Eddie and Simon are going with me to get some feed supplement. Let's hit the road, boys, so we'll be back in time. We want to help the mares, if they need us, and I want to start our imprint training so those foals will know us and trust us from the moment they're born."

"I'm outta here!" Simon sprang from his chair and shot through the kitchen door, letting it slam behind him.

Eddie, his fifteen-year-old brother, headed toward the jackets and hats that hung on wall pegs. "Well, there's the speed of light and the speed of sound—and the speed of Simon," he remarked as he grabbed his youngest brother's coat along with his own. "At this rate, we'll be to Cedar Creek and back before those mares can turn twice in their stalls."

"Enthusiasm is a gut thing," Jerome replied as he came over to hug Amanda. "Anything you need from the mercantile, Aunt? Maybe a big bag of raisins for my favorite kind of pie?"

Amanda laughed as her twenty-four-year-old nephew wagged his eyebrows at her. The money from Jerome's mule business had seen her through some tight times after her first husband had died, leaving her to raise three young daughters. Now that she'd remarried, Jerome was taking to Wyman's boys with a sense of fun and responsibility that was another big help to her. "Bring whatever you think will taste gut," she replied.

"Raisin-filled cookies," Wyman hinted wistfully. "And with that luscious thought, I'll head to the barn. Reece Weaver's supposed to call me with a progress report on my new grain elevator."

Amanda felt a rush of goose bumps when Wyman smiled at her. With his dark hair and a thick, silky beard framing his face, he was such a handsome man—and a wonderful provider for her and their children. "Jemima and I plan to get some baking done today to stay ahead of you fellows with your bottomless stomachs," she said. "So it can't hurt to sweet-talk the cooks."

"I'm going to kiss this cook instead," Wyman murmured. He quickly brushed her lips with his, and then waved Eddie and Jerome out the door ahead of him. "You ladies have a gut rest of your morning. Oh—and you, too, Pete!" he teased as he playfully clapped his middle son on the back. "See you and Lizzie after school."

As the three fellows left the kitchen, Amanda joined Pete and Lizzie at the counter, where they were closing the lids of their coolers. "Denki to you both for packing your lunches," she said as she slung an arm around each of them. "You've really smoothed out my morning, doing that."

"It's the easiest way to get exactly what we want to eat," Lizzie pointed out. She elbowed her new brother. "Pete made *three* ham sandwiches."

"I sure didn't want any of your stinky tuna salad," Pete insisted. "The barn cats will probably follow us to school yowling for your lunch." Then he sighed. "Another week. Another five days of Teacher Dorcas."

Amanda frowned. "You don't like the teacher here at your new school?"

Pete shrugged. "I don't think she likes *me* much. She finds ways to point out that I'm not as far along in math and spelling as the rest of the eighth graders."

"She's not really picking on *you*, Pete," Lizzie remarked. "She thinks that the boys in general are lagging behind the girls."

"Give Teacher Dorcas a little more time," Amanda suggested, squeezing his shoulder. "It's always an adjustment, getting used to a new teacher after you've been in a different school for so long."

As the two thirteen-year-olds donned their winter coats and hats, Amanda noted that they resembled each other enough to be twins, even though Pete was a Brubaker and her Lizzie was a Lambright. "Make it a gut day," she said as they started out the door, "and we'll see you this afternoon."

"Bye, Mamma," Lizzie replied, while Pete gave her a wave.

As Amanda turned back toward the long kitchen table, she was pleased to see that Vera, Wyman's eldest, had been putting away the breakfast leftovers while the four-year-old twins, Cora and Dora, had scraped and stacked everyone's plates. "Well, now that it's just us girls, the real work can get done!" Amanda teased as she lifted Alice Ann from the wooden high chair.

"I a helper!" the toddler crowed. "Me—Alice Ann!"

Amanda felt a surge of love as the little blonde hugged her. "Jah, and it's gut to hear you talking, too, punkin," she murmured. Wyman's Alice Ann, three years old, had been traumatized when her mother was killed in a hay-baling accident, and because she'd begun to speak only recently, every word sounded especially sweet.

"We're going to work on the laundry," Vera joined in. At seventeen, she was tall and slender—and she'd become well versed in running a household after her mother had died. "Alice Ann's going to help me sort the clothes by colors, and then hand me the clothespins when we hang everything out to dry."

"A never-ending job, the laundry," Amanda remarked as she lowered the toddler to the floor. "And while you start the dough for the bread and piecrusts, Jemima, the twins and I will fetch the morning's eggs."

Her mother-in-law from her first marriage nodded as she ran hot dishwater into the sink. "Better you than me. These cold November mornings make my legs ache, so I'm happy to stay inside."

"Then can we bake cookies, Mamma?" Dora asked eagerly. "Chocolate chip ones?"

"And butterscotch brownies? *Please?*" Cora chimed in. "We don't *like*—"

"Dat's raisin cookies," her twin finished the sentence with a grimace.

Amanda laughed, hugging her look-alike daughters. How could she refuse them when they brightened her days—and had already started calling Wyman their dat? They were just at the age to wear their hair twisted into rolls and tucked into buns . . . growing up so fast. "If you think you can do all the measuring—"

"Jah, we can!" they said together.

"We'll make your goodies after we redd up your room and Simon's," Amanda replied. "So let's get out to the hen-house. The sooner we finish our work, the sooner we can play."

As her girls scurried ahead of her to the low-slung build-ing that was adjoined to the barn, Amanda felt a deep sense of satisfaction. A few weeks ago, her mornings at the Brubaker place had been chaotic and stressful, but when Wyman had decided they would move to her farm in Bloomingdale, everything had fallen into place as though God had intended for them to be there all along. She mar-veled at how the first light of this fine autumn morning made everything sparkle. Out in the garden, the last of the pumpkins were ready to be picked and made into the filling for holiday pies. The maple and sweet gum trees glistened with bursts of red, orange, and gold to form a glorious back-drop behind the white gambrel-roofed barn. As the horses and mules in the corral whickered at the twins, Amanda couldn't help but smile. Her life was so good now . . .

Wyman paused in the unlit barn, watching the wall phone's red message light blink. Had Reece called while he'd been outside seeing Jerome and the boys off? Or had someone else left a message? What with Jerome running his mule-breeding business here, it might be a good idea to get a new message machine that allowed callers to leave their voice mails for specific businesses and family members.

But then, some districts' bishops spoke out against such an updated message system, saying it allowed for keeping secrets. In a lot of Amish towns, two or three families had shared a phone shanty alongside the road for generations. *You've gotten used to the phone being in your elevator office rather than in another fellow's barn,* Wyman realized. *This is just one more minor adjustment—like learning a new phone number after having the same one all your life.*

Wyman pushed the PLAY button. If the message was for Jerome, he would jot the phone number or the caller's name on the pad of paper Amanda kept on the wooden bench beneath the phone. "You have one new message," the voice on the recorder announced.

"Jah, Wyman, this is Reece Weaver, and we've gotta talk about some more up-front money," the contractor said in a voice that rang around the barn's rafters. "Started digging your foundation, and we're gonna have to blast through solid bedrock, which jacks the price *waaay* up from what I quoted you last week. Got some issues with EPA and OSHA regulations that'll cost a lot more, too, so that seven hundred thousand we figured on won't nearly cover building your elevator now. Better gimme a call real quick-like." *Click.*

Wyman's heart thudded. He'd left Reece's written estimate in the house—not that it would answer any of the questions spinning in his mind. Wouldn't a commercial contractor know about environmental and safety regulations—and the possibility of hitting bedrock—before he'd written up his estimate? And why on earth had Reece gone into detail about money, when anyone in the family might have been listening, instead of waiting for him to call back? As Wyman glanced around the shadowy barn, he was relieved that only the horses and mules had heard the contractor's message. The seven hundred thousand dollars he'd spoken of—money from the sale of the Brubaker family farm as well as from the Clearwater elevator's bank account—was all he could spend on a new facility. He'd kept money back to see his family of twelve through the coming year until his Bloomingdale elevator was bringing in some money . . . but Reece's strident words made it clear that he intended to demand a significant price increase.

Wyman pressed the number pads on the phone, hoping he and Reece could settle this matter immediately rather than playing telephone tag. After assuring Amanda that he could support her; her mother-in-law, Jemima; and their blended family of eight kids, he did *not* want any more details about money left on the phone, where she might hear them and start to worry. Finally, on the fourth ring, someone picked up.

"Jah, Weaver Construction Company," a woman answered.

"Wyman Brubaker here, and I need to speak with Reece about—"

"He's out on a job. I'll take your message."

Wyman frowned. More than likely this was Reece's wife, because the company had been a small family-owned business since Reece's dat had started it more than thirty years ago. "He just called me not five minutes ago, asking me to call right back," Wyman replied. "I'd rather not discuss the details of my elevator with—"

"Oh. You're *that* Wyman Brubaker," the woman interrupted. "I'll page him, and he'll call you back as soon as he can." *Click.*

And what did she mean by snipping and snapping at him that way, as though he were an inconvenience rather than a customer? Wyman's stomach tightened around his breakfast as he hung up. There was nothing to do but wait for

Reece to call back, even as every passing moment allowed him to think of things that didn't set right about this situation—

The phone rang and he grabbed it. "Jah? This is Wyman."

"Reece Weaver. So you see where I'm coming from, far as your job costing more?" he demanded. "How about if I stop by, say, around noon? Another hundred thousand should cover the blasting and the—"

"A hundred thousand dollars?" Wyman closed his eyes and curled in around the phone, hoping his voice hadn't carried outside the barn. It took him a moment to corral his stampeding thoughts. "I don't understand why you didn't know—*before* you started digging—about that bedrock, and why you didn't call me—*before* you started digging—about maybe changing the location of the elevator," he said in a low voice. "That's a huge difference from the price you quoted in your estimate."

"Jah, well, the excavation crew I use is only available this week, before they go to jobs with other contractors," Reece replied hastily. "Can't get them again until the middle of January, see, so I didn't think you'd want to wait that long."

The middle of January? Nobody poured concrete then, so his facility would be delayed by months if he waited that long. Wyman drew in a deep breath, trying to compose himself. "It seems to me that bedrock would be the ideal foundation for an elevator anyway," he said. "It's not like I need a basement—or even a crawl space—under the silos or the office building."

"Yeah, but see, the new EPA regulations are making us do a lotta things different these days," the contractor replied. "Nothing's as easy as it was when Pop put up your elevator in Clearwater. That was about twenty years ago, after all."

Wyman blinked. Norbert Weaver's friendly, reliable service had been the main reason he and his partner, Ray

Fisher, had wanted Weaver Construction to build their new facility, but it seemed that some of the family's values had died with the company's founder. Wyman heard the hum of equipment in the background. Could it be that Reece was pushing for more money because he had several big projects going on at once? The founder's son had acted quite accommodating and professional last week, when they'd discussed the plans for this new elevator . . . and Wyman realized that because he, too, was feeling pressured, he wasn't handling these details well over the phone.

"Tell you what, Reece," he said, trying to sound reasonable and relaxed. "I need to discuss this situation with my partner before we proceed. How about if I meet you at the elevator site tomorrow morning?"

"I'll be outta state on another big job. Won't be back around Bloomingdale until Friday."

Wyman caught himself scowling yet again. But he would not be pushed into paying out more money until he'd talked with Ray about this new development. "What time on Friday, then?"

"You really want to wait? My excavation crew'll most likely be gone by then, or they'll charge me double time for squeezing your job in over the weekend," the contractor replied. "You know what they say. Time is money."

No, time is time, *and this is* my *money we're talking about.* Wyman let out the breath he'd been holding. "Three o'clock this afternoon, then. But don't come to the house," he insisted. "Meet me at the elevator site so we can talk about our options."

"See you then. With at least half of that hundred thousand bucks." *Click.*

Wyman sank onto the wooden bench near the phone. How had this opportunity for his future changed so radically? Just a few weeks ago the details of his move to Bloomingdale had effortlessly come together because, he believed, God was directing him to start a new life with his new blended family on Amanda's farm. He'd sold the Brubaker home place to the Fisher family for less than market value because he and Ray had been best friends since childhood, and so that Ray's son could move there to expand his dairy operation when he got married.

The transaction with the Fisher family had been seamless, on a handshake. Wyman had felt confident that he could afford a new facility—in addition to the elevator he and Ray had run since they'd been young and single—or he wouldn't have dreamed of stretching his family's finances so thin. They had agreed that Weaver Construction would do the work because they wanted to support other Plain businesses in the area.

Had they made a mistake? Maybe they should've gotten a bid from another construction company . . . but it was too late for that now. They had already put down more than half the money up front.

Wyman punched in Ray's phone number, hoping his level-headed Mennonite partner would offer him some advice. Because Ray had already borrowed a large amount to buy the Brubaker place, Wyman had insisted on financing the new elevator with the money from that sale and the Clearwater business account, without expecting Ray to kick in any more. Out of sheer Amish tradition and principle, Wyman refused to get a loan from an English bank to make this deal work—or to feed his family. Generations of Brubaker men had remained staunchly self-sufficient, supporting one another rather than going to outside sources for funding.

The phone clicked in his ear. "Hullo?"

"Jah, Ray. How was your weekend?" Wyman relaxed, knowing he could trust his partner's feedback, his sense of perspective. "I suppose you and Sally and the boys are gearing up for Trevor's wedding . . ."

* * *

On the other side of the barn wall, Amanda listened as her husband chatted with his partner. She and the twins had been gathering eggs in the adjoining henhouse, and when she'd heard Wyman holler, *"A hundred thousand dollars?"* she'd sent the girls outside to scatter feed. It wasn't Wyman's way to raise his voice. His calm demeanor and sensible approach to problems were two of the traits that had attracted her when they'd courted.

"Got a call from Reece Weaver this morning, and I don't know what to make of it," Wyman was saying into the phone. "He's telling me he needs another hundred thousand dollars—half of it *today*—because he ran into bedrock and some other unexpected issues . . . Jah, this is on top of the seven hundred thousand on his bid."

Amanda sucked in her breath at such a large amount of money. Wyman was a careful planner, a solid businessman, and his rising voice said it all: he was upset about this new development—and very concerned about where so much additional money would come from.

"When we were going over the items on his bid, didn't you think Reece had covered all the angles?" Wyman asked. "I can't have him coming by the house or leaving any more phone messages about needing money, so I'm meeting him at the elevator site this afternoon . . ."

Ah. So Wyman was protecting her from this situation, was he? Amanda understood that because, like any Amish husband, he believed it was his responsibility to support their family. But she knew firsthand about making their pennies stretch far enough . . . about the fear that she might not be able to pay the propane bill or buy shoes for her three young daughters. For four years after her first husband had died, she'd been their sole support by making pottery to sell in area gift shops.

Wyman sold his home place, left everything he'd loved all his life, so you could be happy here in Bloomingdale, Amanda reminded herself. *You can't let him face this crisis alone . . . even if he won't tell you about it. He may be the head of this family, but* you *are in charge of keeping everyone fed and together, body and soul. Better get back to work at your wheel!*

Amanda stepped away from the wall as the twins bustled into the henhouse with the empty feed bucket. In the cold air, the wisps of their breath framed their precious faces. "Let's take the eggs to the house, girls. Maybe Vera or Mammi will help you bake your cookies," she said gently as she stroked their pink cheeks. "Your mamma's going to start making her dishes again."

Chapter 2

Always a bridesmaid, never a bride.

It was barely five o'clock in the morning, not nearly day-light yet. As Emma Graber peered at the white-draped ta-bles in the greenhouse, where the wedding feast for her brother James and Abby Lambright would take place later today, the familiar saying made her sigh. This traditional Thursday ceremony in mid-November marked the fourth wedding Cedar Creek had celebrated this fall, and now that her brother was finally marrying her best friend, Emma felt her inner clock ticking.

Life was passing her by. She'd always pictured herself wed to Abby's nephew, Matt Lambright, but he'd married Rosemary Yutzy in September, leaving Emma to lament all those years she'd spent pining for an unrequited love and caring for her aging parents. Was she now doomed to re-main a maidel? She'd been paired with Jerome Lambright as a sidesitter at Amanda and Wyman Brubaker's wedding, and she'd spent most of that day—and a few occasions since then—avoiding his flirtatious looks and remarks. He'd be around all day today, too, and Emma was feeling edgy about his presence. Jerome seemed awfully flashy, showing off with his mule teams . . . acting way too full of himself. But was she a fool to shy away from his attention?

Emma told herself such concerns had *not* kept her awake half the night—that she'd been dressed for the wedding at four this morning because the local women had agreed they'd prepare the food early, to discourage Abby from helping at her own wedding. Indeed, the back door of the glass-walled greenhouse swung open, and the bride stepped inside as though she intended to work while no one could catch her at it.

"Gut morning, Abby! All ready for your big day?" Emma called out.

Abby's startled laughter rang in the large high-ceilinged room. "Jah, and I don't know what to do with myself, Emma!" she admitted as she strode between the tables. "Mamm and Barbara and the rest of them keep insisting I'm not to cook or cut pies or—"

Emma caught her best friend in a hug, reveling in the way Abby returned her embrace. "See there? It's not as easy as you think, accepting help from other folks," she teased. "Consider this whole day—all the food and the work your friends want to do—as their gift to you, Abby. I expect to see you smiling alongside James, enjoying yourself until the last guests go home tonight."

"I've heard *that* a time or two." Abby glanced across the road toward the Graber house, which was as lit up as the Lambright place. "And how're your folks doing this morning, Emma?"

"Dat's spinning like a top and Mamm's fussing over every little thing. What with having our two sisters' families staying over last night, I've been reminded how large gatherings are getting harder for Mamm to handle." She let out a sigh.

"Jah, we've got a houseful, too," Abby murmured. "But I'm so glad both of your folks are alive to celebrate this day with us. Mamm's not saying as much, but I suspect she's wishing Dat were here to—"

Hoofbeats and the rumble of wheels made them turn to watch a wagon and two other horse-drawn rigs pull into Lambright Lane. Their lanterns and headlights glowed in the indigo sky as the horses' breath rose from their nostrils. "This'll be Beulah Mae bringing the steam tables, no doubt," Emma said as she rebuttoned her coat. "Makes it mighty handy, having her restaurant and Lois's bakery in town to do most of the cooking for these big events."

"Jah, that's Preacher Abe climbing down from the first wagon," Abby confirmed. "I'll get Sam so the menfolk can assemble our serving line."

Emma went outside with her, waving as the Nissleys, Lois Yutzy's family, and Amanda Brubaker and her girls emerged from the various vehicles. Even though these ladies had prepared most of the food ahead of time, they still had a lot to do before they'd be ready to serve nearly three hundred people. Guests would start arriving around sunup for the eight o'clock church service that preceded the wedding. As one of Abby's sidesitters, Emma was hoping to help with some of the work before she spent the entire morning seated beside the bride.

The next couple of hours sped by. The ladies from around the neighborhood had cooked for so many weddings that the flurry was well organized. Lois Yutzy carried in the white tiered wedding cake she'd made in her bakery, where several women had also helped her bake the bread for today's feast. While Lois arranged the cake on the eck, the raised corner table where the wedding party would sit, Beulah Mae Nissley was supervising her husband, Preacher Abe, and Abby's brother, Preacher Sam Lambright, as they constructed the metal steam table. Amanda Brubaker's two older daughters were setting silverware bundles and glasses on the dinner tables, while other women began slicing loaves of fresh bread.

Emma looked up from the silverware she'd been wrapping in paper napkins and hurried over to open the greenhouse door. "That's quite a load of pies!" she said as Rosemary, her neighbor, pulled her tall-sided cart inside. After marrying Matt Lambright a couple of months ago, Rosemary was already off to a busy start with her home-based baking business.

"Jah, my new oven can handle a dozen pies at a time," Rosemary replied pertly. She smiled as her toddler, Katie, and her young sister-in-law, Beth Ann, burst in to help set the table. "It seems that no matter how many pies I make for Lois's shop, they sell out every day. And, of course, Matt, Katie, and Titus work hard at being my taste testers."

When Rosemary wheeled her cart toward the dessert table, Emma felt a stab of jealousy. After having learned the hard way that Matt didn't love her, Emma was wishing he hadn't moved his sheep to the farm next to her house when he'd partnered with Titus Yutzy. All of them seemed so *happy*—and that rubbed her the wrong way, too.

Get over it, Emma chided herself. It did no good to regret the years of affection she'd wasted on Matt. When she realized it was after seven o'clock, she decided to go home to be sure Mamm and Dat were dressed and almost ready to head over to the Lambrights'. What with her two sisters' families staying with them, her parents were easily distracted.

When Emma stepped outside, however, she spotted James walking between their parents. He called to her with a knowing grin, "The folks were ready early, so they wanted to come on over—to greet folks as they arrive, you know. Our sisters and their tribes will be along shortly."

There was no missing the bright excitement on Mamm's and Dat's faces. They'd been waiting for years to see their only son married, and they couldn't be happier that he was so in love with Abby Lambright. "Jah, better claim your seats early," Emma teased as she met up with them. "It might well be standing room only at Sam's place today."

"It's the wedding everybody hereabouts has been waiting for," her dat exclaimed as he clapped James on the back. His dark eyes sparkled in his wrinkled face. "And we'll be planning for *your* wedding next, Emma. Ain't so?"

"Just saw the Brubaker fellows coming up the road, matter of fact," her mother chimed in. "And sure enough, Jerome's driving a matched pair of Percheron mules. Looks like a successful man come courting, if you ask me."

Well, I didn't ask you! Emma almost blurted. It was bad enough that Abby and James had paired her with Jerome Lambright to serve as their sidesitters today—another obvious matchmaking ploy. There was no time to respond to her parents' remarks, however. She guided them off the lane and onto the frosty grass to make way for some other families' incoming rigs.

Then two tall black mules trotted up alongside them, and the windows of the large enclosed buggy came down. "Gut morning, you Grabers!" Jerome called out, as Wyman Brubaker and his three sons, seated beside and behind Jerome, joined in with their own greetings. "It'll be a little chummy, but we've got room to take you folks on up to the house if you'd like a ride."

"Jah, this is the *man* rig!" five-year-old Simon crowed. "But we'd let *you* ride, Emma!"

"And you, too, Eunice," Jerome added quickly. He smiled at Emma's mother, and then his eyebrows rose playfully as his gaze lingered on Emma.

Could these people be any more blatant about coaxing her into Jerome's company? For the past month, Jerome had been showing off his mules and making eyes at her, and meanwhile befriending her gullible parents. After all her refusals of his attention, why didn't they realize that Jerome just wasn't her type? Emma kept hold of her mother's elbow and worded her response as politely as she could. "I've got pies to cut," she insisted.

Her dat let out a laugh. "I'll ride with you, Jerome. We fellows might as well have our fun today, because you can bet the women will insist on working."

"I'll join you, too." James helped their father step up into the buggy's open door. "We'll see Mamm and Emma come time for church to start."

"This'll be your final trip up this lane as a single man, James," Jerome teased. "Last chance to ride off into the sunrise before you're yoked to Abby forever."

"Ah, but Abby's yoke is easy and her burden is light," James quipped as he climbed in behind Dat.

The smile on her brother's face touched something deep inside Emma. James was *beaming*, far more excited and open about his feelings than he'd been when he'd nearly married Abby's sister last year. And Abby seemed to be floating on clouds these days, too.

So many new couples . . . so much joy in Cedar Creek, Emma mused as she and Mamm walked toward the greenhouse. *Will I find my own happy ending soon? Or will I be left out of the storybook altogether?*

Jerome unhitched the buggy alongside Sam Lambright's barn and corralled the mules where all the guests' horses would spend the day. James and Merle Graber and the Brubakers were chatting with other fellows, but he strode straight toward the greenhouse rather than visit with them. Emma was being her usual skittish self today, but he was a man with a plan. He hoped he'd devised a way to get her out on a date—without it seeming like one. Ever since he'd met this pretty but reclusive brunette last month, and had immediately become lost in her honey brown eyes, he'd sought to spend time alone with her. She was so unlike the other girls he'd been attracted to.

But clearly, Emma wasn't impressed with him. *Why not?*

As he entered the greenhouse where Preacher Sam's mother, Treva Lambright, sold plants, pumpkins, and gift items, the glass-paneled building sparkled in the sunlight and buzzed like a beehive. The contents of the greenhouse had been cleared out and long tables had been set up, covered with white tablecloths, and arranged with glasses and silverware. Several women and girls chatted as they transferred food to rectangular metal pans for the steam table and placed cookies on serving trays. Jerome headed for the table in the back corner. Few men dared to venture into the food-preparation area before a wedding, but the older ladies greeted him with knowing smiles as he stepped up beside Emma.

"Emma, may I ask you a huge favor?" he said in a low voice. "It's something I don't want to mention when Abby and James might overhear me."

Emma looked up from cutting a pumpkin pie. "What kind of favor?" she asked.

Jerome smiled. How perfect was this? Aunt Amanda, his niece Lizzie, and Eunice Graber were working alongside Emma, cutting and placing slices of pie on plates, so he had his own cheering section. Curiosity lit their faces as he continued.

"I need help picking out a wedding gift for Abby and James," Jerome said earnestly. "I'm a clueless bachelor when it comes to such things, but as the sister of the groom and the bride's best friend, you surely must have some gut ideas about what to choose. After all the help those two have given my family these past few months, I want to show my appreciation with a really fine gift."

Emma looked like a startled deer, her hazel eyes widening in a face that was turning pink. It was a pretty face, too, and with her hair tucked neatly into a starched white kapp and a dress of royal blue beneath a filmy white apron, she could well have been the bride. *Maybe someday,* Jerome mused as he held Emma's gaze.

"You mean we'd be . . . shopping?" she asked hesitantly.

"Jah. I'm not much gut at crafting something of wood, or choosing household items," he replied with a shrug. "If we could pick a day sometime soon to drive around to some furniture stores, maybe—"

"Ah, but with James being so busy in his carriage shop," Emma interrupted, "and since he and Abby will be spending the next several weekends visiting relatives to get their wedding gifts, I'll need to stay at home with the folks."

Jerome watched Aunt Amanda's expression and then Eunice's, biding his time. The next few moments of silence didn't bother him at all because he'd expected Emma's usual excuse—and, indeed, he respected her for the way she looked after Eunice and Merle. Emma centered a spoked metal cutter over another pie and pushed it down to make eight equal wedges, acting as though she had settled the matter of going shopping with him.

"It just so happens that Jemima and the girls and I are making quilts as our gifts to the newlyweds," Amanda said with a purposeful glance at Eunice. "We'll be starting them this Saturday—"

"Oh, I'd love to help with those quilts!" Emma's mamm blurted.

"So if you'd like to join us, Merle could visit with the men while Jerome and Emma shop."

Eunice's eyes lit up behind her pointy-cornered glasses. "Better yet, why not have Jerome drive you girls into Cedar Creek and we'll have the quilting frolic at *our* house! He's got to come into town anyway, ain't so?"

"That would give us a chance to buy the batting and more thread at the mercantile, too," Lizzie remarked as she carried away a tray of plated pie.

"I can't see well enough to thread a needle or to cut straight edges anymore, but I sure do love frolics," Eunice remarked wistfully. "We've got long worktables, and I could get our lunch ready while the rest of you sew. Seems to me this would be a wonderful-gut chance for all of us to work on James and Abby's gifts while they're not around to watch us, too."

"Perfect!" Amanda declared. "And this way Wyman and the boys won't have to endure an all-day hen party."

"But—but *I'd* like to help with the quilting, too." Emma's brow puckered. "That's something I never have the chance to do unless—"

"Unless we have another quilting frolic at my house the following Saturday!" Amanda looked extremely pleased with herself for making this plan dovetail like the patchwork pieces they were discussing. "We can't possibly finish in one session, after all. So, Emma, if you'll drive your folks to Bloomingdale on the twenty-eighth, we'll make a day of it. It'll be like an extension of Thanksgiving, with all of us together."

Jerome could practically see the wheels spinning in Emma's mind as she searched for another way to evade him. Yet—without him saying a single word—his aunt and Emma's mother had neatly sewn up his plans and stitched her into a corner, for they had given Emma her wish, too. Meanwhile, Amanda and Eunice had provided him a second day to visit with her, even if he wouldn't be sitting with them while they quilted.

"So Saturday morning, then?" he asked gently. "Day after tomorrow?"

Emma released the breath she'd been holding. She didn't look overjoyed, but at least she was accepting the situation. "Jah, looks that way."

"I really appreciate your help, Emma," Jerome said. Then he winked at her. "And *maybe* we'll even have some fun!"

Chapter 3

As Bishop Vernon Gingerich stood up to give the wedding sermon, Emma shifted on the pew. Jerome was looking directly at her, silently seeking her attention. With the wall partitions taken down to expand most of Preacher Sam's main floor into one huge space for church, nearly three hundred people had crowded onto the pew benches, but the center area, where the preachers stood, was very small. Emma sat with Abby in the front row of the women's side, just as Jerome flanked James on the men's side about ten feet across from her. Nothing blocked Jerome's line of sight.

Emma had nowhere to hide.

"Brothers and sisters," Vernon began in his resonant voice, "I have had the honor of preaching at hundreds of weddings in my thirty years of ministry, yet still I ask our Lord's presence and guidance as He brings pertinent words to my tongue. I must say that the man and woman I join in holy matrimony today are an inspiration to us all. They stand before us as examples of the fruits of the Spirit: love, joy, peace, long-suffering, gentleness, goodness, and faith." The bishop's white-bearded face lit up as he glanced at the bride and then at the groom. "It's a privilege to behold the love and respect James Graber and Abigail Lambright have for each other, and to lead them in their vows later in the service."

Abby blushed as red as a rose at the compliment. She grabbed Emma's hand, and Emma squeezed back. When Emma glanced over at her brother, James looked a little amazed by the bishop's praise, but his love for Abby radiated from his face. All around the room, friends and family nodded in agreement with Vernon's sentiments.

Jerome, however, was gazing directly at Emma, as though the two of them were alone in the room. Flustered, Emma looked away. Why was he paying such insistent attention to her? Surely he realized she'd agreed to go shopping with him only because she couldn't get out of it. She was doing it as a favor to Abby and James more than as a way to be with him.

"Love is patient and kind," Vernon continued in a low, rolling voice. As he extolled these virtues, paraphrasing the beloved passage from First Corinthians, he pointed out that while both James and Abby had shown the Cedar Creek community many examples of those traits as single folks, marriage might expand their understanding of what it meant to accept each other's little quirks and habits, once the novelty of being newlyweds wore off.

You *are patient and kind,* Jerome mouthed at Emma. Then he smiled sweetly at her.

Emma's cheeks prickled with heat as she lowered her gaze. Such a compliment was the last thing she'd expected from Jerome. Or was he just flirting with her?

"I'd like those of us who've been married for a while to reflect back on when we were in Abby and James's place," Vernon went on. "I guarantee that as the years of joys and heartaches have accumulated, we've gained a different perspective on the love Paul the apostle speaks of in the Bible. When we reflect upon how love bears all things, believes all things, hopes and endures all things, we realize how very innocent and inexperienced we were when we took our marriage vows, even though we believed ourselves to be totally, irrevocably in love with our new mate."

Several of the folks in the room were nodding. Even though Emma knew better, she glanced at Jerome again.

His face brightened as he met her gaze. *Love bears all things, believes all things,* he mouthed. *Hopes all things, endures all things.*

Emma's breath caught. Was Jerome telling her that he understood her trials and tribulations as she cared for her parents, yet he still hoped to spend time with her? Or was she reading too much into his silent messages? He looked especially handsome today in his black vest and trousers with a crisp white shirt.

As the bishop wound down his sermon, Emma's heart was pounding so loudly, she wondered whether Abby could hear it. Jerome was being discreet enough that most folks wouldn't notice the attention he was paying her, but she still felt as though he'd been whispering those words about love directly into her ear. No other man had ever acted so . . . enthralled.

But why was she getting caught up in Jerome's romantic gestures? At twenty-four, he hadn't yet joined the church, and he'd backed out of two engagements. Falling for him would surely leave her disappointed and heartbroken. And why would she want to get serious about a fellow whose mule-breeding business was in Bloomingdale, an hour's drive away—too far from Cedar Creek to make dating him a practical idea?

"And now faith, hope, and love abide, these three," Vernon paraphrased in a rising voice. "But the greatest of these is love. Abby and James, if you will rise and stand before us, we will begin that most sacred and beloved of ceremonies that will bind the two of you into one heart and mind from this day forth."

Emma sighed. Hearing the wedding vows for the fourth time within the last few weeks only reminded her that she wouldn't be repeating these words after Vernon anytime soon. And while Jerome's attention was making her all fluttery inside, she didn't want to encourage further eye contact with him during the ceremony. Why should she let him believe she was interested in him? *He assumes I'll be like dozens of other girls who've gone head over heels when he noticed them. After the ceremony, I'll stay busy helping with the meal instead of sitting beside Jerome at the eck table. It's for the best. I'll be seeing him on Saturday, after all.*

Emma couldn't escape the traditional signing of the marriage certificate immediately following the ceremony, however. When the crowd rose to congratulate the newlyweds, she hurried over to the little table, took up the pen, and wrote her name on the witness line as Jerome waited for his turn.

"It's my job to tell the servers the wedding has ended," she said breezily. Before he could protest, Emma skirted the crowd and hurried toward the greenhouse, across a lawn strewn with fallen leaves of red and gold. She inhaled the crisp, refreshing air. Sam's house had gotten stuffy with so many folks crammed together for nearly five hours, and it felt good to get up and move.

"And it's *my* job to check the eck before the bride and groom arrive," Jerome teased as he caught up to her. Rather than opening the door of the greenhouse for her, he stepped in front of her and leaned against it, holding Emma's gaze yet again with his deep brown eyes. "Why are you running away from me, Emma? I have only the best intentions," he insisted gently. "Did it bother you when I admired your patience and kindness—the way you bear all things and believe all things?"

How should she respond to that? She didn't want to fall for his glib compliments and the winsome expression on his face, only inches from hers. "*You* might be hoping all things," she murmured, "but you're setting yourself up for disappointment, Jerome. I take my responsibilities to my parents seriously."

"Emma," he entreated her in a lingering whisper, "I respect you immensely for keeping your family fed and cared for. But your folks would be a lot happier if you'd get out and enjoy yourself more. They've told me so."

Emma's mouth dropped open. *Get out and enjoy yourself more?* She was inclined not to believe him, yet she could well imagine Dat and Mamm telling him that, because they adored Jerome and enjoyed the time he spent with them. Still, Emma wasn't falling for it. "We really need to get inside before the crowd arrives," she told Jerome. "You have your jobs, and I have mine."

Jerome didn't budge. "I just want to have some *fun* with you, because I really *like* you, Emma. Won't you please give me a chance?" He held her gaze for a few moments more, then cleared his throat. "I've heard you were sweet on Matt Lambright all through school, and I'm sorry he didn't return your affection. That had to be a hard pill to swallow, when he married Rosemary and then moved right next door to you."

Emma wished she could disappear. While Jerome had probably learned about her feelings for Matt from her parents as well, it still rattled her that he knew so much about her love life—or lack of one. "I don't need your pity, Jerome," she snapped.

"Pity?" His eyebrows rose. "On the contrary, I admire your longtime loyalty to Matt. It strikes me as . . . very special. I'd like to make up for the good times I suspect you've missed out on—but now I've embarrassed you." He sighed as he opened the door for her. "I'm sorry, Emma. When I really want something to work out, I tend to speak before I think."

Emma's pulse was pounding, and as she entered the airy, glass-walled greenhouse, she hoped the ladies who'd been preparing the meal didn't notice her red face. To settle her nerves, she inhaled the tantalizing aromas of the traditional chicken and stuffing "roast" and the creamed celery. After what Jerome had said about her unrequited affection for Matt, it would be even more difficult to sit beside him for the entire wedding feast, in front of everyone. She really needed to keep herself too busy to—

Why are you so upset? Jerome's a nice fellow, complimenting you and expressing his concern. You could do worse than spending your time with such a good-looking, successful man.

Emma blinked. That sounded like something her mother would say.

Okay, so Jerome came on a little too strong—but he apologized. Maybe you don't know how to respond to his attention because you've hardly dated anyone, while he's been engaged twice . . .

Why were her feelings riding such a seesaw? This wasn't the time or the place to let Jerome's attention distract her. Emma focused again on the tables that were set for the meal and on the things she could do to make this day totally wonderful for Abby and James.

"It was a beautiful wedding!" she called out to Beulah Mae, Lois, and the other helpers who'd remained there to oversee the final food preparations. "Folks'll be coming over any minute now."

The cooks and servers bustled about, lifting the covers from the metal pans in the steam table and checking the food one last time. The bread and slices of pie were already on the tables, so Emma helped fill the water glasses as the first of the wedding guests stepped through the door. Abby and James entered the greenhouse, and the whole place seemed to light up with the joy that shone on their faces as they gazed at each other.

That's how love's supposed to be, Emma mused as she took her place beside Abby on the eck. *I want nothing less for myself.*

Once the helpers had served the wedding party, the other guests made their way through the buffet line. As Emma began to eat the delicious chicken and stuffing, creamed celery, and other delectable dishes, she realized just how ravenous she'd become during the long morning's activities. "The ladies outdid themselves on this meal," she remarked to Abby.

"Jah, they did. And to think they accomplished everything without *me*!"

Emma laughed with her best friend and squeezed her hand. "I wish you and James all the happiness your hearts can hold."

Abby flashed her a radiant smile. "And I wish you the same, Emma. Every woman should be as delighted as I feel right now, knowing God has given her exactly the right husband to share her life."

Tears sprang to Emma's eyes, but they were tears of happiness for Abby . . . weren't they? Or was she once again despairing of ever finding a man to love her the way James adored Abby?

Emma sighed. Jerome was sitting at her other side, eating in silence. Even though his earlier remarks had made her uncomfortable, he hadn't been unkind—and maybe, after two unsuccessful engagements, he, too, was wondering if he'd ever find the right person to love. Emma was trying to think of a way to engage him in conversation again, when Rudy Ropp, who owned the dairy farm down the hill, stepped up to the eck.

"Say there, Jerome, that was quite the picture of your eight-mule hitch in the latest issue of the *Connection*," he remarked. "Looks like you trained a team of prize-winners."

Jerome's smile lit up his whole face. "Jah, when the mules'

owner sent me that photo, Jemima insisted on sending it to the magazine. Seems that mule team's already won a couple of competitions. Come January, they'll go on to the *big* shows at the National Western in Denver."

Titus Yutzy and Mervin Mast came up to the eck then, to add their comments. "I recall the day you were strutting that team's stuff, hauling a wagonload of folks down the county road," Titus said.

"Jah, it was as fine a parade as I've ever seen, even if it was just your one wagon," Mervin joined in. "I rushed outside to see what was making that *thunder* down the road, and there came your team, with every mule stepping in cadence—like you'd trained them to march to music!"

Emma took a bite of her pumpkin pie. She remembered that day because she had been riding in that fancy wagon as Jerome drove those mules. And it *had* been an awesome experience—*and Jerome had to trick you into coming, coaxing Mamm to ride so you'd be the only one left at home if you didn't join them.*

She blinked. Maybe she really did need to get out more . . . but right now, keeping busy seemed the best way to dodge her confused thoughts.

Although as a member of the wedding party Emma was entitled to enjoy an afternoon of visiting rather than helping during the meal, she stood up to scrape plates. "I'm doing this so *you* won't, Abby," she informed the bride. "I hope James will keep you so occupied visiting your guests that you don't wash a single dish or fetch so much as a cookie for anybody today."

As Abby laughed, James slipped his arm around her shoulders. "That's my plan, Emma. We'll resume our responsibilities tomorrow, come time to clean up. I figure on enjoying our big day now that the serious part is over."

Emma agreed wholeheartedly, just as she found particular fulfillment in making herself useful. Because the Graber and Lambright families were hosting so many guests from all over the Midwest today, a second shift would eat the meal after this bunch of folks had finished their pie—and that meant a lot of dishes to be gathered up and washed. Then, after the singing and games this afternoon, several of the guests would remain for supper and the cutting of the wedding cake.

Emma picked up a dish bin and started down the table where folks had first been seated and were starting to leave. She chatted with some of them but remained focused on piling the dishes carefully in the bin so they wouldn't break. Lost in thought, she looked up to find Matt Lambright smiling at her from his seat at the table. Rosemary's toddler, Katie, had settled into his lap, looking ready to snooze, and the sweetness of this father-daughter scene took Emma's breath away.

"Another happy day in Cedar Creek," Matt remarked. "We've been waiting for James and Abby to tie the knot for a long time now."

Emma got so choked up, she couldn't answer him. She grabbed the dish bin to go empty it so she didn't have to behold Matt's satisfied smile as he hugged Katie close.

Chapter 4

Wyman Brubaker rose from the table feeling very full—he'd eaten a heaped plate of the wedding roast, mashed potatoes with creamed celery, and his favorite green bean casserole with the crunchy onions on top, along with some salads. But even after completing the meal with a slice of cherry pie, he felt . . . anxious. In the past few days, he and his partner had talked on the phone several times and had decided not to give in to Reece Weaver's demand for more money, but still he'd lain awake at night, wondering how he'd support his family through the winter. Now it was time to seek advice.

"See you boys around," he said to Eddie and Pete, who were devouring second platefuls from the buffet line. Wyman rested his hand on Simon's head, amazed at how much food his five-year-old had tucked away. "And you, Son, will be making everyone remark about how well-behaved you are today, jah? No more stunts like you pulled when Amanda and I got married."

Simon feigned wide-eyed innocence as he reached for his pie. "But, Dat, I didn't pull the tablecloth off that table on purpose! I was just excited."

"Rowdy and out of control is more like it," Wyman insisted. He'd never forget the ominous crash of plates, glasses of water, and potted plants that had brought his wedding dinner to a halt last month while the servers scurried for brooms. "I'll be visiting with the men, but don't think I'm not watching you."

"Jah, Dat's got eyes in the back of his head," Pete warned his little brother.

"And Amanda's already got you so figured out, she knows when you're going to do something ornery even before *you* do." Eddie widened his eyes ominously, gazing at Simon.

"Jah, like you guys never pester Lizzie, or smart off, or break stuff." Simon forked up a big chunk of pumpkin pie and jammed it into his mouth.

"And those are just a few of the things I expect *not* to see this afternoon, got it?" Wyman said in a purposeful voice.

As he made his way between the tables, Wyman greeted several folks he knew—even some from as far away as Clearwater, where he'd spent his entire life until he'd moved to Amanda's farm in Bloomingdale a few weeks ago. When he spotted Vernon Gingerich leaving the greenhouse, however, he walked faster to catch up with him. The white-haired bishop from Cedar Creek had offered to talk with him about adjusting to life with his large, blended family, and he valued Vernon's practicality about financial matters as well.

Once outside, he was pleased to see that Sam Lambright was also stepping over to speak with Vernon. Surely these two stable, established businessmen—one ran the Cedar Creek Mercantile and the other owned a herd of fine black Angus cattle—would offer some words of much-needed wisdom.

"Say, can I bend you fellows' ears for a moment?" Wyman called out as he followed them across Sam's leaf-strewn lawn.

Bishop Gingerich flashed a beatific smile that exuded boyish happiness blended with venerable wisdom. Wyman raised a hand in welcome as the two church leaders waited for him to catch up. And now that he'd gotten their attention, he had to confide in them, didn't he? No more trying to shoulder his doubts alone, thinking it was the manly way to handle his troublesome situation with Reece Weaver.

"All settled into Bloomingdale?" Vernon asked him. "One of these days I'd like to make it over that way to look at Jerome's mules. Might be in the market for one."

"He'd be happy to work with you," Wyman replied.

Sam, the taller of the two preachers, gazed directly at him as though already detecting his troubled thoughts. "And how's your new grain elevator coming along? That's a major project, but you've got the perfect location for it."

Wyman glanced around to be sure no one could overhear. As well-loved as Vernon was, it was only a matter of time before other folks would want to visit with him. "That's exactly what's on my mind, Sam. Have either of you fellows had any dealings with Weaver Construction in the past few years?"

"Can't say as I have," Vernon replied. "They do mostly commercial construction, the way I understand it."

"Jah, and folks around these parts usually have our Amos and Owen Coblentz build their homes and cabinets and such," Sam continued with a nod. "I noticed you frowning during the wedding—and I was hoping it wasn't because I'd said something that upset you during the first sermon."

Wyman chuckled. He should've realized that Sam and Vernon, two very astute spiritual leaders, would sense when he was troubled. "I wish it were that simple—and something I could go back and do differently," he replied.

"Reece Weaver's dat built the elevator in Clearwater several years back, so naturally my partner and I wanted his Plain family to construct the new one. But Reece isn't cut from the same cloth his father was."

"The younger generation often takes on a whole different attitude," Sam agreed.

Wyman sighed. "*Attitude* isn't the half of it. When Reece first went over his estimate with Ray and me, everything seemed to be spelled out. I paid him more than half of the total amount so he could get started right away. Used the money from selling my place in Clearwater."

Vernon's eyebrows rose. "It's usually not prudent to mix business money and personal money, I've found."

"True enough, but it kept me from having to take out a loan," Wyman explained. "I banked the rest of the money from my farm, figuring it would get us through this winter until the new elevator was up and running. But when Reece called Monday to say he needed another hundred thousand dollars immediately, due to some unforeseen EPA regulations and having to blast through bedrock, I nearly keeled over in the barn."

Both preachers' faces expressed dismay. "Reece should've known about those regulations, and what the geological survey of your place said, before he finalized the deal," Vernon stated.

"Jah, I'm not familiar with current building codes, but I don't like the sound of that at all," Sam said with a shake of his head. "What did you do, Wyman?"

"I talked with Ray, and he thinks we should stand firm—or pay Reece only part of that extra expense until the foundation is poured and we know the actual costs from the heavy equipment operators." Wyman felt himself getting wound up all over again and took a deep breath to settle his nerves. "Reece insists his crew will only be available for my job for a short while, and I want my concrete poured before winter sets in, so I'm at the mercy of his schedule."

"Hmm . . . maybe that's what Reece *wants* you to think," Vernon remarked. "Did you give him the money?"

"A hundred thousand dollars would have left me seriously short for getting us through the winter," he admitted. "I took him twenty-five thousand and said he'd have to proceed with the job like we'd already planned. He was none too happy."

"Is it too late to hire a different contractor?" Sam queried.

Wyman exhaled loudly. He'd asked himself time and again if he should've taken bids from other fellows, and the two preachers seemed to echo his misgivings about the way Reece did business. "He's already started digging, so I can't think he'll give any of my money back. And by the time I could hire someone else—"

"You'd be getting into heavy frost, and the ground would be freezing around your concrete," Vernon agreed.

"I—I don't want Amanda to worry that I've overextended us, after I assured her I'd be able to support our blended family." Wyman glanced toward the greenhouse. Through the glass panels, he saw his wife working alongside local ladies as the second shift of guests sat down to dinner. "Amanda's such a fine woman, and my kids are settling into their new routine at her place. We've been through a lot lately, considering how that storm last month sent a couple of trees through our house in Clearwater. What if that had happened *before* I married Amanda? We Brubakers would've been in a bad way—and we wouldn't have had a home to move into."

"And just as the Lord led you to Amanda, He'll show you the way through this problem with your contractor," Vernon said, squeezing Wyman's shoulder, his blue eyes glowing with compassion. "I wouldn't sell your new wife short, far as being able to handle a tight winter, either."

"Jah, she got her girls and Jemima through four tough years after Atlee died," Sam pointed out. "And with Jerome's mule business doing so well, he'll be helping out, too. We Lambrights look after one another, and now you and your kids are *family*, Wyman."

"But you've already restocked our Bloomingdale kitchen— replaced the food we lost, as well as the kids' clothes, after the storm hit our other house," Wyman protested. "And you gave Eddie a job painting your store—"

Sam held up his hand, gazing purposefully over Wyman's shoulder as though someone were approaching from behind him. "Don't be too proud to ask for my help, understand?" he murmured.

"We'll keep your troublesome situation in our prayers," Vernon added solemnly. "It's the least—and the most—any of us can do for one another. And speaking of your fine wife, here she comes."

Wyman turned to watch Amanda stride across the lawn, with her gray shawl draped over her dress of deep plum. Her smile lifted his spirits, and he felt grateful for the way this woman believed in him and had so greatly improved his life. "Did the ladies give you time off for gut behavior, my dear?" he asked, extending his hand.

Amanda grasped his fingers and included Sam and Vernon in her wide smile. "I thought I'd take a break, to see what the kids're up to while I got some fresh air," she said. "It's such a wonderful day, celebrating Abby and James's marriage, but it *has* been several hours since I started cooking this morning."

"And I can't thank you and your girls enough," Sam said. "What with Abby not helping today, Barbara and Mamm and my girls appreciate some extra hands."

"Vera and Lizzie were pleased to come—and Jemima, too," Amanda added. "At home, they've taken on the laundry and most of the chores, because the Bloomingdale bishop is allowing me to make my pottery again! So today's wedding is a chance for them to be with friends. It's a nice outing, even if they've been just as busy as I have."

"So Lamar Lapp's a more lenient bishop than Uriah Schmucker, is he?" Vernon asked with a smile. He clasped his hands behind his back, assuming a pensive expression.

"As long as I paint with muted colors and stick to useful, practical pieces, Lamar's letting me put the new kiln and wheel Wyman bought me to gut use, jah," Amanda replied as she squeezed Wyman's hand.

"And you're all right with her pottery making, Wyman?" Sam asked. "Some fellows insist that their wives focus on the kids and the household."

"I see this as a way for my kids to take on more responsibilities—as you fellows discussed with me earlier," Wyman replied firmly. "I'm grateful that Amanda's able to carry on with a productive activity she loves, too. We'll never forget the day Uriah smashed a bunch of her dishes in front of the younger kids, claiming her skills were sinful. After that incident, I lost all faith in him as a spiritual leader."

"I'm glad to hear you're at your wheel again, Amanda, because now I have a fine gift idea for James and Abby!" Vernon focused intently on her, a grin twitching at his lips. "I'd like you to make a set of gut, sturdy everyday dishes—plates, bowls, and mugs as well as platters and serving pieces—in whatever color you think Abby will prefer," he said as he reached into his vest pocket. "And I'm going to advance you a down payment."

Amanda's eyes widened with delight. "I'd be happy to do that! How many place settings?"

"Eight sounds like a nice round number," the bishop replied as he took out his checkbook.

"And I'm going to ask you for another eight place settings," Sam chimed in. "Barbara and I were just talking about what to give the newlyweds, and Vernon's hit on the perfect idea. Abby and James will be delighted with dishes you've made, Amanda—and this way, they'll have enough for when all of us come for dinner. My checkbook's in the house, so let's head up there and I'll give you a down payment as well."

Wyman sensed his wife's excitement, and he wanted her to enjoy this moment. "I'll see you in a few, Amanda," he said. "I get suspicious when everything's quiet and Simon's nowhere to be seen," he added wryly.

Sam and Vernon laughed and continued toward the tall white Lambright home, with Amanda walking between them. The folks who'd eaten dinner in the first shift were clustering in the yard, some of them also heading to the house to visit. Wyman greeted many of them as he strolled toward the barn, where the young people had gathered.

While he suspected the two preachers had ordered dishes partly to assist him with his tight financial situation, Wyman wasn't about to protest. Amanda was clearly pleased about making dinnerware for Abby and James, and this sort of order was always preferable to selling her pottery on consignment in gift shops. Even though Sam and Vernon hadn't given him any specific ideas about dealing with Reece Weaver, Wyman felt relieved, as though he'd released some of his burden simply by discussing it with them.

As he'd figured, Eddie and Pete were playing a rousing game of volleyball with other kids out by the corral, while Lizzie and Vera were seated on hay bales inside the barn, visiting with several girls. Alice Ann slumped in Lizzie's lap, napping after a busy day that had started in the wee hours. That left Simon, Cora, and Dora to account for . . .

What a pleasure to discover the twins scurrying around the yard behind Abby's small house, playing hide-and-seek with other young children. Abby's niece, Ruthie Lambright, and her best friend, Beth Ann Yutzy, encouraged them to hurry and find new hiding spots, while Simon stood against the side of Abby's home with his eyes covered. "Ten, eleven, twelve . . . ," he called out in his husky little-boy voice.

Why was it no surprise that Simon was peeking from beneath his hands, watching the kids hide? Rather than disrupt their game by allowing his son to spot him, Wyman turned toward some fellows who were loudly congratulating Merle Graber on his son's marriage. "James looks mighty happy," Titus Yutzy remarked.

"As well he might!" Merle crowed. "No finer girl in the world than our Abby, after all."

"So now the countdown toward the grandkids begins," Rudy Ropp remarked. The dairyman clapped James's dat on the back as Preacher Abe Nissley guffawed.

"As well as the countdown to when Sam informs Abby she'll no longer be clerking in the mercantile," Abe added. "Won't be the same, shopping there without her greeting us from her upstairs sewing nook."

Wyman considered this. Although it was a deeply ingrained Amish belief that wives should not work outside the home, Abe's Beulah Mae ran Mrs. Nissley's Kitchen and Rudy's Adah worked several days a week at the Fisher Cheese Factory near Clearwater. His Amanda made her pottery at home, however, so she would be on the premises for him and the kids—just as she'd earned the family's living at her wheel while taking care of her first husband during the illness that took his life.

As Amanda came out of the Lambright house, her expression rivaled the brilliant afternoon sunshine. Wyman's heart swelled as he went to meet her. His dear wife's outlook had improved so much since they'd moved into her farmhouse in Bloomingdale. He was again reminded that God's hand had led them there—and that the Lord would guide his dealings with Reece Weaver, no matter how disastrous his financial situation seemed.

"Have I told you how your smile lights up my life?" he murmured as Amanda grabbed his hands.

Her grin widened. "Would you look at *this*?" she said in an excited whisper. "Barbara was in the kitchen putting more food in the oven when Sam fetched his checkbook, and she ordered a set of pie plates, mixing bowls, and a couple of pitchers for her Phoebe's upcoming birthday," she exclaimed. "Then Bessie Mast wanted some serving pieces, and Lois Yutzy ordered a salad bowl set for her sister—and she wants me to sell my work in Mother Yutzy's Oven! Then Sam said that when I had *time*, he wants another display of my pieces in the mercantile. I had to make a list to keep all my orders straight!"

She handed him a fistful of money and checks. Wyman's eyebrows rose as he made a quick count. "This is incredible," he murmured. "You've got more than five hundred dollars here."

"These are just down payments, Wyman," she said earnestly. "When I complete the orders, we'll have that much more—plus what my new displays for Lois and Sam bring in later. And with Christmas coming, several other ladies in the kitchen said they'd be calling me with gift orders."

Although this pottery money was a drop in the bucket compared to what he'd need to complete his grain elevator, her giddiness was contagious. And Wyman couldn't miss the way Amanda had said *we*.

"You'll need to buy clay and glazes," he reminded her, "so I don't expect you to contribute to the household—"

"Phooey on that! I still have the cash from the pottery that sold in the mercantile before Uriah Schmucker smashed the rest of it." Amanda grabbed Wyman's hands, crumpling the money between them. She gazed up at him with her expressive eyes. "I can tell you're worried about making the money stretch until your elevator's up and running. And what with all the jars of food from your house and my garden this past summer, and the meat that's in our freezers, I want you to stop worrying *right now*. The Lord *will* provide, Wyman."

Wyman thought his heart might fly out of his chest. While

Amanda's pottery money would buy a lot of groceries, he still felt bad that his wife was handing over her income. He'd made a point of not discussing the finances with her after Reece's phone call . . . "So, what makes you think—"

Amanda's lips twitched. "You talk in your sleep, dear man—when you're not tossing and turning," she said slyly. "So let's be grateful to God for this new opportunity, and to Lamar Lapp for being lenient as well. It'll all work out for us. Jah?"

As she playfully jabbed his chest with her finger, Wyman couldn't help but laugh out loud. How could he possibly argue with this determined woman as she gazed up at him with such joy and challenge on her pretty face? On impulse, he kissed her—and then he kissed her again, even as some of the older fellows across the yard hooted and whistled. "Yes, dear," he teased.

"Louder."

Wyman chortled. "Yes, Mrs. Brubaker," he declared. "You and the preachers and the Lord seem to have me outvoted. Who am I to argue?"

"That's better. Now slip this money into your pocket," she said breezily. "I'll get back to helping with the dinner so someone else can take a break."

Wyman watched her practically *bounce* back to the greenhouse. *And who could've seen this coming?* he mused. *I came here feeling strung out and stretched too thin, and now I'm solid again. Right with myself and the elevator situation, even though it's not nearly settled yet.*

"Your bride looks mighty perky," Mervin Mast called out as Wyman approached the fellows who were still chatting with Merle Graber. "So how's life treating you at your new place?"

"Couldn't be better," he replied. And thanks to Amanda, he believed his life would improve beyond his wildest imagination.

Chapter 5

"Abby-girl, is this a dream, or are we really finally married?"

Abby sighed contentedly as James stood behind her at the kitchen counter on Friday morning. With his arms wrapped around her and his head resting on her shoulder, she was living out her own dreams after their months of courting—after the past several *years*, when she'd been in love with James Graber and he hadn't had a clue. "Jah, it's true," she whispered. "For better or for worse, you're stuck with me now!"

"Stuck *on* you is more like it," he teased as he turned her in his arms. "Much as I loved seeing all the family and friends who came to celebrate with us yesterday, I couldn't wait for them all to leave."

As she gazed into her new husband's handsome face, Abby tingled with joy. Her maidenly worries about their first night together had evaporated like steam from fresh-baked bread. And even though Vernon Gingerich had preached about how love grew stronger and more resilient over the years of a good marriage, she couldn't imagine feeling more *at one* with James than she did at this moment. "It was a long party and a short night," she agreed, feeling somewhat weary from their big day. "But tonight we can catch up on our sleep."

"Sleep?" James countered. "How can I even *think* of dozing off with you beside me? It was wonderful-gut to be here in your little house, just the two of us, for our first night together."

Abby's face prickled with warmth. "Let me rephrase that. Tonight we can get to bed earlier."

"I like the sound of that, honey-girl," he murmured as he gazed into her eyes. He kissed her then, as though he never wanted to let her go. "It would be nice to break with tradition and stay home, rather than leaving tomorrow morning—and these next several weekends—to collect our gifts. This nest is so cozy . . . I could slip back into our room right this minute . . ."

Abby returned his kisses until the teapot on the stove let out a shrill whistle. "We'd have Sam and the others pounding on the door if we did." She filled the teapot and replaced its lid to let the bags steep, thrilled that James's feelings mirrored her own so closely. "We've got quite a lot of redding up to do today. You'd think, after all the weddings I've helped with this fall, I'd be used to how much *mess* comes with hosting nearly three hundred guests."

"We'll have a lot of help—and for that, I'm grateful that our families live across the road from each other," he said as he took two plates from the cabinet. "Are these fried pies on the counter for our breakfast, I hope? If they're your lemon-pineapple ones, you might not get any."

Abby laughed as she opened the oven door. "You're the man of the house now, so I suppose you can have whatever you choose. But I just happen to have a pan of breakfast casserole here, all warm and full of cheese and bacon and onion and—"

James inhaled appreciatively. "Maybe I can have a fried pie for dessert, then. And when did you have time to put a casserole together?" he quizzed her. "These past few days you've been working in the store and sewing wedding dresses for your mamm and sister and Emma, not to mention making those fried pies for last night's supper."

Abby shrugged. "Haven't you figured out that the women in your life just *do* these things as part and parcel of every day? Or did you think little angels came in and made the food appear with a flicker of their wings?" she teased.

"I know *you're* an angel. Does anything else really matter?"

Her heart stilled as she met his gaze. "Oh, James, you still say the sweetest things," she whispered.

"You expect me to stop, now that we're married? I don't *think* so." He glanced toward the window in the front room and sighed. "Looks like your brother and some of the others are already headed over to the greenhouse. Guess we'd better get moving, or they'll think we're slackers."

While they quickly ate their breakfast, Abby couldn't stop smiling. As Cedar Creek's carriage maker and the only son in his family, James was anything but a slacker. And with such a kind, considerate man by her side, she anticipated a marriage that followed the idyllic scenes of her fondest daydreams. They dressed and stepped out into the brisk November morning just as the sun peeked over the horizon. Alongside Sam's tall white house, the plowed garden was bare now that the last of the pumpkins and winter squash had been picked. The red and golden leaves sparkled with a hint of frost. Down in the hilly pasture, along the cedar-lined creek, her nephew Matt's sheep were milling about in woolly clusters.

"Isn't that a picture?" Abby murmured. "I never tire of seeing those mama ewes and their wee ones."

James grasped her hand and leaned close to murmur in her ear. "Someday *ewes* going to be a mama with wee ones," he quipped.

Abby laughed and kissed his cheek. It was such a wonderful thing, to show her affection for her new husband in public now—but it didn't go unnoticed. A loud whoop came from Sam's front porch, where her nieces Gail and Ruthie were stepping outside.

"Two little lovebirds sitting in a tree," twelve-year-old Ruthie sang out, "K-I-S-S-I-N-G!"

"Tease me all you want," Abby shot back. "One of these days, I hope *you* will be this happy."

When they entered her mother's greenhouse, their neighbors' pleasant chitchat echoed in the high-ceilinged glass building. Sam and Matt were taking down the long tables. James's parents were helping Rosemary gather the soiled white tablecloths, while little Katie and Beth Ann were picking up litter from the floor. As James joined the men, Abby went over to help Emma sort the mountain of clean silverware that was piled on the counter.

"Gut morning, Mrs. Graber," Emma murmured. "And how's the bride doing after her big day?"

"Couldn't be better." Abby saw that her friend had started piles of clean knives, forks, and spoons, so she began placing them in their wooden cases. "I'm glad we have a wedding wagon in Cedar Creek, so we don't have to worry about returning all this silverware to women around town. And denki so much for all your help yesterday, Emma—even though you could've taken the day off to just be a member of the wedding party . . . along with Jerome."

"I was happy to help," Emma insisted, but then a shy smile twitched at her lips. "I'm going out with him tomorrow. It's not a date, exactly, but we have a . . . mutual mission."

"Gut for you!" Abby was aware that Emma had been resisting Jerome's attention, so this was welcome news. "Care to let me in on what you'll be doing?"

"Oh, just . . . going for a ride," Emma replied. She glanced back to see how her parents were doing with the tablecloths. "A *lot* of folks asked me for ideas about wedding presents yesterday. What would you and James like? Or need?"

Abby shrugged. "I can't give you much of an answer, I'm afraid. What with my house being as full as it needs to be—"

"Jah, it's the same at our place," Emma remarked. "It's hard to choose gifts for a couple that already has everything."

Chuckling, Abby put the lid on a box filled with forks. "I set up housekeeping because I'd figured on staying a maidel for the rest of my life, running my Stitch in Time business while I helped Sam manage the store."

"And your days at the mercantile are numbered, too, Abby," Sam declared as he took down the table behind her and Emma. "I can't allow you to work there now that you're married—especially now that I'm a preacher. But you knew that, of course."

Without turning from the counter, Abby kept stacking spoons in their wooden box. This was a subject she and James had already worked out between them. Even though she'd anticipated Sam's attitude—his insistence on following the *Ordnung* and Old Order ways—it stung her that he was bringing it up the day after the wedding. It sounded as though he expected her to move her sewing machine and supplies out of her upstairs nook *today*. "Preacher Abe's wife runs a restaurant," she countered. "Beulah Mae deals with English and Plain customers, just like I do at the mercantile."

"But she's finished raising her family," Sam pointed out. "And while Abe doesn't let on, the income from his truck farm and orchard dribbles in pretty thin once the apple sea-

son's over. I've got a gut cash flow year-round, so I can't
justify keeping you on."

Oh, but his words hurt. Abby *loved* working in the store,
helping customers and making out the orders. She'd been
restocking bulk baking ingredients and dry goods in the
back room since she was younger than Ruthie. She'd been
strategizing about this subject for a while now, so she tried
another idea. "Barbara's still midwifing, so I thought—"

"Don't start with me on *that* subject," Sam interrupted.
"I've told her she's to cut back, but she's the only person in
town with any medical expertise. Several women have insisted they'll not let anyone else assist with their babies,
so . . . well, it doesn't sound fair, I know, but her birthing
skills are more essential than your help at the mercantile."

So that was the way of it? Abby nipped her lip, feeling
more disappointment than she cared to admit. She made
one last attempt to change her brother's mind. "Who will
you hire to do the ordering and take the inventories?" she
asked. "Now that you've assumed your preaching duties,
you're not in the store most days until noon or—"

"My mind's made up, Abby. This will be your last week
of working at the store. I'll depend upon Gail, of course,
but I've begun looking for other reliable help as well."

And whom might Sam find to replace her? Abby knew
better than to pursue the subject any longer. What with Sam
being her older brother, the owner of the store, and a district
church leader, his decision overrode her protests on three
counts. Emma patted her wrist in sympathy as the two of
them finished boxing up the clean silverware. They loaded
the wooden containers into a pull cart and then headed
out the back door to where the big wedding wagon was
parked. As Emma pulled the cart up the ramp into the
wagon, Abby pushed from behind until they were inside.

"I'm sorry about your having to quit at the store, Abby,"
Emma murmured. "It won't be the same, shopping without
you there—and I know you'll miss it, too."

Abby struggled with the lump in her throat. But what good would it do to be upset? She slung her arm gratefully around Emma's shoulders as they stood inside the shadowy wagon. "Denki for understanding about that," she murmured. "What would I do without you?"

Emma slipped her arm around Abby's waist. "I'm glad you'll still be living here in Cedar Creek now that you're married, Abby. So many of our friends have moved away after hitching up with fellows from other districts."

"Jah, weddings change things amongst friends," she murmured. "It's a blessing to me that we're sisters now, Emma, and that we'll always have each other to turn to."

"That's how I see it, too." Emma squeezed her, and then they began fitting the cartons of silverware into the cabinets that were built into the wagon's walls. "And you know, we have a couple of spare rooms at our place where you can set up your Stitch in Time business. Sam couldn't object to that, as it would be no different from Rosemary baking her pies at home. And Mamm and Dat would be glad for your company during the day, too."

Abby considered this as she slipped another case of silverware into a slot. "That's a gut thought. When I move out of the store's loft, I surely won't have room for all those sewing supplies at *my* tiny place."

"We'd love it if you and James wanted to live with us, too," Emma continued in a wistful voice. "But I can understand why it's special to have your own little hideaway. Mamm and Dat can be troublesome, what with their picking at each other and—"

"Your parents are *not* the reason we're living at my house, Emma," Abby insisted. "And you know we'll be there the moment you need us, too. James and I never intended for you to have to watch over your folks all by yourself."

"Jah, James says he'll be over every day to check on us."

"And so will I," Abby insisted in a burst of inspiration,

"because—if it's okay with your folks—I've just now decided to move my Stitch in Time business into whichever
room you'll let me have. That's a gut solution for all of us,
Emma, and I appreciate your offer."

Abby raised her eyebrows playfully, considering another
issue she suspected was on her best friend's mind. "So if
I'll be working at the house, you'll have no excuse not to go
out with Jerome, jah? He had eyes only for you yesterday."

Emma let out an exasperated sigh. "He and I had a *chat*
about that," she blurted. "He's a nice enough fellow, I suppose, but sometimes *he* believes he's pretty special, too. I'm
not sure *what* to think of him, truth be told."

Abby closed the cabinet, sensing she'd said enough
about Jerome. She and James had agreed to let the couple
work things out between themselves. "Well, now that we've
packed away the silverware, the fellows can load the tables
and folding chairs. The wedding wagon'll be ready for
whoever's next to get hitched, once we wash all those tablecloths."

"No time like the present," Emma agreed. "Or had you
figured on being at the mercantile when Sam reopens it this
afternoon?"

As they rolled the empty pull cart down the wagon's
ramp, Abby considered her reply. James wanted to work for
a while in his carriage shop, so she had planned to put in
her usual Friday afternoon hours at the mercantile . . . but
her situation had changed.

"Let's you and I get going on the tablecloths. Sam can
run the place with just Gail there today—as practice for
when I'll be gone," she added mischievously. "Maybe this
sounds prideful of me, Emma, but I predict that my brother
will be asking me to come back for the Christmas season,
only a couple of weeks away. Gail does her best, but *nobody* can run that place alone, especially when Sam gets
called out to tend a church member's needs."

Emma chuckled. "I can't imagine who he'll get to replace you, Abby. Far as I can recall, only Lambrights have ever worked there," she remarked as they paused alongside the wedding wagon. "What with Phoebe married now, and Barbara midwifing, and your mamm running her gift shop, and Ruthie still in school, he's down to just Gail."

The back door of the greenhouse opened and Sam stepped outside. He looked at the two of them with a purposeful expression on his face, as though he'd been waiting for them to come out of the wagon. "Emma, would you consider working in the mercantile?" he asked. "If you started on Monday, Abby could show you how we do things while she's still there next week. James has reminded me that you've kept his carriage shop books for years—and your parents have just assured me that they'd get along fine while you'd be working," he continued earnestly. "It would ease my mind to have someone I know and trust as a new employee."

Abby's mouth dropped open. "We—we were just talking about how I'll probably be moving my sewing business into a room at the Graber place, so I would be there with Eunice and Merle," she murmured.

But she stopped there. Although she loved Emma dearly, Abby wasn't at all sure her best friend had the temperament or the day-to-day storekeeping skills Sam was looking for. But her brother had already said he wasn't going to listen to any more of her protests . . . so she would say no more.

Chapter 6

Emma stood speechless, staring at Sam. Apparently he'd had *quite* a conversation with her family while she and Abby had been in the wedding wagon. Abby had just removed her excuse of staying with the folks, and her parents had assured Sam they could get along without her, but she had never considered working away from home. "I—I have no idea about running a cash register, or—"

"Abby and I will be working right alongside you to get you off to a solid start," Sam assured her. "You've been shopping in the mercantile all your life, so you're familiar with where we keep everything. And folks hereabouts know you and like you, Emma. They'll be patient while you're learning the job."

Emma's pounding pulse drove all rational thought from her mind. Shopping at the mercantile was one thing, but dealing with customers and answering their questions was another challenge altogether. "I have *no* idea about the hardware department, or plumbing fixtures, or—"

"Anybody I hired would have to learn such things. I know it'll take more than a day or two for you to catch on," Sam said with an encouraging smile. "But if you come in early so we can train you a little each day without any customers around, you'll know how to handle most situations before the holiday rush starts."

Holiday rush? Emma could recall times when Abby had gotten awfully frazzled from working with Christmas shoppers—English folks who got pushy or rude when the mercantile ran out of the merchandise they wanted. Questions and doubts whirled in her mind, but she couldn't just stand there while Sam waited for her decision. "Can I think it over? This would be a—a *big* change for me."

"I wouldn't have asked you if I didn't think you could handle the job, Emma." He squeezed her shoulder. "Let me know soon, though."

When Sam went back inside the greenhouse, Emma turned to Abby. "Did you have any idea he wanted *me* to work in the store?" she asked in a tight voice. "I don't feel any too gut about stepping into *your* shoes, Abby, knowing how much you love waiting on customers when I can't hold a candle to—"

"We all have to get beyond that," Abby replied. "If Sam wants you to work, we'll trust his judgment. And jah, the hour or so before the store opens each morning would be the best time for showing you the ropes. No interruptions that way."

Emma let out the breath she'd been holding, agog at this new development. "We have a lot to talk about while we wash the tablecloths."

As she and Abby went inside to gather all the laundry from the wedding feast, Emma's mind felt as split as a cut pie, with the pieces flying in all different directions. She sensed her parents' curiosity, but she wasn't ready to talk to them about possibly working in the mercantile—not until she'd considered all the angles of such a huge, unexpected decision.

"What do I need to know to work in the store, Abby?" Emma grabbed the handle of the pull cart, which was loaded with dirty tablecloths, and the two of them started across the Lambrights' yard. "I hate to waste Sam's time if I'm not qualified. And everyone knows it'll take *three* people to accomplish what *you* do in the store."

Abby waved her off, considering her answer as they went around to the back of the house. "Can you figure change and count it back?" she asked. "We'll teach you how to run the cash register, of course, but sometimes I find it just as easy to total the small orders on paper—especially if the line's getting backed up. There are times when we really could use a second cash register, but Sam won't hear of that."

Emma considered her reply. "My math's pretty solid. I've been keeping our home checkbook and James's business account for a long time. If we practice making change, I think I'll be all right with that part."

"Jah, I think so, too."

They entered the mudroom, where Abby ran water into the ringer washer while Emma checked the tablecloths for stains. She was grateful for this time to discuss these details while it was just she and Abby, because she trusted her best friend to tell her the truth about the job. While Emma was flattered that Sam thought she was capable and competent, there was no denying that working in the mercantile would be a big responsibility. "So . . . what's the worst part about running the store? What do you think I'll have trouble with?" she asked.

Abby's eyebrows rose as she thought about her answer. "It's really important to greet people when they come in. You'll want to ask how you can help them, of course," she continued as the washer began agitating. "But you have to look them in the eye—especially the folks you don't know—so they realize you're aware of their presence. It cuts down on shoplifting."

Emma's hand flew to her mouth. "You mean people *steal* from the store? What should I do if I see that happening?"

"Do *not* go up to them and accuse them of anything," Abby warned her quickly. "The best thing is to let Sam know that you suspect something, and he'll handle it. During the Christmas shopping season, a lot of little items get stuck into purses and coat pockets. It's best to keep circulating, to keep talking so everyone knows you're around.

"It's mostly English," Abby continued above the noise of the agitating washer. "They tend to think that we Plain folks aren't bright enough to figure out what they're doing, or that because we don't keep our inventory on a computer, we won't miss the merchandise they take."

As Abby tucked the ends of the first tablecloth into the wringer and began to crank, squeezing out the excess water, her expression became more serious. "Your trusting nature might give you some problems, Emma. It's like the scripture from First Corinthians that Vernon preached on during the wedding," she went on in a thoughtful tone. "You're patient and kind. You bear all things and believe all things. And when you work with the public, you need to question more and accept less. You'll have to stand firm when folks dish up their *attitude*, too—and when they try to return things without a receipt. I suspect that part won't come easily for you."

Emma sighed. Abby made it sound like she'd need to cultivate a whole new personality. But at least she was being honest. "Mamm and Dat have told me a time or two not to be such a doormat," she admitted. "I'll have to work on that."

Abby smiled ruefully. "That's a difficult thing to practice. Usually, you get yourself into a tight spot you can't get out of before you realize somebody's taken advantage of you. I've done *that* plenty of times over the years."

Emma guided the wrung-out tablecloths into the laundry basket, careful not to let them touch the floor. Abby's references to the wedding scripture made her think about when Jerome had been mouthing those same words about patience and kindness and bearing and believing. *What will Jerome think if you work in the store? He said you should get out and enjoy yourself more . . . but this job will be a commitment. It'll be hard work with no time to play.*

But it sounds like an adventure, too! another voice rang in her mind. *Won't he think you're more outgoing—more interesting—if you have something besides Mamm and Dat to talk about?*

"Shall we hang these out while the washer works on the next load?"

Emma blinked. Abby's question had cut through her musings while she was curling the last wet tablecloth on top of the others in the laundry basket. "I really need to think this through," she murmured, yet her voice was rising with excitement. "A lot of people are depending on me to give the right answer to Sam's offer."

They lifted the bulky laundry basket between them and stepped out the door to where the long double clothesline spanned the yard between the back porch post and the nearest shed. It was rigged up with a big pulley on either end, so they could hang up a tablecloth and then spin it away to bring empty line in front of them without leaving the sheltered spot beside the door.

"Ooh, it's gotten chilly enough that I want a heavier jacket," Abby said. "Shall I bring you one, too, Emma? Now that the wind's picking up, it's feeling like winter."

"Jah, the cold's cutting right through this old barn coat," Emma replied. She began hanging the tablecloths as she waited for Abby to return. Beyond the outbuildings, the maples and sweet gums had shed their leaves. With their bare branches swaying, the trees looked desolate against a sky that was clouding over. Emma shivered.

Cold. Lonely. That's how I'll be feeling while Abby and James are away for so many weekends, collecting their wedding gifts, Emma mused as she cranked the clothesline pulley. *If I'm at home with the folks for another winter, what'll I have to show for my time? If I worked at the store, I'd be right across the road if Mamm or Dat needed me. And I'd be getting out more, the way they—and Jerome— have been hinting at. Abby has always made working in the store look like so much fun . . .*

When Abby returned, she and Emma talked of other things and finished laundering the tablecloths. All the while, Emma envisioned herself helping customers in the Cedar Creek Mercantile—restocking the bulk cereals and baking supplies, filling out order forms the way she'd seen Abby do dozens of times.

I can do this job—and Sam thinks so, too! I can put a smile on my face and talk to people—and I can accomplish something besides listening to Mamm fuss at Dat while he ignores her, day after day! What do I have to lose by trying?

When she and Abby had hung the last tablecloth, Emma chatted a little longer with her best friend rather than jogging straight over to the store. She had her answer for Sam! And she wanted to talk with him about it before she told anyone else her decision.

"So, where are you and James going this weekend?" Emma asked while they put away the laundry supplies. "Most likely, several folks at the wedding lined up weekends for you to come see them."

"Your sisters convinced us to visit them and their families in Queen City while it looks like the weather will be *gut,*" Abby replied. "We're all packed, so we'll be leaving early tomorrow morning for Sharon and Amos's. We'll spend Saturday night with Iva and Dan, go to church with the whole bunch of them, and then head back to Cedar Creek on Sunday afternoon."

Emma smiled, thinking how this plan would work so well for the gals who'd be quilting at the house tomorrow. "It'll be a real adventure for you two, visiting different folks' homes every weekend."

But I'll have my adventure, too!

Emma said her good-byes and then quickly strode down Lambright Lane to the mercantile. Sam had posted a sign on the door about being closed all day yesterday and until noon today for the wedding, so only a few vehicles sat in the parking lot. The bell above the door jingled cheerfully when Emma entered. Sam looked up from the catalog he was studying, and her heart thudded with nervous excitement.

"I—I'll take the job!" she blurted. "I've talked to Abby and I think I can do it!"

"I'm pleased to hear that, Emma," he replied. He peered over the top of his rimless glasses, reminding her of Abraham Lincoln—except younger—when he smiled at her. "This is a big load off my mind. I'll see you Monday morning around eight."

"Jah, I'll be here. Denki for thinking of me, Sam."

Emma stepped outside again, squeezing her eyes shut in sheer excitement. *I have a job! Who could've imagined that Sam would want* me *to work for him?*

As she headed across the blacktop toward home, she couldn't stop grinning. This news would certainly give her something to talk about over supper with Mamm and Dat tonight. And tomorrow when Jerome took her shopping—well, she would have to think of just the right way to tell him that she had taken his advice to heart.

"That was a very sensible thing to do, Emma," Mamm said with a nod. She passed the bowl of creamed peas, gazing at

Emma through her pointy-cornered glasses. "Since it seems you're not inclined to pay Jerome any attention, it's best if you've got a job to fall back on. Abby and James will be starting their family, living their own lives. And your dat and I won't be around forever."

"That's no way to talk!" Emma protested. She struggled to keep smiling even as her confidence faltered. "If you and Dat weren't getting on so well, I wouldn't have considered Sam's job offer for a second. I—I just thought that with winter coming on, it might be gut to have something—oh, never mind."

Emma exhaled in frustration, gazing down at her plate of simmered chicken and boiled potatoes. Even with the green peas she was dishing up, it was a bland meal—*as plain and unexciting as your life will be, with James and Abby living across the road and gone most weekends.* She should have known Mamm would put a negative twist on her reasons for encouraging Sam to hire her.

When Dat coughed and cleared his throat, Emma focused on him. Although he was in the early stages of Alzheimer's, he'd seemed very alert and mentally together of late. Would he relapse now that the excitement of the wedding was behind them?

"And what do *you* think about me working in the store, Dat?" Emma asked. "Do you think I can handle the responsibility, and dealing with so many people? Abby makes it look so easy . . ."

A hint of doubt flickered in his eyes, but her mother answered before Dat could express his opinion.

"Merle, we've talked about this," Mamm reminded him. "And if Emma's given Sam her answer, there's no going back on it."

Dat pursed his lips, but then he smiled at her. "We'll miss having you around all day, Emmie-girl," he replied carefully. "But your mamm's right. You're too young to spend your life just hanging around home. We'll get by."

Emma sighed. Wasn't this the way it always went, with Mamm speaking for both of them and Dat going along with it?

"You've got a gut head on your shoulders," her father continued. He patted her hand, encouraging her. "If you find out that working at the mercantile's not your cup of tea, at least you gave it a try. I know you'll do your best."

And what kind of answer was *that*? By the time Emma had helped Mamm clean up the dishes and they'd all gone upstairs to bed, her excitement about working at the store had lost its sizzle. Had she answered Sam too soon? Had she bitten off more than she could chew, considering how crowds and strangers—especially English—intimidated her? And what if Jerome thought she'd been foolish to accept Sam's job offer? She'd envisioned his approval, his encouragement, because she'd be getting out more, but maybe that wasn't a valid reason for making such a major change.

In for a dime, in for a dollar. You've never been a quitter, Emma thought as she dropped her nightgown over her head. If she'd made a mistake by accepting Sam's offer, and he'd misjudged her abilities, they would figure that out soon enough.

Tonight she needed her rest. Spending most of the day with Jerome tomorrow, dealing with his confident affection and his determination to date her, would require all the energy she could muster.

Chapter 7

As Jerome stepped toward the Grabers' front porch on Saturday morning, Cora and Dora scurried around him, leading little Alice Ann to the door as fast as her short legs could toddle, which made him laugh. Lizzie and Vera hefted a box bulging with colorful fabrics between them, while Amanda carried covered pans of food for their dinner. All the way from Bloomingdale, the women in his life had been chatting and laughing, eager for this day of quilting. Their buoyant mood had lifted his spirits as he anticipated his outing with Emma . . . which would be much more than a shopping trip, if he had his way about it.

"It's going to be quite a frolic," Jerome remarked as he steadied Jemima on the stairs. "I hope Merle can handle all the clucking you hens will be doing."

Jemima stopped to focus on him. Her face lit up within the curved brim of her black winter bonnet. "Merle will be glad it's our clucking rather than Eunice's pecking, ain't so?" she teased. "And we're bringing most of his dinner, so our visit won't be a total hardship for him."

Jerome had to chortle at that. But it was the young woman holding the door who made him stand taller and put on his best smile. "Gut morning, Emma! The frosty air's putting roses in your cheeks. How are you?"

"I'm gut. And Mamm's the cheeriest I've seen her in a long while—or at least since James and Abby got married," she added playfully.

Did he dare hope that Emma's fine mood reflected a change of heart? Jerome let Amanda and Jemima step inside ahead of him; then he lingered in the doorway. In her crisp pleated kapp, wearing a mustard-colored dress that accentuated her hazel eyes and the hint of ginger in her brown hair, Emma looked even prettier than she had at the wedding. "And the newlyweds are on their first gift-collecting visit?" he asked.

"They left early this morning for Queen City," she said as they entered the house. "Abby doesn't have a clue about what will be going on *here* all day, either. It's not easy, keeping such secrets from her."

"I hope we'll locate a gift they'll cherish every bit as much as the quilts these ladies will be making," Jerome replied as he removed his hat. "And I'm pleased you'll get to work with them next Saturday, too. You're a gut sport to help me with my shopping today, Emma."

Jerome glanced around, immediately feeling at home. Even though a long worktable and chairs now took up the center of the front room, the recliners, sofas, and tables were of the same vintage he'd grown up with—which meant everything looked a little worn, but comfortable. A woodstove at the other end of the room put out enough heat to make the house feel cozy, and a sweet cinnamon aroma filled the air.

Merle ambled out of the kitchen, a grin on his weathered

face. "You folks got an early start. These ladies must've been prodding you along, Jerome," he remarked.

"They were eager to be on the road, jah—and it smells like you've been baking all morning, Merle," Jerome teased. "What'd you make me?"

Emma's dat laughed. "Sure you don't want to stay and find out? What with those casserole pans Amanda carried in, you and I could be the taste testers while the girls do their quilting."

"Don't go getting any such ideas, Jerome!" Eunice's voice came from the kitchen. "We all want to see what sort of wedding gift you and Emma find on your shopping trip today."

When Eunice stepped out to stand beside Merle, Jerome went over to greet them. They were such a dear pair, as faded and worn as their sofa, yet their eyes sparkled in their weathered faces. "You two look mighty perky this morning," he remarked. "So, how many years has it been since *you* got hitched?"

"Way too many," Emma's dat murmured.

"Never mind him," Eunice said as she straightened her glasses. "It's been sixty-three years. We went ahead with it even though my folks had their doubts. I was barely seventeen, you see," she added coyly. "Somewhat younger than Emma."

Jerome couldn't miss the hint, nor did Emma's exasperated sigh escape him. "Well, congratulations! The Lord's been smiling on you both for a long time, and I wish you many more years together."

He ambled toward the long table where Emma was helping the girls unpack their big box. She was handling the colorful fabrics with a wistful smile, obviously wishing she could sew today. "We can leave anytime you're ready," he murmured.

"Jah. I'll fetch my coat."

A few minutes later they were exchanging good-byes

with their families. Then, *at last*, Emma was settled on the seat of his enclosed buggy . . . although she was up against the door, as far as she could possibly get from him. Jerome clucked to his mules, and as they took off down the county blacktop, he considered ways to loosen her up, to return the smile to her face. It would be a long, tedious day if she wouldn't look at him or talk to him, but he knew better than to mention her unrequited love for Matt Lambright again. He'd kicked himself for that careless comment several times since the wedding.

"That's Sparky and Winona," he said, nodding toward the mules. "I'm training them for a fellow in Lancaster."

Emma's brows rose. "Pennsylvania?"

"No, no—north of here, near the Iowa border," he replied with a chuckle. "I bred my donkeys to his Palominos, which is why they have the tawny coats and blond manes. You don't see that too often in a mule."

"Ah."

Jerome waited, but Emma had no further response. *It wasn't your best idea, talking about breeding, dummy,* he chided himself. *Why would Emma care about mules, anyway?*

After a few minutes they passed Nissley's Ridge and the Mast place, leaving Cedar Creek behind. "I thought we'd try the two furniture stores over toward Clearwater, and maybe the antique mall," Jerome suggested. "But if you've got a better idea—or specific gifts Abby might've mentioned—I'm all ears."

Emma shrugged, watching the passing countryside. "When I told her people were curious about what to get them, Abby said she and James have everything they need. Which comes from Sam's owning the mercantile, I suppose."

It wasn't a helpful answer, but at least she'd strung together more than two words. Was Emma shy around guys? Or was she afraid of *him*? Even if she'd been sweet on Matt, surely other fellows had taken her out, or given her rides home from Singings when she'd been younger.

About ten minutes later—an awfully long, quiet ten minutes—Jerome pulled into the parking lot of the first furniture store. Wyman had told him the Yoder brothers who ran the place specialized in bedroom and dining room sets and that they also did custom work. He'd no sooner pulled up to the hitching rail than Emma was opening her door. "Let me help you, Emma."

"I'm fine," she insisted as her feet hit the ground. "It's always me who's getting Mamm and Dat in and out when we're on the road, after all."

Jerome sighed. He'd envisioned reaching up for her, grasping her hands or, better yet, placing his hands at her waist so he could hold Emma's gaze for a moment, giving her his best smile. Most girls loved that. As he hurried to tie the mules to the rail and follow her inside the store, Jerome wondered yet again what he could do to bring Emma out of her shell.

When he stepped inside, the rich scent of lemon oil and the huge display room of glossy wood furniture encouraged him. What woman didn't love to wander down aisles of beautiful tables, chairs, and chests, imagining such pieces in her own home? It was far too early to suggest that maybe someday she'd be choosing new furniture as his wedding gift to her—that idea spooked *him* a bit, so it would probably send Emma running back to Cedar Creek without the buggy.

Yet in truth, he'd already allowed his daydreams to wander in that direction. Emma was such a sensible girl and a good cook, too. He'd met few daughters who were so devoted to their parents, so he figured she'd be just as committed to loving her husband and children someday. Compared to the two other young women he'd nearly married, Emma Graber was well-grounded—already a member of the Old

Order church—and she'd make some man a fine wife . . . if she'd only allow him to make up for embarrassing her the other day.

Jerome exchanged greetings with the young Plain woman at the front counter and then went in search of his companion, who had disappeared behind a row of tall china cabinets. As he rounded the corner, he stopped to observe her. Emma was running her finger along the plate rail of a stunning walnut hutch, and her awestruck expression touched him.

"That's a gorgeous piece," he remarked as he came up beside her.

When she read the price tag, however, she dropped it as though it had burned her fingers. "Ach, I never dreamed— how can anyone afford to pay so much?" she whispered. "Maybe we'd best go somewhere else."

Jerome smiled patiently. As he glanced at the tag, he thoroughly enjoyed the way his shoulder brushed hers, even though Emma still wore her heavy black coat and bonnet. She carried a faint cinnamon scent that made him want to nuzzle her neck, and he had to refocus his thoughts. Twenty-three hundred dollars didn't seem outrageous, considering the size and workmanship of this hutch and the fact that Amish fellows had made it with such attention to the turnings and decorative details.

"As I told you at the wedding, I want to give Abby and James a *very* nice gift," he murmured. "They were such a help to Amanda's family after last month's storm tossed those two trees into Wyman's house."

Emma's mouth formed a perfect O. She was finally looking at him, but her incredulous stare wasn't what he'd been hoping for. Did she think he was showing off, flaunting his wealth? Spending above his means to impress her?

When Emma moved on down the aisle, past other hutches and sideboards, it occurred to him that she might have a point. Considering how long it took him to earn two thousand dollars, maybe he shouldn't spend that much on a wedding present for friends.

"You're right, Emma," Jerome said as he followed her past a large selection of dining room tables and chairs. "These pieces are too big for Abby's house anyway—and James did say they were living there, ain't so?"

"Jah, that's the plan." Emma stopped to admire a beautiful sleigh bed, crafted of oak, displayed between a matching dresser and a tall armoire. When she noticed him smiling at her, she hurried away, as though his wild, private thoughts were written all over his face.

Jerome sighed. Was he that easy to read? Thank goodness he'd refrained from suggesting they might test the mattress—just teasing her, of course. He could well imagine Cora, Dora, and Simon launching themselves onto these beds when their parents weren't watching, but this was Emma Graber. It seemed she'd lost the childlike sparkle he longed to see in her honey brown eyes.

As they came to another corner of the store, however, Jerome noticed several smaller items that might make better gifts. "How about a clock?" he asked as they approached a wall covered with timepieces in several styles. Some had pendulums, or cuckoo birds and moving dancers, and other models played songs while the sections of their faces moved to the music. As they struck the hour, several of the clocks began to chime or play familiar tunes—a sound he'd always delighted in. While the Amish didn't allow musical instruments and didn't hang fancy artwork on the walls of their homes, most families owned a special clock or two. They were a necessity, after all—especially since folks weren't supposed to wear watches.

But Emma was already walking away. "Abby's got a clock that belonged to her dat in the front room, and James gave her a new one as his engagement gift," she replied over her shoulder.

Jerome refused to give up. The Yoder store was filled with fabulous pieces, and he enjoyed browsing even if nothing seemed appropriate for the newlyweds. "These wall-mounted shelves are attractive," he remarked as he studied a couple of them. "And here's a little corner cabinet—small enough to fit in any home, and useful as a lampstand as well."

But Emma had already gone around the corner and was heading toward the store's entrance. Rather than giving in to her skittishness, Jerome ambled between several styles of wooden rocking chairs—and what family couldn't use one of those? These rockers were small enough to fit where recliners and upholstered chairs would not, and every couple needed one when the kids started coming along. When the bell above the door jangled, however, Jerome quickened his pace. He got outside just in time to watch Emma's backside disappear into his buggy.

Jerome climbed into the rig and took up the traces. Maybe it was best to ask the question that niggled at him rather than try to second-guess the young woman who had once again scooted against the opposite door. "Emma, are you still upset because I got too personal at the wedding? Or are you *afraid* of me?"

Her breath escaped in a cloud of vapor. "No! I—it's just that, well . . . I've never gone furniture shopping," Emma admitted in a strained whisper. "I had no idea how expensive things are."

"Well, you've got that right," Jerome replied. "But when folks buy Amish pieces, they look to have them for a lifetime. So maybe we should skip the other furniture place, eh?"

"Jah. *Please*."

How could he help Emma relax? When they'd been mingling amongst guests at two weddings and at her mamm's birthday party last month, he would never have guessed she'd be so skittish when she was alone with him. It was best to stick to conversation, even though Jerome longed to slip his arm around her shoulders—if only because the morning was turning colder and damp. The gray clouds rolling across the sky suggested snow.

"Surely we'll find something in the antique mall," Jerome said as he steered the mules back onto the pavement. "It's fun to look at all the old stuff, even if some of it's basically junk that didn't sell at somebody's estate auction."

But when they stepped inside the old barn that had been renovated into a consignment shop, Jerome sensed that the two floors of booths crammed with odds and ends might overwhelm Emma even more than the furniture store had. She walked ahead of him with her hands stuffed into her coat pockets, as though she feared she might break something.

Jerome frowned. Emma's shyness was wearing him thin. While she glanced into each booth as they passed it, she wasn't taking time to really *look* at anything.

"Say, what about this drop-leaf table?" he asked. He lifted one side to snap it into place, smiling at its efficient design. "This is only a foot wide—would fit against the wall as a lamp table—yet it opens out to seat six, the tag says. And it comes with these sturdy wooden fold-up chairs. It would be gut for when James and Abby have folks over for dinner."

Emma shrugged. "Most likely if they have company, they'll include Sam's bunch and the parents and me," she replied. "So we could eat at Mamm and Dat's big table or in Barbara's kitchen, the way Abby's done since she moved into her little house. But jah, it's a clever piece."

For another twenty minutes they moved from booth to booth, following the same pattern: Jerome pointed out an item he liked and Emma nixed it. While she had kept him from choosing gifts that would be inappropriate—and had saved him the two thousand bucks he'd have spent on a china hutch—she'd also spoiled the fun he usually had while poking around in antique stores. As they stepped outside again, he felt tiny flutters of moisture hitting his face.

"Shall we get some lunch?" Jerome asked once they were seated in the rig. "There's a vintage-style diner just down the road . . ."

"Or we could go back to Cedar Creek," Emma remarked in a hopeful tone. "Between what Mamm and I fixed and what Amanda brought, there's plenty enough for us to join them."

Jerome smiled. "But you've spent your morning with me and saved me from making a lot of mistakes," he said gently. "I'd like to treat you to a meal you didn't have to cook yourself. Will that be all right?"

Emma smiled as the color rose in her cheeks. "Well, since you put it that way . . ."

He was thankful that once they were seated in a red leatherette booth with a chrome-edged table between them and a miniature jukebox on the wall, Emma took off her black coat and bonnet. In her amber cape dress and a cream-colored apron that fastened behind her neck, she looked much more attractive and . . . inviting.

Jerome was pleased when she ordered a patty melt with fries and a side of tomato soup. At least she wasn't going to be finicky about her food, like some girls were. After he ordered the blue plate special, which was meat loaf, he tapped on the wall-mounted jukebox. "Pick a song, Emma. We can listen while we wait for our lunch."

As she flipped through the selections, Jerome fished out a quarter and put it in the slot. "F six," she murmured.

In a few moments, "See You Later, Alligator" filled the small diner. As Emma tapped her fingers on the tabletop, keeping time to the old rock-and-roll song, she looked as happy as Jerome had ever seen her. At last, he'd found something they both enjoyed, even if the church didn't allow them to play such music at home.

"Dat took James and Abby and me to a horse auction

once, when we were around ten or eleven," she recounted. "We ate lunch at a place similar to this one, and Dat played this record on the jukebox—and it's stuck with us ever since. Even on days when he can't recall what he ate for breakfast, he knows every word to this song."

"It's a snappy tune," Jerome agreed, tapping his toes. Just for fun, he wanted to catch Emma's feet between his and give them a quick squeeze, but he thought better of it. "It's nice to have that memory from when your dat was younger and stronger. My mamm and dat died when our house burned to the ground, when I was just ten."

Emma's eyes widened. "And how was it that *you* didn't—I mean . . ."

The concern on her face coaxed Jerome to grasp her hand. "I was staying overnight at a cousin's house," he replied. "The firemen said the old furnace exploded, and because the house was built of very dry wood they'd saved from a barn they'd torn down, my folks were gone before they knew what hit them. That's when Aunt Amanda and Uncle Atlee took me in—and probably why I get such a kick out of your dat."

"You didn't lose any brothers or sisters, I hope?" Emma murmured. "If something happened to James, I'm not sure I could bear it."

Jerome felt comforted by her concern, even though the accident had happened more than half his lifetime ago. "No, it seems they broke the mold when they made me," he said with a chuckle.

For a moment, Emma's gaze lingered on his. Such an unusual shade of brown her eyes were, similar to a mixture of honey and cinnamon. Too soon, she eased her hand away. "I'm sorry," she murmured. "That was a horrible thing to endure when you were so young."

Immediately she clammed up, and once again Jerome wished he'd selected his topic of conversation more carefully. Their food came, and after a few minutes of silent grace stretched into a lack of conversation that felt unbearably strained, he tried again. "So, what do you like to do for a gut time, Emma?"

She looked at him over the top of her thick hamburger sandwich, which dripped with cheese and fried onions. "I—I don't know," she murmured. "I haven't thought much about it."

What could he say to *that*? Was Emma truly so housebound with her parents that she never even got together with girlfriends? Or was she evading another date with him?

As Jerome scooped up another bite of mashed potatoes drenched in rich brown gravy, he thought it was more likely that Emma didn't remember how to enjoy herself. She'd grown past the age of attending Singings . . . but surely fellows around Cedar Creek and Clearwater had asked her out. Had she turned them down, waiting for Matt to realize how she felt about him? Jerome didn't press for answers, because Emma was intently studying her soup cup as though she wanted to look at anything but him.

Or did that hint of a smile twitching on her lips mean she was looking for a way to tell him something?

When Emma had gone several moments without saying anything else, Jerome fell back on an idea he'd had in mind as a last resort. "You know, I've got three newborn mules at home, none of them spoken for yet," he mused aloud. "I think I'll train one of them to harness for Abby and James. They're every bit as dependable as a thoroughbred for pulling a buggy, and usually less temperamental."

Emma flashed him a smile. "Oh, that's a fine idea, Jerome. Something only you can give them," she replied. "And I was thinking I'll crochet them an afghan. Abby's so busy with sewing for her business, she doesn't have time for much handiwork."

"She'll like that. And it's something James can curl up with as well." Jerome felt as relieved as Emma looked, to have this decision made—even though it meant that he had no more specific reasons to ask her out. Crocheting was something she could do at home, with her parents . . .

"Although," Emma continued in a low voice, "I won't have much time for crocheting, either, considering how I'll be working at the Cedar Creek Mercantile. Starting on Monday."

Jerome's fork clattered to his plate. "*Really?* I never would have guessed—I mean—" He searched desperately for words that wouldn't hurt her feelings. Words he wouldn't regret. "Well, that's quite a surprise, Emma! You didn't let on at the wedding, so—"

"Sam asked me yesterday. Now that Abby's married, he doesn't want her working there, you see." Emma's face turned a pretty shade of pink. "My first inclination was to say no, but—well, after you told me I should get out more, I decided to try it. So, see? I *was* paying attention to you, Jerome."

Jerome gazed at Emma, corralling his thoughts about how shy and sheltered she was. Her eyes were sparkling, and she looked excited about taking the job. It had taken a lot of gumption for her to accept Sam's offer, so he didn't want to imply that she might not be suited to dealing with the public or to handling the pressures of the upcoming holiday shopping season.

"Gut for you, Emma," he said, reaching across the table to squeeze her hand. "We should all try new things every now and again. Sam couldn't have asked a more steadfast, dependable person to help him out."

Emma's blush deepened, and she withdrew her hand from his. "Denki for saying that," she murmured. "I know I'll have to face some challenges, but—but I'm determined to make it work."

Who could've seen that *coming?* Jerome mused as he paid for their meal. During the ride back to Cedar Creek, Emma asked how things were going at their farm in Bloomingdale, now that Wyman's family had joined them and eight kids lived there. This was the kind of light, easy conversation he'd been hoping for all morning. It made him wonder if Emma had been so quiet while they were shopping because she'd been looking for a way to share her news, which again pointed out how bashful she was. He hoped she—and Sam—wouldn't be disappointed if their arrangement didn't work out.

As the mercantile and Graber's Custom Carriages came into view, Jerome hoped to pin down another time when he could take Emma out—especially now that she'd be working. He slipped his arm behind her, along the top of the seat, but he'd barely halted the mules at the Grabers' front porch before she sprang from the seat. Emma hurried into the house, slamming the door behind her.

Women. Who can figure them out? Jerome hitched Sparky and Winona to the front porch railing, realizing what an uphill effort he faced if he wanted to date Emma on a regular basis, much less begin courting her. Would she ever fit into his dreams of having a family . . . or would she require more time and effort than he was willing to invest?

Chapter 8

When Eunice's kitchen was cleaned up after their dinner of casseroles and cake, Amanda paused in front of a china hutch where several pieces of her pottery were displayed. "It's quite an honor to see my pieces set up this way," she remarked as her hostess came to stand beside her.

Eunice's face lit up. "These were gifts from my eightieth birthday party," she recalled fondly. "The blue and red backgrounds—and all those pretty daisies—perk up the whole room, ain't so?"

"They do," Amanda agreed. "That was quite a nice party, and I was tickled to be there when you opened so many pieces of my pottery that folks hereabouts had bought for you."

"I know our *Ordnung* forbids us to engage in art for its own sake," Eunice said with a sigh, "but it was still a crying shame that the Clearwater bishop made you put away your paints. I'm glad our Vernon is a more progressive leader than Uriah Schmucker."

Now that Wyman had moved their family to Blooming-dale, Amanda could smile about the confrontations she'd endured with Uriah—especially the day she'd come home to find that he'd smashed several dishes while he'd forced the younger children to look on. "I'm back in business—working on orders from folks who came to Abby and James's wedding," she replied happily. "While our Blooming-dale bishop, Lamar Lapp, wants me to paint with more sub-dued colors, I'm pleased to be at my wheel again. And if you can keep a secret," Amanda added, leaning closer to whisper in Eunice's ear, "I'm making a complete set of dishes for James and Abby. It's a gift from a couple of fam-ilies here in town."

"Oh, they'll love that!" Eunice exclaimed. "And I can't think God will object to the way you lift everyone's spirits with your work, either. Why, every time I look at these pieces, I feel downright *joyful*!"

What a huge improvement for often-crabby Eunice. And didn't *joyful* describe their entire morning? Amanda noted how Jemima was stitching another flower basket together on the treadle machine, looking more contented than she had in a long while. Vera and Lizzie were sitting with Gail and Ruthie Lambright at the worktable, fitting together more sections of their colorful flower basket quilt as they chatted. Sam's girls were quizzing her daughters about Pete and Eddie, giggling about how cute they were.

The younger girls were having a fine time, too: the four-year-old twins, Cora and Dora, were seated on either side of Merle at a card table, playing Chutes and Ladders. He held Alice Ann in his lap and was talking about the rewards they reached by climbing the ladders and counting along with them as they moved their markers. Amanda could al-most put Wyman's recent financial concerns behind her: her sense of perspective had been restored by making a simple, inexpensive gift from fabric scraps and by the love she felt while she was surrounded by friends and family.

The front door flew open to admit Emma in a gust of cold air that sent snowflakes swirling into the room. She hurried straight over to the table to see what the girls were working on. "My stars, you've gotten most of this quilt top pieced already," she remarked as she removed her black bonnet. "That flower basket design's always been one of my favorites."

"What did you get for Abby and James?" Ruthie quizzed her.

"Better yet, how was your date with Jerome?" Vera asked eagerly.

As the front door opened again, Emma hurried toward the kitchen. "Nothing," she blurted as she passed behind her mother and Amanda. "And I doubt we'll ever go out again."

Amanda frowned—not just because Emma seemed so upset but because Jerome's stricken expression told her he'd overheard Emma's remark. "That doesn't sound any too gut," she murmured.

"Not what I wanted to hear, either," Eunice said with a shake of her head.

Jerome walked over to the worktable to see the quilting they'd accomplished. He ran a finger over some of the flower basket squares they'd pieced. "Looks like you girls had yourselves a fine, productive day," he remarked, although his voice lacked its usual lilt. "The snow's really coming down, so we'd best pack up and head home before the roads get nasty."

As though they sensed Jerome's downturn in mood, Vera and Lizzie quickly gathered the fabric scraps, supplies, and the almost-finished quilt top into the box they'd brought. "I bet Lizzie and Jemima and I can finish this top before our frolic next Saturday—and if we take it with us, there's no chance of Abby seeing it," Vera remarked.

"Sounds like a gut plan. I can't wait to work on the second one," came Emma's voice from the kitchen. "Mamm and I won't breathe a word to Abby. She'll be busy putting in her last week at the mercantile anyway."

After Jerome helped Merle take down the worktable, Amanda retrieved her baking pans and herded her five girls and Jemima toward the buggy. Lizzie and Vera sat in the back with Cora between them, while Dora and Alice Ann each claimed one of their laps. Jerome helped Jemima into the passenger's side of the front seat after Amanda had climbed in, and then he swung into the right-hand side to drive. It was a tight fit for three adults, especially with Jemima's big hips and Jerome's broad shoulders, so Amanda sat forward on the seat.

Sitting this close to her nephew, Amanda couldn't miss the tension in his jaw or the tightness in the muscled thigh that was wedged against hers. As he urged the mules out to the road, it was clear he didn't want to discuss his shopping trip with Emma. It was going to be a long, tiring ride if he stewed about it all the way home, so when the twins began retelling Merle's silly jokes and riddles to Vera and Lizzie in the backseat, Amanda eased Jerome into a quiet conversation.

"How'd your mules do today?" she asked. "They seem to be taking to the harness and working as a gut team."

Jerome let out a mirthless laugh. "Jah, Winona and Sparky behaved just fine," he remarked under his breath. "It's Emma I can't figure out. I understand she's been sheltered—she had never shopped for furniture, so wasn't expecting such sticker shock." He looked into Amanda's eyes and shook his head dolefully. "I made a point of keeping my hands and my kisses to myself all morning. Except—much as I *wanted* to hold her—I'd barely slipped my arm along the seat behind her when she bolted for the door."

Amanda patted his knee. "She comes by some of that honestly. Her mamm's extremely frugal and modest, you know—except today Eunice was as chipper as I've ever seen her."

"Jah," Jemima agreed. "No talk of her aches and pains. No complaining about Merle. She was having a real gut time."

"Which tells me Emma could get out more if she wanted to," Jerome mused aloud. "Maybe she doesn't *want* to socialize . . . Maybe she's content to remain a maidel. If there's no getting her past that idea, I might as well look elsewhere for company."

Amanda considered this. Jerome *loved* to go on dates; he wore his heart on his sleeve as he showed his girlfriends a good time. Yet it seemed his feelings for Emma might already be following the same downhill path as his two previous engagements. "Could be she's a late bloomer," she murmured.

Amanda paused to be sure the backseat conversation remained lively, so the twins wouldn't pester Jerome about his dilemma. "I've heard that Emma was in love with Matt Lambright all through school. Maybe she's still not over him getting hitched to Rosemary Yutzy last month."

"Jah, James told me about that a while back," Jerome said with a rueful shake of his head. "And maybe Emma's skittishness is partly *my* fault, for bringing up that subject at the wedding. Not only did I step in it; I stuck my foot in my mouth before I thought about how such talk might embarrass her."

Such an insightful remark made Amanda smile to herself. She could recall when Jerome was all bluster and all about himself—although she'd been relieved both times when he'd broken off his engagements. Her nephew was like a kid at a swimming hole, leaping into romances without first looking to see what jagged rocks lurked beneath the surface of a serious relationship.

"And did you hear that Sam's asked Abby to stop working at the mercantile?" Jerome asked in a low voice. "Emma's replacing her."

"No!" Amanda blurted. "Eunice didn't say a word!"

"My stars!" Jemima exclaimed. "If Emma feels like a mouse when she's with *you,* she'll really be looking for a hidey-hole when the store gets busy."

"Jah, that was *my* reaction. And once again, I blew it—dropped my fork and acted shocked before I could stop myself," Jerome replied with a sigh. "Bless her heart, Emma said she'd taken my suggestion to get out more. So now she probably thinks I consider her incapable or incompetent. And that's not true at all."

Amanda tried to imagine quiet, reserved Emma Graber dealing with customer complaints and handling a long line at the checkout counter with Abby's cheerful aplomb. Maybe Eunice hadn't mentioned anything about her daughter taking the job because *she* didn't think it would work out, either. Or maybe she just thought it was Emma's place to announce her new position.

"Well, Sam has known Emma all her life," Amanda remarked, "so we should trust his judgment. No doubt she has strengths and abilities we've not seen in the short time we've known her."

"I've got to hand it to her," Jerome agreed. "She's determined to meet this challenge and see it through. But now I've got two strikes against me—and if Emma's working, she'll have less time and inclination to go out with me. Must be losing my touch," he added with a short laugh.

"You'll figure it out," Amanda assured him as they rolled on down the county road. "Emma would make somebody a gut wife. It's just a matter of her figuring out if she *wants* to be a wife, and if she wants to be *yours.*"

By the time supper ended that evening, Emma was ready to pinch off her parents' heads. "Enough about Jerome, all right?" she snapped as she and Mamm cleared the table. "I *know* you think he's a gut man with an established business, and I *know* you adore him because he spends a lot of time with you and Dat. And jah, those are fine qualities for a husband. But I've *had* it with everybody's matchmaking."

Emma realized her frustration was getting the best of her, but she had to express her feelings before she popped like an overfilled balloon. "Truth be told, I was starting to *like* Jerome—and then, before I'd even gone on one date with him, you figured I'd become a maidel, so you told Sam I could work in the store! I can't please everybody, Mamm—or please *anybody*, it seems. So maybe you'd better let me sort things out for myself, all right?"

Her dat knew to retreat to his recliner in the front room without further comment. Mamm, however, withered on the spot. Her shoulders drooped, and the dish she'd been scraping clunked to the table. Then she began to cry—not just sniffling and blinking but big tears accompanied by a mournful wail.

Emma kicked herself. Her mother had been in a rare exuberant mood after quilting with the Lambright girls and Amanda's family, and now she looked utterly devastated. With a sigh, Emma wrapped her arms around her mamm and pulled her close . . . and couldn't help but notice that she was getting shorter.

"I'm sorry, Mamm. I shouldn't have used such a nasty tone," Emma murmured. "But please try to understand my side of this. You and Dat don't want me to end up alone, I know—but wouldn't hitching up with the wrong man be even worse? Jerome's like a horse charging out of the barn. And with everyone having us paired up before I've even gotten to know him, well—I've had enough."

Her mother eased away, removing her glasses to wipe the tears from her red-rimmed eyes. "I know I carry on sometimes—"

So true, Emma mused.

"But now that James is married, I'd feel better knowing you were taken care of before I die."

Emma's eyebrows shot up. "Mamm, what brought *this* on? You're nowhere near death's door," she insisted. "Matter of fact, you've perked up since you turned eighty. And you *know* James and Abby will look after me, no matter what. I'll always have a home."

Her mother sniffled loudly. "Jah. That's true."

"How about if you keep Dat company while I redd up?" Emma offered. "I think we're both tired after a busy day."

Nodding sadly, her mother shuffled into the front room.

Emma sighed, wishing she could take back her harsh words. But why should she pretend things would click between her and Jerome? While their shopping trip had gone better than she'd expected, he still seemed overconfident to the point of being flashy. And he'd been ready to buy that china hutch for more than two thousand dollars—as a *gift*! For all she knew, he was in debt up to his ears, even if he appeared prosperous and financially stable.

There was no mistaking what Jerome thought about her working at the mercantile, either. He'd tried to cover his astonishment, but his expression had said it all: he thought she was totally wrong for the job.

Trouble is, both he and Abby are probably right. Their reactions confirm my own doubts about coming out of my shell to deal with people—lots of people—every day.

As she squirted soap into the hot water she was running, Emma sighed. As a grown woman, she still wanted to tackle the mercantile job as a challenging adventure, to prove she could do it. Yet the shy child inside her quaked at the thought of making too many dumb mistakes with the cash register, or getting tongue-tied when a stranger complained about something. Maybe she should tell Sam she'd changed her mind . . .

Emma's shoulders slumped. She was exhausted. She would pray on this situation and make her decision tomorrow.

When she'd finished the dishes, Emma was ready to

apologize to her parents for her snippy words, but they'd already gone upstairs to bed. These winter days it got dark by five o'clock, so the urge to hibernate was stronger for all of them. She was glad she and Dat had tended the livestock before supper, so now all that remained was . . . an evening alone with her thoughts.

She missed James. Until these last couple of days, Emma hadn't realized how much happier mealtimes were with him around, and how much conversation and diversion her brother had provided for their parents—not to mention how he'd done most of the outdoor chores. *This won't change, either. He'll stop in every day, sure, but then he'll go home to Abby, across the road . . .*

Emma put out the lamps in the kitchen and left only one burning in the front room. While it would be the perfect evening to choose a pattern for the afghan she would crochet for James and Abby, she didn't feel like going upstairs to fetch her pattern books . . . didn't feel like doing anything except gaze forlornly out the side window, watching the snow fall as she stood near the woodstove. The rolling hills were blanketed with a fresh layer of white that glowed in the moonlight, punctuated by the dark cedars at the distant creek and the ribbon of road that had been cleared by the county plow. Such a peaceful scene Sam's place made as the snow piled higher on the fence rails.

Emma, however, felt anything but peaceful. She liked Jerome, but he was way out of her league. *Why can't he be more like Matt?*

She blinked at that sentiment. Was she thinking about Matt again because, just down the hill, the glow of a lantern between the barn and the house meant he was heading inside after tending his sheep and horses for the evening?

Let him go, she chided herself. *He's devoted to Rosemary and Katie. There's no future in wishing for what will never be.*

Emma vowed to make a fresh start tomorrow. It was a

visiting Sunday in Cedar Creek, with no church service, and James and Abby weren't due home until late afternoon. She and Mamm had already put together a bacon, cheese, and hash brown breakfast casserole, and a roast was ready to go into the oven for dinner, so she would spend the day enjoying her parents' company . . . maybe encourage them to join her at some board games. Or she might hitch up the sleigh and take them for a ride! The new-fallen snow was perfect for such an adventure, and the fresh air would do them all good.

She went upstairs to bed with a lighter heart and the best of intentions.

On Sunday morning, Emma hummed as she slid the breakfast casserole into the oven before going outside to tend to the morning chores. It was a beautiful day for a sleigh ride. She was thinking about which blankets to take along when Dat came up beside her. His hair was still rumpled from sleeping, and his flannel shirttail stuck out around his suspenders. He slung his arm around her waist, wearing the oddest expression.

"Emma, your mamm . . . well, she went home to Jesus in her sleep last night. Peaceful as you please," he murmured in a faraway voice. "I sure hope I go that easy when it's my time."

Chapter 9

Had the casserole not already been in the oven, Emma would have dropped it. She grabbed for the kitchen counter. "Dat, you can't be—surely she's just sleeping really hard."

"Tried shaking her shoulder, but . . . well, she's already cold. I'm sorry, Emma."

"Sorry?" she blurted, and then clapped her hand over her mouth. Her thoughts spun out of control even as she suspected her dat was having one of his off days, not thinking clearly. The proper response was to go upstairs and check on Mamm herself, yet her throat clicked like a casket latch when she swallowed. Truth be told, she was petrified at the idea of being anywhere close to a dead person, much less touching one . . . much less determining that her poor, dear mother had indeed passed on.

I didn't get to say good-bye . . . I was so mean and hateful last night . . .

No! Mamm's been perkier than ever lately, just like I

told her yesterday. This is not *happening—not while James is away and . . .*

Emma inhaled deeply to corral her frantic thoughts. She fought back sudden tears. "I'd better see about her," she murmured, even as her stomach knotted. "Are—are you all right, Dat?"

Stupid question! she chided herself. Yet as he wrapped his gnarled fingers around her hand, her father seemed amazingly calm. *My stars, he believes he woke up beside a dead woman. Yet he's leading me toward the stairs as though he knows exactly what he's doing . . . as coherent and purposeful as when James and I were kids.*

Emma willed herself to walk up the stairs and then toward the bedroom at the end of the hall. She resisted the urge to turn and run . . . prayed that Mamm would be sitting on the side of the bed, pulling on her black stockings and fussing about sleeping so late.

But, no. By the light of the lamp Emma lit, she could see that her mother was gazing at the far wall but wasn't seeing anything. As Dat gently lowered her eyelids, Emma turned away, clutching herself to keep from screaming. She suddenly felt lost and terrified and sick to her stomach and ready to flee the room and—

"We'd best call the funeral home," her dat murmured. "But I don't suppose anybody's there this early of a Sunday morning."

Emma turned to stare at him. How could Dat remain so calm and collected? Why did he seem so rational when she felt like jumping out of her skin, ready to babble like an idiot if she opened her mouth?

"It's all right, Emmie-girl. You feel everything all at once, like a hamster running crazy-fast on a wheel, when you look death in the face for the first time." His wrinkles deepened in a sad smile. "I was there when both of my folks and a couple of brothers passed on, you see. Experience doesn't make it any easier, but it sets you up for what needs to be done."

Emma let out the breath she didn't realize she'd been holding. "We have to call James and—and—"

"That's a hard one," Dat replied with a hitch in his voice. "How about if I notify the undertaker, while you go over and tell Sam what's happened?"

"Jah, I can do that." Purposely not looking at the figure in the bed beneath the quilt, Emma went for the door. "Put on your heavy coat and boots before you go to the phone shanty, Dat. The snow's deeper this morning."

"Jah. I'll be all right, dear."

I'll be all right. How could her dat say that, knowing he'd lost the woman who'd been by his side for more than sixty years? As Emma descended the stairs, nearly blinded by her tears, she was again amazed at his presence of mind—yet grateful he wasn't wandering around in circles or talking nonsense. Or maybe he was in shock. She'd heard that folks went through the motions in their grief, and then later couldn't recall taking care of funeral details or—

We'll need to clean the house and cook for company and sew Mamm's white burial dress and call everybody and clear the driveway and—and—

By the time Emma had rushed across the road and onto the Lambrights' porch, she was in such a state that when Barbara opened the kitchen door, Emma blurted, "Mamm's gone! I don't know what to do or who to—and how will I get everything—"

"Hold on, dear," Barbara murmured as she gently grasped Emma's shoulders. "Are you saying your mother took off without telling you where she went?"

When Barbara turned to look at Sam, who was rising from the far end of the table, Emma realized she'd burst in on the family's breakfast. Ruthie, Gail, and Sam's mother, Treva, also came over to see why she was in such a dither. Surrounded by so many concerned faces, lifelong friends who immediately reached out to rub her back, Emma snapped. Crying uncontrollably, she buried her face in Barbara's shoulder.

Sam's wife held her close. "Fetch my medical bag, Sam," she said quietly. "Let's get on over there."

Emma wasn't sure who did what, but during the next few hours all the overwhelming details were taken care of. She was vaguely aware that someone had rescued the casserole from the oven and that Sam had called both Sharon and Iva, her elder sisters, to come back to Cedar Creek with James and Abby.

"This is no time for you to start work at the store, Emma," Sam insisted when he came back from the phone shanty. "We'll wait for a better time, all right?"

Emma nodded gratefully. Next thing she knew, Matt and Titus were plowing the driveway. Rosemary and Treva were sitting on the sofa with her and Dat when men from the funeral home near Clearwater took Mamm's body. Emma felt as though she were viewing it all from outside the house, through a foggy window . . .

That afternoon, when James and Abby returned from Queen City with their two sisters' families, Sam offered to host the funeral dinner in Treva's greenhouse. Abby, ever efficient even as she wiped away her tears, said she would sew Eunice's white burial dress tomorrow. Gail and Ruthie agreed to bring black dye from the mercantile to help Emma prepare dresses for her and Abby's period of mourning, while Treva organized callers to notify distant kin that the funeral would be held on Wednesday. With Thursday being Thanksgiving and most of the distant kin not likely to return so soon after attending the wedding, everyone agreed it was best not to wait until Friday for the service. When she returned from the phone shanty, Treva told them that Amanda, Jemima, and the Brubaker bunch insisted on organizing the meal after the funeral so that the Grabers and the Lambrights could accept condolences.

Emma was so grateful for such caring friends, yet she felt more like an observer than a participant in this life-altering event. After the Lambrights went home, Iva and Sharon began making lists of cleaning chores to do before the funeral. When they went upstairs to their parents' room to hunt for the white apron and cape Mamm had worn at her wedding, so she could be buried in them, Dat went up with them to prepare for bedtime. Emma chose to sit with James and Abby in the kitchen.

Her brother took her hand. "Emmie-girl, I'm sorry you and Dat were here alone when . . . Any idea why Mamm might've passed last night?"

"She'd been doing so well lately," Abby remarked with a loud sniffle. "Or at least I *thought* she was feeling all right."

Emma shook her head, as she'd been doing most of the day. "I had no notion that Mamm was feeling poorly, either. When she went up to bed last night, she'd had a really fine day. I didn't get to say gut-bye . . ."

"Jah, I know that feeling," James murmured forlornly.

"And I'll never forgive myself for getting cross about her talk of Jerome and me—" Emma stopped before she revealed the secret about the quilting frolic. "I was going to apologize for being snippy, but by the time I'd cleaned up the dishes, Mamm and Dat had gone up to bed, and—and now I'll never get to talk to her ever again."

Abby and James each grabbed her hands, nodding forlornly.

"This is all my fault," Emma muttered. "If I'd stayed at home instead of—"

Abby gripped her fingers. "Emma, you were *not* wrong to go out yesterday. I'm guessing your mamm was really happy that you took that ride with Jerome—"

"For sure and for certain," James affirmed. "If Mamm passed in her sleep, without waking Dat with any tossing or moaning, it means she was at peace. Ready to meet her

Maker and move on to her reward," he insisted. "Now it's our job to find our own peace, knowing that Mamm's days were numbered, same as anyone's."

"Jah, God called her home, and she was ready to go," Abby murmured through her tears. "We should all strive to live so good a life, for so many years."

James rose from his chair. "I'm going to say gut night to Dat."

"And I'll see what shape Eunice's wedding apron's in," Abby said as she stood up to join him. "Sharon and Iva have surely found it by now."

Emma nodded. She watched them approach the stairs, yet she felt no need to go along. She shuddered at the thought of Dat getting into the bed that Mamm had died in, as though tonight were just like all the other nights of their lives together. And even though her nieces and nephews were getting ready to bunk in the same rooms they always used for their visits, and her sisters' husbands had gone outside to tend the livestock, Emma realized that—once again—she was alone.

Will it always be this way? Alone, even while I'm surrounded by family?

Exhausted and overwhelmed, Emma buried her head in her arms to cry. So much cleaning had to be done before Tuesday's visitation and the funeral on Wednesday. So many details and reminders of Mamm must be dealt with, when all Emma wanted was to bury herself in her cozy bed and not come out again anytime soon . . .

Chapter 10

James remained still, breathing in and out with Abby as she lay curled against him, asleep beneath a comforting layer of quilts. In the soft shadows of their bedroom, he'd been thinking heavy thoughts, and before it came time to act upon them, he savored a few more moments of the peace and incredible love he felt for his new wife. When the clock on the dresser chimed five, she stirred in his arms.

"Abby-girl, are you awake?" he whispered.

She stretched against him. "Jah, I am, dear James," she murmured. "Did you get any rest?"

"Not a lot, but it felt gut to hold you while my thoughts went their ways."

Abby turned and tenderly stroked his jawline, where his stubbly new beard was growing in. "The Lord's with us even on difficult days like today. It'll be hard to say our gut-byes to your mamm, but we'll get through it."

James nodded, grateful for the darkness that masked his tears as they rose and dressed for the day. "How about if we eat breakfast here, just the two of us, instead of going over home? We'll be surrounded by folks and their condolences all day, and . . ."

Abby smiled sadly. She was dressed all in black, with red-rimmed eyes. "Sounds like a fine idea. Some quiet, prayerful time," she replied. "I'll heat that casserole Barbara brought us."

Once again James was grateful for the efficient way his wife began their days. By the time he reached the kitchen, the savory aromas of bacon and coffee enveloped him. As he sat down to a meal he wasn't particularly hungry for, James bowed in thanksgiving and then gazed at Abby as she remained in prayer a few moments longer.

"What would I do without you to get me through, Abby?" he murmured as he clasped her hand. "Mamm was the glue that held our family together."

"That's the way of it in most households," she observed.

"And I'm concerned more about Emma than about Dat," James went on as he spooned up some breakfast. The eggs and bread, dotted with onion and bacon and smothered in melted cheese, gave him more of an appetite, as well as the fortitude to broach a potentially tricky topic. "I know how you love this little nest—and I do, too," he insisted, "but I believe we'd better move across the road. Once Sharon's and Iva's families have gone home, Dat and Emma will be rattling around in that house like two dried peas in a shoe box."

Bless her, Abby met his gaze with a steady smile. "I've already agreed to Emma's suggestion about having my Stitch in Time business there, so moving in will simplify matters," she replied with a nod. "I won't have to shift from one place to the other, from being at work to being your wife, because I'll be at home all the time."

I'll be at home all the time. James closed his eyes against a welling-up of love for the woman who sat across from him. "Denki for understanding, Abby, and for always seeing the positive side of problems that would send some folks into a tizzy."

Abby smiled despite her sorrow. "Moving in with your dat and Emma's the right thing to do. And it's easier because you'll be making the change with me."

Later, as they joined the rest of the family at home, where everyone in Cedar Creek gathered to pay their final respects to his mother, James clung to Abby's hand until he had to take his place on the men's side of the room. He slid onto the wooden bench beside Dat. Although his father seemed tired from the past few days' decisions, yesterday's visitation, and setting up for the service, he appeared calm. Accepting.

"Eunice didn't have to suffer through long-term illness or pain, like so many folks do," his dat remarked. "And for that, we should be grateful."

"Jah, you're right, Dat. She went out in gut spirits and in her right mind."

His father's face, weathered from years of outdoor labor, crinkled with a fond smile. "You were the special light in her life, James. Your mamm loved the girls, of course, but she always loved you best."

James curled in on himself, overwhelmed by the simple statement that he knew to be true. He'd expected to be the one comforting his dat, yet now it was his father's arm around his shaking shoulders that kept him from collapsing beneath the weight of this loss.

When everyone was seated, the bishop began the funeral with several comforting verses of scripture. " 'Seek the Lord and His strength. Seek His face evermore,' the psalmist tells us," Vernon said, allowing his voice to resonate around the room. "And the prophet Isaiah reminds us to 'Fear not, for I am with thee. Be not dismayed, for I am thy God. I will strengthen thee . . . I will uphold thee with the right hand of my righteousness.' "

As the simple service continued, James sat taller. He

took in Vernon Gingerich's eloquent message about eternal life in Jesus. He found strength in the words of the age-old hymns Sam Lambright and Preacher Abe Nissley recited, for the congregation didn't sing on such somber occasions. After the service, they all made their way to the cemetery down the road, walking behind the black horse-drawn hearse that carried his mamm's plain wooden coffin.

They laid his mother to rest on the peaceful, frost-laced hillside where so many other family members and friends had been buried. As he gazed at the bleak hole in the earth, James was aware of how his arms ached from when he and his brothers-in-law had dug the grave by hand. Once again Vernon spoke comforting words from the Bible, keeping his remarks brief because folks were shivering in the wind. As Emma, Iva, and Sharon wept around him, James stood with Abby between him and Dat, knowing they would all draw strength from her in the coming days. Abby would now be the glue that held the Graber family together while he supported them with his carriage shop.

James sighed, clasping Abby's hand as they walked back to the greenhouse for dinner with the rest of the crowd. How could he show his appreciation to his new wife for the responsibilities she would take on so soon after they'd married? How could he express his love for all the ways Abby had rearranged her life to accommodate his needs? While it was customary for the family to eat first, James hung back, waiting while Abby and Emma spoke to the women who were serving the meal. When he noticed Eddie Brubaker going through the serving line, he got an idea.

"I understand your painting inside the mercantile is going well," James remarked. He smiled, gesturing at the teenager's mounded plate. "Takes a lot of fuel to keep you going up and down the ladder, no doubt."

Eddie smiled. "It's not the painting that's the real work so much as clearing the shelves and moving the displays," he remarked. "Sam started me in the upper level so I can get the hang of it before I move downstairs amongst more shoppers."

"The prep always takes more effort than the painting itself," James agreed. "Say, what would you think about painting a couple of rooms at my place? We've talked about you coming over when you've finished Sam's job, but what with Abby and me moving back in with Dat and Emma soon, I'd like to perk up the kitchen and the room where she'll be sewing. Sooner rather than later."

"If it's okay with Sam, I'll get right on it. I'll be going home right after we finish eating to spend Thanksgiving with my family, but then I'm coming back into Cedar Creek." Eddie looked around the crowd, trying to spot the tall, gray-bearded storekeeper. "Truth be told, doing a couple of rooms at your place will be a snap compared to painting the mercantile. What color?"

James gazed around the roomful of friends and family, all decked out in somber black, just as his wife and sister would be for months to come. "I once told Abby she was made of love and sunshine," he mused aloud, "so let's go with yellow. Not pale like butter, but more like—like that lemon meringue pie your dat's got."

James raised his hand in greeting as Wyman Brubaker nodded at him. It was good to see the head of that family appearing more confident and less worried—a state of mind James hoped to resume soon. "I'll speak to Sam for you, and let's not say anything to Abby, all right? I'd like it to be a surprise."

James managed to smile as he imagined the delight on his wife's face when she saw the freshly painted rooms. Spotting Abby in the clutch of women who were refilling the steam table pans, he went to fetch her. Traditionally the men visited together while the women kept these functions flowing smoothly, yet it felt right to relieve Abby of her serving work at Mamm's funeral lunch. Spending time together was the best elixir for both of them on such a difficult day.

He tugged on Abby's sleeve and got Emma's attention as well. "How about if you girls eat with me?" he asked them. "Dat's sitting with Sharon and Iva and their families. Amanda and the neighbor ladies have this meal under control, and you girls' company is exactly what I need right now."

"That's what I've tried to tell her, James," Amanda called over to him. "Your mamm's smiling down on you for thinking of it, too."

And wasn't *that* a wonderful sentiment? James picked up a clean plate, gesturing for Abby and Emma to go ahead of him in the serving line. They had endured the worst now that the funeral service was behind them. Love and sunshine would again grace their days if they allowed the Lord's light to guide them. James believed this with all his heart.

Jerome gazed across the crowded greenhouse, watching Emma as she picked at her plateful of food. Sorrow seemed to envelope and insulate her, as though she were enclosed in a bubble that shut out James, Abby, and everyone else around her. What could he say to make Emma feel better? How could he express his own sorrow in a way that wouldn't send her skittering across the room to escape him? He'd hung back while others had conveyed their condolences, but he wouldn't go home until he'd spoken to her.

Emma rose from the chair beside James and carried her half-full plate to where the servers were scraping and stacking the dirty dishes. It wasn't the ideal situation in which to tell her his thoughts, but Jerome walked over to join her. "Emma, your mamm was a wonderful-gut woman, and I'll miss her," he murmured. "I think my favorite recollection of Eunice was the look on her face when we took that wagon ride to Wyman's place last month, when I was training the eight-mule hitch. She and your dat were the picture of happiness that day, and I'm so glad I got to know her."

Emma blinked, and a smile slowly overtook her face. "Mamm had such a gut time on that ride, Jerome. She talked about it for days."

He nodded, not wanting to ruin a good moment. While he wished he could spend more time with Emma soon, it wouldn't be the proper time to suggest another outing. "And how's your dat doing? He seems to be holding up pretty well."

"He's got a lot of folks to keep him talking now," Emma replied as she scraped another plate. "But I'm concerned that he might become forgetful again once Mamm's absence sinks in. She fussed at him more than we liked, but she kept him on his toes, too."

Jerome bit back an offer to come to the Graber place every now and again, to visit with Merle and help with chores, because Emma would probably see it as his way to be around *her*. After his shopping trip with her, he'd thought a lot about his behavior . . . about how to approach Emma differently. He was glad when Aunt Amanda came over with a pull cart for the scraped dishes, so they could be hauled to the house to be washed.

"Emma, it's only proper to postpone Saturday's quilting frolic," Amanda said, glancing around to be sure Abby wasn't close by to overhear.

Emma sighed forlornly. "Jah, I'm in no frame of mind to drive to Bloomingdale."

"I'll come get you—whenever you're ready," Jerome blurted. He immediately regretted it, too, because Emma stepped away from him.

Amanda smiled ruefully at him and put her hand on Emma's shoulder. "We still want you to come, as I know how much you want to work on our quilts," she insisted.

"But we shouldn't wait too long to finish Abby and James's wedding present, either. As winter sets in, who knows how the roads might be?"

"Jah, there's that." Emma smiled feebly. "Denki for thinking of me. I—I'll let you know, Amanda."

With that, Emma wandered back toward the tables to collect more dishes. Plenty of other girls were doing that job on a day when the daughter of the deceased wasn't expected to help, yet Jerome understood Emma's desire to keep herself occupied as a way to get through this difficult day. He sensed it might be a long while before she recovered from the shock and grief of her mother's passing, for even though they'd bickered and fussed at each other, Emma and Eunice had been very close.

As he watched her walk between the tables, he saw Emma withdrawing into her own private bubble again. Such a pretty young woman she was, even wearing black from head to toe. Jerome sincerely hoped she wouldn't hide herself away in mourning for an entire year, as custom allowed, just as he wondered how he could get back in her good graces.

With a sigh, Jerome grasped the handle of the wooden cart. "Let me take this to the house for you," he told his aunt. "I can do *that* without upsetting anyone, anyway."

"Denki, Nephew." Amanda leaned closer to his ear. "Between you and me, we should use the quilting frolic as our way of prying Emma out of that house, as she surely won't be starting her job at the store yet. Will you help me with that?"

"I'll do my very best," Jerome replied. "It might take all of you Brubakers and a team of mules to keep Emma in circulation now, but we've got to try."

Chapter 11

As Emma, James, and their dat waved good-bye to Sharon and Iva and their families Friday morning, relief washed over her. The Lambrights had hosted all of them for Thanksgiving dinner yesterday, and the men had removed the pew benches from the house, so today—at last—she could collapse. James would return to work in his shop and Abby would be packing up her sewing supplies at the mercantile. The newlyweds wouldn't be moving in until this evening, so Emma figured to relax and let Dat do the same. What with all the food their neighbors had brought, she wouldn't have to cook for days.

Her brother waved one last time at the departing rigs and then steered her and Dat back into the house, out of the cold. Even though he'd taken Mamm's death hard, James smiled as though he had a secret. "Eddie Brubaker will be here this morning to paint the kitchen and whichever room Abby will be sewing in," he said. "It's a surprise for her, but I figured everyone would feel cheerier in a bright yellow kitchen—"

"Bright yellow?" As Emma gazed toward the large kitchen, where the pale blue paint had faded to a dull gray after several years, all she could think of was how much more work this surprise—this intrusion—would mean for her. "What possessed you to choose *that* color? And *today* of all days, when I'm in no mood to shift everything out of the cabinets and off the countertops."

James gently grasped her shoulders. With a new fringe of beard bristling along his jawline, he looked downright rakish, and far too cheerful. "Don't you worry about a thing, Emmie," he assured her. "You three sisters put everything away after breakfast, and Eddie's experienced at using drop cloths and tape to keep his paint on the walls where it belongs. Let him do all the work—that's what I'm paying him for."

Emma exhaled impatiently, but what could she do? James had obviously taken it upon himself to cheer everyone up without consulting her. She shrugged out of his grasp as she felt tears welling up. Oh, but she longed for some private time to let her feelings out.

James, however, seemed oblivious to how he'd upset her. "Now—where had you and Abby figured on putting her machine and sewing supplies? I can be figuring out where to put the furniture from that room—"

"I'll help you with that, Son," Dat insisted. He'd been following this conversation closely, and his bushy eyebrows rose in anticipation. "And while we're shifting things around, what would you and Abby think of taking the big bedroom upstairs and I'll start bunking down here?" He pointed toward the short hallway in front of them. "Seems only right for me to move into the dawdi haus, where *my* folks used to be, and let you become the head of the family now that you're married, James. And it'll be safer, too, what with me not going up and down the stairs."

Emma bit back another protest. Dat had slowed down a lot, and he wasn't always steady on his feet, so it made perfect sense for him to move downstairs. He'd have his own bathroom, too. But all of this changing around meant even more work for her—carrying his clothes downstairs, not to mention cleaning out the dawdi haus closets where Mamm had stored odds and ends.

"Since Wyman is driving Eddie into Cedar Creek this morning, he can help us shift your furniture," James mused aloud. "I can ask Noah Coblentz to help, if we need him. There's not a lot for him to do in the shop today, so we might as well put his younger muscle to work. I say let's do it!"

Emma clapped her mouth shut. Without Mamm or Abby here, she was outnumbered and outvoted. As she went into the kitchen to figure out what she could serve for dinner to whoever would be working there all day, she heard the front door open. Wyman and Eddie greeted Dat and her brother, their voices low and friendly.

"And gut morning from me as well!" Jerome called out. "Merle, when I heard Eddie would be painting at your place, I came along to help him move furniture so you wouldn't have to."

"You're an answer to a prayer," her dat replied in a chipper voice. "James and I were just figuring out who would move my things into the dawdi haus, so I pick *you*!"

Emma seriously considered disappearing into the cellar . . . maybe hiding in a closet so no one would find her. Jerome was the *last* person she wanted to see today. Why did she sense his appearance was no coincidence—as though he'd been looking for a reason to come and coax her into a better mood? Maybe ask her out on another date?

James clapped Jerome on the back. "You've already been a big help to us, what with directing folks where to park for Mamm's funeral and then working with us to take down tables and chairs after the lunch," he remarked. "Denki for all your kindness."

"Your mamm was a special lady," Jerome replied. "It's the least I can do."

Emma gripped the handle on the fridge, blinking back tears. Jerome's voice had quivered a bit . . . His affection for Mamm had always been sincere, and he *had* taken on a lot of the physical labor required for the funeral. She took a deep breath and slowly let it out. *Better improve your attitude. Like it or not, you'll have a houseful of men helping us reshuffle and resettle, all day long.*

As she was assessing which casseroles and sides to serve for dinner, Eddie peeked into the kitchen.

"Hey there, Emma," he said cautiously. "How about if I tape the cabinet edges and prep the kitchen now, and then paint it this afternoon, so you won't be interrupted while you're cooking dinner?" he suggested. "Then, if you'll show me the other room you want done, I could paint that one first."

Emma gave him a tremulous smile. "That's very thoughtful of you, Eddie."

"It was Jerome's idea, truth be told."

Emma caught herself before she overreacted, thank goodness, because then Jerome was peering at her from behind the Brubaker boy.

"It's gut to see you, Emma," Jerome said. "You're most likely exhausted after these past difficult days, so we've all agreed to be helpful today without making more work than we're worth. If you or your dat have chores that need doing, just say the word and I'll see to them."

Emma tried to find a smile. "That's very kind of you," she murmured. "Eddie, I'll let you do your taping here in the kitchen while James and I decide on the other room you'll paint."

With so many fellows helping, the morning passed quickly and an amazing amount of furniture got moved. Dat seemed as happy as a cat at milking time with his new quarters. Emma did her best to keep coffee and cookies available to their helpers and to stay out of Jerome's sight while he and Wyman and James did the heavy lifting. When Abby came in for dinner at noon, James whisked her upstairs to the freshly painted guest room they had converted into her new sewing nook.

As Emma was setting plates on the table, she heard Abby's exclamations of pleasure. Jerome, Wyman, and Dat came into the kitchen to wash up before they ate.

"I understand this is a surprise for the newlyweds, so I'll speak quickly and quietly," Wyman said to her. "Amanda's hoping you can come to Bloomingdale for your quilting frolic next Saturday."

"That's the fifth of December," Jerome clarified. "And my offer to come fetch you and Merle still stands."

"That would be just dandy!" Dat said as he grabbed for a hand towel. "I can't wait to play board games with Cora and Dora—and Simon will be there this time."

"But—but that's so *soon* after—oh, I'm just not ready for any socializing." Emma's cheeks prickled with heat. She hurried over to pull casserole pans from the oven. Why did these fellows think she'd want to *go, go, go*? It was enough of a surprise, dealing with all this painting and moving today, let alone figuring to spend next Saturday at the Brubaker place.

Jerome was suddenly at her side, easing the steaming pan of chicken spaghetti from between her hands. His dark hair glimmered and his eyes sparkled as he focused on her. Even after a morning of hefting furniture, he smelled clean and fresh . . . such an enticing scent.

And why are you noticing how gut Jerome smells? It's Dat who needs your time and attention, Dat you should be thinking of, because he's going to be so lost without Mamm, once all this company goes home.

"I'm sorry if we've upset you, Emma," Jerome murmured. Then he removed the pans of chili mac and ham with pineapple slices from the oven and set them on the table for her. "We were just passing along Amanda's suggestion. Think about it as long as you need to."

She nodded, aware of how *considerate* Jerome was

being today. He was much easier to dislike when he was being his bold, brassy, swaggering self—the sort of man who paraded down the road with an eight-mule hitch, showing them off.

During dinner, Emma concentrated on passing food and filling water glasses—anything to stay busy while the men devoured an astonishing amount of food. Abby seemed tickled about her new lemon yellow sewing room, and about sharing Emma's parents' previous bedroom with James, and about living here with Emma and Dat, as though life had opened a lot of unexpected doors for her. She didn't seem nearly as disappointed that she'd no longer be working at the mercantile, either.

While Emma envied Abby's ability to rise above sorrow—to see the rainbow rather than the rain—such cheerfulness required too much effort from her right now. What she wouldn't do for a nap . . . or time to begin the afghan for Abby and James in her cozy room. She'd found a large bin of yarn when she'd cleaned out the dawdi haus closet—enough to get a good start on her project. But she couldn't sit around crocheting while they had a houseful of company.

As Eddie carried his ladders, paint cans, and rollers into the kitchen, Emma washed the dishes and Abby dried them before she had to return to the mercantile for the afternoon. "It feels strange, seeing my shelves empty in the loft over there," she confided as they finished redding up. "My sewing supplies are all packed, and I'm just waiting for somebody to move my sewing machine over here . . . working on my last order for Sam before I finish being his employee in a few hours." Abby sighed, shrugging. "But it's all working out for the best. Do you have any idea when you'll start working? I can still go over with you and show you how we—"

"Oh, it's way too soon for that," Emma protested. "Mamm's not even been gone a week."

"And Sam's already said you won't be working in the

main store while you're in mourning," Abby agreed gently. "But whenever you feel up to looking at the ledgers, or bagging up the bulk cereals and baking supplies in the workroom, he'd be pleased to have you start."

Emma bit back another objection, sensing a different topic of conversation was in order. With all the commotion of moving Dat to his new rooms and dealing with Eddie's painting, she'd been hit with all the major changes she could handle for one day.

"Well, I'm glad you and James'll be living here with us," she said, trying to sound cheerful. "Are you planning to visit anybody next weekend?" She figured if Abby was going to be home, there was no way she could go to the frolic in Bloomingdale without revealing their quilting secret.

"Jah, we're venturing over past Queen City," Abby replied as she hung her dish towel to dry. "Mamm's cousins there have invited us."

Emma quelled the urge to sigh. She would have to find another reason to miss the frolic next weekend . . .

No sooner had James accompanied Abby back to the mercantile than Eddie was climbing his ladder and coating the back kitchen wall with bright yellow paint. Wyman and Jerome lingered at the table with Dat, drinking coffee and watching the transformation of the room where the family spent so much of its time.

"I bet Abby'll whip up some new curtains, and we'll have us a whole new room," her father said.

"Jah, I painted Amanda's house from top to bottom before we Brubakers all moved in there," Eddie remarked. His roller swished at a quick, even pace. "Fresh paint really does perk a place up—even though none of our rooms are quite this *sunny!*"

"Amanda's looking forward to having you two Grabers out for that quilting visit, too," Jerome chimed in. "She'll have some of her pottery orders ready by next weekend, so I could bring them when I come for you—"

"I'm not going!" Emma blurted. "I'll be crocheting an afghan for a wedding gift, so—so you should tell Amanda and the girls to work on their quilts without me. It's not like they need my help."

The kitchen rang with silence. The men's eyes widened, and Eddie stopped painting to look at her, as though she might send him home at any second.

Emma's shoulders slumped and she swallowed hard. *I've gone and done it now. I sound like a fussy little girl about to pitch a fit.*

Wyman took another cookie from the plate on the table, looking ready to talk Emma out of her decision. Dat, however, had an odd expression on his face. "Got to see a man about a horse," he mumbled as he headed out of the kitchen.

"Guess I'll fetch a few things Amanda wants from the mercantile," Wyman remarked. "I'll be back by the time you're finished painting, Eddie."

"I'll go, too," Jerome said as he took his coat from a peg on the wall. "Need some feed supplement for my mule foals."

Within moments, the house rang with silence. Emma felt awkward hanging around in the kitchen while Eddie worked, so she went upstairs. Her parents' former bedroom was now arranged with James's bed on a different wall, and Abby had already changed the sheets and the quilts. And while Abby's bright yellow sewing room nearly made Emma squint, nothing needed doing in there, either, until the treadle sewing machine came over from the mercantile. Emma had already put fresh sheets on Dat's bed and tidied his new quarters in the dawdi haus, and James had hung his clothes in the closet.

Emma wandered back downstairs and sat on the chair nearest the woodstove. At last, she had the peace and quiet she'd been craving, but she'd overturned everyone else's applecart by declaring she couldn't go to the Brubakers' anytime soon. Was it so wrong to mourn her mother? To allow time for her emotions to emerge, now that everyone else was returning to their normal, everyday lives? Emma wasn't at all sure what shape her days would take now that Mamm wouldn't be talking with her and working alongside her as they shared every little task.

Maybe working in the back room at the mercantile wasn't such a far-flung idea. Doing Sam's book work and filling bulk food bags sounded a lot more appealing than having to face customers . . .

The front door flew open ahead of Jerome, who held a loaded leather wood carrier in each of his hands. Wyman followed him inside, holding the door for her father, who wore a smug expression.

"We're all squared away! I just talked with Amanda on the phone," Dat announced. "She agreed that maybe this next Saturday was too soon, so the quilting frolic is now set for the following weekend, on the twelfth of December. It'll work out just perfect, because she'll have the whole set of dishes finished for Abby and James by then, and Jerome can bring them when he comes for us that morning."

Emma's mouth fell open. "But—*please*, Dat," she pleaded as she watched Jerome stack the firewood. He was smiling brightly. No doubt he was a partner in this little conspiracy. "Sometime soon I'll—"

"Emma, dear, I know you mean well," her father interrupted with more spunk than she'd seen in years, "but I've got to get myself out amongst cheerful folks who are *doing* something, or my recliner's going to swallow me up. I'll have plenty of time for napping by the fire once the snow's blowing and it's too cold to get out."

Dat gazed at her with unmistakable love but unshakable authority. "Your mamm would be fussing at us both if we turned into stick-in-the-mud couch potatoes, and you know it, Emma. So that's that."

Chapter 12

On the Friday morning after Thanksgiving, Amanda sat immersed in her work, watching a large bowl take shape between her hands . . . breathing in time to the steady *whirrrrr* of her revolving pottery wheel. The set of dishes Sam and Vernon had ordered was coming together as though inspired by those men's faith and spiritual leadership. Most of the pieces were glazed and completed, with only the cups and saucers to make yet—thanks to the way Vera and Jemima had been keeping the youngsters occupied this week. The aroma of chocolate chip cookies convinced her it was time to take a break.

"Mamm! Mamm, some guy's coming to the door!" Simon called out from the kitchen.

Amanda stopped pumping the wheel, easing her hands from the wet bowl so she wouldn't ruin it. Simon's voice sounded strident—and outside, Wags was barking in a way that announced a stranger. With Wyman, Jerome, and

Eddie gone to Cedar Creek for the day, she sensed she'd better see who was coming.

As she entered the kitchen, a loud pounding on the door made Jemima and the three little girls freeze in place at the table, their cookie dough forgotten. Simon, too, stood back, staring at the man who was glaring at them through the glass—not his usual excited reaction when someone stopped by.

"Jah, just a minute," Amanda called out to their visitor.

"Get this mutt away from me!" he snapped. "I'm not in the mood to get bit—and you can't afford it if I do."

A tingle of fear snaked up Amanda's spine. "Simon, go around back and call Wags," she said as their mixed-breed German shepherd continued to bark at the man. "Take him into the barn, and let Pete know a stranger's here."

As the boy darted out the back door without a coat, Amanda washed the mucky clay from her hands at the kitchen sink. Who was this man with such a chip on his shoulder? His short hair and clipped beard didn't look Plain, nor did his uncharitable expression.

Lord, guide our words and actions, and please keep us from harm, Amanda prayed as she dried her hands. With a glance toward Jemima, who stood over by the oven with Cora, Dora, and Alice Ann by her side, Amanda opened the door just far enough to talk. "Jah? What seems to be the problem?"

"If you're Wyman Brubaker's wife, you've got a *problem,* all right," the man retorted as he pushed on the door.

Amanda stepped out of his way, again praying that nothing drastic was going to happen now that this irate man had entered her home. "And what might that be? And who are *you*?" she asked, her voice rising. She wouldn't reveal that neither Wyman nor Jerome was home . . . hoped Pete would come out of the barn soon . . .

"I'm Reece Weaver. Does that name ring any bells?" he demanded.

Amanda crossed her arms. It wasn't her way to speak crossly—especially not to men—but if this was the contractor responsible for building Wyman's new grain elevator, her opinion of him was *not* improving. "And what do you want, Reece Weaver?" she asked in a low voice.

"Where's Wyman?"

Amanda held her ground. She didn't reply.

Reece's expression settled into a knowing sneer. "So he's not home, eh? Probably had a feeling I was coming to collect the money he owes me—and he owes me a *lot* in back payments, Mrs. Brubaker," he added, raising his eyebrows dramatically. "Tell him I'll see him in court if he doesn't settle up within the next few days. *Got* it?"

Wyman had told her that work on his new elevator had been delayed by the recent snowfall. The concrete foundation hadn't been poured, as they had originally figured on. The weather couldn't be considered Wyman's fault, and he'd met with Reece a few days before, as he'd been instructed to. So why was this wiry, prickly man acting so huffy? If her husband were here, he'd send this nasty man packing.

Amanda pointed toward the door. "It's time for you to leave," she stated as she advanced toward him. "This is business for you to settle with my husband and his partner, not with me."

Reece backed up and opened the door, chuckling sarcastically. "You don't scare me one bit, little lady."

"And *you*," Amanda said as she stepped out onto the porch behind him, "*you* had better not *ever* come here to frighten my children again, Mr. Weaver. Understand me?"

"Tell Wyman I was here to see him."

"Jah, you can bet I will." Amanda stood staunchly on the porch to be sure this intruder went straight to his truck rather than nosing around the farm. As she clutched herself in the frosty air, Wags shot out of the barn, barking fiercely.

"Go get him, boy! Sic him!" she heard Simon say as he and Pete loped into the yard.

"Wags! Boys, call the dog back," Amanda said sternly, although she was secretly glad Wags was protecting them.

Reece Weaver still had the sense to run the rest of the way to his pickup, but Amanda had a feeling the overgrown pup's attack would only infuriate the contractor more. Why had Wyman and Ray decided this man should build their elevator? She and the boys watched as the truck sped down the driveway toward the road, spewing loose gravel and mud in its wake.

"Who was that?" Pete asked. "Wags sure doesn't like him."

"Dogs are gut judges of character," Amanda remarked. "Come inside for fresh cookies, boys. We need to talk."

As Pete and Simon preceded her into the house, Amanda realized she was trembling from more than the brisk wintry wind. The twins were talking shrilly with Jemima, and Vera and Lizzie had come downstairs to see what the commotion was about.

For a moment, Amanda soaked up the warmth of the sweet-smelling kitchen as she gazed at her family. She'd been very lucky, and probably foolish. Reece Weaver could have grabbed her—could have made more menacing threats—instead of retreating to his truck. But he'd done his share of damage, too.

"Let's sit down," Amanda said as Jemima pulled sheets of cookies from the oven. "You need to know what's going on here, even if your dat's not one to carry on about his concerns."

"Why was that man so *mean*, Mamma?" Cora blurted fearfully. "And what are back payments?"

"And what does it mean, that he'll see Dat in court?" the other twin chimed in.

"Mammaaa!" Alice Ann wailed as she toddled across the floor with her arms raised.

Amanda scooped up her youngest and held her close. Why would any reputable, trustworthy businessman barge into her kitchen and frighten her little children by threatening their father? It was wrong to judge Reece Weaver, but she hoped God was indeed in charge of this situation and keeping track of such a reprehensible man.

"What you need to know," Amanda began as she joined the kids at the table, "is that your dat's new elevator is costing him a lot more than he'd figured on. He doesn't like to let on about the money—"

"And I smell a rat, as far as the money goes," Jemima muttered as she placed a plate of cookies on the table.

"But he's concerned about getting our family through the winter," Amanda continued matter-of-factly. "We believe the Lord will provide—"

"So you're making your dishes again, like when we were little and our first dat went to heaven. Right, Mamma?" Cora handed her twin a cookie and then passed the plate to Lizzie.

"Jah, and we managed just fine back then, didn't we?" Amanda smiled. Her younger daughters were older than their years in many ways because, until she'd married Wyman, they'd grown up without a father.

"So is it true?" Vera asked warily. "Does Dat owe that man a lot of money? He was talking so loud, Lizzie and I heard him through the floor."

Wyman's eldest child, so like him in her looks, got up to fetch glasses and milk for everyone. It was Vera's way to act as a mother to her younger siblings . . . to be more responsible than most girls were at seventeen.

"That business is between him and your dat and Ray Fisher," Amanda insisted. "Our job is to keep things running here at home without wasting anything. We've got plenty of food, and we can be careful about our clothes—"

"And we can jiggle the flusher when the toilet runs and runs," Simon piped up proudly. "Dat says saving water is everybody's job."

Amanda's hand flew to her mouth as a giggle welled up

inside her. Wasn't it just like this boy to help her see the humor in everyday things, even when her nerves were jangled? "Jah, there's that," she replied. "We can all help in our own ways—and I'm so proud of how you're already doing the chores and taking on more responsibilities so I can make my pottery. You're the best bunch of kids God ever put on this earth, you know it?"

Their wide eyes and smiles were all the gratification Amanda needed. Already she felt as though the incident with Reece Weaver was behind them, and taking a bite of cookie—it was still warm, so the chocolate chips smeared her tongue—improved her mood as well.

"Shall we get back to what we were doing?" she asked when the kids had finished their snack. "And again, we should let your dat handle this situation with Reece Weaver. He's the head of our family, and he'll know what's best."

"And you're the neck that turns the head, right, Mamm?"

Once again Simon's response took Amanda by surprise. He was grinning at her with all sincerity, his lips and teeth smeared with melted chocolate—too cute for his own good. But she couldn't let his quick wit become a habit that would get him into trouble as he got older. "And who told you that, Son?"

"Dat did. He says *you're* the head of the household, and we're to do whatever you say."

A pleasant warmth prickled her cheeks. Perhaps Reece Weaver's visit hadn't been all bad, considering what had come of this conversation. "See what I'm saying? Your dat knows best," Amanda repeated wryly. She kissed Alice Ann's cheek and set the toddler on the floor. "Denki for these wonderful-gut cookies, girls. I'm going to finish making a bowl now, and I'll see you all at dinner."

Chapter 13

That evening as Wyman sat down to supper, he sensed an air of anticipation—or was it urgency?—as he gazed at his children's faces. "We had a gut day at the Graber place," he reported after they'd given thanks. "Eddie painted the kitchen and Abby's new sewing room bright yellow—"

"Me, I wuv *pink*," Alice Ann reminded him as she kicked in her high chair.

"And we shifted Merle into the dawdi haus," Wyman continued as he tickled his toddler's plump knee.

"And we got our quilting frolic set as well," Amanda remarked as she passed a big bowl of Jemima's fragrant beef stew. "But I had a feeling it was more Merle's doing than Emma's."

To Wyman's right, Jerome plucked two puffy biscuits from the basket with a resigned sigh. "Emma's understandably upset about losing her mamm," he said. "Seems to me the roles are reversed there. We all thought Merle would be the one to fold in on himself, yet he seems to be in gut spirits. And he's really looking forward to playing games again with you twins, too!" he added, grinning at Cora and Dora.

The two four-year-olds, identical in their deep orange dresses, giggled at each other. "Maybe we should play alphabet lotto this time—"

"Or the Let's Go Fishing game!"

Wyman still couldn't tell Cora and Dora apart, but he adored their enthusiasm. No matter how busy he got, when the twins gazed at him with big brown eyes so like their mother's, he felt all warm and fuzzy inside.

"I'll get to play, too," Simon declared. He spooned up some Jell-O fruit salad, which made a sucking sound that had all the younger kids chuckling. "Merle needs another *man* at the game table—but not a mean fellow like came here today, Dat. Wags chased him back to his truck, though, so now he knows better than to come back!"

As everyone at the table focused on him, Wyman considered his youngest son's remark. "Simon, you've got to control your dog," he warned. "We can't have Wags getting aggressive enough to—"

"I sent that man away myself," Amanda interjected. "While I agree that we need to control Wags, the dog's behavior was *nothing* compared to the way Reece Weaver barged in here, saying you owed him money and threatening to take you to court."

Wyman's heart stopped. Now he realized why everyone seemed more intense than usual. "I had no idea. I—I told Reece he was to deal only with Ray and me," he stammered as this information sank in.

"Jah, that's what Amanda told him, too," Jemima remarked stiffly. "It's none of my business, but I don't trust that man any farther than I could throw him. And I was ready to do just that, after he pushed into the kitchen, past Amanda, and talked about you that way in front of the children."

"Jah, that was his name," Simon said under his breath. "Reece Weasel."

Out of the mouths of babes. Once again Wyman wondered how he and Ray had been so mistaken about the contractor they'd chosen. "I'll call Reece after supper. This has to stop—and just so you'll know," he added as he gazed purposefully at everyone around the table, "I do *not* owe him any money, nor do you need to worry about him taking me to court. I've kept my part of the contract all along."

The kids dug into their supper, seemingly satisfied by his assurances. As Amanda met his gaze, Wyman sensed she intended to continue this discussion later, between the two of them. But there was no unsaying or undoing what Weaver had set into motion.

"Dat, I, um, called about a couple of ads I saw on the corkboard at the bulk food store this afternoon," Vera said, with a hopeful smile. "They're for cleaning houses a couple days a week. I'd like to take the jobs—if it's all right with you, of course."

"And I'll handle the laundry and cleaning on the days Vera works," Lizzie said. "I can do it when I get home from school, so Mamm can keep up with her pottery orders."

Wyman's eyes widened. Not so long ago, when they'd blended their two families, Lizzie had been the most unsettled of all the children. Now she seemed happy to shoulder more of a load than most thirteen-year-olds would care for.

"And—and since Eddie's got a steady painting job," Pete piped up, "I could quit school and help out, too. I could—"

"Don't you even *think* about quitting school, young man," Wyman said sternly. He was ready to challenge Pete's idea about *helping out* as well when it hit him: his kids now believed the Brubaker family had money troubles. It was one more insidious seed Reece's visit had apparently planted, like a cocklebur in a rose garden.

"We had a family talk after Mr. Weaver left," Amanda admitted, "but only so I could assure everyone that we'll be just fine this winter if we don't waste food and clothing and such. Bless you, Vera and Pete, I didn't mean you had to go looking for work. Honestly, I didn't."

"But I want this job," Vera insisted. "I've heard some of my friends talk about cleaning houses—"

"For English?" Wyman asked. He didn't like the idea of his attractive young daughter working in strangers' homes.

"Mennonites. The Schrocks and Cletus Yoder, just down the road," his daughter replied brightly. "I figure if I make my own spending money for fabric and shoes and such, there'll be more to go around for the rest of the kids' clothes."

While it pained Wyman to hear his daughter talk of covering her personal expenses, he admired her willingness to work. Perhaps taking this job would teach Vera more about budgeting money than she might otherwise learn by staying home. "I haven't had a chance to meet those families since we've moved here, but—"

"I've sold some mules to Cletus," Jerome remarked. "He's got a passel of sons farming with him, but no girls to help around the house."

"Leon Schrock's kids are all married, and his wife's in a wheelchair," Amanda said. "Both of those families have lived in these parts for as long as I can remember."

Wyman saw the yearning in Vera's face. She'd taken on the full responsibility for the kids, the housework, and the meals after his first wife had died, so she could certainly handle whatever the Schrocks and the Yoders wanted her to do. And she asked for so little. "All right, then; give it a try," he replied, touched by the happiness that lit up her face. He looked at everyone else then. "I appreciate your new commitments and contributions. It's a lesson in humility for a man who's always supported his family, and yet Jesus tells us that accepting the help of others is better than floundering—or failing—alone."

When they'd eaten their fill of the hearty stew and biscuits, Wyman wasn't surprised that Pete left the table in a huff. He'd gone through the same phase at thirteen, feeling alienated and off-kilter, so he caught up to his son as they headed to the barn to do the livestock chores.

"I didn't mean to sound so angry about your getting a job, Pete," he began. "Your intentions are the best, and I know how you miss Eddie when he's in Cedar Creek all week. But if you stop going to school, you'll lose out on important skills you'll need when you have your own farm—your own family to support. It'd be a shame to quit when you'll be all finished with school come next May."

"Jah. Whatever." Pete slid the barn door aside on its track with more force than was necessary. "I could be learning real-life skills from *you*, Dat, or—"

"If you'd ask her, maybe Teacher Dorcas could give you some worthwhile tasks around the schoolhouse, since you're amongst the oldest fellows there," Wyman suggested. "She'd probably be less inclined to criticize your lack of interest in math and spelling if you volunteered for—"

"I'm building a stage and a backdrop for the Christmas Eve program," Pete interrupted. His eyes flickered with interest, but then he shrugged dolefully. "Once I've finished that, though, she'll probably start finding fault with me again. I really *am* trying, Dat."

Wyman hadn't yet met the Bloomingdale schoolteacher, and he didn't want to undermine her authority by excusing Pete from doing his best in school. He sensed his son was going through the same difficult phase that he had endured at thirteen—no longer a boy but not yet a man. "That sounds like the perfect project for you, Pete. You and Eddie did a real gut job building the extra bathroom in our Clearwater barn, before we sold that place," Wyman replied. "When you're Eddie's age, you'll know better how you'd like to earn your livelihood. Maybe you'll want to work at the elevator, or you'll line up an apprenticeship, but until you've graduated—" He reached out to squeeze the kid's shoulder, but Pete dodged his show of affection and hurried toward the other side of the barn to start the horse chores.

As he stepped up to the phone on the barn wall, Wyman decided to call Ray Fisher before he talked with their contractor. Perhaps his partner in Clearwater had received a visit from Reece as well, and they needed to keep their stories straight. He dialed and waited until someone picked up the phone, relieved that the Fishers were in their barn doing chores, like he was. "Jah, Ray, it's Wyman. Got a minute?"

"You betcha. What's up over Bloomingdale way?" Ray asked in his usual jovial tone.

"Nothing gut, far as Weaver's concerned," Wyman replied with a sigh. As he recounted the day's incident, he felt his pulse speeding up all over again. "I wish I knew what to do about this guy, Ray. Where'd we go wrong?"

"You know," Ray replied, "I heard the other day that Reece has left the Mennonite church. Gone English, apparently, after a run-in with his preacher. Which matches the pattern we're seeing—confrontation rather than cooperation."

Wyman considered this. "Do you suppose Reece has stretched himself too thin and he's having financial problems?"

"We shouldn't speculate about that—and I sure *hope* his business isn't in trouble, since he's behind on our elevator," Ray replied with a short laugh. "But Weaver's problems don't justify his intimidating your family. How about if I call him and ask when he figures to pour our foundation . . . and maybe fish a little? Better yet, I could stop over at his place in person. He doesn't live but a mile from here, as the crow flies."

"You're the best friend a fellow ever had," Wyman murmured.

"Nah, that's *you*, Wyman!" came Ray's immediate response. "Trevor's new Holsteins are settling in, and he's got that old barn shaped up—and the house is enclosed now, where those two trees landed on it. He wouldn't be nearly so far along with his dairy herd and having a place of his own if you hadn't offered us such a gut price on your farm."

"Well, I wanted you folks to have the first shot—"

"Puh! Trev's future fell right into his lap—and he didn't have to move elsewhere to find land, thanks to you," Ray insisted. "And now Tyler's excited about managing our computer and marketing programs at both elevators—being full-time with us instead of having to find additional jobs. You've helped both of my boys in ways I couldn't have done myself."

As he hung up, Wyman couldn't help smiling. His outlook had improved immensely, and he felt that he—with a big assist from God—had made a real difference in the Fisher boys' lives while he'd improved his own family's future as well. It was just a matter of getting through this temporary snag with Weaver.

Wyman returned to the house, gazing up at the full moon, which shone like a golden coin in the indigo sky. Lizzie, Vera, and the twins were tending to the dishes. Simon and Alice Ann snuggled beside Jemima on the sofa as she read them a story. As he entered the room where Amanda was removing fired plates from her kiln, contentment settled over him like an old quilt. She looked up at him, a question in her bottomless brown eyes.

Wyman kissed her thoroughly. He studied a plate she'd made, running his fingertip around the deep blue edge that set off the cinnamon-colored center. She'd created a different pattern to comply with their bishop's instructions to use subtler colors—and truth be told, he liked this new look a lot better than the daisies she used to paint. "You do mighty fine work, Mrs. Brubaker," he murmured. "With your pottery and with our kids, too."

Amanda's smile made him melt like butter. "And how was your call to Reece?"

"It's all gut," Wyman replied, setting thoughts of Reece Weaver behind him. "Even if the finances will be tight for a while, I'm a wealthy man as long as you're by my side."

Chapter 14

On Monday morning, Emma got up a little earlier than usual and paid particular attention to looking her best. Even though she was wearing black from her kapp to her shoes, she wanted Sam to believe she was ready to move past her mamm's death and work at the mercantile. It seemed she'd spent the weekend watching the clocks and wondering why their hands didn't move. Maybe Dat was right. Maybe it was time to look ahead rather than staying stuck in a rut of sorrow, and with Abby sewing at home and James resuming the livestock chores, Emma wouldn't have as many tasks to occupy her time.

And maybe Jerome would find her more interesting—more compatible with his progressive ways—if she proved she could handle working at the mercantile. Images of his handsome face and kind smile had been on her mind a lot these past couple of days. Emma regretted the fuss she'd made on Friday, when he'd encouraged her to join the

Brubakers for another quilting frolic. He'd had her best interests at heart. Everyone did.

Emma went downstairs determined to begin this day with a better attitude. She had to believe God's plan for her life included something other than suffering and loss, something to make her look forward rather than back.

She was turning the bacon in the skillet when Abby came into the kitchen. Emma smiled, hoping her new sister-in-law would go along with her decision. "I'm heading over to the store after breakfast to see about starting work for Sam," she said. "I think it's time to give it a shot before he hires somebody else."

Abby's eyebrows rose, but then she smiled. "If you think you're ready, Sam'll be glad to have you. Your dat and I will get along just fine."

Emma thought she detected a hint of wistfulness in Abby's answer. "It's a big switch for you, not being amongst the customers all day," she remarked as she took the skillet from the burner. "I wish we could work there together."

Abby shrugged. "Sam's made his decision. I still think he'll want me to come back when the store gets busier, but now that I'm married *and* mourning your mamm, that's two reasons for him to find somebody else, ain't so? God'll show us all the path we're to travel."

Dat seemed inclined to sleep in, so after a quick breakfast with James and Abby, Emma put on her coat and bonnet. Butterflies fluttered in her stomach as she walked across the county blacktop to the mercantile. Knowing Sam and Gail would most likely be stocking shelves at this hour, before the store opened, Emma slipped in the back door to the workroom. Her heart pounded as she called out, "Sam? It's Emma."

She peered out into the main store, which was dimly lit, with only a few of the gas fixtures burning. Sam was standing across the huge room, hefting bags of sidewalk salt into display bins. "Gut morning, Sam!" she spoke out. "You're already hard at work, I see."

The storekeeper turned, his eyes widening when he recognized her. "Emma—gut morning. Is everything all right over at your place?"

"Jah, with Abby and James living there now, we're as right as rain, for the most part," she replied. "I—I was wondering if you still want me to work. Abby said it would be in the back room, most likely, and that suits me fine—*if* you still want—"

"Happy to hear it. *Real* happy." He tossed the bag of salt from his shoulder into the bin and approached her with a smile. "We got behind on the bookkeeping last week, so I'll bring out the ledgers and the receipts, and we'll look at them together. You're an answer to a prayer, Emma."

She smiled. Sam's remark was a fine start for a new day, a new week . . . a new chapter in her life. She hung her wraps on a peg in the workroom, and a few moments later they were seated at a small table surrounded by big bins of rolled oats, noodles, baking mixes, and other staples. Emma had always liked this room because it smelled like the sugar, spices, and herbs they scooped into plastic bags before they stocked the shelves with them.

"Gail's running late," Sam said as he opened the big black accounting book. "She says she's helping Barbara clean up after breakfast and getting Ruthie ready for school, but I suspect she's flirting with Eddie Brubaker. Having him stay at the house while he's painting the store is a practical arrangement, but it changes the family dynamic a bit."

Emma chuckled. And wasn't it good that something tickled her? "Eddie's cute, so I'm not surprised Gail's sweet on him," she remarked. "He's a gut worker, too. I didn't realize how faded our walls were looking until he painted the kitchen and Abby's sewing room—even if James chose a bright yellow that almost makes me squint."

"Eddie's a fine young man," Sam agreed. He opened a

shoe box full of folded cash register receipts and removed a lined tablet, a small calculator, and a couple of pencils. "Here's how we keep track of each day's receipts and whether customers paid cash or used credit cards," he began.

Emma nodded, following his finger along the columns in the ledger . . . listening carefully as Sam explained the accounting system he had probably learned from his dat as a young man. "This isn't much different from the way James's books are set up," she said, "except folks pay him larger amounts for fewer items."

Sam raised his face to the ceiling. "Thank you, Lord," he murmured happily. "Gail gets flummoxed at the sight of all these figures. By the time she's recalculated each day's totals and she's gotten a different number each time, she throws up her hands."

"Jah, these daily cash register tapes are pretty long," Emma said as she unfolded one, "but your system makes sense to me."

"Glad to hear it." Sam glanced up as Gail and Eddie came through the back door, laughing and pink cheeked from the cold. "Look who's here—our new bookkeeper," he said.

"Oh, but it's gut to see you!" Gail exclaimed as she hugged Emma's shoulders. "I'll be real quiet while I'm bagging up baking supplies on the big table. I'm *so* glad you're taking over the books, Emma."

"Once you've got us caught up on the receipts, I'll show you how to handle the inventory and ordering," Sam went on. He looked at Emma as though considering what to say next. "While I'd be ecstatic to have you working every day, I know that'll be an adjustment for you."

"And I really should be at home whenever James and Abby leave for their weekend visits," Emma pointed out. "Dat had a little spell yesterday afternoon. Woke up from a nap, and it took him a while to recall that Mamm wasn't there and that the newlyweds have moved into his bedroom upstairs."

"That's bound to happen, after so many changes in his routine," Sam murmured. "You've got a lot on your mind, Emma. How about if we have you come in early like this, on weekday mornings, and before you go home for dinner at noon, we'll decide whether you need to—or want to—come back each day? I don't want you to feel overwhelmed so soon after your mamm's passing."

Emma swallowed the lump that threatened to rise into her throat. "That's kind of you, Sam."

"Well, it's also the way Vernon suggested we do things while you're in mourning," he replied. "It's not proper for you to be working amongst the customers, especially with so many English coming in for holiday shopping. I hope I'll get some responses to my help-wanted ads, so we'll have more sales help soon."

"Me, too," Gail added as she began scooping rolled oats into gallon-size plastic bags. "Even with Grandma helping, we're stretched pretty thin."

Emma nodded. "Jah, it'll take more than one person to replace Abby."

"So she's told me," Sam said with a laugh. "But that's my problem, and I'm glad you're here to be part of the solution, Emma. The *Ordnung* has its rules about women working for a gut reason, and Cedar Creek's a better church district all around if we abide by them." He stood up and stretched, glancing at the wall clock. "I'll leave you to your book work now. You know where to find me if you have questions."

When Sam and Eddie left the workroom, Emma chatted with Gail for a moment before she turned back to the ledger. Some of the entries had been made in Abby's neat, distinct printing, and some were in Sam's smaller script. She was in good company, keeping the accounts for this well-respected family business. *I hope my best work will be gut enough,* Emma thought as she found the oldest cash register tape. It dated back to early last week, before Sam had closed the store to officiate at Mamm's funeral, so she had a lot of days to catch up on.

She was feeling useful, and she was helping Sam after he'd done so much for her family of late. That was something to be thankful for as she faced this first winter and the holidays without her mother.

Better days are surely ahead, she told herself as she began to tap the calculator's keys.

Chapter 15

Everybody tucked in?" Jerome asked as he peered into his rig. It was the Saturday of the second quilting frolic, and he'd left Bloomingdale before daylight to fetch Eddie and the Grabers. "Extra blankets are in the bin under the seats, if anybody needs one."

"Eddie and I are gut to go!" Merle replied from the back. "What with the newlyweds off on another gift visit this weekend, I'm happy to be running the roads, too."

"And I'm glad to get off the ladder for a couple days," Eddie joined in. "I lost track of the cans of paint I went through this week, but the upstairs of the mercantile's nearly done."

"That's a huge job," Jerome remarked as he climbed into the driver's side. "I bet Sam's happy to have you sprucing up his store."

The teenager chuckled. "Sam's busier than all get-out now that Abby's not there," he quipped. "All the Christmas stuff's coming in and getting snatched up practically before he and Gail can put it on the shelves. I'm glad I'm just painting instead of helping them run that place."

As he clucked at his mules, Jerome smiled over at Emma. She met his gaze for a moment, yet she seemed withdrawn . . . paler than usual, all wrapped up in her black winter coat and bonnet. "Whatever's in that pot you brought along smells awfully *gut*," he said.

Emma shrugged. "Nothing special. Chili."

"The pan'll be licked clean, then. Our bunch can go through a lot of chili," Jerome replied. "Everybody's real excited about you and your dat spending the day with us. Vera and Lizzie set up the long table last night, and the first quilt's already in the frame. The little girls made sugar cookies with Jemima yesterday, too. Does Abby have any idea what you and your dat're doing today?"

"Nope."

Jerome listened as Merle chatted with Eddie about who-all he'd met in the mercantile as he painted. What would it take to get Emma out of her shell? "How's it going, having Abby and James living there now?"

"Fine."

Was Emma missing her mamm today? Or was she resentful about the way Amanda and Merle had gotten her out of the house against her will? Maybe a different topic . . .

"I took Amanda's dishes over to Sam's before I came to your place—the set of sixteen he and Vernon ordered, with serving pieces," Jerome went on. "I think Abby and James will like Amanda's new pottery style. The way the cobalt glaze seeps from the edges into the rusty brown centers makes every piece a little different."

Emma's eyes rose. "We've *got* plenty of dishes—but I'm sure Amanda's are really pretty," she added quickly.

Now *there* was a comment he wouldn't share with Amanda, because his aunt had truly enjoyed crafting that set of dishes. As they rolled down the county highway, Jerome hoped Emma's mood wouldn't spoil the other girls' fun today. For the rest of the trip he chatted with the two fellows behind him—mostly about the potential girlfriends Eddie was meeting on the job, while Merle gave his wry commentary about their families and personalities.

While Eddie and her dat were chatting, Emma yawned and then glanced over at Jerome. "I'm sorry I got snippy," she murmured. "I'm kind of tired because I, um, worked in the mercantile every day this week."

When a little grin flickered on her lips, Jerome grabbed her hand. "And how did that go? If you were on your feet all those hours, no wonder you're worn out."

"I worked in the back room, updating Sam's ledger," Emma clarified. "And I bagged some baking supplies so Gail could restock the shelves. Sam's showing me how to make out orders now. My mind's still spinning with all this new information after I go to bed, but one of these days I'll get back to sleeping like I should."

Jerome's heartbeat sped up. Emma did look like she could use some more rest, yet she seemed a lot happier than she'd been the last time he saw her. "Gut for you," he murmured as he steered the mule up the lane toward Amanda's house. "When you're ready to tell me more about your new job, I want to hear all about it."

When they arrived at the Brubaker place, Wags greeted them with boisterous barking. Simon and the twins rushed outside to grab Merle by the hands. Vera and Lizzie exclaimed over seeing Emma as Amanda held the door open for everyone.

"Ach, we've been so busy getting the fabric and food ready, I had no idea it was snowing," she said as she peered outside. "Gut thing Wyman's elevator foundation got poured this past week."

Jerome let everyone else precede him inside, and then he spoke near Amanda's ear. "Emma's got some big news, but I'll let her share it," he murmured. "And don't be surprised if she curls up for a nap later today."

"At least she still wanted to come," Amanda replied as their guests hung up their coats. "Emma can let Vera and Lizzie do the talking and just sew along with us if she's tired. But would you look at her dat!"

Jerome had to laugh. Merle had scooped Alice Ann up to his shoulder while Simon and the twins led him eagerly to the corner of the front room, where the card table was set up for playing Chutes and Ladders.

"I'm gonna be red!" Dora crowed.

"I'm yellow," Cora chimed in as the two little girls shared a chair.

"I wuv pink," Alice Ann chirped as Merle sat down and settled her in his lap.

Merle's face was lit up like a Christmas candle. He kissed the toddler's cheek. "That leaves the green and blue markers for us guys, Simon," he said. "You pick."

"Green means *go*, so that's gotta be me!" the boy replied. "I'll be climbing all the ladders and skipping all the chutes, so the game's already in my pocket."

"If you're so sure I'm going to lose, you'd better have a little mercy and let me make the first move," Merle teased as he spun the spinner.

Amanda chuckled fondly as she watched them from the kitchen. "He can be the grandfather they never had, ain't so?"

"He's the perfect man for that job," Jerome agreed. "Abby and James's kids will never lack for attention, either, as long as he's around." He watched Jemima add the last of her chopped vegetables to a soup pot, inhaling the aroma of the bread she'd baked that morning. "I'll stay out of you ladies' way now, or you might put a needle and thread into *my* hands—and that would make for a disastrous quilt."

"I'm sure we'll see you come time for dinner," Jemima remarked from the stove.

"Wouldn't miss it." Jerome passed through the front room, smiling at Vera, Lizzie, and Emma as they were choosing which colorful fabrics to cut for their second quilt. Then he paused beside the card table to observe the progress of the Chutes and Ladders game. When Alice Ann threw him a kiss, Jerome bussed the top of her blond head. He patted Wags, who was lying near the woodstove, and then went upstairs to work on some bookkeeping.

Jerome opened his ledger but didn't focus on the figures. The quilting table was beneath his room, and because talk drifted up through the open grate in the floor along with the woodstove's warmth, he heard the thrum of female conversation.

"You'll never guess what I've done," Emma spoke up during a brief lull. "I'm working in the back room of Sam's store, doing his bookkeeping and bagging up baking supplies."

When the other quilters exclaimed in surprise, Jerome chuckled. Everyone began asking Emma questions at the same time. She sounded more awake now and seemed tickled to be working—and he was pleased for her.

If she's overcoming her shyness enough to work at the store, maybe she won't be so skittish around me. But now that she's got a regular job, it won't be as easy to find time when she can go out, either.

He would find a way. Jerome considered himself pretty resourceful when it came to convincing young women to spend time with him, and Emma was certainly worth his best efforts.

When he heard laughter outside, he went to the window. Wyman was running errands this morning, so Pete and Eddie had decided to go deer hunting—this wooded Bloomingdale farm offered a better opportunity than they'd had in Clearwater. It was good to see the brothers walking side by side with their bows tucked under their arms. The vapor of their breath floated around their stocking-capped heads as they caught up with each other's news after a week apart. No one else hunted on this property, so if they were quiet and watchful, they stood a good chance of getting a deer.

Jerome went downstairs for coffee—but mostly to steal a glance at Emma. She sat between Vera and Lizzie, carefully cutting a stack of fabric with a circular blade as she followed the lines of her paper pattern. Nibbling on a frosted sugar cookie in the kitchen, he watched the set of her jaw as she concentrated . . . the swift, efficient motion of her hands as she made each cut. Even clothed in black, Emma looked like a late-summer rose: her skin was dewy soft and pale pink, her lips were a delectable shade darker, and her eyebrows were an expressive brown.

Once again dreams of settling down and starting a family taunted him. Twice before he'd believed he'd found the right woman—and twice he'd walked away. Why was he now so drawn to Emma Graber? Was he interested in her as a potential mate, or only because her determination to deflect his attentions presented a new challenge?

Jerome resisted the urge to strike up a conversation with her. Without interrupting the hen party, he headed back upstairs with fresh coffee and another cookie. As he passed the quilting frame, he caught Aunt Amanda's knowing wink: she and Jemima were hand stitching the quilt with the colorful flower baskets on it. Jerome immersed himself in updating his business records for a while . . . Then he heard the back door open, followed by the rapid thump of stocking feet on the stairway.

"Jerome, can you help us?" Pete called out breathlessly.

"Jah, Pete got a really nice deer!" Eddie's cheeks were flushed with cold and excitement as the boys stood in the doorway. "We got it field dressed, but we need to haul it out of the woods."

"Sounds a lot more interesting than this book work." Jerome clapped Pete on the shoulder. "We can take it right over to the locker, and it'll make some mighty fine eating this winter. See there? You're putting food on the table without having to quit school for a job."

Pete rolled his eyes. "Jah, well, I guess Dat and I had *that* discussion already."

The boys shared the details of their hunting adventure with Merle, the kids, and the quilters while Jerome put on his heavy coat and boots. He kicked himself for bringing up the subject of Pete's leaving school, but after they hitched a wagon to a draft mule and started across the snowy field toward the woods, Jerome got an idea.

"What if I paid you to take over the daily chores with my mares and donkeys?" he asked. "Now that the mule foals are here, I'll have my hands full, so it would be gut if someone else tended—"

"Don't go making up a new job, trying to humor me," Pete interrupted brusquely. "Truth be told, I'm fed up with school because Teacher Dorcas and I don't see eye to eye. Teacher Elsie was a pill, but I knew what I could get by with in Clearwater and . . . I'm just ready to be out of the schoolroom and doing something *real*."

Jerome recalled feeling that way, too. He also remembered when Lizzie had gone through a tough time changing schools, those first weeks after her family had moved to Clearwater. When they located the downed buck, however, they turned all their energy to hefting it into the wagon. On the way to the processing plant, the boys gave Jerome a moment-by-moment account of how they'd heard movement in the bushes and Pete had gotten in a perfect shot without having much time to take aim.

By the time they returned home, the snow was coming down in thick, flat flakes. Jerome sent Eddie and Pete inside to see if Jemima had left them something for lunch while he unhitched the mule. As he rolled the wagon back into place, he spotted the old sleigh that had belonged to Amanda's first husband, his uncle Atlee. Could he convince Emma to go riding with him? The hills were covered in a perfect, pristine blanket of fresh powder . . .

Jerome set aside that happy thought. When Emma saw how the snow was coming down, she'd probably insist on heading home to Cedar Creek. Maybe some other time this winter he could talk her into taking that sleigh ride. In his mind's eye, he saw the two of them snuggling together beneath the blankets, with only the clip-clop of hooves punctuating the silence of a perfect winter evening. He wanted to hold Emma close and kiss her, out where none of the kids would spot them and make a fuss.

Jerome sighed. Even though Emma seemed more confident now, he had a lot of persuading to do before *that* would ever happen.

Emma stood up to stretch, surprised at how quickly the day had passed. While she'd been engrossed in sewing, she'd felt closer to her mamm and more grateful for the Brubakers' company than she'd anticipated. Lizzie had taken the kids outside to run off some energy, so she and Vera were clearing away fabric scraps and stacking their finished squares. Amanda and Jemima had gone to the kitchen to start supper.

"We made gut progress today," Vera remarked. "Now that most of our nine-patch squares are sewn together, we'll only need another day or two to finish this second quilt top."

"I'm really glad I got to work it, too," Emma replied. "I was ready to work with pretty colors after concentrating on columns of numbers all week."

After they stashed the table in a closet, Emma and Vera joined the others in the kitchen. As they began setting the table for supper, Emma watched her dat lifting pot lids and sniffing appreciatively while Jemima was nice enough not to scold him for it. Even though he hadn't had a nap all day, he looked alert and very much at home.

"What's this you're fixing?" Dat asked. "When my mamm mixed cornmeal into boiling water, she was making up a batch of mush."

"You guessed it, Merle," Jemima replied as she briskly stirred the thick yellow mixture. "I'll put it in bread pans to set up in the fridge, and we'll have fried mush for breakfast tomorrow."

Dat looked like he might fall over in a fit of ecstasy. "Oh, but that takes me back to my childhood!" he said. "Eunice didn't care for mush, so it's been years since I had any. Apple butter's my favorite topping, but syrup or honey or jelly is gut, too."

"We've got every one of those things," Jemima said with a laugh. "And unless I miss my guess, that snow's getting deep enough that you folks might be here to share this mush with us tomorrow. I'll stir up another batch, just in case."

"Want to head out to the barn with us, Merle?" Jerome asked as he and Pete and Eddie went to the coat pegs. "I've got three little mules out there you'll get a kick out of meeting while we do the horse chores."

Emma saw how her father jumped at the chance to join those fellows, even though he had to borrow a pair of knee-high boots. She couldn't remember the last time she'd seen Dat in such high spirits—but then, why wouldn't he be? The Brubakers were awfully good about including him in their activities.

As she gazed out the kitchen window, watching her dat walk toward the barn with the other fellows, Emma realized how much snow had accumulated. It was halfway up Dat's boots and still coming down! "Oh my, we'd best get Jerome to take us home," she remarked to the other women. "Does your county have a snowplow that clears the blacktop? If we're ready to go after it passes your intersection—"

The heavy clomping of feet out on the porch announced that Wyman had returned and was knocking the snow from his boots. When he opened the door, Simon and the twins rushed inside around him, pink cheeked and ecstatic about the snowman they'd made. Lizzie followed Wyman inside, looking as though she'd had as much fun playing in the snow as the younger kids.

"It's a gut thing you and your dat are still here, Emma," the big man announced as he hung his wraps near the door. "The wheels of my rig were icing up as I drove home. You'll be staying over tonight."

Emma knew better than to argue with Wyman, as it was already getting dark—too dangerous to drive in such weather. Yet her insides clenched. She hadn't brought any extra clothes . . . didn't have Dat's robe and pajamas, much less their toothbrushes. "But what of our horses and chickens? James won't be home to tend them, and we'd figured on being back to do the chores."

Wyman stooped until his eyes were level with hers. With his tall, stocky build; dark, tousled waves of hair; and the thick beard framing his face, he wasn't a fellow *anyone* would contend with, yet his smile reminded her of the teddy bears in the mercantile. "I just spoke with Jerome and your dat out in the barn, and they'll be calling somebody about your chores," he said gently. "So settle in and be our guest, Emma. We're so happy to have you and Merle here."

"Jah, we *love* having company!" Cora said.

"And you can go to church with us tomorrow!" Dora added.

Church! Once again Emma realized she and Dat weren't going to be presentable, wearing the more comfortable clothes they'd had on all day. As she began setting plates around the table for supper, her hands were trembling so badly that some of the dishes landed harder than she'd intended. "I hate to sound like a worrywart," she murmured to Amanda, "but we've not got any clothes for tomorrow, or—"

"I'm thinking Vera or Mamm's dresses will fit you," Lizzie said as she hung up her wraps. "And your dat's about the same size as Eddie."

"We've got a couple of Atlee's Sunday suits still hanging in the back closet, too," Amanda said after a moment. "Truth be told, though, with church set to be clear over at Bishop Lapp's, and his place being a long way down a gravel road that won't be plowed out—"

"We can stay home?" Simon clapped his hands gleefully. "Merle can bunk in my room! It'll be a sleepover—but no girls allowed!"

"And since Lizzie and I each have a double bed," Vera chimed in, "we'll share one, and you can sleep in the other one, Emma. So it's all gut!"

"And we're all safe and sound," Amanda said. "That's the most important part."

Emma managed a smile. Who wouldn't be grateful at the way these friends had so quickly seen to her and Dat's needs? And it *was* a relief not to be heading home on roads that took them an hour in the best of daylight conditions—and she wouldn't have to whip up something for supper when they finally got there, or invite Jerome to stay over at their place because it would be too late for him to drive back to Bloomingdale. This was the first snowstorm of the winter, and it wouldn't be the last, so Emma reminded herself that she'd better be ready for the shoveling and the extra effort the next few months would require.

As Jerome came inside with the other fellows, his expression told her the inclement weather suited him just fine. "Matt Lambright's headed to your place to do your animal chores," he said in a low voice. "And I bet we'll not be venturing to church in the morning, either, so . . . what would you think of a sleigh ride after supper? Now that the wind's dying down, it'll be a perfect evening for one."

Emma got lost in Jerome's intense, dark-eyed gaze. Maybe Dat and Amanda had pulled their strings to get her to the Brubakers' place today, and now Mother Nature was conspiring to keep her here overnight, yet a sleigh ride sounded like the perfect end to this day. "Denki for asking me, Jerome. Everyone's been so kind to us today."

"And that will continue for as long as you'll allow it, Emma," he whispered.

Emma sucked in her breath. Jerome wasn't a foot away, right here in the kitchen where the whole family could see him flirting with her. Yet something about that tickled her as much as it scared her . . .

After giving thanks, everyone passed bowls of kraut and sausages, along with stewed tomatoes, baked acorn squash, and fried apples. Pete and Eddie were telling their dat how they'd gotten their deer when a loud pounding on the kitchen door made everyone jump. Vera hurried over to answer it, but before she got there, two figures bundled in black coats and bonnets, with scarves around their faces, burst inside. The snow and cold air came with them.

"This is the Lambright place, jah?" one of them demanded in a muffled voice.

"We found it, Mamma! Jerome's right there at the table, sure as God made little green apples!" the other one replied.

Emma caught Jerome's confused look as he slowly stood up. Then his face paled. *"Bess Wengerd?"* he rasped as the two women peeled the wraps from their faces. "And Mabel? What brings you all the way from Queen City on such a nasty night?"

"Let me take your coats," Amanda said as she went over to help them. She shared a wide-eyed glance with Jerome, as though she were just as shocked as he was by their arrival.

"I'll set a couple more places," Vera said. "We just sat down to eat—"

"Even if supper was what we came for, I've hardly been able to swallow a bite these past couple of years," the older woman interrupted in a nasal whine. "Just *sick* about the way none of the fellows want to court my Bess, after the way Jerome backed out on marrying her. *Ruined* her reputation, he did—and her chances of making another match, too."

Emma's fork clattered to her plate. The Brubakers all sat straighter as they gawked at this mother and daughter from Jerome's past. Who could have guessed *anyone* would have made such a long drive in the snow—much less two women who would need to stay the night? While Emma felt bad that Jerome had been caught off guard, the evening now promised to be more interesting than she'd anticipated. She had wondered about the fiancées he'd jilted, and now she would have some answers—some insight into how Jerome treated a girl he'd once intended to marry.

Chapter 16

Jerome struggled to corral his stampeding thoughts. Never in his wildest nightmares had he figured on seeing Bess Wengerd and her meddling mother again, but there was no turning them away on such a hazardous night. "Bess and Mabel Wengerd," he announced by way of introduction, "this is the Brubaker home now, on account of how my aunt Amanda has remarried."

He quickly went around the table naming names, until he reached Emma. And how was he to explain *her*, considering how Mabel had so blatantly stated her case against him? "These are our gut friends Merle and Emma Graber from Cedar Creek," Jerome said. "Emma's been quilting with—"

"Merle's been playing games with us kids!" Simon blurted. His brown eyes resembled shiny brown buttons as he took in the two women at the other end of the table. "Him and Emma are sad 'cause Emma's mamm just died, so we've been cheering them up."

"And Jerome's real sweet on Emma," Dora announced.

"And we all like her a *lot*!" Cora chimed in with a decisive nod.

The bottom fell out of Jerome's stomach, but what could he say? In their inimitable way, the twins had only spoken the truth. Mabel Wengerd stiffened as she and Bess focused so intently on poor Emma that her face turned the color of the stewed tomatoes.

"You Grabers have my deepest sympathy," Mabel said stiffly. "We lost my husband—Bess's dat—last spring, so we understand your grief."

"We appreciate your concern," Merle murmured. Then he looked at them more closely, while Wyman was placing two additional chairs at the end of the table for them. "Are you ladies any relation to the Wengerds who run the pallet factory in Queen City? I've got a couple of daughters who live not far from there," he remarked. "Looks to be quite a large operation, and I understand they supply wooden crates and pallets for a lot of warehouses around the Midwest."

Mabel brightened. "My two oldest boys run it, jah," she replied. "Started there after they got out of school, cutting the boards and building the crates and pallets, so they know the business backward and forward."

When the two Wengerds took their seats and began to fill their plates, Jerome sat down as well. He hadn't missed the speculative way Mabel had eyed Merle when she learned he was a widower, but that was the least of his concerns. How could he find out the reason they'd shown up here, out of the blue? He hadn't so much as said hello or heard from Bess in nearly two years . . .

"So, what brings you ladies out this way?" Wyman asked as he resumed his place at the head of the table. "Even in the best of weather, it's a three-hour haul from Queen City."

Jerome gazed gratefully at Wyman for asking the obvious question. He noticed how—just as she had when they were courting—Bess deferred to her mother when it came to the important issues. Matter of fact, Bess hadn't made a peep since she'd first spotted him at the table. And just as she had when he'd been courting her daughter, Mabel Wengerd took her time about responding, making sure everyone was paying attention to her opinions. For a woman who hadn't been able to eat since he'd broken up with Bess, she seemed to have found her appetite readily enough. Mabel forked up two big chunks of sausage, a mound of kraut, and then filled the rest of her plate with fried apples before snatching two thick slices of bread from the basket.

"Couldn't help but notice the write-up in the *Connection* magazine about Jerome's fancy eight-mule hitch," Mabel finally replied. "Before we realized the weather was getting bad, we figured to stop by and offer our congratulations. By the looks of that photograph, you've come a long way with your mule-training business, Jerome. That was quite the impressive team."

"Jah, it was!" Merle replied. "Got to ride on that wagon myself, and every mule stepped in time with the others. It was like having our own one-wagon parade."

As Jerome watched the two Wengerds' faces, he was coming to some unfortunate conclusions. It wasn't his place to judge, or to assume what Bess and her mamm's *real* motivation was for coming all the way to Bloomingdale. But he sensed that his success with his mules, made so public in a magazine, suggested that he was making good money . . . and that he'd be a better catch now, even if he'd supposedly ruined Bess's reputation. Mabel apparently saw their visit as a chance for him to redeem himself—not that he had any such inclinations. While these thoughts crossed Jerome's mind, Wyman's expression suggested that the same suspicions were occurring to him.

"It was a fine, fun hayride we had that day!" Dora crowed. "Jerome brought Emma and her dat and our friends

from Cedar Creek over so we could ride, too!" Cora recounted with a wide grin.

"And he's teaching *me* to drive his mules," Simon added
happily. "Now that we've moved here to our new mamm's
place, we don't never want to leave—because Jerome's
here!"

While the kids were recounting that same exciting
wagon ride with his mules, Jerome pondered the Wengerds'
situation . . . dug a little deeper into his memory of that
family. If Mabel's two older sons now owned their dat's
pallet factory—a large, long-established business—were
they not supporting their widowed mother and unmarried
sister? Even if the business was *not* hugely profitable, Mabel and Bess would still be those fellows' responsibility.

So what's really going on here? As the mealtime conversation continued, with Mabel quizzing Wyman and
Amanda about what *they* did for a living, it all came back
to him: Jerome had always felt Bess and her mother were
joined at the hip, which meant Bess couldn't carry on much
of a conversation unless her mamm was nearby. And when
Mabel said, "Jump," she expected everyone else to ask,
"How high?" and then exceed her expectations.

Jerome had *not* bad-mouthed Bess or in any way ruined
her reputation, for he'd behaved honorably as they'd
courted. She was a very attractive girl, with dark blond
hair, flawless skin, and adoring blue eyes, so why weren't
other fellows taking her out? Had all her dates backed away
from Mabel, just as he had?

"And your bishop allows you to make pottery?" Mabel
asked shrilly. "My stars, in our district such an artsy pursuit
would be considered *sinful!*"

The kitchen got so quiet that the stilted tick of the battery
clock sounded loud. It was time to rescue this situation—
and his aunt.

Jerome gazed directly at Mabel. "We all do our best
with the gifts the gut Lord gives us. And we abide by what

our bishops allow," he stated. "I'm sorry you've lost your husband—and your dat," he added with a nod at Bess. "Ammon Wengerd was a fine man. I missed seeing his obituary, or I'd have sent you a card and a memorial contribution. We'll make a place for you to stay the night, and I'll see that you get home tomorrow when the roads have been cleared."

Bess fluttered her eyelashes as her mamm coyly covered her heart with her hand. "That's mighty kind of you, Jerome," Mabel chirped. "Ammon always regarded you as a fine, upstanding young man."

Jerome put on a patient smile. If the two Wengerd women were getting their hopes up for a romantic reunion between him and Bess, they would be sorely disappointed.

Could this situation get any more bizarre? To avoid further attention from their unexpected guests, Emma kept her eyes on her food as Mabel Wengerd took control of the suppertime conversation. But once everyone finished eating, the men would go to the front room while the women would redd up the kitchen . . . and Bess's outspoken mother would probably make Emma her next target while Jerome couldn't hear what was being said.

Emma felt sorry for Jerome. He'd done nothing to provoke the Wengerds' visit, and while she'd often considered Jerome flashy and a bit on the feisty side, he wasn't the sort of man who'd drag a girl's reputation through the mud. Just twenty minutes at the table with Mabel had given her a pretty good idea of why Jerome had backed out of his engagement, especially if he and Bess had followed the old tradition of not meeting each other's family until after they'd decided to marry.

Amanda stood up, looking a little strained. "Vera, if you and Lizzie will start the dishes, I'll freshen the guest room."

"Jah, we can do that, Mamm." Lizzie went to the sink

straightaway to run the dishwater. Emma decided her best strategy would be to stay busy and keep her head down, rather than getting caught up in Mabel and Bess's scheming.

"Jemima, how can I help you with tomorrow's breakfast?" she asked. "It seems the snowstorm's brought you four more mouths than you'd figured on feeding."

The gray-haired woman smiled gratefully at her. "I'll take some ham slices out of the deep freeze, and let's you and I stir up a batch of muffins. We can use the apples in that bowl."

"Bess, this would be the perfect time for you to get re-acquainted with Jerome, out by the fire," Mabel suggested loudly. "We've got plenty of help here in the kitchen without you, dear."

Emma bit back a smile as she went to the counter where the apples were. Could Mrs. Wengerd possibly be any more obvious about her intentions? She jumped when someone grasped her shoulder.

"Emma, when you've finished in here, will you meet me in Aunt Amanda's pottery room?" Jerome murmured close to her ear. "I'd like a word with you about—"

"Jerome, I'll be *waiting*. On the *love* seat," Bess cooed as she walked right past them. "We have so much to catch up on, you and I."

Emma frowned at the soft-spoken blonde. She didn't like the Wengerds' using Jerome as a pawn—and she didn't want to get caught up in their game playing, either. She'd felt Mabel and Bess sizing her up during supper, considering her an easy crumb to sweep under the rug . . .

"Jah, I'll be there," she replied. "Give me about fifteen minutes, and we'll have Jemima's muffins in the oven."

Bless him, Jerome looked grateful that she'd agreed to spend time with him. Emma wanted to hear his side of the story about his engagement to Bess. Here was her chance to clear away the objections she'd expressed when her parents, James, and Abby had encouraged her to date Jerome.

If this handsome, fun-loving fellow didn't answer her questions about Bess in a straightforward, sincere way, then Emma would know he wasn't worth her consideration.

And isn't it just a wee bit exciting—and daring—that he wants to meet you away from the others? To talk with you instead of with the pretty girl he was once in love with? You might be in mourning, but you're not dead . . .

As she chopped apples and walnuts for the muffins, Emma felt herself anticipating her talk with Jerome, actually looking forward to spending time alone with him. Was it because another—very pretty—young woman was trying to woo him? Or because Emma was sincerely interested in what Jerome would say about his feelings for Bess . . . and maybe for her? By the time she and Jemima had poured the thick, cinnamon-spiced batter into muffin tins, Emma was thrumming with curiosity. She sensed that whatever she learned during this private chat might well change her attitude and set the course for her future outings with Jerome—the course for her *future.*

When Emma entered the lantern-lit room where Amanda made her pottery, however, she was *not* expecting to see Bess Wengerd there with Jerome. At just that moment, the blonde launched herself at him, too—pinning him against a wall, pressing herself against him to claim him with a searing kiss. Jerome stood with his arms outstretched, not holding Bess—but not pushing her away, either.

Emma's jaw dropped. Why was he letting this young woman kiss him if he claimed to be so interested in *her*? Why had she believed Jerome was ready to open his heart and soul?

Look again. Things are not what they seem.

Emma crossed her arms, assessing this evening's surprises. She'd seen through the Wengerds' little games at the table, so why would these women have changed their tactics? They were manipulating Jerome, and she didn't have to tolerate such blatant behavior!

"Bcss, this is *pathetic*," Emma stated as she moved closer to the clinging blonde. "First, you and your mamm show up unannounced, expecting Jerome to court you again—mostly because he's making gut money. And now you've thrown yourself at him. If he hasn't started kissing you back yet, it's not going to happen, honey."

And where had *that* come from? Emma's eyes widened, for she'd never in her life spoken out so brashly, with such a *tone*. But her little speech accomplished what she'd intended. Bess backed away from Jerome and glared at her.

"Puh! What could a handsome man like Jerome Lambright possibly see in a mouse like you, Emma Graber?"

Chapter 17

Jerome thought he'd been hearing things. Was that *Emma* accusing Bess of throwing herself at him? He wanted to shout hallelujah, because the one person whose opinion mattered had seen the Wengerd women for who they were: fortune hunters. These two females had nothing better to do than kiss up to him, thinking that if Bess couldn't lure him back with her looks, then Mabel would shame him into feeling sorry for their bereavement.

But Bess wasn't finished yet. "Seems to me the choice is *yours*, Jerome," she said in a cloying voice. "You know we had a gut love between us—that God Himself brought us together. So why are you wasting your time with Emma?"

The two young women were now facing him—one a blue-eyed blonde and the other a compelling brunette all dressed in black—their arms crossed as they awaited his answer. He could only hope this agonizing moment would settle the situation once and for all.

Jerome cleared his throat. "God may have brought us together a couple of years ago, Bess," he replied firmly, "but your mamm drove us apart. I saw that our marriage wouldn't stand a chance because of her interfering ways, so I ducked out. Not very nice of me, but there it is. The truth."

Bess's eyes got as round as the full moon. Then her chin began to quiver. "Jerome, I can't believe you'd say such a thing about Mamma," she wheedled. "It's you and I who'd be getting hitched—"

"Stop right there." Jerome held out his hand. "I've said all I'm going to say, and my answer is *no*, Bess. So don't embarrass us both by playing any more games."

Thank goodness she took the hint this time. As Bess left the pottery workroom, Jerome knew his rejection would come back to haunt him once Mabel heard what he'd done. But that didn't bother him. At long last, he was alone with Emma Graber, the way he'd hoped to be all day.

Here was a woman who could indeed speak her mind, with a strength he hadn't anticipated. Apparently Emma liked him more than she'd been letting on—or at least she refused to stand by and watch the Wengerds humiliate him.

"Denki, Emma," he whispered.

Emma held his gaze, yet she appeared as dumbfounded as he about what had just happened. "You probably think I'm a buttinsky busybody, telling Bess—"

"Nothing's gained by tiptoeing around the fact that I'd never be happy with Bess," Jerome insisted. "And I'm grateful that you saw through that kiss. I can't believe she'd stoop so low, which means she's getting . . . desperate. Sad, jah, but it's not a situation I'll be fixing."

Emma's tremulous smile did funny, wonderful things to his insides. Jerome held out his hand and was gratified when she took hold of it.

"I used to want . . . I needed to hear—from you, rather than the gossips—about why you broke up with the two other girls you were engaged to," Emma said in a low voice.

"It was worrisome, thinking you might walk out on *me* as well and—"

"Let's not put that cart before the horse." Jerome tightened his hold on her hand, bringing it briefly to his lips. "I sincerely loved those girls, and I didn't take it lightly, walking out on them. Breaking my promises."

Emma's brows flickered. Was that concern on her sweet face? Or maybe envy, because he'd confessed he'd been in love twice before?

Jerome didn't want to spoil his chances of getting to know her better, so he vowed to slow down . . . to allow a solid friendship to develop before they made any other assumptions. This time, he would look before he leaped. It was the only way Emma would allow him to win her affection. Even before she'd been in mourning, she'd been cautious about sharing herself, her feelings, her deepest dreams.

Maybe he could take a lesson there.

"How about that sleigh ride?" he asked. "It's a perfect moonlit evening, and I don't feel like staying around all these *ears* and *eyes.*"

Emma's smile was wistful and sweet. "Jah, I'd really like to go."

Jerome had to hold himself back from kissing her out of sheer gratitude. He led her from the pottery room toward the kitchen, intending to slip out into the wondrous winter night without attracting any attention. But Jemima was taking muffins out of the oven and Simon was helping himself to a brownie from a platter on the counter.

"Where you going?" the boy asked hopefully. "Will you and Emma play outside in the snow with me?"

Jerome tousled the boy's mop of hair. "Not this time, sport. Emma and I are taking a sleigh ride."

"Sleigh ride! In our dat's sleigh?" came a voice from under the kitchen table.

"Oh, but I'd love to ride tonight!" Dora and Cora popped

up from where they'd been playing with Alice Ann, their eyes alight.

Jerome laughed. Why had he believed he could escape without these kids following his every move? "We'll all go for a sleigh ride sometime soon, I promise. But right now I'd like to be with Emma."

"Ah, but Bess, you should be going along, too!" Mabel Wengerd called over her shoulder as she entered the kitchen. Her face looked taut, as though she'd pulled her hair back into an extra-tight bun. "All three of you young people can fit in the sleigh, and it'll keep everyone's intentions *honorable*, ain't so?"

Jerome reminded himself to be patient and to mind his mouth. "There's no one more honorable than Emma," he said. "You'll just have to let the Lord be our chaperone and trust that He's in charge of all our lives. He'll take care of you as well, Mabel, if you believe in His goodness and mercy."

He turned back toward Emma then, before anyone else could delay the ride he so badly wanted to share with her. "Shall we go?" he murmured. "I'm ready if you are."

"It's been way too long since I hitched up a sleigh," Jerome said as he lightly clapped the reins on Sparky's back. "I don't think this one's seen the snow since Uncle Atlee passed, and that's a shame. Are you warm enough?"

Emma burrowed deeper beneath the quilts Jerome had draped over them. Now that she was settled on the plush old seat, leaning into Jerome as the sleigh tilted slightly on the downhill lane, she felt happier than she had in a long time. The full moon was beaming down from a blue velvet sky dotted with diamond stars, making the snow-blanketed pastures glimmer all around them.

"I'm cozy. And I'm having a really gut time," Emma replied with a contented sigh. "Night rides are the prettiest, especially now that the wind has died down."

"Jah, it's a perfect evening," Jerome replied. "I've been hoping for more time alone with you—well, since the day we went shopping, Emma."

As she thought back to that day she'd spent trying to escape Jerome's attentions, Emma let herself relax . . . allowed the breeze from the accelerating sleigh to blow away her former objections to the handsome man who was driving it. The clip-clop of Sparky's hooves on the snow-packed road settled her heartbeat into its rhythm while the warmth they shared beneath the quilts soothed her after a day of surprising guests and revelations. "Denki for giving me another chance, Jerome," she murmured. "You were right at the wedding. I've missed out on a lot of opportunities to go out and have *fun*."

"Emma, it's *me* who's grateful for another chance," he said. "I nearly fell out of my chair when the Wengerds showed up—"

"They *intended* to catch you off guard. They're a nervy pair, if you ask me."

"But if you want to know anything else about why I walked out on Bess," he continued in a heartfelt voice, "*please* ask me. I want to be totally honest with you, Emma. I want you to trust me, as a friend and . . . as a man looking to marry someday."

Emma's heart nearly jumped out of her chest. She almost blurted an objection, saying it was too soon to speak of marriage, but then she caught herself. Most fellows wouldn't offer an explanation of their past romances, and she'd never figured Jerome for a man who could admit to his mistakes. Yet he'd proven that assumption wrong.

"No need to say another word about Bess and her mamm," Emma assured him. "And if you don't want to dig up old bones about your other engagement, well, that's *your* business. Not mine."

Jerome took the reins in one hand and slipped his other one beneath the quilts. When he found her hand, he grasped it . . . swallowed it up in his gloved grip, yet she no longer felt trapped. "The other girl didn't say so until I'd popped the question, but she wanted to join a liberal Mennonite fellowship," he explained. "She wanted electricity in our new home and a car to drive. Even to a fun-loving fellow like me, that seemed like a slap in the face to Aunt Amanda, after the way she and Atlee took me in and raised me up in the Old Order ways."

Emma smiled in the darkness. "You've never wanted a car?"

"Sure I have. What young fellow doesn't?" Jerome admitted. "But I couldn't afford a car in my rumspringa—and maybe that's why I got into mules," he reflected aloud. "It's another form of transportation, after all. And since mules aren't as common as horses, it's a way to distinguish myself. I hope that doesn't sound prideful to you, Emma."

It touched her that he valued her opinion about his livelihood. "James once told me he went into carriage making for the same reason," Emma said. "And the custom carriages he's designed for amusement parks have set him apart from other rig builders, just as you've chosen a different path with your mules. Seems like a smart business decision," she went on with a shrug. "Lots of fellows train horses, after all. No harm in offering a different draft animal—especially when you've got such a way with your mules."

Jerome was regarding her with something akin to awe. "Why, Emma Graber," he teased softly. "I've never heard you string together so many sentences at once—and all of them in my favor, too. I'm glad you feel that way."

Emma's cheeks prickled. She *had* nattered on and on, hadn't she? Yet now that she'd heard Jerome's explanation of his broken relationships, her reservations seemed to be slipping away. Why, for these past several minutes, watching the pristine snow-blanketed pastures go by, she'd even forgotten her sorrow . . . forgotten that she was grieving Mamm's passing.

Mamm adored Jerome! She's probably smiling down on you right now!

When the sleigh hit a bump, Emma let out a whoop and laughed out loud.

Jerome's whoop mingled with hers in the frosty air. "I like the sound of your laughter, sweetie," he said. "If I'm going too fast—"

"Don't slow down! This is—" Emma closed her eyes, trying to think of exactly the right word to describe how she felt. "It's exhilarating. I can't remember the last time I had so much fun."

Jerome scooted against her, still holding her hand. "I'm really glad to hear that, Emma," he replied. "I was a little worried about you earlier, when you were so tired after your week at the mercantile."

"I'll settle into the routine," she assured him as she gazed into his dark eyes. "I really have enjoyed helping Sam and learning so many things about running the store. And I'll sleep gut tonight after getting all this fresh air, no doubt."

Emma nipped her lip, unable to look away from Jerome's intense gaze. Should she share one of the main reasons she'd taken the job? They were having such a good time, yet this sleigh ride was the only opportunity they would have to talk without several other people around them—and she certainly didn't want to discuss her personal feelings where the Wengerd women might overhear them.

"I'm working in the store partly because I like to feel useful and partly because when you said I needed to get out more, I knew it was true," she admitted. "You must think I've led a sheltered, limited life while I've looked after my parents."

"Oh, Emma, not at all." Jerome tugged on the reins, guiding the sleigh to a complete stop on the shoulder of the road. Snow-laced evergreens whispered beside them as his gloved hand tightened around hers. "I've always admired your caring ways, and I suspect your dat would be lost without you, now that your mamm's passed. I think you're a loving daughter—a wonderful woman—*just the way you are*, Emma. But if you enjoy working in the store, that's a gut thing, too. I bet it helps you pass the time."

Emma's heart raced. Jerome understood her needs better than she'd anticipated. His expression suggested he might have something else on his mind as well, and she told herself she would *not* react by skittering away from him as she had in the past.

"While we've got this time alone, I want to tell you something I've not mentioned to anybody else, all right?" His smile was only inches from her face, and in the moonlight he looked a little bit nervous. "I—I'm taking my instruction to join the church."

"Jerome, why—that's so gut to hear!" Emma gripped his hand beneath the quilts. "I never really figured you for a fence jumper."

"Denki for saying that." Jerome let out the breath he'd been holding. "After all the times you've tried to avoid me, I got to thinking that a woman of faith like yourself might have *reason* to run the other way. I've been going to church all my life, living our Old Order beliefs, after all, so it's high time I committed."

Emma felt his gaze pulling her in, holding her on a deeper level. In all the years she'd spent wishing Matt Lambright would realize she existed, she'd missed the chance to talk this seriously with a man. *A woman of faith*, Jerome had called her—even after all the times she'd scurried away from him, expressing doubts about everything from wedding presents to quilting at the Brubakers' because he'd be around all day.

And doesn't it say something that Jerome didn't take his instruction—or leave the church—for either of those other two girls, even after he got engaged to them?

Not long ago, such a thought would have frightened her. Yet as Jerome shook the reins and spoke to Sparky, the sleigh once again glided effortlessly, and Emma felt herself sinking deeper into the seat and settling against Jerome's shoulder.

"I've always known you were a solid sort of fellow," she finally replied. "Sometimes your confidence scares me, on account of how I'm basically a mouse, like Bess—"

"Don't listen to her!" Jerome blurted. "She has *nothing* on you, and she's always up to something tricky. With you, Emma, I don't have to play games or second-guess your motives. You are who you seem to be. And I *like* who you are. A *lot*."

Emma's heart fluttered in spite of the fearful thoughts that raced through her mind. She wasn't used to such serious talk—had no idea how to respond if Jerome kicked the conversation up a notch by alluding to their future. "In my way," she said, "I was as . . . close to my mamm as Bess is to hers, as far as depending on her advice and—"

"Except when it came to me!" Jerome chuckled. "Your mamm, bless her soul—and your dat, too—took to me from the first. Which only seemed to make you that much more determined to hurry off in the opposite direction whenever I showed up. I was starting to wonder if I smelled as gamey as my mules."

Emma laughed so loudly that the sound echoed in the evergreens beside them. She couldn't stop laughing, either, as though Jerome's idea about smelling bad had grabbed her funny bone and wouldn't let go. "I—I'm sorry," she murmured between a couple of final giggles. "I'm not laughing *at* you, Jerome."

"Why not? I'm an odd duck."

"I just . . ." Emma paused. If anything, Jerome had the nicest scent of any fellow she knew. He had a woodsy fragrance she found appealing—and very bracing in the cold air, as they sat so close together. "I must have made quite a sight, running off every time you came my way," she said with a sigh. "I'm not sure why I was so skittish."

"Until tonight, there were a lot of things you didn't know about me. Important things." Jerome gazed into her eyes. He slowly drew his arm from beneath the quilts to wrap it around her shoulders. "You're as cautious as I am impulsive. That would make for a good balance between a man and a wife—but we'll not talk about that just yet."

Emma held her breath. Her pulse started pounding so loudly that Jerome could surely hear it, yet as he guided Sparky from the meadow onto the road again, she allowed her head to rest on his shoulder. Just for this glowing moment, surely it would be all right to savor the moonlight and the company of a fellow who wanted to hold her close . . . wanted to consider a future with *her* instead of with that pretty blonde back at the house.

"I'm determined not to have a third strike against me, as far as engagements go," Jerome went on in a low voice. "And I don't dare hurt you by acting like a clueless kid anymore, either. You deserve better than that, Emma."

She let out a long sigh . . . immersed herself in the sensations of this romantic ride, enjoying Jerome's solid warmth and the way her breathing fell into rhythm with his. The freshly washed scent of the quilts . . . the steady hoofbeats of the mule as it maintained a trot down the snowy road . . . the briskness of the winter night on her face while the rest of her felt cuddly and secure.

And to think you wanted to stay home and catch up on your sleep.

Sooner than Emma wanted, Sparky was pulling the sleigh up the hilly lane toward the Brubaker house. The kitchen window shone with the glow of a lamp, but the front room and the upstairs bedrooms were dark.

"Let's hope Bess and Mabel didn't wait up," Jerome said

with a sigh. "I hope you don't mind that I offered to see them home tomorrow."

"It was the proper thing to do. Especially since I didn't hear mention of any men living at home."

"With Ammon gone, it's just Mabel and Bess." Jerome halted the mule outside the barn door, keeping his arm around her. "Considering how I've made my answer to Bess clear, it's going to be a long, not-so-pleasant ride, but I'm going to ask Eddie and Pete to go along, too. Most likely, the Wengerds' lane will need clearing, and maybe they'll need some firewood split. After those chores are seen to . . ."

"And truth be told, Mabel's older sons should be doing them," Emma murmured.

"Then I can say I did what was right before I left them once and for all." Jerome held her gaze, his eyes mere inches from hers. "But why am I talking about those two conniving women when I'm sitting with *you*, Emma? At last."

She didn't have an answer. As his breath mingled with hers in wisps of white vapor, time stood still. "Denki so much for this sleigh ride, Jerome," she whispered. "And for your patience with me, too."

"May I kiss you, Emma?"

Her anxious thoughts shattered the mood Jerome had created so perfectly on this winter night. Oh, but she *wanted* to kiss him, yet she eased out of his arms. What if he found her kiss lacking? He was probably an expert kisser, so he'd know right away that she was a rank beginner. "Not yet," Emma rasped. "Another time, maybe."

His sad expression filled her with immediate regret.

"It's too soon after your mamm's passing," Jerome murmured. "But I had to ask."

"Denki for understanding," she replied in a tiny voice.

"I'll have that first kiss to look forward to, I hope." Jerome scooted away from her, gazing toward the house. "Will you wait for me while I unhitch Sparky? So we can walk to the house together?"

Relief and gratitude filled her. "Jah. I'd like that."

"Probably the last few moments I'll have you all to myself. No telling who might be peeking out a window."

As Jerome led the mule to his stall, Emma ducked inside the barn door to escape the wind. Her thoughts whirled like the light, loose snow that skimmed the drifts. What a night it had been! She had so much to consider . . . so many images to run through her mind again and again in quiet moments. So many possibilities to pray about.

Is Jerome the one? Do you love him? Could it come to that, if you gave him a chance?

Emma gazed up at the vast indigo sky dotted with sparkling pinpoint stars. She didn't have an answer to that yet . . .

But you're asking the questions.

Chapter 18

As everyone came to the table Sunday morning, Amanda was grateful that Jemima had made a variety of items for their breakfast—substantial food that would fuel the men when they went outside to clear the lane. Why was she not surprised that Mabel Wengerd found fault with this?

"Shouldn't be frying up mush of a Sunday morning," their guest muttered when she saw Jemima at the stove. "That's *work*."

Merle made a face. "You can't think we're going to eat it cold," he said as he took his seat. "Besides, Jemima cooked it up yesterday."

"We've got plowing to do, and we'll eat a hot breakfast," Wyman stated. "Even though the bishop left a phone message last night saying church is called off, we'd be remiss if we didn't get you and Bess home to Queen City—in case your own lane is snowed in," he added in a purposeful tone.

"Eddie and Pete have agreed to come along to help me clear it if need be," Jerome chimed in. "I hope to have our lane and the gravel road passable by the time the county plow goes by on the blacktop. You and Bess should plan accordingly."

Bess appeared resigned to the fact that Jerome wanted nothing further to do with her, but her mother's feathers were still ruffled.

"And what of Emma?" Mabel demanded with a sniff. "Surely she and Merle should consider heading back to Cedar Creek as well, if you're going to such an effort."

"Nah, Merle's staying to play with us!" Simon piped up. "I'm tired of Chutes and Ladders, though, so it's time to get out the Let's Go Fishing game."

"But it's *fun* to watch you slide down the chutes when you land on the squares that're about bad choices, Simon," Dora teased, her eyes bright.

"Sundays are for spending with family and friends," her twin said demurely, "and Emma and Merle are our gut friends."

"But if Dat says we're to clear the lane first, I'm gonna eat *three pieces* of fried mush so I'll be ready to help!" Simon declared. Gripping his fork and knife, he stood them on end on either side of his plate, eagerly awaiting his meal. The twins followed suit.

Amanda turned toward the sink so the Wengerds wouldn't catch her laughing at the kids' insinuations. The Brubakers hadn't discussed their opinions of last night's uninvited guests aloud, knowing how voices carried through the heat grates in the floors and how the youngsters might repeat what the adults had said. But it was unanimous. Sunday or not—snow or not—the Wengerds were going home.

Jerome and Wyman ate without much talk and then excused themselves to go outside. By the time Eddie, Pete, and Simon had finished eating, Merle insisted on joining them. "I can at least feed the horses."

"You can be my helper, Merle!" Simon insisted. "I know where all the rations and buckets and stuff are."

Soon, out of the barn came the plow, a V-shaped blade with a platform where Wyman stood behind the two large mules Jerome had hitched to it. While her husband tended to the lane, Amanda watched her nephew and the two older boys attack the walkways with snow shovels. She was glad Bess and her mamm excused themselves to get ready for their trip home, so she and the girls could wash the dishes without any more of Mabel's negative remarks.

Wyman and Jerome cleared the lane and the unpaved road to the county highway in record time. After the boys had tucked snow shovels, plus Eddie's clothing for the coming week of painting in Cedar Creek, into their own rig, the little procession took off, with Jerome driving the Wengerd buggy. Wags circled the rigs in wide loops, barking exuberantly to send them off. Then he greeted the girls, who were heading outside with Simon to play in the snow.

"Jerome's got a long day ahead of him," Jemima remarked as she watched out the window with Amanda and Emma.

Vera and Lizzie had also gone outside, with Alice Ann in tow. The kids were building an igloo, so Amanda felt freer about talking. "It's a wonder Mabel and Bess didn't run off the road and wreck last night, the way the snow was piling up. They weren't even sure where they were going, by the sound of it."

"Puh!" Jemima said as she put on a kettle for tea. "Sheer orneriness keeps folks like that going when normal, decent people would've known better. But I've sinned by judging them that way, and I ask the Lord's forgiveness," she added. Then she sighed ruefully. "I'm also sorry I sent that photo of Jerome's mule team to the *Connection*, so Mabel could get ideas about the money he must be making."

"You couldn't have foreseen how Mabel would react,

Jemima. None of us were as charitable as we should've been," Amanda admitted. Then she smiled at Emma. "But those two women are behind us now, and everyone else is outside. So . . . what went on in my pottery room last night?"

"Bess came out in quite a huff," Jemima said with a shake of her head. "I'm glad she didn't start pitching Amanda's dishes to the floor."

Emma's cheeks colored, but she managed a smile. "Bess overheard Jerome asking me to chat with him there after the kitchen was cleaned up," she explained. "From what I can tell, she stuck to him like glue while he waited for me. And then she lit into him full-on, pressing him to the wall while she *kissed* him."

"My stars," Amanda whispered. "To spite *you*, no doubt. I'm sorry, Emma."

"I'm surprised it wasn't Jerome who was pitching dishes, then," Jemima remarked. "He was fed up with her foolishness ages ago."

Emma shrugged. "I called Bess out on her behavior. Told her we all knew she and her mamm had come here to sweet-talk Jerome because they thought he was making gut money with his mules—and then she stormed out."

"Gut for you!" Amanda was pleased that Emma had taken such a stand. And it seemed a good sign as well that she and Jerome hadn't returned home last night until after eleven. "It was a perfect evening for a ride in Atlee's sleigh, ain't so?" she hinted.

Emma's cheeks turned rosier. "Jah, it was. Jerome and I talked about a lot of things, and then . . . well, he wanted to kiss me gut night, but—but I was *afraid*," she blurted. "I've never been kissed—not *really* kissed, by a fellow. And I didn't want Jerome to notice if I did it wrong."

Bless you, Emma, you're more sheltered than we thought. Amanda recalled how awkward it had been when she'd first met Wyman and had had to adjust to another man's affections. She stood before Emma, gently grasping her shoulders. "The easiest thing is to let the man lead," she murmured. "But while your mouth follows his, let your heart guide you—and ease you away, if you feel Jerome's taking you too fast."

Emma's eyes widened above her flushed cheeks. Then she looked away, still embarrassed. "*Please* don't tell him I've never— Jerome and I had such a gut talk last night, but if he finds out—"

The stomping of boots outside the kitchen door brought their intense conversation to a halt. Wyman and Merle stepped into the kitchen, their weathered faces a deep red from the cold. "*Now* we can savor our Sunday," Wyman said with a good-natured chuckle. "Is it me, or were those two women the most bothersome biddies we've ever encountered?"

Merle shook his head as he removed his stocking cap and coat. "Eunice had her cranky moments, but Mabel Wengerd takes the cake, as far as trying a man's patience." He paused, watching the kids through the glass in the door as they packed snow around the base of their igloo. "Hate to disappoint Simon, and I hate to be a bother to *you* on your day of rest, Wyman, but I'm thinking Emma and I ought to head home," he said. "We've enjoyed your hospitality more than you know, but I hate to impose on Matt any more, expecting him to look after our animals."

Wyman clapped the older fellow on the back. "Let's warm up with a cup of tea, and then I'll be happy to take you. I bet you're ready for some peace and quiet—and to sleep in your own bed tonight."

Merle chuckled. "Jah, there's that. And you folks start a new work week tomorrow, along with James and Abby." He walked stiffly toward the table as though his arthritis might be bothering him—not that he'd admit it. "I'd like to be home when they get back, to hear about their trip. And that way Abby won't ask us where we went and what we were doing. Your quilts will still be a secret."

"He wants to catch up on his naps," Emma remarked with an indulgent smile, "but it *has* been a wonderful-gut visit."

Amanda set the basket of muffins on the table, along with the goodies that remained from the quilting frolic, while Jemima poured hot water for tea. Within the hour, the Grabers were heading down the lane with Wyman, and the rest of her Sunday—the *rest* of her Sunday—awaited her. Vera, Lizzie, and Jemima were setting up chairs around the quilting frame, while Alice Ann began plucking scraps from the box of quilting fabrics they'd set on the floor for her. It was a satisfying, peaceful scene, after the previous evening with their unexpected company.

At the kitchen window with Simon and the twins, Amanda watched Wyman's rig disappear around the snowbank at the bottom of the lane. She wrapped her arms around the three of them. "You know, a game or two of Let's Go Fishing sounds like a fine way to spend this snowy morning," she said.

"I'll go set up the board!" Simon hurried toward the front room with the twins in his wake, but then he rushed back and grabbed Amanda around the waist. "I'm glad you're playing with us today instead of making your dishes, Mamm! Sit by *me*, okay?"

As Amanda smiled down into Simon's expressive brown eyes, she realized yet again how blessed she was to be a part of this big, happy Brubaker family. What a joy, to be chosen by a child . . . to be welcomed into a simpler, more carefree world for these next few hours. It was an opportunity not to be wasted.

Emma settled against the carriage's backseat, wrapped in the warmth of a quilt, as Wyman and her father conversed in the front. Like Dat, she looked forward to the comfort of her own bed. With all the commotion the Wengerds had caused, she hadn't slept much last night.

No, you were too excited to sleep, she thought with a smile. Hadn't her evening with Jerome assured her that he wasn't interested in Bess, or in anyone except *her*? In her mind, Emma reviewed the highlights of their sleigh ride: the warm strength of Jerome's hand wrapped around hers, the life-changing secrets he'd revealed as they slid effortlessly across pastures of flawless white snow and stopped beside the evergreens, the moment he'd asked her for a kiss . . .

"And while Jerome might jump into things feetfirst, you can't fault him for being lazy or hard-hearted," her dat was saying matter-of-factly.

"You've got him pegged," Wyman agreed. "When I first considered marrying Amanda, I had reservations about Jerome and how his wild notions might encourage my kids—especially Pete and Eddie—to go astray. But he's matured a lot."

"Jah, he's taken to your little ones, for sure," Dat replied. "And what do *you* think of Jerome by now, Daughter? Surely you've changed your tune, considering how late you stayed out with him last night."

Emma's eyes flew open. She'd nearly drifted off, and now her father was gazing over his shoulder at her, expecting her opinion. "Um, jah, he's nice enough," she hedged.

While it had seemed natural to share her concerns—her secrets—with Amanda and Jemima, she wasn't keen on discussing her romantic hopes and dreams with two men. Dat and Wyman would probably tell Jerome what she'd said, and Emma didn't want to jinx her new relationship by talking about it too much. It was awfully early to be making any firm assumptions, after all. Jerome himself had said so.

Dat's raised eyebrows told her he'd expected a more enthusiastic affirmation of Jerome's character and worthiness. Emma closed her eyes again and leaned her head against the buggy wall. Why was it any of Dat's business what she and Jerome had done on their outing?

After they arrived home, Emma threw together a quick dinner of sandwiches, chowchow, and home-canned applesauce to eat before Wyman headed back to Bloomingdale. As she was washing the dishes, her father saw their friend off—and then he was standing at her elbow, peering intently at her.

"You baffle me, Emma," he said with a sigh. "A solid, well-off, gut-looking man is head over heels for you, yet you couldn't care less. Well, it's up to God now," he declared. "Your mother couldn't convince you to take up with Jerome, and I'm washing my hands of this whole disappointing business, too."

With that, he shuffled out to the front room and immediately fell asleep in his recliner.

Emma sighed. When she'd finished in the kitchen, she stood gazing at Dat as his snoring got louder and steadier. In repose, his face looked deeply wrinkled . . . older than she cared to think about. He wouldn't stir again until Abby and James returned.

Was this how their life at home was to be now—too quiet and fraught with constant frustration? Was she wrong to keep her hopeful feelings about Jerome to herself, knowing she'd disappointed her father?

No, Dat's got it right. This whole situation—with Jerome and with Dat—is in God's hands now. I'll deal with it one day at a time.

Chapter 19

Monday morning, Abby focused on the holly-print tablecloth she was hemming, pumping the machine's treadle in her usual steady rhythm. While living in the Graber house was the right thing to do, it still felt *different*. Most days, by the time Emma and James had gone to work and Merle had finished his breakfast—and she'd cleaned up the kitchen by herself—she started her sewing more than an hour later than when she'd been single, working in her nook at the mercantile.

But what's an hour? It's nothing, compared to what Merle, Emma, and James lost when Eunice died.

Abby opened another package of the cranberry red bias tape she was using to finish the tablecloth's edges. A banquet center on the other side of Clearwater had ordered eight of these long tablecloths, and she had two more to finish today so that the banquet manager could pick them up by four o'clock. She was carefully lining up the hem and bias tape edges to begin sewing again when a male voice interrupted her.

"Knock, knock."

Abby glanced up. "Sam! And how are *you* this morning? Everything's all right at home, I hope?"

Her older brother gazed around her freshly painted sewing room. "Jah, the family's fine," he replied. Then he chuckled. "This bright yellow almost calls for sunglasses. Eddie told me it was intense."

Abby laughed. "It's more color than we're used to, jah, but it made James happy to choose it for me. Here, sit down."

As she cleared the nearest chair, which held her sewing notions for the tablecloths, Abby's thoughts spun. Why had Sam come to the Graber house and then all the way upstairs to speak with her? She couldn't recall him *ever* going up to her Stitch in Time nook at the store for the sake of conversation.

"Two things," Sam said as he perched on the wooden chair. He held her gaze, as though figuring out how to express his thoughts. "First, Barbara and I would like you and James to come for dinner tomorrow night—and of course we want Merle and Emma to join us, too," he added quickly. "It's a little party so we can give you our wedding gift, knowing how your weekends are busy with trips for a while."

"My word, Sam, after all you've already given us, what with providing the wedding feast and preaching for us, and—"

"All part of the package," Sam insisted. His smile looked tired, but his eyes sparkled. "We wanted to set aside time to celebrate properly, with just close family. I—I think you and James will really like what we chose for your gift."

And wasn't *that* an interesting thing for Sam to say? Abby noted how the lines around his eyes and the sides of his mouth seemed deeper. Was it her imagination, or had

more salt and pepper crept into what had once been a deep
brown beard?

"Abby, I've prayed long and hard about this," he began
in a low voice, "but I see no way around it. Will you come
back to work at the mercantile? To get me through the
Christmas season?"

There it was, the plea she and Emma had predicted the
day after she'd married James. But Abby swallowed her tri-
umph; Sam had done some deep soul-searching before he'd
come here with his hat in his hand. He was in dire straits at
the store, or he wouldn't have made such a request. "So . . .
things aren't going so gut? Emma's not working out?"

"Oh, Emma's pitching right in," Sam replied. "She's
keeping the ledger in gut order, and she's learning how to
inventory the stock—everything I can possibly have her do
in the workroom. I've wondered if she's not working too
many hours, but she insists on coming back every afternoon after lunch."

Abby nodded. Although Emma had mentioned that it
took her mind a long time to wind down after she went to
bed each evening, she seemed really pleased about taking
on so many responsibilities for Sam. "What about Gail,
then? Surely she's relieved that Emma's keeping your
books so she can be in the main store, helping customers."

With a sigh, Sam leaned his elbows on his knees. "It's
not just Gail's youth and inexperience—I knew about those
things when I insisted that you leave," he admitted. "We've
got more business than ever this holiday season, and—well,
Gail's taken a shine to Eddie Brubaker."

"Ah. So she's distracted."

Sam let out a short laugh. "I knew you'd be difficult to
replace, Abby, but Ruthie can help only after school, and
our mamm can't handle so much time on her feet."

"She's not getting any younger," Abby agreed.

"And when Emma hired on, I stopped running my ads.

So I'm caught shorthanded, with long lines at the cash register and a week and a half to go before Christmas."

Abby considered this. While she loved working in the store and would help Sam in a heartbeat, the piles of fabric around her reminded her of all the sewing orders she had to finish before Christmas. "What-all do you want me to handle? Do you have a number of hours per day in mind?"

Sam looked flustered, as though he'd expected her immediate *yes* rather than questions. "How do you mean?"

"Will you want me waiting on folks?" Abby clarified. "I know how you—and the church—object to married women working in public places."

"It was Vernon who suggested I ask you back through the end of the year, last week when he saw what a pickle I was in. So who am I to argue with the bishop?" Sam replied with a shrug. "I was hoping you'd come back full-time to help customers and run the cash register, as you did before. But with Christmas less than two weeks away, beggars can't be choosers."

Never had Abby anticipated such a sentiment coming from her brother. But she had her own responsibilities to consider these days, too. "What would you think if I put my sewing machine in the back room?" she asked cautiously. "Will I have a chance to work on my sewing orders when we don't have customers in the store?"

Sam's lips quirked. "These past several days, folks've been at the door first thing, and I've practically had to lock them out come closing time. English shoppers seem to keep coming in as long as they see lights on, regardless of the hours we've posted."

Abby recalled Christmas business being that brisk in previous years as well. The stress on Sam's face reflected his additional duties as a new preacher, because there was no predicting when one of their district members would require his attention, or when Vernon Gingerich and Abe Nissley would need to meet about church business.

"I've got a lot of sewing orders to finish before Christmas," Abby said, choosing her words carefully. "I'm also wondering how much time I should spend at the store because—well, with Emma working, Merle likes having me around more than he'll admit. It would be different if Eunice hadn't died."

"Jah, this household would be pretty bleak without you here to liven up the conversation and help with the chores." Sam looked torn. While he was truly concerned about his lifelong neighbors, he also had a very busy store to run.

"How about if I come in around ten o'clock and leave by four?"

The flicker of his eyebrows indicated that he'd hoped for more of her time.

"You know," Abby said softly, "you were right—the *Ordnung* is right—about restricting a woman's working once she marries. After only a few weeks, my priorities have changed. My own preferences have shifted toward the back burner while I help with my new family responsibilities."

Sam smiled tenderly and squeezed her knee. "Never thought I'd hear *you* admit that, Abby," he teased, "although I didn't doubt that your perception would change when you became a wife. I believe God's bringing both of us to these realizations because He wants us to honor each other's best intentions, little sister. So jah—ten to four will be fine."

Sam rose from his chair, giving her a grateful smile. "And denki for helping me out of this tight spot without saying *I told you so*—as Barbara and Mamm have been doing all along."

"You've helped *me* out of many a tight spot, after all," Abby pointed out as she stood to see him off. "I'll see you tomorrow morning, then—and we'll all come for supper tomorrow night. Emma and I will whip up something to bring for the meal."

"Maybe fried pies with your pineapple and lemon filling?"

Abby kept her smile carefully in place as she considered how much time it would take to make fried pies this evening. "For you, Sam, I'll do that," she replied, cherishing the boyish hopefulness that lit her older brother's face.

After he left, Abby resumed her seat at the treadle machine. She hadn't anticipated having such mixed feelings about returning to the Cedar Creek Mercantile—just as there had been a time when Sam wouldn't have admitted he needed her help. Working at the store had shaped her life since she'd been a teenager, when she'd learned how to keep books and deal with all sorts of customers. And the skills she'd acquired from Sam had led to her starting her Stitch in Time business, too.

To everything there is a season, Abby reminded herself as her feet rocked the treadle again. Marriage had multiplied her responsibilities more than she'd ever imagined as a maidel, but as her husband's handsome face came to mind, Abby knew her union with James would be the source of blessings too abundant to count. Still, she wasn't sure how she'd find the time to complete her sewing orders and be a good wife, daughter-in-law, and friend while she relieved Sam's business burden.

With God's help, her efforts would be good enough.

Chapter 20

As Emma sat at the Lambrights' table Tuesday evening, she sighed wearily. Her legs ached from climbing up and down the workroom ladder and standing on the hardwood floor all day to fill bags of baking supplies. She longed to relax in her nightgown and soak her feet in a tub of warm water, but with Vernon Gingerich, Eddie Brubaker, and everyone in Sam's family, along with Dat and Abby and James gathered for dinner, laughing and talking, she tried her best to smile. This was a party for the newlyweds, after all.

"How are things going at the store now, Sam?" Vernon asked as he buttered a slice of bread. His face, set off by a soft, white beard, looked rosy from being out in the cold weather. "I'm pleased that Abby has limited her hours, and that Emma remains in the back room, but I wish this weren't going on while they're in mourning."

"That's why I'm only working until Christmas," Abby pointed out.

"That's the plan, anyway," Sam agreed.

The bishop nodded. "And how are *you* getting along, Emma?" He gazed at her with blue eyes that assessed her warmly. "Sam tells me you've gone above and beyond, as far as keeping up his ledger and working more hours than he'd expected."

"I like the work just fine, jah," Emma replied. "It—it keeps me from missing Mamm so much, I think."

But you've had plenty of time to kick yourself for not kissing Jerome the other night, she thought as the conversation continued around her. *Such a sociable fellow, so accustomed to having much prettier girls playing up to him, will soon tire of a timid girl who rejects his affection.*

Emma took another bite of pork roast, hoping no one would notice how exhausted she was and how her mood was sinking along with her energy level. Only a few days had passed since she and Jerome had been gliding across moonlit snow-covered pastures, laughing together, yet she couldn't seem to summon the same carefree mind-set she'd enjoyed on Saturday night . . . some of the happiest hours of her life.

Why haven't I heard from him? Why didn't he stop by Sunday on his way back from taking the Wengerds home to Queen City?

That was the real issue, wasn't it? And while it was foolish to fault Jerome for not calling her, Emma sighed. The sound of his voice, the reassurance that he really did want to take her out—and court her—would be so sweet, after all these years of being a homebody who didn't go out on dates. And a phone call would dispel the more upsetting moments of her weekend at the Brubaker place, too. Dozens of times during the past couple of nights when she couldn't fall asleep, Emma had replayed that brazen kiss she'd witnessed in Amanda's workroom, and recalled Bess Wengerd's scornful words afterward.

What could a handsome man like Jerome Lambright possibly see in a mouse like you, Emma Graber?

"Are you all right, Emma? You've hardly touched your supper."

Emma jumped when Treva's question, and the warmth of her hand, interrupted her woolgathering. "Jah, I just—I'm *fine*," she stammered, putting a smile on her face. "It's a wonderful-gut dinner. And it was awfully nice of you to include us in the invitation."

Everyone at the table was looking at her. Had someone asked her a question and she'd missed it, lost in her thoughts?

After an awkward silence, Vernon leaned forward to focus on her dat. "And how are you doing on these snowy days, Merle—especially with Abby and Emma both working in the store now?" he asked in his resonant voice. "After I lost my Dorothea, I wandered lost from one day into the next for a while."

Her father nodded in appreciation, and then his face lit up with boyish glee. "This past Saturday, Emma and I—"

Emma coughed loudly, staring at Dat so he wouldn't reveal their secret trip to the Brubakers' in front of Abby and James. He'd been particularly forgetful the past couple of evenings, but he stopped talking when he realized why Emma was staring at him.

"What I mean to say," Dat went on, "is that Emma and I are—well, we're still getting cards and calls from friends who wish us well. It's wonderful to have James and Abby living with us now, but Emma's been my special blessing these past three weeks. A real comfort, she is. Denki for asking, Vernon."

Emma blinked. Dat had talked as though she'd been at home rather than working, and he hadn't mentioned that he'd been spending some time in the carriage shop with James, either, but he'd kept their weekend activities a secret. There was no telling how his mind worked.

"Please let me know if there's anything I can do for you," Vernon remarked kindly. "You folks are at the top of my daily prayer list—and would you look at these goodies!" he exclaimed when Barbara handed him the tray from the sideboard. As he studied all the different cookies, fried pies, and bars on the plate, he flashed Eddie a teasing smile. "I'd best limit myself to one or two so our painter will have enough to sustain his energy on the job. How's it going at the mercantile, son?"

Eddie chuckled. "I've finished the upper level. What with so many shoppers in the store now, emptying the shelves and shifting them around are more of a challenge."

"And what a difference the fresh walls make. I didn't realize how dingy the store had gotten," Sam remarked to the bishop. Then he, too, smiled at Eddie. "It would probably be best if you took the next couple weeks off and resumed your painting after the first of the year. Easier for you and the customers as well."

Vernon was following this conversation with genuine interest. "Seems like you're off to a gut start on a career you seem well-suited for, son."

"Jah, I've lined up a lot of other jobs with folks who've seen me painting while they shop." Eddie paused as the cookie tray came to him. "Hmm . . . are these your brownies with the peppermint patties in them, Gail?"

Gail's face turned a telltale pink. "They are. But Abby brought the fried pies, and the lemon bars are Emma's, and Ruthie made the sugar cookies. You can't help but find something you like there, Edward."

Edward! Emma had never heard anyone use his full name. The two young people had been stealing glances at each other all during supper, flirting so effortlessly. Why was it so difficult for her to believe Jerome wanted to spend his time with her? After all, only a couple of days had passed since she'd heard from him. He did have mules to train and other work to do around the farm.

After the meal, Emma went immediately to the sink to run the water, for washing dishes would keep her more alert and less likely to wonder about Jerome. She was glad that

Treva, Barbara, and the girls were having a lively conversation about what to serve for the Christmas meals rather than paying any attention to *her*. Emma washed the dishes as quickly as she could. The faster they got through this redding up, and then the gift opening, the sooner they'd head home. She longed to fall into bed and get some rest. Tomorrow would be another busy, tiring day at the store, because it seemed no matter how many bags she filled with jimmies, noodles, rolled oats, and other staples, the store shelves needed to be restocked by closing time.

When the kitchen was spotless, the women joined the fellows in Sam's front room. Two large boxes sat beside the sofa, where Barbara encouraged Abby and James to sit. "We hope you'll enjoy this gift," she said as she smiled at the bishop. "Vernon went in on it with us—"

"And I was tickled when the idea for it came up at your wedding," Vernon chimed in. "It's useful and beautiful— and something we're sure you don't already have!"

The newlyweds laughed together. "We're accumulating quite a pile of gifts," Abby said as she pulled something from the box nearest her end of the couch.

James's eyes widened as Abby removed the newspaper that was wrapped around it. "Now that's a fine-looking mug!"

"And these colors!" Abby said as she turned the mug this way and that. "I've never seen a mug with a reddish brown border bleeding into a deep blue center."

"Care to guess who made them?" Sam asked. "We're amazed she completed them so quickly."

Abby's eyes widened as she unwrapped a matching cereal bowl. "Is this Amanda's new style of pottery? Oh, what a gift you've given us!"

"Denki so much," James added as he unwrapped a serving bowl. "It'll be a treat to use these dishes and think of the friend who made them for us!"

"Jah, we won't be saving these for special occasions," Abby said as she unwrapped a dinner plate. "Look how sturdy they are—and every piece a little different because of the way the border blends into the center."

Barbara nodded as she looked on from her rocking chair. "You've got sixteen place settings plus serving pieces, so if you want to keep the rest of them packed until you get them home—"

"We'll unwrap the rest of them later tonight so we can use them right away," James said. "This is a wonderful-gut present!"

Emma watched and listened with a rising sense of anxiety. Even though Jerome had told her Amanda was making the newlyweds a set of dishes, seeing *two big boxes of them* sent her over the edge. "And just where do you plan to *put* them?" she blurted. "The cupboards are full of Mamm's dishes, and I—I want to use *those*!"

As the words spewed from her mouth, Emma knew she'd spoken from a selfish welling up of emotions that was fueled by her exhaustion. The Lambrights' front room rang with a stunned silence. Everyone stared at her as though she'd dashed one of the new dishes to the floor.

But didn't her feelings count for anything? She hadn't said a word when James had wanted the kitchen painted that glaring shade of yellow, but it was another thing entirely that he planned to clear out the cupboards without asking her.

"Of course Mamm intended for you to have her dishes." Surprise and regret clouded James's expression as he gazed at Emma. "I didn't mean for you to think we'd get *rid* of anything—"

"And you know what?" Abby interrupted. "We can wait until you're ready to use these dishes Amanda made—or even wait until you marry someday. We didn't mean to upset you, Emma."

Emma was ashamed of her outburst and her uncharitable attitude, but she wanted to be surrounded by familiar, beloved belongings. Was that so wrong? She sighed, resting

her head in her hands. If only she'd kept her mouth shut . . .
If only she could go home and go to bed . . .

"This same situation came up at the Brubaker place,
when Amanda and Jemima wanted to use some of their
own kitchen equipment but Vera didn't," Vernon recalled.

Before the bishop could elaborate, Dat sat forward in his
armchair. "Jah, I remember that fuss between Wyman's
daughter and Amanda, and I'll not have it repeated at our
place," he declared. "We've welcomed Abby into our home,
and—except for using a room for her sewing—this is the
first time she's asked for any adjustment on our part."

"I'm so sorry," Emma murmured. "I spoke out of turn
without—"

"And I believe the real problem," Vernon interrupted
gently, "is that you haven't had nearly enough time to adjust
to your mother's passing, dear Emma. You've been so busy
helping Sam that you haven't allowed yourself to heal from
your profound loss—and the rest of us haven't allowed you
that time, either."

While the bishop's words rang true, Emma was embarrassed that everyone in the room was watching her so
closely. "There's that, jah, but I really do enjoy the work,"
she protested in a tremulous voice. "I'm just tired from—"

"Too many hours in the store," Sam finished her sentence. "While I truly appreciate the way you've taken over
my bookkeeping, and you've been filling bags of our baking supplies and bulk foods so Gail can wait on the customers, I can tell you're worn out, Emma."

"Working in the mercantile takes a lot of energy," Abby
joined in as she reached over to grasp Emma's hand.
"That's why Sam suggested you could work mornings until
you got accustomed to spending so much time on your feet.
You've done a wonderful-gut job, Emma. It's not your way
to lash out, so I know you must be more exhausted than
you're letting on."

Emma chuckled sadly. "You've always made running the

store look so easy, Abby. But jah, after these past two days of going up and down the workroom ladder, shifting bins and filling bags, I'm tired," she admitted. "Really, *really* tired."

After a few moments of considering the situation, Vernon leaned toward Emma in his armchair. His face was lit up with such compassion, such wisdom, that she couldn't look away from him.

"What if you did Sam's bookkeeping at home?" he asked. "Seems to me you could still be a big help, and meanwhile you'd be keeping your dat company—especially with Abby in the store for the next several days."

Emma considered this. "Well, I've always worked on James's accounts at the kitchen table," she remarked. "I could fill out Sam's order forms, too—and I'd be home to fix the meals that way. With both of us girls working yesterday, it was a rush to put something on the table for supper after Abby and I got home."

"Works for me, having you home again," Dat said with a grin. "Nobody wants to eat *my* cooking, and I was wondering if it might come to that."

As everyone chuckled, Emma felt her shoulders relaxing. As much as she'd enjoyed taking on the challenge of working at the store, Vernon's solution made a lot of sense. She had proven to herself that she could do something besides look after her parents and the housekeeping chores, after all—and she would still be doing valuable work for Sam.

"There's our answer," Sam said with a nod. "And the ledger's all caught up, so I don't want you coming over for the rest of this week's receipts until Friday, Emma. And I won't take any fussing about that."

Relief washed over Emma like a balm. She was pleased that Sam valued her work—and that everyone in the room valued *her*. When she got home, she went to bed and sank into a deep, satisfying sleep.

In her dreams, she sat in the sleigh with Jerome again. And he was smiling at her.

Chapter 21

Jerome was heading toward the phone to call Emma, but when the barn door slid open so a buggy could pull in, he remained in the wide center aisle with one of his recently born mules. Several times since the weekend he'd intended to contact the pretty young lady in Cedar Creek who'd captured his heart—and why hadn't he? In all his years of dating, he couldn't recall wanting to do everything *just right* to please a woman.

"Hey there, Jerome!" Wyman called out. He closed the door and unhitched his horse. "How're your foals doing in this cold weather?"

"They prefer the barn to the corral," Jerome answered with a laugh. He kept his hand on the foal's fuzzy back, reassuring her in the presence of a different man who had a booming voice. "Can't say as I blame them on such a blustery day."

"Jah, Pete and Lizzie were glad for the ride to school this morning, too. Seemed logical to take them, since I was

dropping Vera off at Cletus Yoder's place." Wyman patted
his draft horse as it headed toward its stall. "I have a hard
time believing she's old enough to be working. Seems like
only yesterday she was about as tall as your foal, and just
as skittish."

"Jah, this little girl's jumpy, but she's got the sweetest
temperament of the three," Jerome remarked as he kept his
hand on her back. "Vera seemed excited about working
there, at breakfast. She's a gut girl," he added. "Level head
on her shoulders."

"Cletus's wife was glad to have her. They've got family
coming in for Christmas, so a lot of rooms need freshening
up." Wyman gazed at him then. "I'm thinking about a trip
to the Cedar Creek Mercantile, or anyplace I might find a
gift for Amanda. This being our first Christmas together,
I'd like to get her something special. Any suggestions?"

Jerome's eyebrows rose. If he went along with Wyman,
he could visit with Emma—except he wouldn't really be
able to spend time talking to her alone. "Isn't that the hard-
est part about hooking up with a woman? Figuring out what
she likes?" he teased.

Wyman's laughter rang around the barn's rafters. "It
hasn't gotten any easier with my second wife than it was
with my first," he agreed. "Care to come along? I'm thinking a certain young lady in Cedar Creek would be happy to
see you. Or at least Emma *appeared* to be sweet on you."

Jerome knew an invitation to chat about his love life when
he heard one, but he preferred to keep his budding relationship with Emma to himself. "I don't want to interrupt her
while she's working," he hedged. "And if I'm to have one of
these young mules ready for James and Abby, I'd better keep
working with them while they're so open to learning."

"Jah, mules are like women that way. One day they'll do
anything you ask, and the next day they're liable to bare
their teeth at you." Wyman chuckled. "That would be
Jemima I'm talking about, not Amanda."

Jerome guided the little foal back to the stall where her mother waited. "Some of them don't improve with age," he agreed. "With animals, you can imprint them from birth if you're lucky, but women have had several years to get set in their ways. I've seen a gut many husbands who were getting trained by their wives, rather than vice versa."

"You've got that right." Wyman led one of his other Belgians to the buggy so he'd have a fresh horse for his shopping trip. "If anybody asks, I'll be checking the progress on the elevator. Weaver's crew should be ready to build the bins, now that the foundation is in place. No need to mention that I'm also shopping."

Jerome smiled, watching the foal rush to her mother to nurse. He never tired of observing his mules and mares interacting, for he gained valuable insight into the way each foal received instructions—training methods he emulated, as far as where a mare nuzzled or nipped her baby to guide his or her behavior. When he heard the rapid patter of footsteps on the snow-packed driveway, along with a *woof* from Wags, Jerome was glad he'd turned the foal back in with her mamm. Simon adored the little mules, but he hadn't yet learned to curb his excitement around them.

The barn door slid open. "Dat!" the five-year-old cried. "I saw you drive in!"

Wyman laughed and launched Simon to his shoulder. "Have you spent enough time with the hens this morning, Son? If you can keep a secret—"

"Jah! My lips are zipped!" Simon drew his finger across his mouth.

"I'll take you along to see the new elevator. And then we'll go to the mercantile," Wyman continued in a low, purposeful voice. "Just us guys, all right? You can't let on to the twins, or they'll feel bad that we didn't take them along."

Simon nodded exuberantly, his hands clapped over his mouth.

Wyman grinned, obviously pleased that his boy had

joined him. "See you later, Jerome. Tell Jemima not to wait dinner on us."

Jerome watched the big Belgian back the buggy out into the brightness of a sunny winter day. After he slid the barn door shut, he gazed at the phone on the wall. His hand went toward it, yet he pulled it back.

Emma had him stumped. She'd seemed *so close* to coming out of her shell during their sleigh ride that he'd practically tasted the kiss he'd been longing for. But then she'd gotten scared again.

Jerome recalled how Emma had leaned into him as they'd ridden in the sleigh . . . her dreamy expression as her eyes closed . . . the sound of her laughter. How could he convince Emma to trust him with her emotions . . . her future? Already he'd done more soul-searching about this young woman than about all his previous dates and fiancées put together. He longed to propose marriage to Emma before they even courted, so she'd understand that his intentions were honorable. Yet he understood that she needed his patience and compassion while she mourned her mother.

Did these thoughts mean he was taking the higher, wiser road with Emma because he truly loved her? Or was he following the wrong path altogether? He'd believed he'd found the love of his lifetime in his two earlier fiancées, too.

With a parting glance at his mules, Jerome returned to the house. A pot of soup simmered on the stove, and three fresh loaves of bread sat cooling on the counter, filling the kitchen with a yeasty aroma that made his stomach rumble. The steady *whirrrr* of Amanda's wheel told him his aunt was working on her pottery orders in the adjacent room. The three little girls must be helping Jemima upstairs.

Jerome surveyed the kitchen and the front room. Even with its freshly painted walls, this house hadn't changed much since he'd come here as a boy. *What would Emma think of living here? Merle would settle right in, but would*

*any new bride want to start up amongst eight kids and four
other adults? Even with Emma sharing my room, we
wouldn't have a bedroom for her dat . . .*

And Emma might cling to the notion of remaining in her
own home, too. That would mean he'd have to move his
mules, mares, and donkeys to Cedar Creek . . . which would
involve building a new barn, because the Grabers' was only
big enough to accommodate their horses. Pasture for additional animals would be in short supply, too—and the Lambright land on both sides of the road was already being grazed
by Matt's sheep, so there was no place nearby he could rent.

Jerome sighed. Such responsible thoughts hadn't occurred to him during his two engagements. Clearly he had
a lot to consider before he mentioned marriage to Emma.

Amanda smoothed the edges of four heart-shaped pottery
boxes and then quickly tucked them on the shelf behind her
supplies to dry. With Vera working today and Lizzie at
school, she'd had the perfect opportunity to make these
whatnot containers for their Christmas gifts. The two older
girls' boxes were larger than Cora's and Dora's, and she
would glaze them each a different color. A few days ago,
she'd crafted deep bowls for Wyman and Jerome to catch
their loose change, and she'd made banks in the shapes of
animal heads for the younger kids: a dog for Simon and a
bunny for Alice Ann.

When Wags barked out by the barn, Amanda glanced
out the window to see Wyman's buggy leaving again. She
laughed at how her devious little plan was playing out:
she'd alerted Simon to his dat's arrival, so now he was off
on an adventure, and she could call in an order to the Cedar
Creek Mercantile for a few other presents. With Christmas
coming, Simon seemed keen on following every little hint
about gifts. He was much more likely than the girls to poke

around in the house looking for them, too, so she was being very careful. Crafty as a fox.

And wasn't this anticipation of Christmas a huge improvement? During the past four years, the holidays had felt like *hollow* days, but now she cherished the presence of a husband and five additional children with whom to celebrate the Lord's birth. Then, on Second Christmas, they would play games, go for sleigh rides, and indulge in special treats. Even though they were watching their pennies, the simple pleasures of home and hearth—enjoying time together as a family—didn't have to strain their budget. Amanda was particularly pleased that the money she was earning with her pottery would cover the family's gifts as well as the chocolate, nuts, and other special ingredients Jemima wanted for their cookies and candies.

Amanda reached into the chest where she stored her clay and found the shopping list she'd hidden. If her luck held, she could make her phone call in the barn and the girls would be none the wiser.

When she entered the kitchen, however, the expression on Jerome's face stopped her in her tracks. He was standing in the middle of the room, looking as though he bore the weight of the world on his broad shoulders. "And what's on *your* mind?" Amanda asked. "I hope Simon didn't interfere with your training session."

Jerome flashed her a quick smile. "Did you send him out? He seemed eager for something to do."

"Let's just say Wyman came home—and left again—at a gut time. So I'm calling the mercantile for a few things." Amanda wasn't fooled by the way her nephew had dodged her question, but she knew better than to press him for details. "Do you need anything while I'm giving them my list?"

Once again Jerome's face changed, this time to suggest he knew something she didn't. But wasn't Christmas the time when everyone kept a few secrets?

"Raisins for a pie? Or the makings for a cherry cheese-cake?"

"There's a fine idea! I don't think we've had cherry cheesecake since last Christmas, and the twins love it, too." Amanda fetched her coat from its peg on the wall. "If the girls ask where I've gone, keep them in here, all right? I'll be back in a few."

As she stepped outside into the bright sunshine, Amanda felt exhilarated. She loved the crispness of sunny winter days, and the line of snowmen in the yard was one more thing to be thankful for this year. Once inside the barn, she dialed the number for the Cedar Creek Mercantile's phone shanty.

As Amanda listened to the rings, Jerome's mares and their mule foals shifted in their stalls, watching her. All legs and ears, the little ones appeared alert and curious— black they were, like their Percheron mamms. Amanda couldn't help smiling at them, pleased that the trio looked so healthy—which meant Jerome had been stewing over something else when she'd caught him in the kitchen.

"Jah, hello—this is Abby Graber."

Amanda laughed in her surprise. "And this is Amanda Brubaker. I wasn't expecting to hear *your* voice, Abby! If you could take this shopping list over to Sam, I'd like to pick my order up in a day or so."

"I'm back in the store through year's end, helping with the Christmas rush," Abby replied with her usual cheerful-ness. "Pencil's ready. What can I get for you?"

And wasn't *that* something, Abby working again? Once again circumstances seemed to play right into Amanda's plan. "I'd like three lined tablets—the kind kids use when they're learning to write their letters—and four pairs of stockings and kapps that would fit Jemima, and five cards of hairpins."

"Any baking supplies?" Abby asked. "We just got a shipment of colored sugars and jimmies, along with the bigger bags of chocolate chips. Thank goodness Emma ordered them before she stopped working in the back room, or we'd have run out."

"Emma quit? She seemed so tickled to be helping Sam."

"She had no say about it when Vernon and Sam figured out that she was wearing herself too thin," Abby explained. "But she's doing the store's book work at home now."

"Ah. Well, I bet Merle's happy to have her company, just as Sam's mighty glad to have you helping again," Amanda remarked. Then she glanced at her list again. "Jah, a couple bags of the chips, and two or three bags of your cookie sprinkles would be fun for decorating the girls' cookies—oh, and Jerome wants a big bag of raisins, plus two blocks of cream cheese and two cans of pie filling for a couple of cherry cheese pies."

"Ooh, can I come to your place when you make those?" Abby teased.

Amanda laughed. "Matter of fact, that's a fine idea—for Second Christmas! And bring Emma and Merle—and James, of course."

"Ach, I was teasing you, Amanda. You already have a houseful."

"No, please! We'd love to have you—unless you newly-weds have already made plans," Amanda insisted. "And while I'm thinking of it, cut me enough fabric to make shirts for Jerome, Wyman, and the two older boys—in two colors. Have you got purple, and maybe turquoise, in some no-iron shirting?"

"Jah, we've got those—but I'm hoping you won't want *me* to whip them up before Christmas," Abby remarked. "What with helping Sam again, my sewing orders are running a bit behind."

"Jemima and I can make them after the first of the year. And you know what?" Amanda added as another idea struck her. "If I have Jerome come after these things in a day or so, maybe he'll venture across the road to see Emma."

"He can take Eddie home, too, until after the holidays. We

haven't got room for his ladders, what with the extra shoppers, so he's been helping us in the hardware department—and sneaking peeks at Gail." Abby let out a short laugh. "Far as Jerome visiting with Emma, I *think* she'll enjoy seeing him— although she's not saying much on that subject. She's a tough nut to crack."

Amanda's eyebrows rose. She caught herself before she mentioned how smitten Emma had looked after her sleigh ride with Jerome, as she didn't want Abby to know about the two quilts they'd been working on. "We all have to bloom in our own time," she said quietly. "It took me a long while to consider seeing another man after Atlee passed, and I suspect Emma misses her mamm something awful. You never saw one without the other."

"She was devoted to Eunice," Abby agreed, with a little hitch in her voice. "Even if Jerome doesn't come to see Emma, Merle would be happy to have a visitor. The colder weather has kept him in his recliner of late, almost like a shut-in."

"I'll let Jerome know. He'll be there either Thursday or Friday. Denki so much, Abby."

As Amanda hung up, she wondered how things were going in the Graber household. Merle had delighted in playing with the children and eating cornmeal mush—and in speculating with Wyman about the Wengerds' motives as well. She had a hard time thinking of the sweet old fellow folding in on himself when he wasn't around other people. All the more reason to invite the Grabers for a day of Second Christmas festivities, to take their minds off their mourning.

When Amanda returned to the house, Jerome had the three little girls lined up in kitchen chairs and was putting on their snow boots. "We're going out in the sleigh to cut evergreen branches," Cora announced.

"Jah, because we got the Christmas candles out of the attic!" Dora chimed in.

"And Baby Jesus!" Alice Ann swung her booted feet with an excitement only a three-year-old could generate. "And widdle sheeps!"

When Jerome had helped the toddler to the floor, he smiled at Amanda. "Jemima asked me to carry the box with the Nativity set downstairs, so I figured it was time to fetch the fresh greenery. Our decorating will keep us busy after dinner while you work at your wheel."

"What a fine idea," Amanda replied. "I can glaze and fire Lois Yutzy's salad set—and I can't wait to see the front room when you're finished," she added with a big smile for the girls. "It's wonderful to have such gut helpers."

It touched her heart to watch Jerome button Alice Ann's coat and then playfully heft her to his shoulder as the twins dashed ahead of him. He would make such a wonderful father.

As the trio of girls headed out the door, Amanda pulled Jerome aside. "Just so you'll know," she murmured, "Emma's working on the mercantile's books at home now. Seems the bishop and Sam thought she was wearing herself too thin."

Jerome's eyebrows rose. "Glad to hear it. I was concerned about—well, a lot of things," he added with a smile.

"My order should be ready by tomorrow—or whenever you'd care to fetch it for me," Amanda hinted.

"Jah, I can do that. Denki, Aunt," he replied as he bussed her cheek. "You're the best."

"So you're saying Amanda just called in this order?" Wyman asked as he stood with Sam at the mercantile's front counter.

"Jah, and Abby said she's figuring on Jerome coming for it in a day or two," the storekeeper replied. "But if you've got some shopping to do, I can have everything boxed up by the time you're ready to check out."

"That's better than Jerome having to make a special trip. Let's do it."

Wyman didn't have to see the prices alongside all the items on the page to wonder if he had enough cash to cover them—not to mention anything he'd hoped to find for Amanda's Christmas gift. What could she possibly want with so much fabric, when she had no time to sew? And why couldn't the girls' stockings and kapps wait until next year, considering how they were watching their money so closely these days?

"It's too hectic for Eddie to be painting now, but he's a big help with the customers. I hope it's all right if I keep him into next week," Sam said. "He's got a gut head for figures and the patience for explaining how things work, so I've put him on the payroll."

Wyman's eyes widened. "But he's probably eating you out of house and—"

"Happy to have him," Sam insisted with a wave of his hand. "With the store so busy, he's making my life a lot easier, believe me. I'll have Abby cut that fabric and see you back here in a bit."

The mercantile *was* as crowded as Wyman had ever seen it, and it did his heart good to spot his eldest son over by the snow shovels. With a polite smile, Eddie was demonstrating the difference between a bent-handled model and the regular kind to an elderly English gentleman.

At least one of us is bringing in some money, he thought bleakly. Wyman wondered if Sam was paying Eddie out of sheer kindness—or, Lord forbid, *pity*—because he was aware of the Brubakers' financial straits. His first impulse had been to cancel Amanda's order, at least until he could quiz her about the need for some of the things on her list . . .

"Dat, let's look at fishing gear!" Simon said, pointing toward the display of rods along the wall. "We've got a pond now, so we'll be needing—"

"Not today, Son."

"But, Dat! If the water's going to freeze, don't we need to get the fish out before they die?" the boy went on, his voice rising. "They'll turn into Popsicles, or—or fishsicles!"

Wyman caught himself before he snapped at Simon again. It wasn't his son's fault that he was preoccupied with how little progress Reece Weaver had made on his grain elevator. Nor had Simon phoned in such a long, expensive store order. Wyman stooped to his son's level. "The fish will spend the winter near the bottom, where the water won't freeze," he explained. "They'll have enough oxygen to breathe."

"So can I find a present for Mamm? I want her to have a real nice Christmas."

Wyman's heart flew up into his throat as two brown button eyes gazed into his. It was such a blessing that his boy considered Amanda his mother now. "I want her to have a real nice Christmas, too, Simon," he murmured, searching for words that conveyed the right tone. "But it's not really about the gifts, you know."

"Jah, it's all about Jesus," the boy replied without missing a beat. "But the Wise Men brought *Him* presents—and they were silly perfume things that a baby wouldn't even use."

Wyman choked on a laugh. "We can't judge what men back in Bible times selected as gifts. They were giving Jesus gold and precious oils to—"

"Oil!" Simon dug down into his coat pocket and brought up some one-dollar bills. "I'll get Mamm some cooking oil—'cause it's *gold*, too! Jerome paid me for helping with the horses this week."

Simon's logic beat adult reasoning hands-down, so Wyman started toward the grocery aisle. At least his boy would have a gift he was excited about giving—and maybe something would jump out at Wyman as a gift for Amanda until he could afford something . . . worthy of her. It rubbed him like a burr under a horse's blanket, to be so strapped for cash at this time of year. It galled him even more that this situation stemmed from his own lack of judgment about how thin to stretch his money, and about Reece Weaver's character as well.

Wyman felt out of place amongst the pie plates and measuring cups, and he didn't see anything that Amanda didn't already have. As he followed Simon toward the next aisle, however, he noticed that Sam and Abby were having an intense discussion next to the fabric counter. And when Abby looked at *him*, her face conveyed an emotion he couldn't interpret.

Now what have I done? Wyman wondered if he would ever reach a point where women didn't befuddle him. At least Simon was snatching up a bottle of canola oil as though he'd found the perfect gift—and indeed, Amanda would be pleased with the boy's biblical explanation, and she would put Simon's oil to good use.

"I'm all set, Dat! And I can color a design on the grocery sack, to use it for my wrapping paper," Simon added with a satisfied nod. "But don't tell the girls, okay?"

"I wouldn't spoil your surprise for anything." As Wyman watched his son skip along the aisle, deftly dodging other shoppers as he held his bottle of oil high, he wished for some of Simon's ingenuity . . . just a hint at some little thing . . .

At the end of the grocery aisle, Wyman grasped a jar of dill pickles—*because I'm certainly in a pickle,* he mused. He chatted with Eddie for a few moments, catching up with his son while Abby got Amanda's order together. When she bustled toward the counter with an armload of bundles wrapped in brown paper, Wyman made his way over to check out. It was a treat to watch Simon hand his money up to Sam and then hold the bagged bottle to his chest as though it were indeed as precious as myrrh.

"You've got quite a shopper here," Sam remarked as he punched button after button, tallying Amanda's bill. "Simon chose a brand that's on sale this week—ain't so?" he asked the boy.

"It's all gut!" Simon crowed as he stuffed two dollars back into his coat pocket.

Remember that—it's all gut. The ultimate statement of faith, Wyman mused as he set down the pickle jar and took out his wallet. He sighed inwardly as Abby added a bunch of hairpins—*hairpins,* of which they already had dozens at home!—and waited for the total of Amanda's purchases.

"Comes to a hundred twenty-seven dollars and seventy-five cents," Sam said.

"Oof. I didn't know I'd be picking up all this extra stuff," Wyman murmured as he counted out a fifty and some twenties.

"Your credit's gut with me," Sam replied. "Not a problem at all."

"I pay my bills," Wyman insisted, "and you've been way too generous these past couple of months, as it is. Phooey. I'm shy by a buck and half. This is downright—"

Simon elbowed his thigh.

"Just a minute, Son, I—" Wyman glanced down and his breath caught in his throat. His boy was holding up the two ones he'd just pocketed, smiling like a mop-haired cherub.

"Got you covered, Dat."

A wondrous love for his son filled his heart, as well as yet another lesson about childlike *faith.* Didn't Simon always believe things would work out right—sometimes in spite of adults' nay-saying? Wyman cupped his hand around the boy's downy cheek and then accepted the money. "I'll pay you back as soon as we get home," he said. "I'm pleased you were so quick to share your money with me, Simon."

"I wish some of the other boys who've been in the store lately could see what you just did," Sam added with a nod. "The Lord loves a cheerful giver."

Wyman added the pickles to Simon's paper bag and then grabbed Amanda's bulky bundles and her grocery sack. As they started for home, he was grateful that his boy was such a happy chatterbox today, for it kept the heavier subjects on his mind from bogging him down.

"Will you help me color holly and red bows and ever-green branches on my paper sack, Dat?"

Wyman smiled, picturing himself at the table with crayons—an activity he really didn't have time for. *Why not? Don't you recall how you cherished every moment your dat spent with you at Simon's age?* And designing paper for Christmas packages would certainly be more fun than the phone call to Reece Weaver he had to make when he got home.

"Tell you what," he replied. "If we use one of the sheets of brown paper Abby wrapped your mamm's stuff in, we'll have a piece big enough to wrap your gift and mine, too."

Simon's eyes got wide. "But all you bought was pickles! Is that what you're giving Mamm?"

Wyman leaned sideways until his nose nearly met his boy's. "It's a secret, what-all I'm getting her, so you can't say a word. Promise?"

Simon made a big X across his chest with his mittened finger. "Jah, promise. I can't wait to see her face when she opens *that* one."

Wyman laughed. He could only hope Amanda would accept his explanation of the pickles as readily as she would love Simon's story about the Wise Men and his oil. Considering how most of his morning had gone, he was going to need a lot of heavenly intervention if this Christmas was to be as wonderful as he'd intended.

Chapter 22

I'll be in after I make a phone call," Wyman said as he climbed out of the buggy. "How about if you see what we can have for a quick lunch, Simon?"

"Jah! After I hide my present up in my room," the boy replied as he scrambled down to the floor of the barn. "I'll hide yours, too, okay?"

"That'll be gut. Denki." As his boy slid the barn door shut, Wyman unhitched the Belgian and gathered his thoughts. He'd been stewing over this phone call to Reece Weaver ever since this morning, when he'd seen that *nothing* had been done on his elevator after the foundation for the big bins had been poured. It wasn't his way to be confrontational, but a new tactic was necessary if he was to command his contractor's full attention—and get what he'd already paid for.

Guide my mind and my tongue, Lord, he prayed as he picked up the receiver and dialed. Wyman heard the third ring . . . the fourth, and then the funny ring that signaled he was being transferred into Reece's voice mail. He could picture Weaver recognizing the Brubaker number on the window of his cell phone and refusing to answer—maybe for several more days. So he'd have to leave a message that would get results.

"Jah, Reece, it's Wyman, and I'm not at all pleased at what I saw—or rather, did *not* see—at the elevator site this morning," he said in a rising voice. "Unless I hear your assurances that the bins will be going up by the end of this week, I'll be contacting my lawyer. Christmas season or not, I won't accept empty assurances rather than visible progress on my elevator. Call me."

Wyman's stomach clutched with more than hunger as he hung up. He didn't *have* a lawyer, and the idea of consulting an English attorney went against his religious convictions, but he hoped Reece would take him seriously now. He and Ray had made more than enough phone calls lately, and Weaver's lack of response was gnawing on him. He was beginning to wonder if he'd been altogether wrong to expand his business—much less to choose Reece as his contractor. Considering what he stood to lose if this project went wrong . . .

It's got to go right. There's just no other way.

As Wyman gathered Amanda's bulky packages into his arms, he prepared himself for the next little chat he needed to have, with his wife—now, before the older kids got home. He'd always considered Amanda a prudent, conscientious shopper, but this morning's spending spree had to be addressed if they were to get through the next several months without owing Sam and every other area merchant a bunch of money. He was as averse to running up a tab—being beholden to anyone—as he was to getting into a legal hassle with Reece. He would go right into the pottery workroom and—

"Wyman!" Amanda said in a strained voice as she threw open the door. "Why'd you bring those packages home? Abby and I had agreed that—"

"I was saving Jerome a trip." He reminded himself to remain calm but direct, because it seemed that Amanda, too, was in a confrontational mood.

"But we agreed that Jerome could fetch them in a day or two and pay for everything with money from the pottery orders he'll be delivering for me." Amanda leaned closer and lowered her voice. "Now I suppose Simon knows every little thing I got him and the girls for Christmas."

Wyman's heart thudded dully. As he faced his wife across the top of the bundles he held, he noticed that she'd been crying. Her flummoxed expression suggested she was about ready to start up again. "I had no idea—"

"Jah, and now you've seen some of *your* presents as well."

"Because Sam didn't let on about—"

"Well, Sam doesn't know everything!" Amanda blurted. "And now Jerome has no reason to go into town and visit with Emma, or—oh, just get inside and shut the door! Bring those packages into my workroom before the girls hear you're home and come downstairs."

Wyman had never been one to let a woman manipulate him or make him feel guilty, yet he kept his mouth shut as he followed Amanda through the kitchen. From what he could tell, he'd foiled a little Christmas scheme by going along with Sam's practicality . . . which also explained why Abby and her brother had engaged in such an intense discussion at the fabric table, and then Abby had scowled at *him*.

When he entered the room where Amanda's pottery wheel, kiln, and shelves of supplies were set up, she quickly shut the door behind him. As she opened the closet and pointed for him to put his bundles inside it, Wyman noticed the broom and dustpan near a pile of shattered cobalt and cinnamon-colored pottery on the floor. "Uh-oh. What happened here?" he asked gently.

Amanda exhaled loudly. "Jemima and the girls were decorating the front room, and when I was taking one of Lois's bowls out of the kiln, Alice Ann came up behind me with the Baby Jesus from the Nativity set. She was *so* excited—but she startled me, and then the bowl hit the floor. And so did Jesus."

Wyman's face fell. His toddler was just beginning to grasp the Christmas story, at least the fact that barn animals and a special baby were involved, and she had to be heartbroken. Just as Amanda was.

"I know it's only ceramic," Amanda went on with a sad sigh, "but Alice Ann was beside herself about breaking Jesus, and the pieces are too tiny to glue together . . . and it was from a Nativity that's been passed down in my mamm's family."

Amanda turned away, crossing her arms tightly as she got her emotions under control. After a few moments she faced him again. "I'm sorry I got upset, Wyman," she murmured. "I just wanted this first Christmas to be the best ever for all of us and—"

"We all want that," he murmured.

"I'll pay you back for those presents when—"

"No, you won't," Wyman insisted. "It's not your place to—"

"Please, let's not fight about it!" Amanda blurted. Her shoulders slumped. "Now that I think back, I didn't tell Abby I was Christmas shopping," she admitted. "I'm sorry, Wyman. The whole morning's been jagged around the edges."

"I'm sorry, too, Amanda. I really didn't mean to spoil your surprises." Wyman opened his arms, grateful that his wife entered into his embrace and wrapped her arms around him. His morning had felt pretty jagged, too, and yet as pressing as his problems with Reece and the family finances had felt, those concerns now seemed petty compared to the trauma of breaking the most important piece of a beloved family Nativity set.

As Amanda let go of her tension, Wyman held her closer, savoring her warmth and the way she fit so perfectly against him. Last year at this time, he'd felt desolate and overwhelmed, wishing the Christmas season would pass him by so he wouldn't have to face it—and the kids—without Viola. He'd been financially well-off then, but a broken man nonetheless.

Wyman breathed deeply, inhaling Amanda's clean scent. He held her for a few moments more. Simon and the girls weren't used to seeing the door to this room shut, so they'd soon be knocking on it out of concern or curiosity. It was probably in his best interest to talk about something less emotionally charged—which certainly didn't include voicing his frustrations about Reece Weaver—so Wyman considered his topic options carefully.

"Is there any way I can have a sheet of that brown paper that's wrapped around some of your packages?" he asked. "I promise I won't look at what's in them—and Simon, by the way, didn't see what you got him or the other kids, either. He was too busy picking out his gift for you—and he bought it with his own money, too."

Amanda looked up at him, a smile lighting her face. "Jah, I suppose I could—"

"He's asked me to help him design his wrapping paper," Wyman explained as he thumbed a final tear from her cheek. "I think I'll take a couple of sandwiches upstairs so we men can color in his room for a while."

"Oh, he'll love that, Wyman."

"And I love *you*, Amanda," he murmured, holding her gaze. "Can you forgive me for thinking that my way surely must be right and that I always know best?"

Never would he have asked his previous wife such a question, but Amanda wasn't Viola. Today's shopping episode was one more reminder that *change* was in order—and that such changes started from within. Wyman held his breath as the woman in his arms kept him waiting for her answer.

"Jah, I can do that," Amanda finally whispered. "I love you, too, Wyman."

Wyman kissed her. He noticed that she hadn't asked for his forgiveness in return—but then, why did she need to?

That was another example of his old way of thinking. Instead, his wife had offered him the perfect response to almost anything she would ever ask of him: *Jah, I can do that.*

Because with Amanda by his side, Wyman believed he really could do anything.

Before dawn the next morning, Wyman headed out to the barn as though he intended to get an early start on the chores. After seeing the Nativity set in the front room yesterday, with all the pieces except for the most important one, he'd thought long into the night about how to remedy the situation. The crèche probably dated back to the early 1900s, and the sets being made today were far less detailed. But he had to try. He lit the lantern and then dialed the phone.

"Jah, it's Wyman," he said when the Fishers' answering machine kicked on. "I'd like Tyler to give me a call, about seeing if he can locate something on his computer. It's a Christmas gift, so he'll have to talk to me rather than Amanda or Jerome. Have a gut day—and I wish your family a blessed Christmas."

As he hung up, a sense of anticipation and peace filled him. Chances were slim that a Baby Jesus of the right size and style could be ordered and delivered in the week that remained before Christmas—if ever—but it was a mission Wyman could wrap his heart around. He walked slowly down the center aisle of the barn, gazing at Jerome's mule foals as they slept in the hay near their mothers. The shadowy stalls smelled earthy with manure, and the winter wind whistled through a crack.

Once again Wyman was reminded how humble and lowly the Christ Child's beginnings had been and how blessed he was that his own children had a sturdy roof over their heads and a mother to care for them. Amanda had provided his family with a great many gifts to be grateful for this year.

Behind him, the door slid open. In the lantern light,

Jerome's expression looked tight. "Is Pete out here with you?" he asked.

"Nope, it's just me and the livestock. Why?" Wyman replied.

Jerome shut the door against the wind. "When I heard you go downstairs, I thought I'd shake him awake, so you wouldn't be doing the chores by yourself. But his bed hasn't been slept in. Looks like a bunch of his clothes are gone, too."

Wyman gripped the top railing of the stall to steady himself. Then he hurried along the center aisle, taking a count of their horses and rigs, his heart racing along with his footsteps. "How'd he get out of here without any of us knowing? Or without Wags barking?"

"The dog sleeps in Simon's room," Jerome reminded him. "What with the way Pete's been talking about how useless school seems—"

"And how much he dislikes Teacher Dorcas," Wyman joined in, "maybe we should've seen this coming. Blackie's gone, but none of the rigs, so he's on horseback." He stopped, still puzzled, to stare into the empty stall where their oldest gelding usually stayed. "But where on God's gut earth would Pete *go*? Do you suppose he said anything to Vera or Lizzie?"

"They would've told you or Amanda after they tried to talk him out of it."

As Jerome came to stand beside him, Wyman recalled more incidents and remarks than he cared to . . . times when Pete had expressed his unhappiness, and then *he* had responded with the usual stern fatherly insistence that his son follow the rules.

"You know, this probably started when Amanda and I first married," Wyman murmured. "When the two oldest boys made a fuss about moving to this farm, I told them that if they didn't want to pull their weight in our new blended family, they should get out and make their own way."

"You couldn't have foreseen this, Wyman," Jerome assured him. "Boys go through this stage—just like you and I did at thirteen. But that doesn't mean we took off."

Wyman chuckled ruefully. "Speak for yourself. I recall more than a night or two when I didn't go home, but I was older than Pete—in my rumspringa. I was out with Mennonite or English boys my parents didn't approve of."

"But you eventually faced them and took the lecture you had coming."

"Jah, that's how it worked."

Jerome paused to collect his thoughts. "I suspect Pete'll be back as soon as he misses a few meals. And I can't think any Plain man would hire him or take him in without asking him why he's on the loose, young as he is."

"Haven't heard him mention any gut friends he's made around here . . . and if he's gone back to Clearwater, any of those parents would call me—or at least I hope they would," Wyman reasoned aloud.

"It'll be the same if he's gone to Cedar Creek," Jerome pointed out. "Maybe he hopes to work with Eddie—"

"If so, Sam will call as soon as Pete shows up. And there's no point in taking off down the road looking for him while it's still dark."

"It's probably best to wait him out," Jerome remarked as he grabbed a bucket and headed for the feed bins. "Pete's not world-wise enough to get far."

While Wyman refilled water troughs, he thought back to when he'd come down on Pete for teasing Lizzie—downright flirting with his new stepsister—during her brief time at the Clearwater school and again over the past few weeks, when Pete had wanted to contribute to the family's income. What could he have said or done differently?

But stewing over the past wouldn't accomplish anything. After he and Jerome mucked out the stalls, they went back to the house. He'd never had to deal with the issue of a runaway child before, so he hoped other family members would have helpful suggestions. "Anybody know where

Pete might be?" he asked in the calmest voice he could muster. "Looks like he took off on Blackie sometime during the night."

He realized then that everyone in the kitchen was very quiet. Jemima's brow was furrowed as she took the skillet of bacon from the stove burner. The younger kids began to chatter about all manner of places to look, as though Pete were merely playing hide-and-seek. Vera nipped her lip as she handed him a folded piece of notebook paper. "This was under my door this morning," she murmured.

When Wyman opened the paper, Pete's message made his breath catch in his throat. *Heard about a job, so I'm off to check it out. Don't worry about me.* "As though we could just let him be out there somewhere without worrying," he murmured as he passed the page to Jerome. Amanda came over to him, her face pale and her eyes wide.

"This isn't gut. And so close to Christmas," she fretted. "Pete's been too quiet—too much to himself—ever since we moved here."

"It's not like he buddies up to the boys at school," Lizzie remarked with a frown, "so maybe he headed back to Clearwater."

"We can go looking for him after breakfast!" Simon piped up.

"And on the way to Clearwater, maybe we should stop in Cedar Creek," Vera suggested. "When Pete heard that Eddie was clerking in the store, he looked like he wanted to do that, too."

"Sam'll be calling as soon as Pete gets there, if that's the case," Jemima remarked as she put the bacon on a plate. "He'll not get far without *somebody* letting us know."

"Unless he went someplace amongst English," Lizzie said in a somber voice. "He's talked about trying that life, even though he has no clue about how to survive in their world."

"He can't go far without any cash," Jerome pointed out.

Jemima got a funny look on her face. She took a cocoa can from the drawer of the pie safe and popped the top. "My egg money's gone," she said somberly. "I'd saved up nearly a hundred dollars, too."

Scowling, Amanda quickly left the kitchen. When she returned, her crestfallen expression said as much as her words. "I had more than three hundred dollars in an old teapot in my workroom," she rasped. "I—I can't believe Pete would *steal* . . . unless he doesn't intend to come back. He could go quite a distance on that much money."

Wyman's heart clutched. The money issue put a different spin on letting Pete tough it out until he came home hungry. He didn't think the kid would abandon his favorite horse in favor of a bus or a train—but then, he hadn't gauged *any* of his second son's reactions correctly, it seemed. "I think we'd better pray on it," he murmured.

As the family members took their seats around the table and bowed their heads, Wyman asked God for guidance with a fervor he'd seldom needed. He felt so helpless . . . at a loss for answers. But he was the man of the family, and everyone would be looking to him for direction.

"After I drop Vera and Lizzie off this morning, I'll go out looking for him," he announced when everyone had looked up again. "We've got to have faith that God's aware of Pete's circumstances and whereabouts and that He's working this situation out as a part of His plan—for Pete and for us as well."

Wyman wished he felt more confident about *how* God was guiding his troubled son. Sometimes boys in their rumspringa took off—jobs or not—for parts unknown, but he didn't know of any thirteen-year-olds who'd run away from home. He wished he'd paid more attention, maybe been more sympathetic instead of so prone to lecture his lonely, left-out son . . .

After Wyman dropped Lizzie at the schoolhouse and Vera at Leon Schrock's place, he turned the rig toward

Cedar Creek. Pete probably didn't realize that any responsible Plain adult would call the house as soon as folks hereabouts knew he'd run off. Wyman scanned the countryside as he drove, looking for any sign of a rider on a black horse, but the hour he spent on the road did nothing to soothe his concerns. When he got into Cedar Creek, neither Eddie nor Sam had heard from Pete, either.

"We'll keep an eye out," Sam assured him. "Pete doesn't seem the type to venture out on his own."

"I know it goes against our grain to get the police involved," Wyman murmured, "but maybe I should let the sheriff know that Pete's run off."

Sam shook his head. "As a dat, I understand your thinking, but as a preacher, I'm not in favor of that. It's not like Pete was kidnapped, and he left you a note about taking a job," he pointed out. "Far better to let your Plain friends around the area know what's happened, because they're more likely to spot him, anyway. We'll keep this situation in our prayers, Wyman."

"I told him not to get any wild ideas—to put up with school until he gets out next spring," Eddie said, shaking his head. "He won't get far. Pete's not gut at thinking on his feet. And any money he makes burns a hole in his pocket, so he's basically broke."

Wyman didn't have the heart to mention that Pete had stolen more than four hundred dollars from Amanda and Jemima. It was this theft that lay so heavily on his heart as he got back into his rig and headed to Clearwater. All around the back roads he drove, stopping at every farmstead and getting the same surprised response from folks he'd known most of his life. Nobody could believe that shy, quiet Pete would disappear into the night.

The Fishers, too, said they would call the moment they heard of anyone spotting his son. "Pete's a gut boy," Sally affirmed. "He's just ferhoodled by the changes in his life these past months. We'll keep him in our prayers, that he'll be back home soon."

Wyman thanked them, hoping they were right. After a desperate morning on the road, he found it a welcome bright spot when Tyler found a Baby Jesus figurine on his computer. It wasn't the same as the one Alice Ann had dropped, but the size and style in the photo appeared close enough to complete their Nativity set without looking odd.

"This close to Christmas, there's no telling when it'll arrive—unless you want to pay for express shipping. Might run you twenty bucks or so," Tyler remarked as his fingers flew over the keyboard.

Wyman shook his head. "Seems foolish to waste money I could use for other things. We'll keep our Nativity set displayed a little longer, if need be—extend our Advent and the time of waiting for Jesus. Having the new baby in the manger will be a nice finish for our Christmas season." He counted out enough cash to cover the figurine's price, plus some more to cover the tax and standard shipping.

As he headed back to Bloomingdale, Wyman wondered if this was how it would be with Pete as well—*waiting* until he came home . . . wondering where he was and who he was with . . . or who would even consider hiring a thirteen-year-old kid for any kind of job.

When Wyman got back home, no one had heard anything about Pete. Reece Weaver hadn't returned his call, either. Advent, the season of longing and waiting and watching for a savior, took on a whole new meaning as the day crawled by. In a week, they'd be celebrating Christ's birth, and then the next day was Second Christmas, the merrier of the holidays. But if his son hadn't returned home by then, there would be little joy in the household.

Wyman prayed that his family wouldn't spend this first Christmas together worrying about a lost sheep rather than rejoicing over the Lamb of God.

Chapter 23

Emma finished the border on the afghan she was crocheting for James and Abby and folded it on the sofa with a great sense of satisfaction. She sensed the newlyweds would love cuddling together beneath this coverlet of red, blue, purple, and green as much as she had enjoyed working with such bold colors. With a glance at Dat, who had drifted off in his recliner, she went into the kitchen to stir the pot of vegetable beef soup she was making for their noonday meal. As she looked out the window, Emma thought how bleak and gray this winter morning looked— until a buggy pulled around the carriage shop and up beside the house.

Her heart fluttered. She knew of only one fellow who hitched his rig to a black Percheron mule.

As Emma fetched her coat from the peg beside the door, she glanced into the front room. Dat was still snoozing beneath the copy of the *Budget* he'd been reading. Grinning from ear to ear, she hurried out through the kitchen's back door. "Jerome! What a fine surprise!" she said as she slipped into her coat.

His face lit up. "Emma, it's gut to see you. I've been out looking for our Pete—"

"He's not come home yet?" Emma's smile faded. She stopped a few feet in front of Jerome, noting the concern etched around his dark eyes. "Wyman and Amanda must be beside themselves."

"Jah, my aunt's been calling the folks around Blooming-dale since he went missing yesterday, and Wyman and I have been out looking again this morning," he replied. Then his handsome face eased into a smile. "But I was also hoping to spend some time with *you*, Emma. I—I've missed you this week."

"Oh my," she murmured as her pulse sped up. "I keep thinking about our sleigh ride—"

"Jah, me, too," Jerome interrupted as he grabbed her hands. "And I've almost called you a dozen times—"

"And I hope you didn't get the wrong idea when I didn't kiss you gut night," Emma continued in a rush.

"But I didn't want James or Sam or anybody but you to hear my message," Jerome went on in a breathy voice. Then he laughed, rubbing her bare hands between his gloved ones. "Seems we've both been saving up what we wanted to say, and it's all rushing out at once. So . . . you weren't upset because I wanted a kiss too soon? Or because I didn't stop on my way home from escorting the Wengerds back to Queen City?"

Emma pressed her lips into a line. All the frustrating circumstances he'd mentioned seemed petty now that he'd surprised her with a visit. "Well, I *did* wonder if you didn't stop because you were . . . disappointed in me."

"Oh, Emmie-girl, how could I be disappointed in *you*?" Jerome wrapped his arms around her and swayed her from side to side before loosening his hold. "And yet here I go again, getting too close for your comfort, maybe."

Emma gazed up into his shining eyes. *Emmie-girl* he'd called her—a nickname only Dat and James had ever used, but it sounded particularly nice when Jerome said it. "Well," she said as her cheeks got hot, "if any of the fellows in James's shop happen to be looking out, we're giving them quite an eyeful, ain't so? How about some coffee? And we've got fried pies and lemon bars and—"

"Say no more! I love your lemon bars."

When Jerome kept hold of her hand as they headed back to the house, Emma wasn't sure her feet were touching the ground. She'd felt restless these past couple of days, since Sam and Vernon had insisted she work at home, yet now she was glad she'd been here when Jerome pulled in. "Dat's been napping," she murmured as they entered the kitchen. "He'll be real glad to see you."

"Before we rouse him, maybe I'll just stand here sniffing whatever smells so gut," Jerome replied. He closed his eyes and inhaled deeply. "Soup with beef in it, jah?"

Emma chuckled at his ecstatic expression. "There's plenty for you, if you care to stay. Abby and James usually come home for dinner around twelve fifteen."

"Denki, but I told Amanda I'd get back with a few odds and ends she wanted from the mercantile." He opened his eyes and held her gaze. "So, do you miss working at the store, Emma? It's a shame Sam and Vernon made you quit, if you enjoyed what you were doing."

Emma hung up their coats and went to the stove to stir the soup. "I'm still doing the work I like the most—the bookkeeping—and it's better for Dat if I'm home now that Abby's helping Sam through the Christmas season. And truth be told, I was getting . . . crabbier than I realized." She stopped there, as Jerome didn't need to hear about the hissy fit she'd pitched about using Amanda's dishes rather than Mamm's.

"You were tired when you came to our place last weekend," Jerome agreed as he came to stand beside her. "I suspect none of us realize how much effort goes into running that store, because Sam and Abby just *do* it without any apparent effort. Starting any new job takes a lot of energy until you're used to it."

"Denki for understanding that," Emma murmured. She removed the snap-on top from the pan of goodies on the counter. When she gave Jerome a lemon bar, he took hold of her hand to guide the treat to his mouth.

He held her gaze as Emma held her breath. Standing this close to Jerome felt even more exhilarating than when she'd been sitting beneath the quilts with him in the sleigh. As he bit into the lemon bar and chewed, his smile delighted her.

"While I was all for you working in Sam's store if you wanted to," Jerome murmured, "I'm old-fashioned enough to like it better that you're home again. It takes a lot of effort to keep a household running smoothly, too, and you've always made *that* seem effortless."

Emma's brows rose. "I'd never call *you* old-fashioned, Jerome," she protested, but then he put the unbitten side of the lemon bar to her lips. She took a bite, wondering where he was leading her with this quiet conversation . . . these unexpectedly intimate gestures.

"Isn't this nice? Just the two of us in the kitchen?" he asked as she chewed. "It's cozy here. Real homey. And it reminds me that while I tend to run off at the mouth and look before I leap—like when I almost spent a couple thousand bucks on a wedding gift—you go on quietly about your tasks with such a sense of purpose. When I'm with you, Emma, I feel so much more grounded and—and—"

Jerome stopped midsentence, lowering his lips toward hers.

Behind them, Dat chuckled. "Are my old eyes fooling me, or is Jerome Lambright standing at the stove with my daughter?"

Emma jumped away from Jerome. She'd been *this close*

to kissing him. She should've realized that Dat might interrupt them.

But Jerome didn't seem the least bit flustered. He turned to offer the cookie container to her father. "Merle, it's gut to see you," he said with a chuckle. "You'd better have some of these lemon bars before I eat every last one of them."

"I'm more in the mood for dunking some of Emma's gingersnaps in a mug of coffee," he replied as he took a seat at the kitchen table. "She bakes them nice and crisp so they'll hold together."

Jerome winked at Emma and joined her dat, placing the cookie pan on the table between them. His confident grin belonged to the fellow she'd been running from a few weeks ago, yet he'd mellowed. Even though Dat had startled her at the wrong moment, it felt like the most natural thing in the world to set mugs on the table for him and Jerome and to pour them fresh coffee from the percolator. *Cozy and homey, like Jerome said earlier. It's lucky for me that the two of them are gut friends.*

Emma stirred the soup again while Jerome brought her father up to date about Pete's situation. There was nothing out of the ordinary about this visit from Jerome, yet he was making her feel very special.

"Could be Pete doesn't want to be found," Dat remarked as he took a handful of gingersnaps. "And if the job he mentioned in his note didn't pan out, he could be hiding in barns or any number of places, not all that far away."

Emma turned toward them, frowning. "But how would he eat? And stay warm on these cold nights?" she asked.

Jerome chose another lemon bar. "Pete left in the night, while everyone else was asleep, so he might've packed along some food."

"You'd think folks would notice an extra horse in their barn, though," Dat remarked matter-of-factly. "I'm betting Wyman gets word of him before the weekend's past. Pete'll either slip up and somebody'll catch him, or he'll head on back to Bloomingdale when he's tired of hiding. Then again," Dat added, "Pete might be miles away by now, with no intention of going home. A Bontrager kid I grew up with ran off like that."

Emma blinked. For all her thoughts of how Dat might be losing touch, he was making astute observations—as he always seemed to do when he was with Jerome. It was too soon to be seriously thinking of marriage, yet the benefits of spending more time with Jerome seemed to be adding up for both her and her father. At least she didn't feel like running in the other direction when he flirted with her now.

Emma lowered the flame under the soup pot. While the men kept chatting, she went into the front room to fetch the afghan she'd finished. When she paused in the kitchen doorway with the coverlet made of blue, red, purple, and deep green granny squares, Jerome's expression made Emma hold her breath.

"And what've you got here?" he asked as he rose from the table. "The way those bold colors are held together with black reminds me of stained-glass windows you see in old churches. May I take a better look?"

Emma's heart danced. She had hoped Jerome would like her afghan, but she hadn't anticipated the intensity of his interest as he unfolded it so they could hold it between them. "I've been crocheting this for Abby and James's wedding gift—which has been a lot easier now that she's working in the store again," Emma added.

"And they'll *love* it." Jerome held her gaze for a moment. "Here's another reason I'm glad we didn't buy something on our shopping trip," he continued. "Nothing in the stores compares to this beautiful gift you've made with your own hands, Emma. See there? You might've been hurrying past all the stuff I wanted to look at, but you were *right* about what Abby and James would rather receive."

Emma blinked. Jerome had just put a new spin on their awkward shopping trip. His difference in perspective made her feel better about that day, and it also cast a new light on his personality. Whereas she'd once considered him flashy and overconfident, Emma now saw a fellow who was trying to improve her perception of herself . . . a man who appreciated her quiet, reserved temperament.

After Jerome finished his coffee, he put on his coat, blowing Emma a kiss as he went outside to his rig.

"The more I'm around that fellow, the more I like him," Dat said. "I'm glad Jerome's in it for the long haul and not giving up on you."

Emma smiled to herself as she tucked the afghan into a trunk so Abby and James wouldn't see it. Once again Dat was spot-on with his observations—and she, too, was thinking Jerome's visit had done them both a world of good.

After they'd eaten their noon meal and Abby and James had returned to work, Emma pawed through her bin of yarn. Over the years, she and Mamm had crocheted several projects, so surely she could do something useful with these partial skeins, especially now that Jerome had shown such an interest in her handiwork. When she unfolded the yellowed instruction sheet Mamm had used to make stocking caps for James and Dat, Emma felt as though she'd found buried treasure.

The perfect gift idea! Dat's poor old cap is hardly fit to wear to the barn.

Soon she was settled on the sofa with her feet up, forming row after circular row in navy blue—almost as though Mamm were sitting with her, passing a winter's afternoon beside the woodstove. By the time Abby came home at the end of the day, Emma was finishing off the final row of the cap.

"What do you think?" she asked as she held it up. "Dat needs a new hat for these cold days, and I thought James could use one, too."

Abby took the hat between her hands, looking it over. "You've crocheted all this since dinner? You've got flying fingers, Emma!"

"It's a simple pattern," she pointed out. "Doesn't take much thought—"

"And it would make a gut gift for Jerome, too, ain't so?" Abby asked with a knowing grin. Then her eyes widened. "What if you were to make some of these in kids' colors to sell in the store? Folks would snap them up."

Emma's eyebrows rose. It would be a nice change of pace to work with brighter colors. "Well," she hedged, "if nobody buys my hats, I can always donate them to the mud auction next spring—"

"Ach, but you're silly sometimes," Abby teased. "Haven't you noticed what English kids—even girls Gail's age—are wearing these days? Bright colored parkas with caps like these. Some of them have earflaps with braided pigtails on the ends, and some even have animal faces or big flowers on them. We've got patterns for those in the store. What do you think?"

"I think I'll make a quick trip to the mercantile!" Emma replied. "I need to fetch Sam's receipts for the week anyway, and crocheting hats will give me something to do while you and James go to Breckenridge for the weekend."

Emma slipped into her coat and bonnet and crossed the snow-packed road. The mercantile's parking lot was jammed with cars and buggies, and when she stepped inside the store, she was amazed at the number of folks who'd come to Cedar Creek to shop. As she made her way toward the yarn goods section, Emma paid close attention to what the kids and teenagers were wearing on their heads. To her surprise, even a few young men sported the kind of knitted hats with earflaps and pigtails that Abby had mentioned—and none of the caps were in the dark, dull colors that filled her yarn bin.

Emma found an instruction booklet for earflap caps that included a couple of other styles as well. What a treat it was to shop for yarn in such fresh colors! The basket on her arm was soon stuffed with variegated and solid skeins in neon pink, lime green, aqua, lavender, and bright white. She hoped Abby was right about people wanting her homemade hats, because she'd have to sell several of them to earn back what she'd be spending.

"You've got quite a collection of colors here!" Gail remarked as she rang up Emma's order. "I bet I know what you'll be doing this weekend."

"Jah, you guessed it," Emma replied. She didn't want to reveal her plans for these flashy colors, because everyone who crocheted had met up with patterns that didn't turn out the way they looked in the pictures. Even so, just imagining the different styles of hats she wanted to try made her itch to start one *right now*, instead of eating supper. And wasn't *that* something!

When Abby and James stepped into the house early Sunday afternoon, after the threat of snow shortened their visit with cousins in Breckenridge, Abby felt a difference in the atmosphere. Although the skies were clouded over, Emma was humming while she took a rectangular pan of chocolate cake from the oven. A pot of heavenly smelling potato soup simmered on the stove. Merle was poring over the latest issue of the *Budget* at the kitchen table, reading snippets to Emma just as he'd once done with Eunice.

"This is a cozy scene," James remarked as he hung up his coat. "What-all went on while Abby and I were away?"

"You didn't miss a thing," Merle insisted.

Emma's lips twitched with a secretive grin. "You'll find out when you go upstairs to unpack."

Abby nearly asked if Jerome had stopped by again, but Merle would have mentioned that. "I'm headed that way right now, and then I'll be down to help with dinner. Whatever you've got in the oven smells awfully gut."

"I'll be right behind you, Abby-girl, so don't go hefting that box," James said as he clapped his dat on the back. "The Graber cousins send their best—and they gave us enough linens to last the rest of our lives, I think. Sheets, kitchen towels, and even a quilt they said your mamm made years ago, Dat. They found it in a trunk and wanted you to have it."

The catlike expression on Emma's face sent Abby upstairs while James and his father took a look at the old quilt. During the ride to and from their visit, Abby had wondered if Emma's fingers had been flying with her crochet hook, and the display on the bed made her gasp with surprise. Not only were four girls' hats laid out, but a large afghan with a wedding card on it was there as well.

Wishing you happiness for your life together, Abby and James. Denki for all you do for us, and for the way you encourage me. Much love, Emma.

"Ohhh," Abby murmured as she unfolded the afghan. As she studied the intricate argyle pattern in red, blue, purple, green, and black, she realized that some of the squares were solid and some were half one color and half another— forming two triangles within the square—arranged to make the overall pattern. It had taken some time and Emma's close attention to make the design come out right.

The girls' hats made Abby giggle as she held them up. One was lavender with a big white flower and lime green leaves, while another was striped with alternating bands of variegated and solid aqua. The other two caps had earflaps— a bright pink one with a pig's face on top and a white one with a lamb's face. Abby popped those two over her hands like puppets and hurried back down to the kitchen.

"Emma, these are too cute!" she exclaimed. "I'll take all of your hats to the store tomorrow, and I'm guessing these two with the faces will be gone before the day ends."

"Oh, Abby, sometimes you carry on—"

"I'm not kidding! We've got nothing like this in the store!"

"I did have great fun making them," Emma admitted. "I'll crochet more if you want them, maybe an aqua donkey and another pig. That one's the funniest."

Abby hugged her best friend tight. "Denki so much for the beautiful afghan, too," she murmured. "I've not seen that pattern anywhere, and the colors are so bold. I'm glad we're sisters now, Emma. You and your dat have made me feel so at home here."

Emma eased away from her embrace but kept her hands on Abby's shoulders. "Sometime soon let's pack away Mamm's old dishes and put the ones Amanda made you in the kitchen cupboards," she said. "It would be a shame to keep them boxed up, pretty as they are. I'm sorry I got so upset about them the other night."

Abby sucked in her breath. "Oh, Emma, are you sure?"

"Jah. Let's do it." Emma's hazel eyes glowed as she returned Abby's gaze. "Crocheting those hats was a great idea. While I worked, it was almost like Mamm was sitting beside me. I feel a lot better now—like I'm moving forward. What would I do without you, Abby?"

What a lovely sentiment, one she didn't want to diminish by replying with a snappy answer. Abby glanced toward the stove and the counter. "Chocolate cake and potato soup—treats that make a wintry night special. I can't wait to dig in!"

Emma reached for a long knife and went to the counter. "Actually, it's dark chocolate fruitcake bars, with candied cherries and nuts and coconut. I thought it was time we enjoyed some Christmas goodies."

Abby snatched the first bar that came out of the pan. The mouthful of warm, chewy goodness felt like the beginning of a much happier holiday than she'd anticipated after Eunice passed away. And for that, she was very grateful.

Chapter 24

As Jerome pulled his rig into the stable Sunday evening, he felt heavyhearted. He'd spent the day visiting with every family he knew around the Bloomingdale area, inquiring about whether they'd seen Pete, while Wyman had once again hunted for his son in Cedar Creek and Clearwater. This marked the fourth day of Pete's disappearance—far longer than any of them had anticipated. He wasn't looking forward to going inside without the teenager in tow.

When Jerome stepped into the kitchen, he was surprised to find Amanda there alone. Her face lit up for a moment and then fell again when she saw that he, too, was by himself.

"I stopped at every house for miles around," he murmured, "but nobody has any idea about Pete. I'm really sorry."

Amanda shrugged listlessly. "Wyman got the same report from Sam and Ray and the others out that direction. We must've really misread our boy, as far as how upset he was," she replied with a sigh. "Maybe it's time to notify the police. I—I've been praying that Pete's safe, rather than . . . out in the cold, hungry or maybe *hurt* or—"

"Going down that road only leads to troublesome assumptions, Aunt," Jerome murmured as he rested his hands on her shoulders. "We're leaving it in God's hands, jah?"

"That's the better answer." Amanda looked up at him with a stronger smile. "Did you get some supper someplace? We ate a littler earlier tonight so Wyman could take the kids out in the sleigh. It's a nice evening for that."

"Gut. The little ones will have a fine time and lift their dat's spirits as well."

"I'll warm you some of Vera's split pea soup. How about a sandwich to go with that?" Amanda said as she opened the refrigerator.

"And can I have a side of your advice as well?" Jerome eased into his place at the table, hoping a few moments alone with his aunt might help him see his future more clearly.

Her raised eyebrows made him chuckle. "And what's on your mind, dear? You've done all you possibly can, as far as looking for Pete, so—"

"It's about Emma."

"Ah." Amanda's expression wavered between curiosity and hopefulness as she ladled cold soup into a small pan. "I've got some pottery orders to deliver to Cedar Creek as well as pieces to sell in Sam's store, if that gives you a gut reason to see her again. From what you told me, your last visit went really well."

"I'll take your pottery in for you, sure," Jerome replied, wondering how to word his concerns. "But while I think my instincts are right this time, about Emma being a better match than either of my two earlier girls—"

"I agree with you there."

"It struck me the other day that I don't have a lot to offer her," he continued earnestly. "Sure, I can take Emma out, and I think I'm convincing her I'm a worthwhile kind of guy, but *then* what? Where's the proof that I can make a gut life for her?"

Amanda's brow furrowed. "Whatever do you mean, Jerome? You're a fine man with a gut business and a heart big enough to love young and old alike."

"But where would we live, if indeed Emma would have me?" Jerome gave his aunt a moment to consider the ramifications beneath the surface of his plea. "If I were to move my mule-breeding business there to the Grabers', I'd need to build a much larger barn, and—"

"You don't want to live *here*?"

Amanda's question—her disappointment—pierced his heart. "Oh, it's not that at all," he insisted. "But I'm pretty sure Emma would only come if she can bring her dat along . . . and as I count up the bedrooms, I run short. And while I'm glad Wyman and his kids have come here . . ."

"The house *is* awfully noisy and full now, compared to what we were used to," Amanda agreed. "And while Merle would be happy to be surrounded by the kids' hubbub, Emma's quieter. More private."

Jerome flashed Amanda a relieved smile. "Denki for understanding that, Aunt. I don't want you to think I'm ungrateful or unwilling to be here with you any longer."

Amanda slid into the chair beside him and slung her arm around him. "I know better than that, Jerome. But there can be too many hens clucking in one kitchen, I think. And you deserve to rule your own roost as well."

He chuckled, secretly pleased that she was knuckling his scalp like she'd done when he was a kid. "Jah, I've heard it said I can be pretty cocky. Emma's implied as much, more than once."

"You're *confident*, but not to the point of being too proud or vain," Amanda assured him. "And let's not forget that when I first married Wyman and we moved to Clearwater, I intended for this house—the whole farm—to be yours because it belonged to your uncle."

Jerome's pulse thrummed as he gazed into Amanda's eyes. While they had discussed this subject before her marriage—before the Brubakers had decided to live here, rather than in Clearwater—he hadn't felt it was his place to bring it up again.

"You've been awfully gut about accepting the way all of our lives have changed these past couple of months," his aunt went on in a firm voice, "so I want you to consider the bulk of this land as your own, Jerome. It's only fair—and it's not like Wyman will ever farm it, except to raise hay for the horses just as you already do."

"You're sure he'll agree with that?" Jerome quizzed her. No sense in getting his hopes up, knowing how her new husband saw things from a more traditional Old Order male perspective. "Wyman's the head of the household—"

"And I will always be the neck that turns the head," Amanda teased, playfully tapping his chest with her finger. "I have no doubt that James and Merle—and Wyman and I—will help you with the money for a house, too."

"Oh, I've got a gut start on the money part. It's knowing *where* to build a home that's been the holdup." Jerome grasped Amanda's shoulders, smiling excitedly. "You have no idea how many doors this opens for me, Aunt! Your telling me these things is the best Christmas gift ever."

"Glad to hear it. I'd better stir your soup before it scorches."

As she rose from the table, Jerome silently thanked God for the way this conversation had changed his entire outlook. The large bowl of soup Amanda set in front of him made him inhale appreciatively, and as she sat down beside him to make his sandwich, he smiled gratefully at her. "Can I ask you something more? Something . . . women understand better than guys do?"

Once again her eyebrows rose expressively. "This is *you*, asking me how to handle women?" she teased.

Jerome let out a short laugh. "I used to think I knew what I was doing," he confessed, "but with Emma, well . . . after she gave Bess Wengerd a piece of her mind and then went on that sleigh ride with me . . ."

"She came back with rosy cheeks and a big smile," Amanda recalled. "I thought you'd won her over, for sure."

"Me, too, until—until I asked if I could kiss her. She said *no*." Jerome sighed. "I was making progress with her on Friday, too, but Merle walked in on us and she jumped away from me."

What had his love life come to, that he was making such an inglorious confession to his aunt? It was fine to have the promise of land and a new home, but he wouldn't need those if Emma wouldn't kiss him.

Amanda slathered mustard on a slice of bread before arranging cold pork roast on it. "I know something about that, from Emma herself. But if I tell you this, Jerome, you *must* respect her feelings—keep this information to yourself—or you'll lose her," she insisted. "Emma will be too embarrassed, too upset with you and me both, to ever see you again, I suspect."

Jerome lowered his spoonful of soup back to his bowl. "All right. I'm listening."

His aunt slowly drew the knife through his sandwich in an X, as she'd done when he was a boy. Then she looked into his eyes. "Emma has never been kissed, Jerome. She *wanted* to kiss you after your sleigh ride, but she was afraid she'd do it wrong and ruin her chances with you."

His mouth dropped open and then closed again. "You don't say," he rasped. He quickly reviewed crucial moments they'd spent together: the way Emma had seemed so afraid of him when they'd shopped; her refusal to kiss him after their sleigh ride; her hazel-eyed gaze as they'd shared a lemon bar but nothing more. "I can't believe the boys in Cedar Creek didn't take Emma the long way home after Singings and didn't introduce her to smooching in the seclusion of their rigs."

Amanda slid his sandwich toward him. "A woman her age doesn't admit such a thing unless . . . unless she's every bit as concerned as *you* are about this relationship," she said.

"Just one more thing Emma missed out on while she was waiting for Matt to notice her," Jerome murmured.

"Even before they marry, girls are at the mercy of the men in their lives," Amanda remarked pensively. "To me, this proves what a respectable, decent young woman Emma has always been. She just needs someone like you, Jerome, to show her how happy she can be . . . to show her how love can change her entire life."

Jerome's breath escaped him in a rush. "Now you're scaring me, laying all the responsibility on *me* for—"

"Puh! Since when have you ever been afraid of a kiss?" Amanda's tone was light, yet she held his gaze as surely as she was holding him accountable for the secret she'd just revealed. "Emma's waiting for a gut man like you to help her become the woman and wife she was meant to be. It's all in how you handle it."

His thoughts were spinning wildly. Jerome felt as though an invisible barrier had just been lifted, revealing his entire future. *Emma has never been kissed! She's not afraid of me— she's unsure of herself.* And didn't that fit with everything else he knew about the elusive young woman in Cedar Creek?

"If you need another reason for going there—besides to visit with Merle, of course," Amanda said lightly, "Jemima and the girls have nearly finished the quilts we've been making for Abby and James. Emma will want to see them, since she and her mamm helped piece the tops, and you can give them to the newlyweds while you're there as well. So, see? Pottery, quilts, and Merle. I've given you three reasons for visiting Emma again without making it seem like you're chasing her."

"Not to mention land and a future home. Denki for the way you've always looked after me, Aunt." Jerome grinned and grabbed a section of his sandwich. He believed he had a better chance of winning Emma's hand and heart now— and a lot more to offer her than he'd anticipated.

Chapter 25

"Have a gut day with your cleaning, Daughter," Wyman said as he pulled the buggy into the Yoders' lane on Monday morning. "This is your last day to work until after Christmas, jah?"

Vera nodded glumly. "I'm to get paid today, too, but that doesn't seem nearly so exciting, with Pete still missing. I've prayed and prayed."

"Then you've turned your brother's situation over to God, and that's the best any of us can do," Wyman insisted as he gently lifted her chin with his hand. "No need to carry your problems into the Yoder house. Working cheerfully and well is the way to spend your day. I'll be back for you around two."

"Thanks for the ride, Dat."

As Vera opened her door to get out of the rig, Wyman noticed a couple of younger fellows—Cletus's sons, by the looks of them—coming around the side of the machine shed. He waved at them, but they were too focused on his daughter to notice.

"Vera, Vera!" one of them called out.

"Come right here-a!" the other one added with a laugh.

Wyman stiffened. This was his seventeen-year-old girl they were taunting—but she had the sense to ignore them and head straight for the house. When she'd gone inside, the fellows finally waved to him and then headed into the barn, so Wyman turned the rig toward the road again.

He'd gotten a call from the locker that Pete's deer was processed and ready for pickup, so that was his next stop. Amanda and Jemima were pleased about having the deer meat, and they were planning to serve a venison roast when Eddie came home from the mercantile to celebrate the holidays . . . not that Christmas would be the same with Pete still missing.

Better follow your own advice. It's in God's hands, and He knows exactly where your boy is, Wyman reminded himself. *Better follow your instincts about those fellows catcalling at Vera, too.*

Wyman turned the rig around in the next wide spot in the road. He was still kicking himself for not reading Pete more clearly, or being more aware of Reece Weaver's irresponsible ways, so he wasn't taking any chances where Vera was concerned. As his reason for coming back, he would step inside to express Christmas wishes to the Yoders, and if everything appeared to be on the up-and-up for Vera, he'd leave. It didn't hurt to get a look at the house where his daughter was working her very first job, after all.

Wyman drove back into the lane and stopped alongside the tidy two-story white house. As he stepped up to the porch, he noticed how the windows sparkled in the morning sunlight, probably because his Vera had cleaned them recently. What he saw going on in the front room, however, propelled him through the door without bothering to knock.

"Who are you and what do you think you're doing?" Wyman demanded as he strode toward the two young men he'd seen earlier. They were standing on either side of Vera as she gripped the handle of a broom, and their playful grins told him *exactly* what they had in mind as they flirted with his pretty daughter. "Where's your mamm? Or your dat?"

At close range, the two brothers looked to be twenty-something, both of them sporting English haircuts and clothes. They backed away from Vera, but they didn't seem particularly contrite. "The parents got called down the road to help a neighbor," one of them replied.

The other one hooked his thumbs into the belt loops of his jeans. "We were just making sure Vera could find all the tools she needed."

"Vera, get your coat." Wyman gestured toward the door, holding her gaze.

"But, Dat, I—"

"No buts. I'll call later and explain to Mrs. Yoder why you won't be working here any longer."

His daughter's distressed expression tore at him, but as Vera fetched her wraps, Wyman was glad he'd walked in when he had. Scowling at the two young men, he held the door for his daughter and followed her out. She scurried toward the rig with her shoulders hunched, and by the time he'd taken the driver's seat, she was crying inconsolably.

"Nothing was going on," she protested as Wyman drove them toward the road. "The Yoder boys were only teasing me. I was handling it just fine—"

"I know you believe that, Vera," he countered gently, "but you were outnumbered. I was the same age as those fellows once, and I—"

"And now I won't get my pay, and I'd hoped to—"

"Money's nothing compared to your safety, Vera. Your reputation, too," Wyman added ruefully. "It would break my heart if I so much as *suspected* those fellows had taken advantage of my dear, innocent daughter. I'm sure Cletus and his wife will see it that way as well."

Vera gulped and sniffled, not answering him.

Wyman sighed. Why were so many unfortunate things happening with his kids? Just when he thought he'd gotten his family settled into the farmhouse in Bloomingdale, all manner of problems were cropping up. He didn't attempt further conversation as he went to the locker and then loaded boxes of white-wrapped packages into the back of the buggy. It was only nine thirty when they returned home, yet Wyman already felt the day had gone sour.

Vera hurried toward the house, her feelings still hurt, as he went into the barn for a wheelbarrow. He was grabbing a box of frozen meat from the back of the buggy when he heard horses' hooves and creaking wheels making their way up the lane behind him. Wags dashed out of the barn and began barking raucously.

"Say there, Brubaker! You remember the parable of the lost sheep?" a familiar voice called out.

Wyman straightened to his full height, not looking behind him. That reedy remark could only have come from Uriah Schmucker, the bishop of the Clearwater district he'd moved away from—and whose farewell had consisted of slamming the door in Wyman's face.

Now what? Why has Uriah come such a distance to torment me, on top of everything else that's happened? Considering the way this bishop had smashed Amanda's pottery at the other house, he couldn't welcome this fellow with open arms. But he couldn't ignore Schmucker, either.

"Wags, hush!" Wyman pointed at the overgrown puppy until he sat down beside the barn door, his tail thumping wildly. When he turned, his heart nearly sprang from his chest. Pete—*his Pete!*—was stepping out of the passenger's side of the buggy, looking rumpled and somewhat sheepish, indeed. But he was home, and all in one piece, and—

Wyman couldn't think for running. He grabbed the boy in a bear hug, aware that he was babbling, but he didn't care. "We thought you were—Pete, we've been so worried that you'd—where have you—"

For the briefest moment, his son hugged him back before shrugging out of Wyman's embrace. "Hey, Dat."

All the air left Wyman's lungs, but he refrained from launching into a lecture. Uriah Schmucker was standing there, assessing their reunion with a smug smile.

"Remember this boy, do you?" the bishop teased. "Seems he's been hiding out in one barn or another, with his friends sneaking him food. It was the gelding that gave him away." Uriah gestured toward the large black horse tethered behind his rig. "I heard tell that you'd been to Clearwater a couple-three times trying to find him, so here he is—your prodigal son. A Christmas gift, a few days early."

"You have no idea," Wyman rasped as he willed his pulse to return to normal. He extended his hand, keeping his other arm around Pete. "Can't thank you enough, Uriah."

The wiry fellow cleared his throat in a way that suggested there was more to his story. "Pete, I'm sure the rest of your family will be happy to see you—and they'll be glad when you've had a bath, too. Don't forget your duffel."

Pete nodded. He kept his head low as he untied Blackie, fetched his belongings from the buggy, and then headed into the barn.

Uriah stepped closer to Wyman, one eyebrow raised. "On the way here, your boy told me you've gotten into a money crunch. Says you've forbidden him to quit school so he could help out."

"He's only thirteen," Wyman protested, his hackles rising. "I told him he couldn't—"

Bishop Schmucker held up his hand for silence. "And you did the right thing, Wyman, at least where your son's concerned," he added. Then his lips flickered. "But if you haven't figured out that Reece Weaver's as crooked as a dog's hind leg—"

Wyman bit back a retort. He wasn't happy that Pete had revealed their financial difficulties, but perhaps Uriah could shed some light on how to handle his elevator situation.

"And that he jumped the fence and went English because there was more profit in it," the bishop continued in his nasal voice, "then you got what's coming to you. Weaver took advantage of your trusting Amish nature and work ethic, which he himself abandoned after his dat passed on."

Wyman considered this information. Schmucker hadn't told him anything he didn't already know, but the bishop's words had the ring of experience. He glanced up, waving at Pete as the boy headed for the house. "So how do you know so much about Weaver?" he asked. "You're right. I chose him because his dat built our elevator in Clearwater."

Uriah rolled his beady eyes. "Weaver built a hog-confinement building for me. Couldn't trust him any farther than I could throw him, and I was ready to throw him out after his first week on the job."

There was more to this story than Uriah was telling, but Wyman sensed he wasn't going to hear it. And since his former bishop had been good enough to escort his son home, there was only one polite thing to do. "Would you come in for coffee? The girls were baking Christmas cookies this morning . . ."

"Got to move along. Just wanted to be sure your Pete made it home. Boys that age get grandiose notions of what they can do and how far they can go," Uriah added with a laugh. Then he nailed Wyman with an intense gaze. "Don't wait too long to do something about Weaver. *He's* got grandiose notions, too. Merry Christmas to you, Wyman."

"You've just made that wish come true for my entire family." Wyman held Uriah's gaze for a moment. Moving out of this domineering bishop's district had been the only way he could've held his new family together, but Schmucker had done him a tremendous favor today. Maybe more than one . . .

As Uriah's buggy rolled down the road, Wyman finished loading the venison into his wheelbarrow. Then he went into the barn and picked up the phone.

"Jah, Ray, it's Wyman," he said when the *beep* came to leave a message. "How about you set us up an appointment with your attorney to deal with Reece Weaver? I'm not cutting him any more slack, after some information I just got from Uriah Schmucker—who, by the way, brought our Pete home just now," he added happily. "I'll look forward to your callback."

As Wyman returned to the loaded wheelbarrow and pushed it toward the house, a tremendous weight had been lifted from his shoulders. Sure, he needed to have a talk with Pete to be sure the kid had no plans to run off again, and most likely he and Amanda would need to smooth Vera's ruffled feathers. But hadn't this day taken a big turn for the better? It never ceased to amaze him how the Lord could make everything work out for the best.

Chapter 26

"Pete, I'm sure glad you came home," Simon said, grinning at his older brother. "Homemade pizza's my favorite, and we don't have it nearly often enough!"

Amanda watched both boys help themselves to another slice, marveling at how much food all the kids were tucking away tonight. Profound relief had filled the kitchen the moment Pete had walked in. After everyone had exclaimed over him, and while his dat was still outside talking to Uriah Schmucker, Pete had quietly apologized to her and Jemima and returned all but a few dollars of the cash he'd taken.

Amanda considered the missing money an investment in his maturity, for Pete then admitted to her that he'd made a foolish mistake, taking off in the night. He seemed genuinely touched when she'd asked what he wanted for supper, to celebrate his return. Freshly showered and wearing clean clothes, he was the picture of contrition as he closed his eyes over another mouthful of cheeseburger pizza.

"So did you really sleep in a barn?" Cora quizzed him.

"Jah, what if a horse *pooped* on you?" Dora added with wide brown eyes. Then she and Alice Ann got the giggles.

"Poop!" the toddler crowed. "Horsey poop!"

"Alice Ann, that's enough, honey," Amanda murmured near her ear.

Pete looked down at his plate as though he'd rather forget about his days away from home. "I was in the Slabaughs' loft, silly," he replied. "Tim and Toby, my gut friends in Clearwater, were figuring to join their older brother, who works on a ranch in Kansas. They were going to take me with them, but . . . well, it didn't work out that way."

"We're glad to have you back, too," Amanda remarked as she pulled another pizza from the oven. "Sometimes plans like that sound a lot better than they really are."

"I hope you've gotten that out of your system for now," Wyman said with a purposeful gaze at his son. "Plenty of time for getting out in the world when you're older."

"Jah, jah," Pete replied with an impatient sigh. He'd endured his father's interrogation earlier, and he'd apologized again for the worry he'd caused them, too. "I've *told* you I'll stay in school, so I don't know what else I can say—"

Amanda set the steaming sausage pizza on the hot pad in front of Pete and removed the empty pan. She squeezed Wyman's shoulder when she saw the color rising in his face. "We're all thankful it turned out the way it did," she insisted as she gazed at her husband, "and we're happy for Vera that Cletus Yoder came by with her pay after he found out what happened there this morning, too. Forgive and forget seems like a gut plan for the rest of our evening."

Wyman relaxed as Amanda sliced the pizza, and then he reached for a slice. "Could be you're right, Wife," he murmured. He winked at her. "I'm hoping that big platter of sugar cookies on the sideboard is for our dessert."

"Jah, my name's on the yellow star with the sprinkles," Simon said.

"Pink angel cookie!" Alice Ann piped up. Then she joyfully jammed a chunk of cheese pizza into her mouth, smearing sauce all over her chin.

When everyone had finished eating, Lizzie and Vera ran the dishwater while the twins scraped and stacked the plates. Amanda convinced Jemima to sit down and work on their second quilt for Abby and James, knowing how the colder weather made her mother-in-law's ankles ache. Wyman, Jerome, and Pete headed to the barn for the livestock chores, while Simon raced outside for a final romp in the snowy yard with Wags. It felt so satisfying to have everyone settling into their usual routine again that Amanda was in the mood to think toward the two upcoming holidays.

"Vera, what favorite dishes do you kids and your dat enjoy most for Christmas?" she asked. "With all of us together for the first time, I'd like to celebrate with foods both families like best."

"Let's have a turkey!" Lizzie replied without missing a beat.

"White Christmas pie," Jemima called from the front room.

"Dressing with walnuts and raisins," Vera replied. "We go through a lot of that. And the boys love corn-bread casserole, and Dat likes the cranberry salad you make in the grinder with apples and oranges."

Amanda nodded, keeping a mental list. "Jah, Jerome loves all of those, too. And he's partial to sliced yams and apples baked with marshmallows over them."

Dora's eyes lit up. "Marshmallows! Let's have the lime Jell-O salad with pineapple—"

"And the different-colored baby marshmallows, jah!" Cora finished. "And it's green, for Christmas!"

"We'll be sure to have all the ingredients for those," Amanda replied. "We'll ask the fellows for their ideas when they come in. What with Christmas Day and then Second Christmas meals, we'll go through every bit of that."

"Can we invite Merle?" Cora asked in a hopeful voice.

Amanda leaned down to stroke her daughter's cheek. "What a thoughtful idea, honey. I asked Abby earlier if they'd like to come, but she didn't give me a for-sure answer," she replied. "They might go to visit their family in Queen City, you know."

Dora giggled. "We can make it Jerome's special project, to ask Merle—so that *really* he can see Emma again."

Not yet five and already a matchmaker. Amanda had noticed Jerome looking like a man with a plan today, so perhaps Dora's idea would come to pass without any obvious nudging on their part.

As the girls finished in the kitchen, Amanda lit more lamps in the front room. She smiled at Alice Ann, who'd perched on a chair beside Jemima's frame to watch her quilt. The little pixie in pink was running her index finger over the part that was completed, following the simple loops of the quilting stitches that made the basic nine-patch design look a little more special.

"What with my helper beside me, I figure to finish this before I go to bed tonight," Jemima said. "I recall helping my mamm with quilts this way when I was a wee girl."

"Me, too," Amanda said. "I loved seeing how the colors went together in the different designs and picking out the fabrics we'd use from leftover pieces of the dresses Mamm had sewn for me."

Alice Ann reached in front of her, pointing to a square. "Pink," she stated. "Like my room."

And wouldn't it be a good project for all of them to work on after the holidays—a quilt for when Alice Ann graduated to a big-girl bed? Amanda returned to the kitchen and jotted a note about calling Abby to ask her to gather up some pink fabric remnants from the store. The fellows returned from the barn then, swarthy cheeked and chatting amongst themselves.

Wyman smiled at her. "Remember how Pete and Eddie built the bathroom out in our Clearwater barn because you girls were always in the bathroom upstairs?" he asked. "Well, we've figured out how to use the leftover wood from that project."

"Birdhouses!" Simon piped up. "I've never seen *any* of those in Sam's mercantile!"

"Treva would probably sell some in her greenhouse store as well," Amanda added. "I think that's a fine idea!"

"And remember the flowerpots and wind chimes I pieced together from chunks of your broken pottery, before Uriah Schmucker made me stop?" Vera said from the sink. "I'm going to make them again! I'd rather do that than clean houses, anyway, and—well, I hope you don't mind that I saved the pieces of that bowl you broke the other day."

When Amanda saw Wyman's pleased expression, she smiled as well. "I thought your first ones were wonderful, Vera. I saved all those broken pieces from when Uriah smashed my dishes in Clearwater, too. So you have a couple of boxfuls to work with, in a lot of colors."

"We Brubakers are becoming quite a cottage industry," Wyman said as he hung his heavy coat on its peg. "I'm all for that—especially during the winter."

Amanda smiled at this turn of events, and at the improvement of the emotional atmosphere as well. As Wyman and Jerome headed into the front room, Pete and Simon following, she sensed their family might enjoy its first peaceful evening in several days. She was about to put away the cookie sheets and baking utensils for Vera and Lizzie when it suddenly seemed like a good idea to head for the bathroom.

She made it just in time to vomit into the toilet. Amanda felt sweaty and light-headed. As she leaned against the bathroom wall, she wondered if something in the pizza had upset her stomach, or if . . .

Quickly rinsing her face with cool water, Amanda waited for her head to stop spinning. This wasn't the first little spell she'd had lately, but it was too soon to say anything. With a smile on her face and a prayer in her heart, she returned to where her family was gathering around the Nativity scene in the front room.

As Jerome read the familiar passage from Luke that told of Mary and Joseph's journey to Bethlehem, Wyman felt a sense of satisfaction settle over him. His runaway son was home and had a plan for earning an income. His eldest daughter had decided that working at home was the better option for her. He and Ray had an appointment with the attorney tomorrow. Alice Ann had eagerly climbed into his lap to cuddle. The pieces of this Christmas season were falling into place like a jigsaw puzzle designed by God Himself.

" 'And she brought forth her firstborn son, and wrapped Him in swaddling clothes, and laid Him in a manger,' " Jerome read in a low, heartfelt voice, " 'because there was—' "

" 'No room in the inn'!" Simon recited with childlike excitement. He'd been moving the pieces of the Nativity set on the table while Jerome was reading, shifting the sheep and the cow and rearranging Mary, Joseph, and the Wise Men around the wooden stable.

Alice Ann looked up at Wyman with a perplexed expression. "But Jesus broke," she said mournfully. "On the floor."

"That was a little *statue* of Jesus, just like the figures of Mary and Joseph and the animals are statues," Wyman explained carefully. With a three-year-old, everything was literal, and the religious concepts were more than she could grasp. "The real Jesus—His spirit—is everywhere, sweetie.

He's right here in our home—in this room—with us, even if we can't see Him."

Alice Ann gazed around the walls and up at the ceiling, her finger in her mouth.

"He's in our hearts," Amanda joined in as she placed a hand on her chest, "and He'll live there all our lives if we ask Him to. Jesus can be everywhere at once, with every one of us."

Alice Ann placed her hand on her chest, and then on Wyman's, as if comparing. "In there?" she whispered.

"Jah." Wyman felt a rush of goose bumps as his little girl tried to understand this important concept. "So without the glass baby in the Nativity scene just yet, we can say Mary and Joseph are *waiting* for Jesus to come, just like we waited nine whole months for you, Alice Ann, while you grew in your mamm's belly."

"Jah!" Simon blurted. "We thought you'd never come out so we could see who you were!"

"Just like I was waiting to see Cora and Dora," Lizzie said with a grin. "But I'm mighty glad they weren't born in a cold, smelly barn."

"And then there's Simon, who sometimes *acts* like he was born in a barn," Pete quipped.

Simon arched his eyebrow playfully. "That was a bad one, wabbit," he teased. "I was born in the same place *you* were, ain't so?"

Wyman chuckled, pleased that the kids from both sides of their blended family were helping explain this mystery to Alice Ann. "But even though Jesus was born amongst the stable animals, God worked everything out for Mary and Joseph and Jesus, so they could be a family—just like we are."

Alice Ann's eyes lit up. Family was a concept she understood.

Wyman bussed her cheek and went on. "So we wait for Baby Jesus's birth every year at Christmas—"

"There?" Alice Ann pointed her tiny finger at the Nativity set.

Wyman's breath caught. Did he dare promise this impressionable young child that their porcelain Holy Family would be complete by Christmas Day? "He'll come when the time's exactly right," he replied carefully, glancing at each of the older kids and adults, hoping they'd keep this Christmas mystery alive until the new Christ Child was delivered to the house.

"Gut," Alice Ann pronounced solemnly. "I wanna see Him!"

Wyman shared a smile with Amanda. The light from the oil lamp glowed around her like a halo this evening as he waited with great love and longing for *her* to bear a child. Now *there* would be reason for celebration, the concrete evidence that their family was growing—the sign and seal that God had chosen to bless them with new life that would strengthen their bonds in a very special way. As he held Amanda's gaze from across the room, he dared to believe that this fondest wish would soon come true.

Chapter 27

Emma stirred chunks of cooked chicken into the broth and homemade noodles that were bubbling on the stove. Behind her at the kitchen table, Dat's hammer went *tap-tap-tap* against a few more black walnuts before he picked the nutmeats out of the shells. With the sky looking so heavy and gray, both of them were feeling a little slow and cranky . . . at loose ends, without anything to talk about. Christmas was only three days away, and Emma supposed she should mix up some cranberry bread and coffee cake for when they drove to Queen City to see her two sisters' families, but she wasn't in the mood to dirty more dishes or—

"Emma! Emma, you'll never guess what!" Abby called from the front room. The door closed behind her with a loud *whump* as she jogged into the kitchen, her cheeks aglow from the cold air. "I sold every last one of your crocheted hats today and took orders for two more! Didn't I tell you they'd be a hit?"

Emma's spoon came to a standstill in the pot. "My stars, you just took them to the mercantile this morning—"

"And I've got to get back over there, too, after I grab a quick bite. I'm taking an early lunch break so I can cover the checkout while Sam's out on preacher business." Abby laid some money and a scribbled note on the counter beside Emma. Then she strode over to the refrigerator, bussing Dat's temple as she went.

"Uh-oh," Emma's father murmured as he pried a large chunk of nutmeat from its shell. "Nobody likes getting a visit from the preacher. It means he's strayed off the path."

"Nope, it's not that kind of visiting," Abby replied as she carried sliced ham, bread, and cheese to the table. As she sat down, she was smiling. "Vernon's bought some hams and other groceries so he and Abe and Sam can deliver them to a few families who're struggling. Christmas kindness rather than correction."

"And I'm grateful that they don't need to stop at our place." Dat had quit shelling walnuts to watch Abby fold a slice of fresh bread around some ham and cheese. "I don't suppose you'd make *me* one of those, Abby-girl? Just half a sandwich to hold me over until Emma's chicken and noodles are ready?"

"I could probably do that, jah," Abby teased.

As Abby sliced more bread, Emma opened her mouth to protest about Dat spoiling his appetite for dinner—but then the realization struck her. *Isn't that exactly what Mamm would've said? And didn't you get tired of her fussing at him, while he did what he pleased anyway to frustrate her?*

Emma blinked. While she ached for her mamm something fierce, she did *not* miss the way her parents had bickered over every little thing, and maybe she didn't have to perpetuate that pattern. Dat looked perfectly happy, letting Abby fuss over him. And *she* had hats to crochet—orders from folks who wanted to *pay* her for doing something she enjoyed. Now *that* was something worth thinking about!

When Emma picked up the money, counting two twenty-dollar bills, her eyes widened. That came out to ten dollars per hat—and it more than covered what she'd spent for yarn. Abby's note was an order for two more earflap hats, one with a big flower and one with a lamb face.

Turning toward the stove again, Emma grinned like a kid at Christmas. She didn't have *time* to feel lonely for her mother. Once she completed these two orders, she might even post a card on the mercantile bulletin board so anyone who shopped at Sam's store would know whom to call for afghans or baby blankets or more hats. What with keeping Sam's ledger and orders current, and crocheting items for the store, her winter days would pass a lot faster. While she hadn't liked it when Vernon and Sam had told her she could no longer work in the store's back room, Emma had to admit that she was glad to be at home again with Dat, keeping meals on the table for the four of them.

"Oh! And there was a phone message from Sharon," Abby said as she got a plate for Dat's sandwich. "Seems she and Iva caught a stomach bug, so she wants us to stay home over Christmas rather than traveling all that way and maybe catching whatever they have."

"I'm for that," Dat agreed quickly. "Truth be told, that ride to Queen City's getting mighty hard on my backside. But I know how you girls and James would rather spend the day amongst all those folks instead of being stuck here with me."

"Merle! Don't you ever say such a thing again," Abby scolded. "If we're confessing secrets here, I've spent enough time in a buggy these past several weekends, making our wedding visits, that staying home for Christmas sounds like a dream come true."

"And I have hats to crochet," Emma murmured. Then she let out a giggle. "I have *hats* to crochet! Denki, Abby, for such a gut suggestion that'll help me get through this holiday without Mamm. What would we do without you?"

Dat grabbed Abby's hand. "We don't want to know the answer to that question," he replied. "So it's settled! We'll stay home and do whatever we please for Christmas Day— and Second Christmas as well, if you like. I can wear my baggy old brown sweater and my slippers all day without anybody fussing at me!"

"And since we're not going anywhere," Emma mused aloud, "I might wear that new green dress you made me, Abby. While black's still the proper color for being out and about—"

"What a wonderful-gut idea," Abby crowed. "I'll wear green, too."

"Maybe this first Christmas without Mamm will be easier to get through in a brighter color," Emma finished in a pensive tone. "Working with those perky shades of pink and aqua yarn has really improved my mood, you know?"

"I can see that, and I'm *glad*," Abby affirmed. "After I come home this afternoon, we'll figure out what-all we want to cook for our Christmas dinners."

Emma nodded happily. Despite the gray sky, she felt as though a door inside her had opened to let in a beam of warm, golden sunshine . . . the sense that she could spend each day exactly the way she *chose* to. Dat was getting along well, and he wouldn't stop her from crocheting or working at anything she enjoyed. And she had a feeling Jerome might pay her another visit sometime soon.

Maybe I'll kiss him if I have another chance—but I'm leaving that up to You now, Lord.

Chapter 28

As Wyman sat with Ray in Graham Lock's nicely decorated law office, he inhaled deeply, trying to settle his nerves. He'd just shown the Clearwater attorney their estimates for the elevator costs and told him how Reece Weaver had demanded more money yet had stopped working on his elevator—and how Reece wasn't returning his calls anymore, either.

"Your timing is perfect," the portly attorney said, "as you're not the only area businessmen asking for legal advice about Mr. Weaver's business practices. You can take him to court, but I have a suggestion that might get you better results—faster and cheaper than filing a civil suit."

"Reece was threatening to take *us* to court if we didn't give him another hundred thousand dollars," Wyman said with a sigh. "I've given him too much of my trust and my money—I can see that now. My family will get by this winter, but I can't afford for this elevator not to be completed by spring."

The attorney took a sheet of paper from his desk drawer. "A regional television station has just started working on a piece about this situation. Ever heard of the program *Eight Gets It Straight*?"

Wyman shrugged. "We don't have a television."

"We do, but I rarely watch," Ray added. "What do you have in mind?"

"It's called investigative reporting," the attorney explained in a businesslike voice. "A reporter named Cole Calloway, from the Channel Eight TV station, will be interviewing customers who've gone through these same difficulties with Reece Weaver, and meanwhile a video crew will film the construction projects he hasn't completed. The idea behind this sort of news story is to expose unscrupulous or illegal business practices and get restitution for the consumers who've been defrauded."

Wyman glanced over at Ray, who seemed as befuddled by this information as he was. Words like *unscrupulous*, *illegal*, and *defrauded* made Reece's behavior sound a lot more serious and widespread than he'd been thinking, which confirmed that he and Ray weren't the only fellows who'd taken Weaver at his word and regretted it.

"Thousands of northeast Missouri viewers will see what Reece is doing," Graham went on, "and because he's been bilking people who might be their neighbors, he'll be out of business unless he makes good on what he's promised his customers. It's an added twist that Weaver's cheating so many Plain customers when he's Plain himself, so this story will get a lot of attention."

"*Used* to be Plain," Wyman clarified. "He's jumped the fence, I hear."

"TV reporters can *expose* guys like Weaver?" Ray asked.

"It's considered a public service. And in this rural area, viewers realize how important it is for family men like you to stay in business," Lock continued. "After all, if your grain elevator goes under, Lord forbid, your family will be adversely affected, yes, but so will the farmers who store and sell their crops with you. That's *news* here in our neck of the woods."

Lord forbid, indeed, Wyman thought. He wasn't in the habit of telling God what to forbid and what to allow, but he felt a tiny ray of hope because he wasn't facing this uncomfortable situation alone. "And this Calloway fellow's going to have Reece talking about his unfinished projects on TV? I can't see him doing that."

Lock chuckled as he clasped his hands on his massive desktop. "I doubt Weaver will confess his wrongdoing on camera, but if he's *smart*—if he wants to clear his name and stay in business—he'll complete his customers' construction and get squared away with them," he replied. "That way, on the final segment of the show, viewers will see film clips of the finished projects while the reporter announces how Weaver has fulfilled his contracts."

Wyman listened intently, hoping he fully understood what the attorney was telling them. "So . . . what if Weaver *doesn't* make good with his customers? What'll we do then?"

"Excellent question," Mr. Lock said with a nod. "Your best recourse would be to file a civil suit—probably together with the other unsatisfied plaintiffs. I sincerely hope the situation doesn't get that far," he added emphatically. "I've seen and heard enough to suspect that Weaver's been demanding additional money from one customer so he can buy materials for other customers' jobs."

"Robbing Peter to pay Paul," Ray murmured.

"Yes, sir. Quite often, these cases will be settled out of court, but if Weaver reaches the point where he no longer has the money to complete some of his projects"—the attorney shrugged, his expression glum—"some of his customers will get burned. I hope, for your sakes, it won't come to that."

Wyman let out a long sigh as he exchanged a glance with Ray. "So what do we need to do to get in on this TV investigation?"

"I'll give you Cole's number," Lock explained. "He'll want to shoot film footage of your elevator site, and maybe interview you—"

"Nope, can't do that," Wyman insisted as he raised his hands. "We Amish don't believe in going before a camera."

"But Tyler could." Ray's voice rose with excitement as he smiled at the attorney. "Our Mennonite fellowship allows the use of technology, and my son Tyler handles the computer end of our business. It's okay for him to be filmed."

"And Tyler would be a gut one for explaining anything the reporter wanted to know," Wyman agreed. "When would he need to be ready?"

The attorney smiled as though Wyman and Ray had just unlocked the door through which he'd been hoping to enter. "Since this project is getting under way and I don't want you to miss out on it, would you like *me* to set up the interview? Might be quicker and easier."

Wyman's mouth dropped open. "If you'd do that for us, I'd be mighty grateful. This is way out of my league, far as knowing what to expect or what to do."

"Unfortunately, Weaver's using your lack of legal experience to his advantage, which is why I'm happy to help you fellows. I'll call the station right now," Lock said as he grabbed his phone. "Meanwhile, here's the list of other folks who are already part of this investigation. Since their participation is a matter of public record now, you might be interested in whom you're joining forces with. You probably know some of them."

Ray took the piece of paper the attorney slid across his glossy desk, and Wyman scooted his chair closer to his partner's so he could read it. "Uriah Schmucker?!" he blurted when he saw the name at the top of the list.

Graham Lock chuckled, still waiting for someone to take his call. "Mr. Schmucker got this whole ball rolling. Apparently Weaver completed his hog-confinement building in a hurry and hasn't returned to make the final adjustments that Mr. Schmucker requested several months ago. Schmucker suspected Weaver was also shortchanging some of his Amish friends and church members, so he met with several area bishops about it a few weeks ago. They gave him the go-ahead to pursue the investigation, as long as he stayed off camera."

Lock swiveled in his chair and began to speak into the phone, so Wyman turned his attention to the other names on the paper. "Jah, there's your cousin Josiah . . . and doesn't this Schwartzentruber fellow live over toward the Illinois border?" He let out a low laugh. "When Uriah brought our Pete home the other day, he railed at me for being so stupid as to work with Weaver. Told me not to put up with his shenanigans too long but didn't let on that he'd gotten a television station involved."

"Well, I've never been able to figure out Uriah's methods," Ray replied. "Maybe he didn't tell you because he's still peeved about you Brubakers leaving his district after selling your farm to us Mennonites."

"Jah, there's that."

"Are you okay with what we're getting into here?" Ray murmured. "We'll be publicly broadcasting how much money Weaver took us for, and how we've been duped, when it's mostly English folks who'll be watching the show. Some of them already think we Plain folks are a brick or two short of a load."

"True enough, but it's not like we'll be the only ones revealing that information. I should've *known* to pay the suppliers for my elevator materials myself, and to keep their receipts, rather than figuring Reece would manage that much money like he was supposed to." Wyman's tone was rueful. "*My* mistake . . . and jah, thousands of folks will know it now—some of them the farmers we do business with."

Wyman considered his partner's question again, putting it into Old Order perspective. "Jesus himself exposed crooked tax collectors and overturned the tables of the money changers in the temple," he murmured. "He took a big risk, pointing a finger at the corrupt religious leaders of His day, but it was the right thing to do. I believe God led us here today for a gut reason. We won't be helping only ourselves by taking Weaver to task, after all."

"And the price is right. Won't cost anything unless we have to go to court later."

"Jah, I heard that part loud and clear," Wyman murmured. "And I think our customers, Plain and English alike, will respect us for taking action rather than losing out on the major investment we've made."

Just then Graham Lock turned around to face them again, still holding the phone to his ear. "Can your Tyler meet the crew at the elevator site on Monday the twenty-eighth? Middle of the morning?"

"We'll both be there," Ray replied.

"I'll go, too," Wyman confirmed. "I'm really curious as to how all this will play out, while he's shooting the film and afterward."

The attorney spoke briefly into the phone again and then hung up with a satisfied smile. "You're all set up with Cole. He'll have some legal and informational statements for you to sign—think of them as permission slips—when you arrive. And he's just told me that Reece Weaver has gotten word about this investigative report and has threatened to sue Channel Eight if they broadcast it."

Wyman let out a short laugh. "Of course Reece would say that. Is there any way he can stop the interviews and the filming?"

"Cole Calloway and his station are dedicated to running this sort of story," Lock explained, "because it'll attract thousands of viewers to their program and because everyone wants justice to be done. If Weaver's to keep his dirty laundry off the air, he'll have to make good on a lot of botched jobs awfully fast, because Cole's already begun filming."

"We really appreciate your help with this," Wyman said. "I had no idea, when we came in here, how we might salvage this situation. You've given me a mighty fine Christmas gift, Mr. Lock."

The attorney hefted himself from his chair and extended his hand across his desk. "Honest, hardworking men like you two are the backbone of America, and of our local economy as well. I'll be glued to Channel Eight while this story runs. You never know what interesting details might be revealed," he added with a grin. "Local investigations are always more interesting than the fictional crime-show series on national TV because they involve folks we know."

After they exchanged a few more pleasantries with the attorney, Wyman stepped outside into the brisk December day. As he and Ray walked toward their vehicles, he filled his lungs with crisp, cold air and savored the sunshine on his face. "Well, I never saw *that* coming," he remarked.

"It's like Lock said," Ray replied. "Timing makes all the difference. And it's like you said, too—the gut Lord got us to Lock's office right when we were supposed to be there. I have a feeling the situation's going to get worked out now."

"Jah, I feel a lot better about it, too. Merry Christmas, Ray, and may God bless your family in the New Year as well!"

"The same to you, old friend. And we'll see you Monday—I wouldn't miss this filming adventure for anything!"

On the drive back to Bloomingdale, Wyman reflected on the amazing turn of events. When Christmas arrived on Friday, he would have much to thank the Lord for during their day of quiet reflection. And if the Grabers joined them on Saturday to celebrate Second Christmas, he would have this wonderful news to share with them.

Instead of heading toward Cedar Creek, Wyman took the back roads that ran alongside the railroad tracks. He passed several wooded English hobby farms used mostly for hunting, as well as Plain farms where the fields had been cleared for the season. The simple white homes and red barns looked tidy against the snow, and he waved at each horse-drawn buggy he met. When he reached his property on the outer edge of Bloomingdale, he halted his horse beside the sections of foundation that had been poured for his elevator.

Wyman now believed that the round metal walls of his new grain bins would indeed rise, section by section, until they stood like silver towers in the sunshine. He had a hunch that once the Channel Eight reporter convinced Reece Weaver that his unethical business practices would be revealed to thousands of viewers, those costly problems concerning the EPA and blasting through bedrock would disappear like snowflakes in the wind. He drew a deep, easy breath. Somehow, with God, Cole Calloway, and Graham Lock assisting him, Reece Weaver *would* be held accountable.

Wyman continued down the gravel road toward home. Through the bare branches of the trees, he could see the tall white farmhouse on the hillside—and now that it accommodated four adults and eight kids, wasn't it the warmest, coziest place on God's good earth? As he pulled the rig up into the lane, a brown UPS truck lumbered off the county highway, coming toward him. This was the only residence for a long way down the gravel road, so he halted the horse and hopped out of the buggy. Maybe Amanda had ordered more clay and pottery supplies. *Or maybe it's a baby!* he thought with a hopeful grin.

"Coming to the Brubaker place?" he called out when the driver pulled to a stop.

"Yup, got a box for Wyman Brubaker," the fellow said as he reached down for a parcel. "If my memory serves, that would be you, right?"

"Jah. Thought I'd save you the trip clear up the hill," Wyman replied.

"I appreciate it. I've been running a lot of long hours," he remarked as he handed a padded brown envelope out the door. "So many folks do their Christmas shopping online now, our trucks'll be out late into the next couple of evenings."

Wyman's pulse accelerated as he grasped the small package. "Merry Christmas to you! You've certainly made *our* Christmas more special, bringing this so fast."

"Glad to hear it. Merry Christmas back atcha!"

Wyman hurried back into his rig to open the shipping bag. The small box inside it was illustrated, and as he gazed at it, he was grateful that Tyler Fisher knew about computers—and that he'd been kind enough to pay the extra money for express delivery without letting on he was doing so.

Taking out the tiny figurine, Wyman smiled at the delicate Baby Jesus lying in the manger filled with hay. *You came into the world at just the right time, way back then, and now You've shown up at my house so Alice Ann can have her own little miracle for Christmas. Denki, Lord.*

Wyman eased the figurine back into its box. As his plan for Christmas Eve came to mind, he smiled and urged the horse up the hill toward the barn.

Your timing is perfect, Graham Lock had said to him and Ray this morning. But really, it was God who had timed these details to perfection.

Chapter 29

As Jerome drove through the countryside toward Cedar Creek, he couldn't help grinning. It was December 23, and while he was delivering Amanda's pottery, as well as the two completed quilts for James and Abby, it was his more romantic mission that made his heart pound. He'd brought along the mule foal he was giving the newlyweds, as well as three kids who were eager to visit with Merle. He was hoping their presence might keep Emma's dat distracted while he spent some time with her.

"Look at those black-and-white cows!" Dora piped up as they turned off the main highway and onto the county blacktop.

Jerome smiled. "Those are Rudy Ropp's dairy cows," he explained. "He milks them twice every day, and then a big tanker truck takes his milk to the cheese factory over by Clearwater."

Both of the twins let out a little *oooh*. "So . . . if you

want chocolate milk, do you have to have brown cows?" Cora asked.

"And pink cows for strawberry?" Dora added with a giggle.

Simon clapped his hands against his head. "You get those flavors from the syrup bottles in the fridge, silly," he replied. "It's a gut thing you don't want to be farmers when you grow up."

Jerome chuckled. The kids were buzzing like bees today, excited about visiting the Grabers. They were also in that rising state of expectation all kids entered as Christmas drew closer. He suspected Simon had been snooping for presents hidden in the closets and blanket chests, but he hadn't said a word about that to Wyman or Amanda. He'd done the same thing when he'd been Simon's age, even though gifts had never been the emphasis of their Christmas celebrations.

And what will you give Emma?

The question came at him again. Several times he had wondered what would please her most . . . what would convince her that he was a man worthy of her attention. *You'll know it when you see it. The right gift will show itself if you believe it will.*

"Next stop, the Lambright place," Jerome said above the kids' teasing conversation. "If you'll run to the door and tell them we're here, I'll unload the pottery."

"We'll take the cookies!" Cora said.

"And sing them a Christmas carol like we did for Bessie Mast and Lois Yutzy," Dora added as she gazed eagerly at the tall white house.

Jerome pulled the buggy to a halt in front of Sam's place, and the kids shot out of it with their goodies and their excited smiles. Barbara and Treva greeted them at the door and exclaimed over the plate of cookies, and as Jerome carefully carried the packed boxes to the porch, he cherished the sounds of "Silent Night." Even in broad daylight, nothing touched him quite the way that carol did, sung in young voices that were slightly off-key but earnestly sincere.

After he visited with the Lambright women and wished them a merry Christmas, Jerome waved the kids back to the rig. He opened the side door of the horse trailer he'd hitched behind the buggy, clucking at the foal inside. Even though the trailer was only large enough for one horse, the little mule looked tiny inside it—but she seemed to be holding up well on this first trip, when her mamm was in the buggy harness rather than beside her. "You're a gut girl," Jerome murmured as he stroked the foal's forehead. "I'll let you out in a few, and I think a couple of folks will be mighty excited to meet you."

He gazed across the road toward Graber's Custom Carriages and the home situated a short distance behind it. His pulse sped up. He hoped the right words would occur to him when he got a chance to speak with Emma alone. *Last time you were with her, you didn't have a lot to offer her. Things have changed for the better.*

Jerome inhaled the frosty air to settle himself and then climbed back into the buggy. He hoped that *he* had changed for the better over the past few weeks as well.

"Now we're going where the *real* fun is," Simon crowed. "But let's don't sing for Merle. Guys aren't as wild about that caroling stuff as old ladies are."

Jerome choked on a chuckle, recalling how he'd viewed adults when he was Simon's age. Perhaps he owed some of his inner transformation to the presence of Wyman's kids in his home . . . to the way they spoke right up, expressing their joy and frustration and opinions without holding back. Eddie and Pete and Simon never pretended to be any different from who they were.

And that's how you should approach Emma. Be the man you are, because even if she's too shy to say so, she really does like you. You've seen it in her eyes.

Once they'd crossed the blacktop and entered the carriage shop's parking lot, Jerome explained his plan to the kids. "Rather than pounding on the door and maybe waking Merle from a nap," he said as he held Simon's eager gaze, "let's show James and Abby their foal first. That way, if they invite us to stay for dinner, it won't seem like we showed up at this time of day figuring to eat with them."

Simon's smile sobered. "But what if they don't ask us? Will they eat their dinner while we stand there—"

"*Now* who's being silly?" Dora asked as she elbowed the boy. "Of course they'll invite us for dinner."

"Because every time we see the Grabers, we eat!" Cora exclaimed. "But we want it to be their idea. We just came to deliver gifts and to see Merle. Okay?"

Chuckling, Jerome marveled at the wisdom of these young girls. "Jah, that's what I was trying to say, and it looks like our timing's gut, too. Here comes Abby from the mercantile, probably taking her dinner break."

"Hope she's been making fried pies," Simon said as he opened the rig's door.

Abby's curiosity brightened her rosy cheeks as she strode up the carriage shop's short driveway. "Jerome, what a fine surprise, to see you—and you kids!" She hugged the twins and tweaked Simon's stocking cap. "What on earth could be in this trailer, or are you delivering a *lot* of pottery orders for Amanda?"

Simon jumped up and down, his brown eyes sparkling. "It's a little—"

"*Surprise,*" Cora insisted as she clapped her hand over his mouth.

"Jah, something for you and James," Dora added sweetly. "We brought your wedding presents!"

"Well, let's go fetch James so he can see them, too," Abby suggested. "Simon, will you come into the shop with me?"

Simon didn't take the hand Abby offered him, but he

was delighted to be going into the carriage shop. Jerome opened the double back doors of the horse trailer and spoke softly to the foal as he lowered the ramp. "Shall we stand alongside your mamm for a few?" he murmured as he un-hitched the foal's tether. "You're doing real gut, little girl."

The foal nickered as Jerome gently backed her out of the trailer. When she caught sight of the mare in front of the rig, she brayed and hurried to stand beside her mother. The twins gathered around the foal and stroked her back, speaking quietly as Jerome had taught them.

"And what have we here?" James said as he came toward them. He was slipping into his coat, looking very pleased to see his visitors, while Abby and Simon walked alongside him.

"What a pretty sight, the sleek black Percheron mamm and her nubby foal together," Abby remarked. "Your little mule's doing real well for as young as she is."

Jerome smiled, pleased with her compliment. "I'd like you two newlyweds to have her, soon as she's weaned and broken to the lead—and I'll train her, if you'd like."

"This little mule's for *us*?" James's eyes widened as he looked at the foal again. "That's a very generous gift, Je-rome."

"And you'll train her, too?" Abby ran her hand gently along the foal's neck. "But we'll *pay* you for training."

"Nope. She's my wedding gift to you, along with my gratitude for helping our family make the move to Blooming-dale, and for selling Aunt Amanda's pottery in your store again," Jerome added as he smiled at Abby. Then he leaned closer to the couple. "And if you could give me some time with Emma today, I'd really appreciate it."

James chuckled. "Consider it done."

"Jah, we can arrange that," Abby agreed as she glanced toward the house. "Emma's crocheted hats are selling as fast as I can take them to the store, and she's mighty tickled about that, but you'll be the frosting on her cake, Jerome.

She's happier now. More at peace about her mamm's passing and—well, I think you'll see a difference."

"Glad to hear it," Jerome murmured. "And how's Merle doing?"

"Oh, he'll be excited to see these kids," Abby said as she grinned at them. "Let's go in and tell him and Emma you're here, shall we?"

"Jah!" Cora exclaimed as she and Dora hurried around the side of the rig. "We brought him—"

"A cookie plate," her twin finished. "And we can sing carols, too."

As Abby and the three kids hurried toward the house, all talking at once, Jerome smiled after them and said to James, "Hope we won't be putting Emma out, showing up when she wasn't expecting four extra folks for a meal."

"Puh! Emma and Abby have already baked enough breads and goodies—there's plenty to share. And by the way," James added, "tell Amanda we'll be pleased to come for Second Christmas. What with my sisters' being sick, we're staying home on Christmas Day, so we'll be ready for some fun at your place."

As Jerome and James led the mare and the foal to the barn, Jerome inhaled the cold winter air to settle himself. Countless dates he'd been on over the years, but today felt different. *Bigger.* As though he might be finally walking down the right path toward his future.

Although dozens of times he'd imagined proposing to Emma, it was much too soon for that. Jerome didn't know for sure *what* he would say or do, so he prayed that whatever came out of his mouth would be appropriate, proof that his feelings for Emma were sincere and long-lasting. When he'd fetched the two wrapped bundles from the rig, he and James went inside the Graber house. It was a joy to see Merle laughing with the kids—and humorous, because the back of his hair was standing on end from napping in his recliner. He was asking Simon which cookies were the best, making a game of it, and making each child feel special.

Abby came out of the kitchen and winked at Jerome. "No time like the present."

"And no present like the time," Jerome quipped as he removed his coat. "Denki, Abby. I won't be but a few—"

"Don't hurry. The kids can help James and me open those other gifts—so many presents!" she added when she saw the wrapped bundles on the sofa.

Jerome inhaled the homey aromas of freshly baked bread . . . something rich and beefy . . . something sweet. He peeked around the kitchen door frame to gauge Emma's mood. The rise of her expressive eyebrows and the bustle in her step suggested that she was more flustered about having dinner guests than James had let on. But she looked so pretty and efficient, and she was wearing a dress the shade of nutmeg rather than black.

"Emma, it's so gut to see you again," he murmured as he entered the kitchen. "Please don't go to any extra trouble— whatever's bubbling in that pot smells fabulous."

"Let me just stir up another batch of biscuits to go with our stew and—"

Jerome couldn't help himself. He gently took hold of Emma's shoulders and turned her so she was facing him. Her measuring cup fell from her hand into the flour canister, and her hazel eyes widened as she gazed up at him. She had a little spot of flour on her cheek, and it was all he could do not to kiss it away.

"Oh!" Emma gasped. "Jerome, I—"

"I've been wanting to give you something for the longest time, Emma," he murmured, "and if you don't like it, I'll leave you to your cooking and I—I'll never bother you again."

Before she could question him, Jerome lowered his head and kissed Emma very gently. It was just a brief brushing of lips, but the velvety sweetness of her mouth made him dip down for another sip, like a bee sampling the nectar of a delicate flower.

"Oh!" Emma gasped again. She gazed at him full-on, as wide-eyed and fetching as a young girl. The roses blooming in her cheeks, and the way her breathing accelerated with his, told Jerome she'd liked his kiss.

"I—I've wanted to do that since the first moment I saw you, Emmie-girl," Jerome insisted softly. "I'm a different man when I'm with you, happier and more settled. I've said it before, but it bears repeating. You're sensible and down-to-earth. And you balance out my tendencies to act first and think later."

Emma's cheeks blazed, yet she didn't look away from him. "And you encourage *me* to come out of my boring, predictable shell to try new things," she whispered. "I felt so gut last time you were here, Jerome, when you fussed over the afghan I'd crocheted. Not many fellows would do that or . . . have such patience with me."

He sucked in his breath. She was responding even more sweetly than he'd hoped, standing between him and the stove without trying to break away. Did he dare speak of all the wondrous ideas that were whirling in his heart? "It's not just who you are that makes me want to be with you, Emma," he murmured earnestly. "It's who I am when I'm with you."

"Will you kiss me again, Jerome?"

His breath left him in a rush. His eyes closed, and when his lips found hers, Jerome knew the answer to every question his heart had ever asked. Emma responded shyly, but she wanted his kiss now . . . accepted him in ways she hadn't before. Knowing Emma had never been kissed by anyone else made this moment feel especially sweet— downright sacred, because she was entrusting so much to him.

Jerome suddenly believed he could move heaven and earth if Emma asked him to. He could let her determine the course of their courtship and take it at her own speed, too. And when had he ever allowed a woman such control over his life?

"Amanda's given me some land, so I'm going to build us a house on the farm in Bloomingdale—if you'll have me, that is," he added in a tight voice. He smelled something getting too hot and reached behind Emma to yank the stew pot off the burner. "But we've got time to sort all that out, jah? Will you let me court you now, Emma? Please?"

Emma was aware that her first batch of biscuits needed to be taken from the oven and that the stew had scorched, yet her worries evaporated like the steam coming from the pot on the stove. Why had she been so reluctant to kiss this man before? Why had she believed Jerome Lambright was a bounder who was too full of himself to even notice a shy mouse like her?

Once upon a time those things were true. But both of us see our lives, our futures, differently now.

Emma eased herself from Jerome's grasp and turned to face the oven. The look on his face tickled her. He thought she was stalling, not going to answer his courting question, but it wouldn't hurt him to wait, would it? She could let him think, for just a few moments, that she might not gush out a *yes* like his previous fiancées probably had. Emma removed the golden-brown biscuits and set the pan on a rack to cool. Then she returned to the stove to pull the wooden spoon through the stew, assessing how much of it had stuck to the bottom.

Finally, Emma smiled up at Jerome. "I think we'll still have enough for everyone if you don't eat any," she teased. "Or we can scrape yours from the bottom, where it stuck while you were distracting the cook."

Where had this playfulness come from? When had she ever teased any man, especially about something as serious as his dinner?

Jerome appeared dumbfounded, as though he'd taken her silly threat seriously. From the front room came strains of the children's singing—"Away in a Manger," it was— and her dat singing along. A move to Bloomingdale might be beneficial for both her and her father, but it was too soon to discuss that, even though Jerome had mentioned building her a home. Still, Emma's heart fluttered. *He's got plans for his future, and he wants you to be a part of it!*

Jerome thumbed away something on her cheek. "Flour," he murmured. "You look really pretty today, Emma. Like a rose blooming in midwinter. You've got that kind of strength and determination, you know—to bloom where you've been planted, no matter what the season or the situation. That's just one of the things I love about you."

Her mouth fell open, but no sound came out. Somehow she caught her breath and corralled her runaway thoughts. "I—I *do* want you to court me, Jerome. But I'll be in mourning for a while longer," she reminded him. "I've put away my black dresses to enjoy Christmas."

"And I'm glad to see that," Jerome affirmed. "We'll take our courtship at whatever pace suits you. I just wanted you to know that I'm hoping you—and your dat, if that's best— will join me in the new home I'm planning. It's all I've been able to think about lately."

When he hugged her, Emma wrapped her arms around his sturdy body and held on tight. For a few heavenly moments, she envisioned herself standing on a new front porch with this handsome man embracing her. She sensed that the expression on her face resembled the way Abby looked when James hugged her and spoke so lovingly to her. And it felt *wonderful*, this affection. Better than she'd been able to imagine.

"Oh!" a little girl exclaimed from the doorway. Then she giggled and began to sing. "Jerome and Emma, sitting in a tree—"

"K-I-S-S-I-N-G!" her twin finished.

Cora and Dora began to clap wildly as Emma eased away from Jerome to smile at them. Simon joined them then, sniffing loudly. "What's on fire? It smells like that time Vera's biscuits were burning and—"

From either side of him, the twins clapped their hands over Simon's mouth. "You're not supposed to talk that way," Cora insisted in a loud whisper.

"Jah, when we're company at somebody's house, we're supposed to eat what's set in front of us," Dora reminded him. Then she grinned at Emma. "We're sorry about what Simon just said. We're still training him to think before he talks."

Emma laughed out loud, and Jerome joined her. "Gut luck with that, girls," he remarked. "Some of us fellows have taken a long time to learn that lesson."

"It's all about the training, ain't so?" Emma teased. Then she gazed up into Jerome's deep brown eyes, loving the happiness she saw there . . . the same joy and affection she was feeling now, at long last.

Chapter 30

At breakfast the next morning, Amanda paused to gaze around the table at her family. *This is what Christmas Eve should look like,* she mused as her gaze lingered on each person. Eddie was home from Cedar Creek, looking happy to be here yet more mature and confident than before he'd done his painting and clerking at the mercantile. Beside him, Pete was smiling as Eddie regaled them all with a tale from the busy shopping season at the store. Simon, Cora, and Dora sat spellbound, listening to their brother's story as they ate their French toast and scrambled eggs.

"Why do I suspect you spent a gut bit of your time gawking at Gail?" Lizzie teased him. "Fannie Lehman's been asking about you at school. Thinks you're never coming back to Bloomingdale or the Singings."

"Jah, Fannie's asked me the same thing," Vera teased as she passed the bacon platter. "She's got her eye on you."

When Eddie shrugged, Pete let out a laugh. "Just my opinion, Ed, but stick with Gail," he said. "Fannie and her sisters will be at the school program tonight, and you'll see how moony-eyed they are."

"Kinda like Jerome and Emma," Dora said with a giggle.

"Or Mamm and Dat," Simon remarked.

Amanda covered a laugh when her youngest son flashed her a brown-eyed smile from across the table—probably to distract her as he wrapped his hand around at least three more strips of bacon. And yet it made her heart flutter to think the kids considered her and Wyman as *moony-eyed* as a young couple.

Wyman's gaze confirmed his agreement with Simon's observation. He winked at her, even as he gripped Jerome's shoulder. "So you and Emma came to an . . . *understanding* when you were at the Graber place yesterday?" he teased.

Jerome looked like the cat that had swallowed the canary. "Oh, Emma and I have always understood each other," he hedged as he snatched one of the slices of bacon from Simon's plate. "But jah, I've brought her around to my way of thinking."

"And kissing," Dora said with a knowing look at her twin sister.

"Jah, right there in Emma's kitchen," Cora confirmed.

"Kisses!" Alice Ann piped up, kicking gleefully in her high chair. "I wuv kisses!"

Jerome looked down the table, fixing the twins with his teasing yet purposeful gaze. "Someday—if you're lucky—you'll have fellows who can't help but kiss you, too," he said. "Meanwhile, it's best not to go telling tales on folks who're sweet on each other, because those stories tend to get *repeated*," he said with a roll of his eyes in Alice Ann's direction. "If Emma knew you were talking about her this way, she might run off like a scared rabbit. And then we'd all be sorry, ain't so?"

Amanda smiled. While Jerome hadn't raised his voice, he'd made the children aware that gossip could lead to undesirable consequences—a lesson all of them could take to heart. The shine in his eyes announced his progress with Emma, and that lifted Amanda's spirits. Jerome was a fine young man, and Emma would make him a devoted wife. She wanted nothing more than for them to be happy.

"I'm glad the Grabers are coming for Second Christmas," Jemima said from the other end of the table. "What with this being their first Christmas without Eunice, it'll do them gut to be amongst other folks and in a different place for the day."

"Jah, that first round of holidays without Dat was tough," Lizzie said somberly. She looked at Vera and her new brothers, and then her gaze lingered on Wyman. "This'll be our best Christmas ever, all of us having fun and being together as a family."

"Amen to that," Wyman said as he smiled fondly at Lizzie. "We've had our troubles, but we've made our way through them. I'm looking forward to the program at the school this evening, attending with our new friends here in Bloomingdale. I trust you and Pete have learned your parts?"

Lizzie's face lit up. "Jah, Fannie and I, being the oldest girls, put the program together, and we're reciting a poem we wrote to introduce each of the different sections. We'll have recitations about Mary and Joseph's trip to Bethlehem and Baby Jesus's birth."

"Baby Jesus!" Alice Ann crowed. "At school!"

"He's everywhere, little girl," Wyman assured the toddler as he chucked her little chin.

As Amanda spread apple butter on another slice of French toast and cut it up for their youngest daughter, she saw a secret sparkling in her husband's eyes. Had he found a new ceramic figurine for the Nativity set? She wasn't going to ask, because she didn't want to spoil Wyman's surprise if he had or disappoint their little girl if he hadn't. It seemed awfully *soon* for him to have found that replacement piece, as she didn't think he'd done any shopping.

With God, all things are possible.

The Bible verse filled Amanda with gratitude and wonder, because this peaceful scene at the breakfast table, where all the kids and adults chatted so happily, hadn't seemed possible a few weeks ago. It was indeed the Lord's hand at work, transforming her kids and Wyman's, along with Jerome and Jemima, into the big, happy family for which she'd prayed so earnestly.

"How about you, Pete?" Eddie teased. "This'll be your last school program. Did you write a Christmas essay and memorize it? Or will you duck out before—"

"Pete's going to make us all glad we came tonight," Wyman stated. "Our new friends and neighbors will be pleased that he's part of the Bloomingdale community now, too."

"Jah, because Pete's been our carpenter," Lizzie spoke up. "So instead of the chalkboard with the alphabet above it, you'll see the wooden backdrops of Bethlehem he built and painted for us, to go along with the enactment of the Christmas story. And the raised stage he constructed will make it easier for everyone to see the littlest kids. Teacher Dorcas says the scenery's so gut, she wants to store the flats away to use every year."

"Gut for you, Pete!" Jerome said.

"I'm pleased to hear you got those finished, Son," Wyman affirmed.

"So, did that get you out of having to memorize and recite?" Eddie asked as he stabbed another slice of French toast from the platter.

Pete grinned as though recalling some of the Christmas recitations his older brother had given when they'd lived in the Clearwater district. "I'm changing the scenery a couple times during the program," he replied. "I've worked long enough at building and painting the backdrops after school that Teacher Dorcas says I've done my part already. I didn't argue with her."

Eddie's dark eyebrows rose. "Now, why didn't *I* think of doing that when I was the oldest scholar? You're a genius, Pete."

"Jah, you *wock*, Peter Wabbit!" Simon exclaimed.

Amanda smiled. It was wonderful that Pete had found a way to contribute to the Christmas Eve program using his God-given gift for construction, and she was certain that designing and painting such scenery would have drawn only negative attention from Uriah Schmucker were they still living in Clearwater.

As everyone rose from the table, Amanda went to the pie safe to prepare the desserts and casserole dishes for tomorrow. Even though Christmas didn't fall on a Sunday, it was important that their prayerful observance of Christ's birth not be interrupted by a lot of cooking or other work. Wyman had asked for a sour cream raisin pie, the boys had requested a meatball sandwich casserole for tomorrow's dinner, and the younger children wanted Jemima's chicken soup with homemade noodles for supper tonight.

As she measured out flour from the bin in the pie safe, Amanda felt Wyman come up behind her. He leaned in close, kissing her behind the ear before he whispered, "How about you and me making a cocoa and pie date for after the kids are tucked in tonight?"

Goose bumps tingled up Amanda's spine. "I can do that, jah," she murmured.

"I've got a surprise for you."

"Me, too," Amanda replied with a furtive laugh.

Again he nuzzled her. "I love you so much, Amanda."

She turned and clasped his handsome face between her flour-coated hands. "And I love you, Wyman."

Amanda exhaled slowly, aware the kids were watching them while they cleared the table and ran the dishwater. But wasn't it the best example she and Wyman could set, to allow their children to witness deep, true love between a man and a woman?

* * *

Later that evening, after a particularly moving program at the school, and after thanking Pete and Lizzie for their contributions to it, Wyman took great pleasure in tucking the four youngest kids into bed after listening to their prayers. Eddie and Pete had challenged Vera and Lizzie to a late-night game of Settlers of Catan downstairs at the game table, and Jerome and Jemima had retired to their rooms. As Amanda spent a moment with Simon, the twins, and Alice Ann, he went downstairs and quickly retrieved the small box from his coat pocket.

The front room, bathed in the glow of the gas fixtures and warmed by the woodstove, seemed cozier than usual . . . a welcoming place for the holy child who'd been born in a barn on a chilly night. As Wyman gently placed the new figurine in the tabletop stable, between His earthly mother and father, emotion choked him.

What an honor it was to bring this symbol of Baby Jesus into their home again, in time for his children to find Him on Christmas morning. As Wyman gazed at the baby's tiny face and outstretched arms, he felt as though Christ were gazing up at him in gratitude and welcome. It was silly to think the ceramic baby had any human qualities—a reminder of why the Old Order restricted graven images. Yet his heart was moved by the open, loving smile on the baby's face.

In the stillness of the moment, he felt his spirit lift.

"Oh, Wyman," Amanda murmured as she came up beside him. Her hand fluttered to her heart. "Denki so much for this fine surprise. It was silly of me to be upset when the other figurine broke."

"But now the Holy Family is complete, just as our family is," he murmured. "We have Tyler and his computer savvy to thank for this."

"We have many, many things to be grateful for." Amanda's

eyes glimmered in the lamplight as she gazed at the Nativity set. Then, with a prayerful sigh, she gazed up at him. "Is it time for that pie and cocoa you mentioned earlier?"

"A fitting finish to a satisfying day." Wyman slipped his arm around her shoulders as they headed into the kitchen. As Amanda poured milk into a pan on the stove, he stepped into the pantry and found the wrapped jar he'd hidden behind the other boxes on the shelf.

"For you, dear wife," he murmured as he set it on the counter beside her. "I bought this that day I picked up your Christmas gifts at the mercantile, thinking I knew best—and I ran short on cash," he explained with a sigh. "It comes with the promise to give you much more worthy gifts every chance I get."

Amanda's smile warmed him as she turned the jar this way and that. "You made the wrapping paper, too? Seems I'm not the only artist in the family."

"It was Simon's idea, and his coloring, mostly," Wyman admitted. "It's so amazing to see the way he's taken to you."

"He's such a joy. I have an idea you were a lot like him when you were his age." She slipped her finger beneath the taped edge of the brown paper, careful not to tear the holly and candy canes their son had drawn with his crayons. "Oh my. Pickle spears."

When Amanda burst into a fit of giggles, Wyman wondered what she found so funny. Or was his gift, and the idea behind it, as totally ridiculous as he'd feared?

"I—I'd be in a real *pickle* without you, dear Amanda," he murmured earnestly. "Had I not overridden your plan for Jerome to pick up your order and pay for it with—"

"You were doing your best, Wyman, at a time when you were trying to keep our family solvent. How can I fault you for that?" Once again she looked at the jar of dill spears and giggled.

"I really will find a more fitting gift, Amanda, but—"

She laid a finger across his lips. Her deep green eyes

fixed upon his with such an intense love that Wyman sucked in his breath.

"It seems you've already given me the greatest gift of all, Wyman."

He questioned her with his eyes, for her expression, her tone, left him strangely unable to speak.

"I'm pretty sure I'm expecting."

Wyman blinked. Then he grabbed her and held her close, a sob escaping him. "I—oh, Amanda!"

"Let's keep this between us until we're certain," she whispered. Amanda was holding him so tightly, he felt her heart beating against his stomach as she rested her head on his shoulder. "But meanwhile, your pickles are the perfect solution for those cravings I'll get, ain't so? Jerome had to fetch a couple of jars of dills from the store every week, along with peppermint stick ice cream, while I was carrying the twins."

As Wyman closed his eyes and marveled over the way his wife fit so perfectly against him, a joyous serenity settled over him. Amanda had found a way to transform his hastily grabbed gift into the perfect offering, and once again he gave thanks for the way this woman had blessed his life.

"You're absolutely right, dear wife," he murmured, kissing her lightly on the lips.

"Shall we celebrate with cocoa and pie? Something tells me we'll have company, once the kids smell our cocoa."

Wyman chuckled. "I'm a happy man, sharing this sweetness with my family. Merry Christmas, Amanda."

"Jah, dear husband, merry Christmas to you, too—and to our big happy family."

Chapter 31

The sun brightened the horizon with pink-ribbon clouds, making the snow glisten on the trees. With the barn mucked out and the mules and horses fed, Jerome and the two older boys started back to the house to spend Christmas Day immersed in contemplation of Christ's birth with the rest of the family. Wyman had mentioned that he'd like to be in the house when the wee ones got up this morning, and Jerome had been happy to allow him that pleasure. As he stepped into the fragrant kitchen, filled with the aromas of a breakfast casserole, coffee, and cinnamon rolls, Jerome let the warmth of this home, and the love of his expanded family, seep into his chilled limbs.

"Merry Christmas, Aunt Amanda, and to you as well, Jemima," he said as he and Eddie and Pete hung up their coats.

"And a blessed Christmas to you boys, too," his great-aunt replied as she pulled a steaming pan from the oven.

"Jah, it's going to be a wonderful-gut day," Amanda said. When she smiled so warmly at him, it felt like a hug.

Jerome remembered Christmases past, when he'd been an orphaned boy clinging to the affection Aunt Amanda and Uncle Atlee had shown him as he'd mourned his parents. He also recalled when he'd reached Pete's age, thinking that an entire day of Bible reading and quiet reflection was more than he could tolerate. It had been *impossible* for him to sit still, and even more unbearable to put up with baby Lizzie's fussy spells, so he'd looked for every excuse to slip outdoors. Even feeding the chickens and gathering eggs had seemed like entertainment on those endless Christmas Days. In his teenage frustration, he'd hurled a few of those eggs against the side of the barn just for the satisfaction of watching them splatter. Then, of course, he'd quickly cleaned them up and fibbed to Jemima about how some of her hens had taken the day off from laying.

Jerome smiled. It was a relief to be beyond such frustrations and wonderful that Amanda and her girls had moved past their grief and into a new family this year as well.

The rapid clatter of feet on the stairs announced that Simon and his three younger sisters were eager to greet Christmas. A loud *ohhhhhh!* rang in chorus around the front room.

"Baby Jesus!" Alice Ann cried. "Baby Jesus comed to our house for Kiss-mas!"

As Jerome peered out the kitchen doorway, Amanda and Jemima left the stove to join him. He slung his arms around their shoulders as they beheld Simon, Cora, and Dora gazing in wide-eyed wonder at the new baby in the manger. Vera and Lizzie smiled as they descended the stairs, while Pete and Eddie also seemed genuinely in awe of the Nativity set's newest addition.

Wyman rose from his armchair to join the children, maintaining an air of solemnity even as his lips twitched with a grin. "Jah, kids, here He is," he said. He lifted Alice Ann to his shoulder before she could snatch up the fragile figurine in her eagerness. "The Lord's come into our home, and when we let Him into our hearts, all will be right with the world."

"I know!" Cora said. "Let's sing 'Away in a Manger.'"

Dora clapped her hands. "And then 'Silent Night,' even though it's daytime."

As the little girls' voices swelled in the sweet, timeless melody, Simon joined in, and so did Wyman and the four older kids. Jerome felt Amanda quiver as she leaned into him. She swiped at a tear and whispered, "Oh, isn't that a sight?"

"Jah, it is," Jemima agreed in a breathy voice. "All the kids singing together like they've been doing it all their lives."

Jerome hugged the two women, his heart swelling with the music that filled the front room. He resisted the urge to sing along, allowing the sweet younger voices to fill him with a sense of wondrous love. *This is what it's all about,* he thought. *And I hope someday it'll be my kids . . . Emma and I gathered with them, telling them the Christmas story and teaching them these dear old songs.*

As the last notes of the first carol drifted, and Dora's clear voice took up "Silent Night," sunbeams shone through the window where Jemima's Christmas cactus sat. Its waxy green branches were especially full of blooms this year, as though the plant also sensed this was a very special Christmas. The deep pink flowers swayed in the air current from the furnace, shimmering in the sunlight.

Jerome suddenly had an idea.

"Do I remember correctly that your Christmas cactus belonged to your mamm, Jemima?" he murmured.

"Jah, it goes way back to when she was about to marry," she replied. "The young fellow who became my dat gave it to her as a Christmas gift when they were courting."

Jerome's heart sped up as he carefully phrased his request. "It's probably not the right time to mess with that plant's roots, but do you suppose we could put a section of it in one of Amanda's pots? I've been trying to come up with a gift for Emma, and—"

"Oh, what a wonderful idea!" Amanda exclaimed.

"You know, I've been meaning to transplant that poor root-bound cactus for the last couple of years," Jemima said. She smiled up at him, her wrinkled face alight. "It's not the best time, like you say, but I think the plant will forgive us if we pot a starter for your Emma and then put the rest of it in a bigger container. I'd be pleased for her to have it."

What better blessing and benediction could he hope for? Jerome kissed Jemima's temple, his pulse thrumming with the rightness of the idea. "Denki, Aunts," he murmured. "I can't wait to see her eyes light up tomorrow when I give it to her."

The next morning was dawning cold and clear as Wyman, Simon, Eddie, and Pete did the chores. Wyman took deep satisfaction in spending this time with his boys before the Grabers arrived later that morning. He shared a special kinship with his three sons as he watched Eddie and Pete growing toward manhood while Simon was leaving his early childhood behind, getting ready to start school next fall.

"You boys all did a fine job of observing our quiet, worshipful time yesterday," Wyman said. He poured a bucket of water into one of the troughs, smiling as his youngest son hefted a heavy bucket of feed. "What did you like best about our Christmas, Simon?"

Simon's eyes sparkled in the dimness of the barn. "It was *cool* that Baby Jesus showed up just in time," he replied. "And it was a better Christmas than last year because

I had Cora and Dora to play with—and because we have a new mamm."

"Jah, those are gifts we're all enjoying this season," Wyman agreed.

"Even if they're all about *girls*," Pete teased his little brother.

They all laughed at that observation as they kept working. "And how about you, Pete? What have you liked best?" Wyman asked. "I for one am truly thankful that you're home with us instead of on that cattle ranch in Kansas you mentioned."

Pete let out a short laugh as he untied another bale of straw. "Well, the Christmas Eve program came out better than I thought, considering how Lizzie and Fannie Lehman kept bossing me about how to paint those backdrops after I built them."

"Your scenery really looked gut," Eddie remarked. "You've got a fine eye and a steady hand for the detail work."

Wyman caught the satisfaction on Pete's face. "And how about you, Eddie? You've had a busy season, what with painting and clerking in the mercantile."

"While I'm grateful that Sam gave me the job," Eddie said, "there's no place like home, far as spending time with regular folks. The Lambrights are fine, fun people—"

"Especially Gail?" Pete teased.

"But living with Preacher Sam in a house full of women is another thing altogether," Eddie went on with a chuckle. Then he focused on his father. "If my painting business does well, I want James to build me an enclosed wagon big enough to hold my equipment, with a built-in bunk for when I'm working a distance from home."

Wyman's eyebrows rose. His son seemed awfully young to be living on the road, yet he didn't want to discourage such a forward-thinking idea. "Start saving up your money for that," he replied. "I appreciate how all you kids have been pitching in to help pay the family bills this winter—"

The ringing of the phone on the barn wall made all of them look up. Simon raced over to grab the receiver before the message machine kicked on. "Hello? This is Simon Brubaker . . . Okay, Dat's right here. Just a minute, please."

When Simon thrust the receiver in his direction, Wyman set down his water bucket. "You did a nice job of answering that, Son," he said. No doubt Amanda and the older girls had been coaching him on his telephone etiquette.

The boy pressed the receiver against his coat. "It's Reece Weaver, Dat. He sounds kinda . . . jumpy."

Jumpy. And wasn't *that* an interesting observation from a five-year-old?

"Jah, Reece." Wyman mentally prepared himself for whatever his contractor had in mind, calling so early in the morning—and on Second Christmas, too, as though he'd forgotten that Plain people celebrated it. "Gut morning, and merry Christmas to you."

"It'd be a lot merrier if you'd tell that television reporter to *back off*," Reece replied. "I can't believe you're joining in on that *farce*, Wyman."

Wyman considered his response. He wanted a fair shake from this contractor, but he was also setting an example for his boys. "When I tell the farmers who bring their grain to my elevator what I'm going to charge them for drying their corn and what I'll pay them when I sell their crops," he began, "I stand by my agreement. I expect nothing different from you, Reece."

"What if I have your elevator finished by the end of the year? And consider your account paid in full?" Weaver shot back. "Would you get that Calloway fellow—and that Clearwater attorney—off my case?"

"I'd have to see that to believe it," Wyman replied.

"Seems you have *several* customers awaiting completion on their jobs, which date back before mine. There's no way you can get to them all by the end of this week—nor could you do a gut job on my elevator in just six days."

"You *saw* that list?" Reece demanded shrilly. "I'm going to *sue* that Lock fellow for—"

"Those names are a matter of public record," Wyman interrupted firmly. He was *so* glad he and Ray had seen the attorney before Reece called him this morning. "Seems to me your time would be better spent making gut on your construction projects rather than taking Graham Lock to court. You're right about one thing, though," he added. "I'm not paying you another dime until my elevator's completed, and then I'll only give you the balance of what we originally agreed to. No more surprise fees."

Wyman sighed as Reece ranted for a few moments more. "Tell you what," he said when he could get a word in edgewise. "Ray and Tyler and I will be at the site Monday morning with the reporter. If you want to look like a more reputable contractor, be there with your construction crew. The way I understand it, Cole Calloway will keep following your progress until every one of the fellows on his list is satisfied," he insisted. "If you fall short, thousands of people will know about it. It's the sort of accountability you should have been showing all along, Reece—just like your dat taught you when he was bringing you into the business."

The silence on the line suggested that Reece was finally listening, taking him seriously now.

"After all," Wyman went on calmly, "we agreed to have my elevator finished in the *spring*. I expect your top-quality work rather than a shoddy job done in a hurry to get Calloway off your case, as you put it. We're talking about sophisticated mechanical and technical equipment that has to be properly installed. My business will go down the drain just like yours has if I'm constantly shutting down for repairs."

Wyman paused again, letting Reece absorb what he was saying. His three sons had stopped working to follow this conversation closely, as well they should. "This might be just another job to you, but my family's welfare is riding on this project," he continued. "If you can't properly complete my elevator, I want most of my money back and I'll get another contractor. But I won't let you off the hook, Reece. Nobody wins if you don't come through with what you promised."

A long sigh came over the phone line. "Stay with me, all right? I'll see you Monday."

"All right. We'll go from there."

As he hung up, Wyman took a deep breath to settle his nerves. Confrontation and disagreement went against his nature and his religion. But at least now Reece was facing the consequences of his unethical behavior.

"I won't belabor the point," he said to his boys, "but we reap what we sow. If you're ever tempted to do less than your best work, or to cheat people out of their money with false promises, I hope you'll think back to how Reece Weaver has affected our family. And if you realize someone's taking advantage of you, I hope you'll stand up to him a lot quicker than I did."

Wyman smiled at Eddie, Pete, and Simon. "End of sermon. Let's finish up here and go in for breakfast," he said in a lighter voice. "I'm ready to have some fun!"

"And open presents!" Simon exclaimed. "I can't wait another minute!"

When he got inside, Wyman wasn't surprised to find all the girls in the kitchen, eager to enjoy their Second Christmas celebration. Even Jemima was in a fine mood as she helped Amanda, Vera, and Lizzie set out steaming bowls of hash browns, sliced smoked sausages, scrambled eggs, onions and green peppers, and cheese sauce for making breakfast haystacks. After the blessing, Wyman took par-

ticular pleasure in watching the kids dig into their food—
all of them healthy and so much happier than they'd been
last year at this time.

His gaze lingered on Amanda, sitting to his left. Was it
his imagination or was she fuller in the face, already
abloom with the life growing inside her? When he squeezed
his wife's hand, she shared his purposeful gaze, as though
silently saying her thoughts were aligned with his.

After the meal, everyone gathered in the front room.
Wyman, Jerome, and the older boys agreed that the purple
and turquoise fabric Amanda had wrapped as gifts would
make great shirts, and they liked the catchall containers
she'd made them, too. Jemima was pleased to receive her
new kapps and black stockings. Lizzie, Vera, and the twins
exclaimed over their heart-shaped ceramic whatnot boxes,
and when the younger kids unwrapped the lined writing
tablets, Simon seemed eager to practice his alphabet—
mostly so Cora and Dora wouldn't get too far ahead of him
at learning their letters. Alice Ann squealed as she unwrapped a pair of faceless Amish cloth dolls, mostly because the girl doll wore a dress of bright pink.

While other presents were being unwrapped, Wyman
watched closely as Simon handed his gift to Amanda. The
odd-shaped bottle hadn't been easy to cover, so it looked
clumpy with all its tucked corners and tape. But Amanda
complimented their boy on the paper he had colored, then
held up the bottle of cooking oil with a wide smile. "How
did you know I just used up the last of my oil, Simon?" she
asked brightly. "This is a wonderful-gut present!"

Simon flashed her an adoring grin. "The Wise Men
brought precious oil and gold to Baby Jesus," he explained
earnestly. "Seems like a dumb thing to give a baby, but *you*,
Mamm—I know you'll make gut things with that oil. Like
fried pies, ain't so?"

As laughter filled the room, Wyman delighted in how
his youngest son had presented such an unusual gift in his

inimitable way and how Amanda grabbed Simon in a hug and loudly kissed his cheek.

Vera then walked over to the china hutch and pulled a slender, wrapped rectangle from behind it. As she handed it to Wyman, she glanced toward Amanda. "All of us kids worked on this for both of you, Mamm and Dat," she said. "We hope you'll like it."

Amanda's face lit up with curiosity as she came over to stand beside him. The children got quiet, anticipation on their faces as Wyman offered Amanda an edge so they could unwrap the gift together.

"It's a list of our names to hang beside the front door!" Amanda exclaimed as she tore away the last of the paper.

"I'm glad you kids thought of this," Wyman said. "With so much going on lately, it slipped my mind that the plaque at the Clearwater house was destroyed."

"And it needed updating, just like the one at this place," Amanda pointed out. "Denki so much, to all of you!"

Wyman felt a rush of emotion as he read THE BRUBAKER FAMILY across the top, followed by his name and Amanda's together, and then the names of everyone else in the household, from the oldest to the youngest. He was secretly pleased that a lot of space remained at the bottom for new additions.

"I was tickled that the kids asked if they could include me on the list," Jemima spoke up. She was smiling as brightly as Wyman had ever seen, looking ten years younger.

"Jah," Jerome said as he clasped his great-aunt's shoulder, "we carry the Lambright name, but we're pleased to be considered a part of the Brubaker household."

"Pete made the frame and the wooden plaque. And Eddie painted it," Vera began.

"But Lizzie did the lettering, because she writes prettier than I do," Eddie said.

"And Vera made the little flowerpots along the sides of the frame with pottery chips," Lizzie continued eagerly.

"And it was Simon who got us the shelled field corn for the centers of the flowers."

"We twins glued on the dried beans and macaroni shells for the petals," Dora chimed in.

"And you'll never guess who wanted the pink buttons in the corners," Cora added with a grin.

"Me, Alice Ann!" the toddler crowed as she climbed into Wyman's lap. She touched each of the buttons with the tip of a tiny finger. "Pink! I wuv pink!"

As Amanda's hand fluttered to her throat, she looked as ready to cry as Wyman felt. "It's perfect, kids," he murmured. "You each used your special abilities to make this such a special record of our blended family."

Everyone in the room basked in a moment of collective happiness. Wyman smiled at each one of the kids then. "I bet we can hang this on the wall before the Grabers get here," he said. "They'll get a kick out of hearing how all of you kids helped with—"

"So, Mamma, does this mean our name is Brubaker now?"

"Like yours?"

Cora and Dora stood together, clasping hands as they gazed intently at their mother. The soft brown tendrils escaping from their buns to frame their little faces made them look all the more precious, so much like their mother that Wyman could envision the lovely young women they would become. He and Amanda had discussed this subject before they'd married, but he felt it best to let her respond to her daughters now that they had raised the issue.

"Your new dat is adopting all three of you girls. It's just a matter of waiting for the legal paperwork to come through." Amanda smiled at Cora and Dora. "Would you twins like to start going by Brubaker? That way, by the time you go to school, your new name will feel like a natural part of you. We can practice writing it on your new tablets."

The twins looked at each other, smiling simultaneously. "Jah, that would be gut," Dora said.

"Everyone at church and school will know we're Simon's for-sure sisters, then," Cora pointed out. "That'll be real special."

Wyman kept his chuckle to himself as he watched Simon formulate his answer to Cora's endearing remark. His youngest son was all boy, yet he and his new look-alike sisters were practically inseparable.

Amanda was smiling at her teenager, continuing her discussion before the younger kids sidetracked it. "This adoption situation is a little different for you, Lizzie," she said gently, "so we're leaving up to you which name you want to go by."

"You've been a Lambright for more than thirteen years," Wyman added, "so I'll understand if you keep your father's name. You don't have to choose right now. It's a big decision, and you're grown-up enough to make it."

Wyman smiled at the slender girl as her face got pink around the edges. While Lamar Lapp had counseled him to announce that Lizzie would become a Brubaker when the adoption was final, the Bloomingdale bishop's well-meaning advice had sounded like something Uriah Schmucker would say. Wyman sensed that Lizzie would be best left to decide on her own. She was looking down now, her long lashes brushing her cheeks as she twirled the string of her kapp around her finger.

"It was my idea to make the new plaque with 'the Brubaker Family' across the top," Lizzie murmured. "I want all of us kids to be real brothers and sisters now, with the same last name."

The front room rang with a sanctified silence. The older kids were nodding in agreement. Wyman was so overwhelmed, he couldn't speak.

"Well, glory be," Jemima murmured. "If that's not the sweetest thing I've ever heard from our Lizzie."

"Jah, Lizzie! You said that real gut," Dora exclaimed as she grabbed her older sister's hand.

"It's like us girls got a new last name for Christmas," Cora said as she joined their little circle.

"I *suppose* we'll claim you," Pete teased as he and Eddie began to pick up the torn wrapping paper around the room.

"Even if you're *girls*," Simon declared. "But can we stop all this yacking now? Merle's gonna be here any minute!"

As the kids began straightening the front room, shifting their gifts from the middle of the floor, Wyman stood up and put his arm around Amanda's shoulders. "This is priceless—mostly because it came as a surprise, from the kids instead of us," he murmured as he gazed at the list of all their names.

"I *thought* they might be working on something this week, the way they all disappeared into the basement every now and again," Amanda recalled. "I'm glad I didn't walk in by accident and ruin their surprise."

"And the way your girls handled the name change?" Wyman went on. "I was concerned about how to bring up the topic of their adoption."

"Leave it to the twins to see that the i's are dotted and the t's get crossed," Amanda quipped. "Lizzie's answer was my best Christmas gift. Well, maybe along with your pickles."

Wyman kissed her, chuckling. "It's been a fine Second Christmas already, and it's only nine o'clock. I can't imagine how this day can get any better."

A smile lightened his wife's lovely face as she nodded toward the window. "We'll soon find out. Here comes the Grabers' buggy up the lane."

Chapter 32

Emma clambered down from the buggy with a sense of eager anticipation. Yesterday had been their quiet observance of Christ's birth, but she'd spent a lot more time thinking about Jerome than about the babe in the manger. Surely God had understood, and hopefully He would guide her as she spent time with Jerome today—and for the coming months of their courtship. She and Abby had agreed that their deep green dresses were appropriate for a visit with the Brubaker bunch, and as they picked up the pans of food they'd stacked behind the backseat of the buggy, Emma felt a rush of happiness. While she would always miss her mother, her heart felt hopeful rather than heavy. Somehow, she thought Mamm would approve of that.

"Merle! What took you guys so *long*?" Simon cried as he raced toward them with his coat blowing open. "Merry Christmas!"

"Jah, and merry Christmas to you, Abby, and James!" one of the twins called out from behind him.

"And to you, Emma!" her sister chimed in as the trio scampered through the snow. "Oh, just wait till you see what Jerome's got for you."

Emma laughed, hugging the children who'd circled the four of them with outstretched arms and rosy, smiling faces. They were all chattering at once, as excited as she remembered being at their age.

"You've gotta see my new wooden train, Merle."

"We've got White Christmas pie. And a deer roast."

"Gooey butter cake and a *big* ole turkey."

"Did you bring me some fried pies, Abby?"

"And Jerome says we can take sleigh rides today, and—"

Emma glanced toward the house, and her heartbeat stilled. There on the front porch stood Jerome. He was holding little Alice Ann, sheltering her from the wind by wrapping both sides of his coat around her. Alice Ann waved gleefully, and Emma waved back. What a picture they made . . . such a tall, strong man holding a blond angel whose face beamed with delight. *He'll make a devoted dat someday.*

Emma blinked at that thought. Just a couple of months ago she'd considered Jerome bold and brash, too caught up in showing off his mules to care anything about a tiny child. Yet as he kissed the little girl's golden hair, fixing his gaze on *her* as she started toward the house, Emma had no trouble believing that Jerome would be the perfect man with whom to start a family. *Her* family.

"Merry Christmas to you," she said as she ascended the stairs to the porch.

"Baby Jesus comed here for Kiss-mas!" Alice Ann crowed. "You gotta see!"

Jerome flashed Emma a knowing smile. "It's quite a story," he murmured. "All about how everything works out in God's gut time."

Emma reveled in the shine of his brown eyes and the way he held her gaze as he challenged her not to lower hers. "Jah, we know about things working out just the way they're supposed to," she replied. "I brought you a little something for *Kiss*-mas, too, Jerome."

"Did you now?"

Was his voice husky with anticipation, or was that wishful thinking on her part? Emma stepped into the house, thrumming with the hunch that she was about to spend an incredible day with the Brubaker family, who would someday be *her* family if her courtship with Jerome went the way she hoped it would.

It was surely Your doing, God, because I was just a scared little mouse trying to scamper away from—

Emma's prayer was interrupted by greetings from Amanda, Vera, and Jemima as they relieved her of the pans she was carrying.

"You didn't have to bring anything," Amanda insisted. "What with everyone here asking for all their favorite dishes, we've got so much food."

"Maybe the table will break," Simon cried as he stepped inside with his sisters. "Wouldn't *that* be something!"

Laughter filled the busy kitchen, and as Emma hung up her coat and bonnet, she felt very much at home. Even so, it was exciting to consider what Jerome had said about building a new house. So many happy thoughts had been filling her mind these past couple of days. What a difference falling in love made.

Falling in love! Just when grief might otherwise have swallowed her whole, during this first holiday season without her mamm, Emma's heart was dancing and her outlook on life had changed completely. As her dat preceded Abby and James into the house, it was another joy to see the kids grabbing his hands to lead him into the front room even before he could get his coat off.

"Merle, we got a set of dominoes!" Cora crowed. "All the way up to nine—"

"So we can practice our math!" Dora continued excitedly. "Mamm said you would teach us how to play."

"I'll be happy to," Merle replied, his face alight. "And I'll show you a nifty trick for knowing the number of dots without having to count them every time, too."

As Simon and the twins escorted Emma's father to the game table they'd set up, Vera smiled at her. "Emma, I think your dat's day is going to be a long round of eating and playing, and then eating and playing some more," she said as they began to set the table.

Emma placed a plate at every chair, thankful to be spending this day amongst so many friends. "Denki ever so much for inviting us today," she said, including Amanda and Jemima in her thanks. "Keeping up with four little ones means Dat won't spend his day drifting off in his chair."

"And Emma will have something more than her crocheting to keep her occupied," Abby teased as she began setting silverware and napkins around.

As the women continued visiting and preparing the meal, the men passed through the kitchen on their way to the front room. Her father sat in a chair at the card table with the kids, while James caught up with Eddie and Pete. Wyman was adding logs to the woodstove. When Emma noticed Jerome lingering in the doorway, she smiled at him.

"The kids are looking forward to a sleigh ride today, I hear," she remarked.

Jerome's handsome face eased into a secretive grin. "They'll get their turn," he replied. "Then I figured you and I could take our own ride. If you want to, that is."

As Lizzie and Vera chuckled furtively, Emma felt the color rising in her cheeks. She wasn't accustomed to discussing her romantic plans in front of an audience, but she'd better get used to that, hadn't she? Here in the Brubaker home, moments of total privacy were rare, she suspected.

"I'd like that," she said. Emma went toward her coat, which was hanging on the wall, and reached into its deep pocket. "Seems like a gut time to give you this. It's cold out there when the wind kicks up."

As she handed Jerome a wrapped package, he squeezed it between his hands, his face alight with curiosity. "You didn't have to give me anything, Emma. Just seeing you today is a gift—"

"Truth be told," she murmured as she leaned closer to him, "this is what I was doing yesterday when it was so quiet at our house."

As the wrapping paper split, Jerome's face lit up. "How'd you know my stocking cap was getting raggedy?" he asked as he held up the one she'd crocheted for him. "And a scarf, too? These are fabulous!"

"Purple rather than black," Lizzie remarked playfully. "Isn't *that* special?"

"Well, if there was ever a colorful character in our family, it's Jerome," Amanda teased. She winked at her nephew. "Might be a gut time to show Emma what you put together for *her*, while the kids are busy."

"True enough," Jerome said as he set his new cap on the counter. "I just happen to have a little something stashed in the pantry, Emmie-girl. It was a team effort."

Emma savored the way Jerome lingered over her nickname as he said it. When he stepped out of the pantry closet, she gasped. "Oh, what a beautiful little Christmas cactus! Look at all of those bright pink blooms."

"It's a cutting from the one my dat gave to my mamm when they were courting," Jemima said sweetly.

"A looong time ago," Lizzie teased. "It's a wonder the plant in the window has survived a couple more generations of Lambrights and now Wyman's rambunctious lot, too."

Emma laughed. "Is this one of your pots, Amanda?" she asked as she turned the plant to and fro between her hands. "I really like these colorful chunks along the top of it."

"Vera's been making wind chimes with some of my broken pottery pieces," Amanda explained as she slid a blue enamel roaster into the oven. "It was her idea to press some of those pieces into the clay as I was forming a new pot.

You're the first person to receive one, and I'm pleased about that, Emma."

"What a wonderful gift, with so many family attachments," Emma murmured. "I'll have to find just the right spot for it."

Jerome stepped closer and gently lifted her chin. "Jemima's Christmas cactus has been in that same window in the front room since I came here as a kid," he murmured. "But yesterday, it was like I was seeing it for the first time—and all those pretty blooms glowing in the morning sunlight reminded me of *you*, Emma."

Emma held her breath. When had anyone ever compared her to a blossoming plant? *Glowing,* he'd said. She could tell by Jerome's rapt expression that he meant every word, too.

"I'll be sure we have a big window on the east side of our new home so you can enjoy these blooms when it's cold and snowy outside," Jerome continued softly. "Would you like that, Emma?"

For a timeless moment, the sound of the women working in the kitchen and the men's voices in the front room faded away. As Emma gazed into Jerome's sparkling brown eyes, she felt as though they were the only two people in the world—sharing a lovely blooming plant that had redefined her self-image, just as Jerome had. While she would never consider herself as beautiful as this Christmas cactus, was it so wrong to believe that Jerome thought she was?

Maybe beauty really was in the eye of the beholder. And maybe Jerome could help her see herself—her entire life—through fresh eyes. She trusted him now and believed that his intentions for their future were as honorable as they were exciting.

Emma let out the breath she'd been holding. Jerome had just asked her a very sweet question, after all. While she'd known times when fear and self-doubt would have made her hesitate, now she smiled brightly. "I would like that, Jerome," she whispered. "I'd like it very much."

Acknowledgments

Once again, Lord, You've brought the right ideas just when I needed them, and stood by me as I wrote this book despite many, many distractions. Thanks!

My continuous gratitude goes to Jim Smith of Step Back in Time Tours in Jamesport, Missouri—the largest Old Order Amish settlement west of the Mississippi River. Your research assistance is invaluable, and I treasure your friendship, too!

Special thanks to Joe and Mose Burkholder and to Mary Graber in Jamesport for opening your hearts to me.

Evan Marshall, I so appreciate your guidance and support as I make the most of my writing career. Ellen Edwards, thank you again for your attention to the details that make my books so much better!

Ready to find
your next great read?

Let us help.

Visit prh.com/nextread

Penguin
Random
House